This Red Land

Arthur Dobrin

Nsemia

First Edition: January 2018

Edited By: Verah Omwocha
Cover Concept & Illustration: Arthur Dobrin
Cover Design: Linda Kiboma
Layout: Bethsheba Nyabuto

Published by Nsemia Inc. Publishers
Oakville, Ontario, Canada.
www.nsemia.com

Published and Distributed in Kenya by Nsemia (K) Ltd.

Note for Librarians:
A cataloguing record for this book is available from Library and Archives Canada.

ISBN: 978-1-926906-73-7

Front Matter

This is a work of fiction. Names, characters, places and incidents are either the product of the author's imagination or are used fictitiously, and any resemblance to actual persons, living or dead, business establishments, events, or locales is entirely coincidental.

Portions of this work previously appeared, in significantly different form in *Salted With Fire*, Oxford University Press, Nairobi and *Malaika*, Jomo Kenyatta Foundation, Nairobi.

"26 Ways of Looking At A Blackman," Raymond R. Patterson, in *26 Ways Of Looking At A Black Man and Other Poems,* Award Books, 1969

"A Dream of Whitman Paraphrased, Recognized and Made More Vivid by Renoir," Delmore Schwartz, in *Last and Lost Poems*, New Directions, 1989

"Asphodel, That Greeny Flower," William Carlos Williams, in *Journey to Love*, Random House, 1955

"Bye, Bye, Blackbird," Henderson and Dixon, 1926

"Dancing in the Street," William 'Mickey' Stevenson, Ivy Joe Hunter and Marvin Gaye, 1964

"Hard Times Come Again No More," Stephen Foster, 1854

"Heart to Heart," Rita Dove, in *American Smooth*, W. W. Norton and Company, 2004

"He'll Have to Go," Joe Allison and Audrey Allison, 1959

"I Am a Jew," Abel Meeropol, quoted in "'Strange' Evolution of Legendary Song," Harold Heft, *The Forward*, March 27, 2012

"If," Rudyard Kipling, in *Rewards and Fairies,* Doubleday, Page & Co., 1910

"In My Solitude," Duke Ellington, Eddie De Lange, Irving Mills, 1934

"In the Beginning," Malka Heifetz Tussman, in *With Teeth in the Earth*, Marcia Falk, translator, Wayne State University Press, 1992

"In the Café," Anna Margolin, in *A Century of Yiddish Poetry: Selected,* Aaron Kramer, editor and translator, Cornwall Books, 1984

"In the Midnight Hours," Wilson Pickett, Steve Cropper, 1965

"Lift Every Voice and Sing," John Rosamond Johnson and James Weldon Johnson, 1900

"Little Red Rooster," Willie Dixon, 1961

"Living for the City," Stevie Wonder, 1973

"Love to Love You Baby," Donna Summer, Giorgio Moroder, Pete Bellotte, 1974

"Mellow Yellow," Donovan, 1966

"Peter Quince at the Clavier," Wallace Stevens, in *Harmonium*, Knopf, 1923

"Sadness and Happiness," Dejan Stojanović, with author's permission

"Song of the Open Road," Walt Whitman, in *Leaves of Grass*, David McKay, 1891-1892

"The Mother," Gwendolyn Brooks, in *A Street in Bronzeville,* Harper & Brothers, 1945

"The Place Where We Are Right," Yehuda Amichai, in *The Selected Poetry of Yehuda Aimichai*, Chana Block and Stephen Mitchell, editors and translators, University of California Press, 1986

"There's No Forgetting," Pablo Neruda, in *Conductors of the Pit*, translated and edited, Clayton Eshleman, Soft Skull Press, 2005

"Thirteen Ways of Looking at a Blackbird," Wallace Stevens, in *Harmonium*, Knopf, 1923

"This Land Is Your Land," Woodie Guthrie, 1945

How do accidents of birth and history separate people and make them different?

—Hilton Als, "Exiles," *The New Yorker*

"Twilight Time," Buck Ram, Morty Nevins, Al Nevins, Artie Dunn, 1944

"You Will Hear Thunder," Anna Akhmatova, in *The Penguin Book of Russian Verse*, Dimitri Obolensky, editor and translator, 1965

"[What lips my lips have kissed, and where, and why]," Edna St. Vincent Millay, in *Collected Poems*, Harper & Brothers, 1923

"Who Knows Where the Time Goes?" Sandy Denny, 1967

Zen Buddhism: Selected Writings of Daisetz Teitaro Suzuki, W. Barrett (ed.), Doubleday, 1966

Table of Contents

Prologue:
A Body Falls From a Plane

IN 2009 THE DAILY MIRROR reported, "Neighbours on Back Swinegate in West London were startled in the early morning hours when they heard what they described as a thud or a loud bang on the street. They thought it was a small explosion. Residents in this upscale neighborhood were horrified to discover a twisted body of a black man who appeared to be in his early twenties on the sidewalk with a pool of blood near his head."

"No identification documents were found on the body, and the man's pockets were empty except for a wad of used chewing gum.

Shortly after emergency vehicles arrived speculation as to his identity began when a bundle of Kenya shilling notes was found resting on the needle leaves of a nearby yew.

"One line of inquiry," a police spokesman said, "is that the man was a stowaway who fell from an airplane. As of the moment, the death is currently being treated as unexplained."

Police kept the residents of Back Swinegate indoors for the better part of the morning as emergency vehicles converged on the suburban street.

"There was loads of blood everywhere, all over the street and my car," a homeowner said.

Later in the day, it was confirmed that Kenya Airways Flight 102 from Nairobi had landed in Heathrow moments after the victim crashed to the earth. The young man evidently fell approximately 2,000 feet from the plane on its descent into the airport.

A representative from the Civil Aviation Authority explained that the stowaway was probably dead long before hitting the ground. "It was likely that he was stowed away in the undercarriage compartment. If he wasn't killed when the landing gear retracted on take-off, he would have died from hypothermia and lack of oxygen during the flight. It gets down to minus 40. So he would either have been crushed or frozen to death."

One neighbour told a reporter, "Poor chap must have been desperate."

The police determined that the man was in his late teens, but his identity remained unknown for a week until a child playing in the garden behind her house on Priory Green found Gilbert Joel Kimathi's passport wedged in a raspberry bush.

That evening, an aviation expert explained on the news that a body falling from the sky seemed incredible to those on Back Swinegate, but it wasn't unique. There had been more than ninety recorded attempts by stowaways in plane wheels. "Some stowaways do make it," she said. "But that's on short hops. On long hauls there is very little chance of survival."

The chief operating officer at a refugee council said on a TV interview, "We don't know the circumstances of this particular person, but we know from our work with refugees that people often feel forced to take extreme measures in order to flee their countries."

After British authorities contacted their African counterparts, the Kenyan government looked into the matter. The Immigration officials there were stymied; they couldn't locate a Gilbert Joel Kimathi in their system, and concluded that the passport was a fake. What was this so-called Kimathi person thinking? The fake was so amateurish it would never have withstood examination at the UK end.

There were no matches for the fingerprints faxed by the British to Kenya. Neither were there records to match dental, hair or blood samples. The victim's tattered clothing didn't provide any clues; the shirt, shoes and trousers, ripped and torn from his body, could have been acquired at any upcountry market. The chewing gum sample was tagged as Gogo bubble gum, a popular brand sold throughout Kenya. The victim had no unusual body markings. The photo in the passport didn't match others on the government file.

Without proof positive of the mystery man's nationality—he could have been a refugee from Somalia or Uganda or Sudan—the Kenyan email to the British police stated that there was no basis for them accepting the body. As far as they were concerned, he was stateless. He belonged to the UK, which meant he belonged to the Richmond Borough council, which meant it was responsible for the disposal of the body by cremation.

〰〰〰〰〰
〰〰〰〰〰

AT ONE TIME HE DID BELONG SOMEWHERE, to someone. Lydia Nyamache had named her son Joseck Sokoro.

Lydia sold bananas at the Suneka market, where buses, trucks, cars and motorbikes stopped for tiers of "sugar," the small, sweet fruit that everyone considered the best bananas in Africa. Lydia lived nearby in a two-room house near the sewage treatment plant. It had been her home since leaving her father's place after giving birth to Joseck.

Samwel strongly disapproved of Lydia giving birth. She was barely out of Standard Eight, and without a husband. He didn't disown her, but he no longer permitted her to stay at his compound. Instead, Samwel bought a piece of land for his daughter and grandson with space to grow bananas for an income. Before the house was completed—it had just a cinderblock frame and a partially completed roof—Lydia and Joseck moved in to sleep on a reed mat on the concrete floor. Whatever money Samwel had set aside to complete the house went to pay for his funeral instead when he died of a heart attack. After that, Lydia collected her father's bed and Portman trunk and brought them to her own house. Joseck continued to sleep on the floor. At night the whine of lorries lumbering on the main road competed with the croaking of frogs.

Lydia had intended to buy a sewing machine to begin her own business, but all her money from the sale of bananas and avocadoes at the market went to school fees and supplies for Joseck. The sewing machine would have to wait; metal sheeting to complete the roof would have to wait; glass for the window frames would have to wait.

Joseck disliked school. He preferred the sweat won through work, rather than the heat of a classroom bench shared with a dozen children. He begged his mother to let him bring the bananas to Suneka and stay with her through the day. Lydia, however, insisted that he pay attention to the teachers, learn how to read and get good marks . Despite his drowsiness in dark and stuffy rooms, his middling grades kept him out of trouble,— not a star but a good boy. When Lydia could no longer afford fees for the private school, she reluctantly sent Joseck to Standard Four in a government school. For Joseck, this was an improvement. Since there were too many students in his standard for any classroom on the compound to contain, Joseck and fifty mates sat on the grassy hillside, and no longer struggling with the heaviness of lethargy, his mind wandered far from academics. He wanted to join the clamour of the *jua kali* market across the highway from his mother's banana stand.

Which was easy to do, as teachers couldn't keep track of a thousand children and, in fact, were happy to have fewer pupils. On many days, he slipped away with his teacher's blessing. Lydia, busy with her work, wouldn't see him and before the final assembly of the day, he would return to the school compound to be counted as present.

The *jua kali* men who worked across the road from the vegetable market were self-employed outdoor workers who cut keys, fashioned containers out of metal scraps, kept cars usable with ties of rope and spanners, repaired used toilets and built water troughs, fixed flip flops and shoes with super glue, sold re-worked cast-off junk, made coffins, crafted chairs and tables. They were creative workers who were glad to send Joseck on the back of a pick-up truck with messages into Kisii Town five miles away or have him search for orphaned scraps of material needed to complete their handiwork. They paid Joseck with patience and an apprenticeship in astonishing ingenuity. He most valued his independence.

One day there was a great deal of excitement on the roadside.

"Yes, yes," the oven maker shouted, "last night there was a raid. They burnt down a house and cattle were stolen. Who is ready to get them back?"

There were as many opinions as bananas on a hand, as Joseck sat on a pile of metal sheeting trying to follow the arguments. But nothing happened that day. They couldn't afford to lay down their tools for justice.

News swept through Suneka that the police had shot four Kisiis on the district border and had rounded up herds of Kisii cattle to return to the Maasai, who claimed they were merely reclaiming what the Kisii had stolen from them. "*Chinkororo, chinkororo*. We will rain down on you," the workers in the market shouted. Who initiated the chant of young Kisii warriors never was determined, but it carried on throughout the day and long after sunset by school leavers and young men who made signs, raised fists, danced and sang.

"*Chinkororo! Chinkororo! Chinkororo! Chinkororo!*" From that point on, that's what those were called who pledged to protect the region and avenge Kisiis like the warriors who had saved them from the Maasai, the Kipsigis and the Luo in the past.

The *chinkororo* went on their first retaliatory raid in the Trans Mara. Long before sunrise, Joseck pulled himself to the windowsill, boosted himself through the uncovered part of the roof and clambered down the outside wall of the house without waking Lydia. Two pickup trucks were on the main road. Joseck climbed on board one them and rode with the *chinkororo*, clutching a fistful of stones and a hastily made bow as he squatted, squeezed tightly in with the others. Everyone was still as the pickups followed the red dirt, unlit roads south.

"Stay," Joseck was told, as the motors were quit. A dozen *chinkororo* alighted, ran down a lane, crossed a rise and stepped cautiously into a field of cattle under starlight. Before the livestock bellowing and lowing brought moran to the field to stop the rustling, the *chinkororo* rounded up a calf, lifted it onto the bed of one of the pickups. The trucks sped away, and as they drove back to Suneka the stopped to return the calf to an aggrieved farmer near Nyangusu.

Having caught the Maasai by surprise and the police unaware, the *chinkororo* returned to Suneka before noon and were feted as heroes. They displayed their bramble abrasions, bruises and cuts on their arms and legs to admiring girls. No one questioned why Joseck was unscathed. He basked in the glory along with the others. The *chinkororo* drank gallons of beer with local officials. Politicians saluted them with speeches.

"For your defense of the homeland," saluted one elder. "A little for you," he said to Joseck as he shook his hand and gave him a pile of fresh bills. "The first payment as our new warrior."

After the night raid Joseck attended Suneka Primary infrequently, rarely bothering to show up for roll call. He took his morning groundnuts and tea, packed his bag and slung it over his shoulder to head out, returning in time for dinner.

Lydia didn't ask to see his homework; she never saw him read at home. She didn't get summoned to school, but she knew that Joseck wasn't attending classes, and she didn't try to persuade him to attend to his subjects; she no longer promised him a bright future, if only he would graduate.

〰〰〰〰〰
〰〰〰〰〰

AT THE START OF THE NEW TERM, Lydia conceded that Joseck wasn't meant for school and there was nothing she could do to distract him from the working with his hands. She saw little chance that he would have made the necessary marks for entry into secondary school, and even if he did, it was unlikely she could afford the fees.

In truth, Lydia was glad to be relieved of the burden of paying for a school uniform, books, and school supplies, and was happy for the few shillings Joseck gave her from his earnings.

Joseck never crossed the road from the *jua kali* center to the vegetable market. He was on his own, returning after dark, when Lydia was asleep. After a few years, he didn't return at all.

He told his mother that he worked in the supermarket near the cyber café in Kisii. Whenever Lydia went to Kisii Town, she walked past the crowded car park in front of Nakumatt and down the aisles of canned and packaged foods, pots and pans, and bottles of liquids of many colors. She didn't find Joseck there but always on the town streets or with friends on the steps of the city market.

When confronted with how he spent his time, Joseck replied, "Here and there, with friends. No problem. I'm fine here. Kisii is a good place."

Joseck wasn't completely honest with his mother. He lived with other school leavers, as squatters in an incomplete flat, but he was truthful about having more than enough to eat, although Lydia would have blanched knowing that the food often came from the spoiled fruits and vegetables tossed behind the town market or from filched tins taken from the supermarket, but it was more food than he had at home. He came and went as he pleased. Joseck could never have imagined there could be such freedom.

Work, when he wanted it, came readily. Odd jobs were always available. Quickly his tasks grew into more substantial work as he learned auto body repair and how to fix car engines. His income grew. But why pay rent, why buy food? Whatever he needed he got. After all, everyone knew who he was: Joseck, the boy from the cattle raid, a story that was burnished with each of his retelling. His name would become mythic, remembered with that of other Kisii legends, leaders and defenders of great things, Joseck thought. He and his fellow in *chinkororo* would put a stop to the rising violence in Kisii, the thefts and the murders wracking their community, and they would do what the police would not. They would protect their people; do whatever necessary to bring justice to bear.

He would purchase a plot in the greenest part of the district, Joseck thought, in the richest valley in Kisii and on it there would be tea and coffee and cattle, vegetables and fruit, and he would hire hands to do the labor. The house would be a mansion, as grand as any in Kisii, a pink house with protective walls too high for any thief to scale, a house with an iron railing wrapped around an imposing balcony on the upper story, a house big enough for all his friends with as many rooms as his mother desired for herself and there would be a cook and a housemaid to help her, and on the roof would be the biggest satellite dish bringing shows from everywhere to his TV, and he would hire security guards with rifles and have the most ferocious dogs to protect them all while he drank the finest whiskeys that the supermarket sold.

He would be as wealthy as any *sonko* and hire drivers for his Land Rovers and surround himself with bodyguards, and he would fly whenever he wished, from Suneka to Mombasa to England, in his own airplane.

Every Voice

AN OLD MAN WITH AN OLD horse pulling a dray came to Junius's neighborhood twice a year. "Alte claz, alte claz," he sang out as bells dangling from the wagon clanged with each plodding step of the blinkered mare. Susan would call from the front steps of the rowhouse for the ragman to stop and tell Junius to give him the bundles of worn clothes and rags she had kept in the closet under the staircase.

Although feral dogs that lived in the weeds of the nearby subway and trolley yard also scared Junius with their snarls when they trotted down his street, but at least he could duck into a hallway until they passed, but with the rag-wagon he was exposed, assailed by the fetid smell and flies. He was frightened by the peddler who grunted and scowled. A thick stream of gleet from the nag's nostrils disgusted Junius and the size of the animal, even as it stood mutely indifferent, intimidated him.

Junius tossed the knotted rags onto the wagon as the old man grumbled in his garbled and rough tongue, "Alte claz, alte claz," not bothering to turn to watch Junius run away.

While Junius feared the Alte-Claz Man, as his mother called him, Eldon derided the peddler and his horse.

"That Jew," Junius's friend said.

Junius looked at Eldon, not admitting that he didn't know what he was talking about. The only Jews he knew were those in the bible stories heard at church.

"I know where he keeps the horse."

"The horse really stinks. It has snot coming out of its nose."

"The Jew stinks, too," Eldon added. "He stinks up the street."

Eldon persuaded his friend to follow him down the street under the elevated train tracks, as far as Truxton St., taking him into what for him was a new area. Here were auto repair shops, many garages and, at the end of a cobblestone alley between a row and frame house, a small stable. They clambered onto the roof of a garage littered with greasy parts and tires until they heard the sound of the horse and wagon slowly returning home.

"Let's go," Junius urged. "It's getting late. I need to get home before supper."

"Yeah, OK," Eldon said.

They slid down the back of the roof. The old man saw them and shouted.

"Old Jew!"

Eldon found a rock and threw it towards the wagon. The ragman climbed from the wagon and shouted. Eldon picked up another rock and threw it. The peddler put his hand against his bleeding temple. Eldon scrambled up to the stable roof again. He lifted up a rusted anvil with both arms and tossed it over the side.

When Junius arrived home, his mother didn't turn from the kitchen sink. She said, "You smell to high heaven, Junius. Go wash yourself off, then come to the table." As Junius started for the bathroom, she added, "I don't want you to ever do this again. You know when you are supposed to be home."

Whether Susan spoke to her husband, Junius never knew. Carl said nothing to his son about it that or any other night.

It took many years for Junius to forget the look of the horse sprawled in front of the barn, its lolling tongue, the dray turned on its side, the old man sitting beside his dead mare. Junius had heard there was a factory in Queens where horses were turned into glue. He wondered how they would get the animal there.

No one else that Junius knew referred to his neighborhood as Weeksville and if Junius had asked his parents why they called it by that name, they would have said that's what his mother's parents had called it. She knew traces, scraps, legends, lore and rumors about the area. All she could say that it was an old section of Brooklyn that had also been populated by Negroes. Junius's parents grew up just blocks from each other but his father always said that he came from Crown Heights.

Susan's family had lived in the area for several generations; Carl's came from South Carolina at the turn of the 20th century. By then Weeksville was largely gone, crushed in the pincers of housing projects, most especially the Kingsborough Houses, a 16 building complex with more than 1,000 apartments, just blocks from the Cassels' home cast.

In the living room of the Cassel's row house was a framed photograph that was the only visual reminder of the village that not only had disappeared from view but had also nearly vanished from history's record. The man with the derby standing with his arm crossed in front of the Rapid Transit Boot Black Parlor, Susan said, was his grandfather on his mother's side.

Grandpa Junius wasn't a bootblack or storeowner, his parents told him, but a lawyer with an office on Utica Avenue. Junius Gibson's clientele were blacks and Jews.

When Carl and Susan married, they took the second floor of the Pacific Street rowhouse. Grandpa had his bedroom on the top floor. Susan insisted that they eat dinner together, even if it meant waiting into the evening for Carl to get home from the wharves. Junius remembers references to ministers and tailors, schoolteachers, storeowners, nurses, a woman doctor. They joked that the nearby Fulton Street subway was the second Underground Railroad in the neighborhood; they also referred to the trains that ran above Atlantic Avenue from Long Island to downtown Brooklyn as the 'Overhead Railroad.' Junius didn't make the connection to the neighbor's past.

His grandfather died when Junius was five and he took the top floor bedroom. Without a few photos of him as an older man, he wouldn't remember what he looked like.

There was still a third possibility for his name, he realized. A newspaper clipping that was filed between the pages the photo album reported that 14-year-old George Junius Stinney had been executed after confessing to the murders of two white girls. A brief note, also tucked into the album, addressed to Carl read, "This poor boy is from Alcolu. No Afro Americans allowed in court. Jury out ten minutes. You may know the family."

Table conversation often centered around Carl's work at the docks and whether Local 968 should amalgamate with white longshoremen, the changing nature of the neighborhood and talk of moving to a more congenial area on Long Island where work was steady, —"There's airplane building out there. The guys say there's work."—never talk about lynchings or burnings or executions or Jim Crow, but they were all present, like an invisible riptide digging deeper into the shoreline of their lives.

The Cassel's worshipped at the Bethel Tabernacle African Methodist Episcopal Church, where each Sunday the congregation sang: "Lift every voice and sing,/ till earth and Heaven ring,/ ring with the harmonies of liberty"— though the liberties Junius soon pursued weren't what his parents longed for. Church fell away. Under the railroad trestle on Atlantic Avenue and in a concrete tunnel that near the railroad yard, he lifted his voice with the Sparrows, the group he had formed; ran his hand under a girl's blouse behind the abandoned houses on the unnamed alley; listened to singers through open windows at nearby clubs. He knew every song on the charts and knew nearly every girl within a quarter mile.

The Cassel's parked their newly bought two-year old used 1955 two-tone Pontiac Starchief in front of their stoop. After washing the aqua and white car, Junius would sit behind the wheel, eager for the day when he would be able to drive himself. When Carl said they were going for a ride out to the Island to see for themselves what others were talking about, Junius agreed. Carl, with his pencil-thin mustache neatly brushed, wore his summer suit. He loosened his striped tie as he sat behind the steering wheel. Susan sat in the middle of the bench seat in her Sunday best, her pageboy brushing her shoulders, her hat fixed primly upright, while Junius put his elbow out the open window, hoping to be seen by friends as they followed city streets to the parkway entrance at the foot of the cemeteries.

Carl gave Susan his fedora to hold.

'Faster,' Junius wanted to tell his father, who gripped the steering wheel tightly, his mouth pulled tight, not allowing the car to budge beyond the 25 mph speed limit, but still it was thrilling enough to sit in the thing of beauty as it hugged the narrow twisting pass through several cemeteries that arched on either side, ridges filled with crypts and tombstones. Junius had been to one of the cemeteries before, for grandpa's burial. His mother said that another ancestor was buried here, in one of the graves, which one she didn't know as time had effaced the records but probably in the Cedar Vale, where the Colored Troops of the Civil War were put to rest.

The highway straightened out as it merged with Grand Central Parkway in Queens and Carl pressed the pedal a little harder to edge towards the 35 mph speed limit as the Pontiac took Junius further from home than he'd ever been, the tree-lined roadway transporting him to the factories on the Long Island flatlands.

"This is where Sam works now," Carl said, staring at the gates of a sprawling complex that seemed as big as the Breakwater Piers as they sat in the idling car. "He likes it. It's steady, you know you've got work every day, and it's cleaner. No more banana boats. No stink can be like that, no matter what. No rats. It's good steady work, Susan."

Carl smiled as he looked at the directory sign that pointed to dozens of warehouses, hangars, office buildings, factories and storage sheds. Junius hoped one of the military fighter planes arranged on landing strips would soon take off.

"He's talking about moving out here. It got me to think about things, too. It's not good on the docks. No more. I don't see a future there. It's going from bad to worse. It'd be nice to live out here. You know, with the GI Bill we can do it."

Carl drove miles on streets that turned in circles—Blacksmith to Weaver to Saddler, one section where streets were named after girls, another after flowers. They found Cadillac, Buick and Mercury. Pontiac Place was near Susan Court, an auspicious sign, Carl said aloud. Several times they wound up where they started. There were swimming pools but no basketball courts, cars but no pedestrians. Stores were clustered together and school grounds were much like Junius imagined a college campus to be like.

"What do you think, Susan?"

"It's not for us."

Carl pulled the car to the curb and put his hand on his wife's shoulder. Susan didn't turn her head.

"Those were rednecks, Susan. The Myers stuck it out. It's OK. I've seen rougher on the piers. That was Pennsylvania. It won't be like that here."

Susan admired Carl's courage, the way he had never backed down from the thugs at the wharves or the white union leaders. He stood firm against Local 1814's attempt to siphon off black stevedores from his local.

"Why look for trouble?"

"It's not like that here. I think it's time for us to get a better place."

"They're very small. The houses are very small," she insisted, dragging her words for emphasis.

"$100 down, $65 a month. That's what it said. It's a good deal. We can easily swing it."

Susan didn't want to leave Weeksville; Carl knew that. She had been the bookkeeper and office manager at a used car dealership for years. But the neighborhoods were already going to hell in a hand basket, as the dealer said. Cars on the lot had been vandalized and the office had been held up at gunpoint.

Perhaps Carl was right, it was time to go. If he could get better work on the in the suburbs, maybe life could be better, even if it meant uprooting a lifetime of generations.

The new amalgamation of locals would mean that his lot would be thrown in with that of white longshoremen and that couldn't be good.

"Those new containers, Susan, they'll be the death of all of us on the docks. They're going to put most of us on the unemployment line."

Maybe, she thought, maybe it wouldn't be so bad living somewhere new, leaving the dead behind. The housing projects erected just blocks from their home had already changed the neighborhood she and Carl had once known so well.

Junius wished he hadn't agreed to come along. He opened the car door and turned to put his feet on the street, his back to his parents, his chin in his hands. He looked at the stores in the strip mall. They were closed but not shuttered; no grates, just locked doors.

"They're small, I agree. But we're already out here. No harm just asking around and seeing for ourselves. Isn't this what we want? A backyard, a place to put the car."

"If you ask me, our car will be just as happy remaining on the street. And what do you plan to do with a backyard? Our front stoop is just fine." Susan touched Carl's hand. "We'll talk later."

Carl reached across her lap to the glove compartment and removed a page torn from the classifieds. He read the address aloud.

"Junius," he called. "Find this for me, son."

Junius spread the street map they had been using across his lap and directed his father back to the broad boulevard that separated the north from south subdivisions.

The office was the development show room, with models of the several style houses available, the model trees fully leafed, the grass perfectly green. Toy cars were in every driveway, a few tiny white people walked the streets. Carl filled out a form and handed it to a receptionist and they waited without speaking to one another.

The receptionist took the paper to an agent. The agent glanced up at the Cassels from his desk piled high with brochures and files. He continued to open and close folders, looking at his wristwatch and rubbing his neck. More than a half-hour later he called them.

"Mr. Cassel, Mrs. Cassel? Nice to meet you. Please, here, take a seat," he said, pointing to folding chairs. Junius stood behind his father. The agent rose, his jacket hung over the back of his chair and reached across the desk to shake Carl's hand. As he sat down, he cinched his tie. "What can I do for you today?"

"We came to see a model house."

"Sure. Where do you live now?" he asked,

"Brooklyn."

"Rent?"

"We own a house."

"So it's time to move on to something better."

"We're thinking it may be a good time for us to move."

"You're interested in buying?"

"That's a possibility. We've got to see if we like it."

"Tell me about the place you live in now, Mr. Cassel."

Carl described their eight-room, three-storey house.

"This would be a big change for you. Are you sure?"

"That's why we need to know the particulars. And see a house for ourselves."

"Of course, Mr. Cassel," the agent agreed. "Our houses are smaller, but there are advantages, as you know. Fresh air. Trees. Grass. It's a great thing moving out here, especially coming from Brooklyn like you do." He paused for a moment, a tic the Cassels knew well. The agent continued, "But I have to tell you. These houses here, right now there aren't any for sale."

"None? None at all?"

Carl felt the pressure of Susan's hand on his thigh.

"Not right here. But there are plenty not too far from here, built by the same developer. I'm happy to show you them. Just as nice as these models."

"Let's go, then, Carl," Susan said, "This isn't the place for us. I've seen enough, haven't you?"

Susan could feel the heat rising from her husband.

"Which development then?" Carl asked. "This one seems fine to me."

"You wouldn't be happy here, Mrs. Cassel, even if I could sell one to you."

"If you had one to sell?"

"It's not your kind of place. But there are others just as nice where that would be more to your liking."

"I like it here," Carl said sharply.

"I understand, Mr. Cassel. Listen," he said, leaning across the desk, "I know what you are thinking. But I know about living with your own kind. I'm a Jew myself, so I understand about these things, you see."

"Yes, I do."

"There are other neighborhoods where I know you'll be more comfortable, in the village I want to show you, near the parkway and railroad station. Models like we have here. Come on. I have a car here. We can all fit in. I'll show you."

"No, you won't, not today," Susan said in the same soft but stern tone that she used to discipline Junius. "We have to get home."

She took Carl's hand.

"This is some set-up you got," Carl said, shaking the agent's hand. He put his hat on as he stood. "It reminds me of South Carolina, if you know what I mean. People with their own kind. There're nice places there, too, for your kind. I'm sure you'd be comfortable there. But not me."

On the ride back to Brooklyn, Susan said, "The houses really are small. We can fit two of them in our house."

If Carl wasn't worrying about Monday's shape-up in a semi-circle around the hiring foreman and feeling like a nigger again, and if Susan hadn't closed her eyes to steady her breathing, they might have seen a faint smile on Junius's face and they may have even heard him singing to himself a song he was practicing with the Sparrows: "I'm searchin'/ I'm searchin'/ Searchin' every which a-way/ Yeah, yeah/ But I'm like the Northwest Mounties/ You know I'll bring her in someday/ Gonna find her/ Gonna find her."

Big Red

〜〜〜〜〜
〜〜〜〜〜

AMONGST LENA'S EARLIEST MEMORIES are those of her father in their Brighton Beach kitchen reading the *Daily Worker* aloud to her mother, Ida, who prepares dinner for the three of them in a room scarcely bigger than a prison cell.

She also remembers the frequent japery with Henry, the air hazy with his cigarette smoke, her father miming wealthy doctors by searching through Ida's black purse as though it were a medical bag. Her father taps Lena's chest, orders her to stick out her tongue and pronounces her very sick. He pretends to count money in large denominations while Lena collapses to the floor crying for help.

"Another ten dollars," he demands from Ida. Ida doesn't smile, as she watches the pan blacken under a slab of searing brisket.

Lena clutches her chest, gasps for breath and falls silent.

Taking on a new role, now Henry histrionically whispers about taking poison pills from his municipal hospital pharmacy warren and drops the invisible medication into the china coffee cups of doctors who identify not with labor but with the capitalist class. Lena springs up like a Jack-in-the-box toy and applauds her father's heroic deed.

Ida is expressionless. She turns the meat onto the other side.

When they aren't playacting, Henry dandles Lena on his lap as he tells her tales of slain beasts in dark forests. Nicotine stains his right forefinger and thumb. With each word Lena inhales the smell of tobacco and mint.

For two summers Lena was sent to Camp Kinderland, a children's program, run by the International Workers Order. They were glorious times away from the small Brooklyn apartment. Her hopes for returning for a third summer were dashed when the camp in Hopewell Junction, in upstate New York, was seized by the U.S. government, when it determined that Kinderland was run by a communist organization.

Pamphlets and books filled the tiny apartment. The *Daily Worker* covered the living room chairs and floor, the glass coffee table, the bottom of the armoire in her parents' bedroom and on top of the mahogany console radio-phonograph, the only piece of furniture that anyone could call luxurious. As an adult, Lena could only guess that the reason the papers were never tossed out was the fear that the government was going through their garbage. She didn't ask as a child.

Photography books most interested her. At first Lena stared at the photographs of concentration camp liberations and war scenes from the siege of Leningrad, finding the pictures haunting and even beautiful, like the fairy tales that left her more thrilled than afraid. She often imagined herself standing hands on hips looking into the skies over Russia for warplanes, daring them to shoot, saving the world from Nazi terror.

She doesn't recall when their skits stopped or when he no longer mugged for her and instead railed at the thumbnail size TV shoved into a corner next to the radiator. Was it the year he cloistered himself in the apartment after being fired by the hospital for his refusal to answer the panel's questions? Perhaps later, when he took the endless subway commute to the drugstore in downtown Manhattan, a position found through a second-hand comrade, which paid him off the books at less than he made as a city employee, a place he deplored two blocks from Wall Street.

"At least I have work," he explained weakly. His small smile never returned, replaced by permanently pursed lips. Later in life, Lena wondered how he ever managed to smile after he changed his name the year before he was married, from Herschel Morelowitz to Henry Morrell, two years before her birth.

Lena remembers his rimless eyeglasses but not the color of his eyes, his baggy trousers but not how tall he was. She remembers that for what seemed forever he didn't replace the missing lens, the one broken by his brother-in-law, Leo, during a fight over how he treated Lena's mother, a fight that turned from ideological tangles to curses both personal and political.

"May your shit and pus turn as red as you," Uncle Leo shouted. "If you love Russia so much . . . "

Henry leaped from his chair, his face purple with rage, a condition Lena often associated with his denunciations of America's latest depredations. Leo's first blow shattered a lens in Henry's glasses and bent the wire frame. Blood trickled from Henry's nose; he stepped on glass shards as he slowly sat on the floor, stunned into silence.

This was the beginning, Lena thought, of her mother's withdrawal from Henry's rigidity and anger and it was the time Lena furiously lost herself in books. She had read every Meridel Le Sueur history and novels several times, the only children's books allowed in her household, and had enough of Abe Lincoln's mother and Johnny Appleseed and Sparrow Hawk. She couldn't find a book about the Russian Night Witches, the women pilots of the Soviet Air Force and long into her adulthood she thought that this was her father's own creation, a fable made just for her. Done with every book that interested her, she insisted her mother get her a child's library card so she could spend Saturday's undisturbed by the domestic eruptions around Henry's self-pity, his soul like cold steel and his reasoning just as hard, as in his insistence on wearing glasses with one lens, the second lens being a capitalist swindle—"You can see just as well with one"; his implacable attacks on Ida's bourgeois desire for a bigger apartment or even one whose windows faced out onto a street, not a courtyard—"That's why we have parks."

Henry wore his one-lens eyeglasses as a badge of political courage. Lena remembers him squinting with his left eye so as to allow the remaining lens to do its job—"just as good, like a monocle," he said until it was pointed out to him that monocles were associated with capitalists and aristocrats.

Only authors approved by the Party were allowed in the apartment, writers coming and disappearing, permitted one week, banished another, although Fast and Wright were always on the nightstand between her parents' twin beds. One day when rummaging through her mother's dresser drawer Lena found two Steinbeck novels, *The Pearl* and *Canary Row* placed under winter sweaters, an astonishing discovery since Henry had recently accused the author of insufficient ideological commitment and backsliding into anti-Marxism.

Folksongs, especially by Negroes—spirituals, in particular, which Henry explained weren't really about religion but were coded messages of freedom—were permitted. His favorite singer was Paul Robeson whom he held up as one of the greatest Americans ever to live. Popular music was beneath comment. Henry dreamily sat in his chair listening to Prokofiev sonatas on the Zenith console.

Lena listened to many children and folk songs until her father disposed of Burl Ives' six-album set of "Historical America in Song" because Ives had betrayed the revolution by favorably testifying before the House Committee on Un-American Activities.

Lena continued to sing her favorites whenever Henry wasn't home. "Jimmy crack corn and I don't care / Jimmy crack corn and I don't care / Jimmy crack corn and I don't care / My master's gone away."

Ida didn't care.

Lena didn't understand who made the lists that her father insisted upon following, but it didn't matter. At the library she roamed alone, appreciating the enforced silence. Her solitude opened doors to more places than she thought possible at home.

No longer conversation or even derision but memorized poetry ruled the table, while Ida sat sullen and Lena swam in the sound of meanings she didn't understand. "Your thoughts/ dreaming on a softened brain/ like an over-fed lackey on a greasy settee,/ with my heart's bloody tatters I'll mock again;/ impudent and caustic,/ I'll jeer to superfluity."

"A softened brain, a greasy settee," and with those phrases Lena began to wend through every book of poetry in the children's section and found none satisfying, this only fueling her desire for something raw and beautiful and mysterious, which she uncovered in "The Raven" and Poe's short stories. Barred from the adults-only section, the books on the forbidden side grew in allurement, beckoning her. Lena knew how many days remained before she was allowed into the sanctum. Until then whenever an adult book lay unattended, she put the book on her lap and, hunched over, devoured it as quickly as she could. She leafed through each one she found, getting dizzy on new words whose sounds she repeated like music, not understanding most of what she read. She put some under her coat and brought them home, hiding them under her bed. When she finished the purloined book, she placed it upright against the library's entrance.

The Party arranged for Henry's funeral. Ida and Lena took the subway to the Bronx and, in a parlor under the shadow of a rattling El, testimonials soared to high oratory and inspiration that only undiluted idealism can provide. Nothing personal, nothing about Henry's life, his work, his family, nothing Lena could recognize, no Ida, no Lena, Henry simply another comrade in the good fight against the ruthlessness of a system that would one day soon find itself in the ashcan of history. Her father was a soldier in the long march. That he marched off the subway platform was never mentioned, not by the men in their somber suits and not by Ida, then or ever.

A large man, nearly handsome, whom Lena knew as an occasional visitor to her apartment, walked her and her mother to the Grand Concourse, expressed his sympathies, shook their hands and paid for the carfare home.

Months later the police released his belongings to Ida. They never explained what interested them or what they thought they could learn from it. It certainly had to do with the trials and deportations of Communist Party-USA members, but Ida never asked or protested.

Before the week was over, newspapers that had accumulated for years, including the issue that made reference to Henry's death in the middle of a story about the need for the city to acquire the entire subway system, went out to the trash with kitchen scraps.

Ida took work in a tea-packing factory within walking distance of the apartment and Lena's friends began to call her Big Red because she was the tallest girl in the class and had shockingly red hair that tumbled thickly to her shoulders. Her father had been bald and her mother's hair was auburn and she sometimes wondered about the hair color of the seltzer deliveryman whose services were long ago discontinued. As an adult she learned that many children wished for an alternative beginning. But now, in high school, only the covers of books bound her parallel universe.

In high school Lena made friends who enjoyed the pleasure of words as much as she did. She joined the Abraham Lincoln High School student newspaper. As a sophomore, her assignments were minor but she was published, two items highlighting upcoming events. Without an assignment and under her own initiative, Lena turned in a lengthy article critical of the cafeteria food. This seemed banal enough, as there wasn't a student who didn't complain about it. Lena didn't mind the food as much as she objected to the costs. Her editor, a senior, liked it. The student advisor didn't.

"We can't publish this," he said to her. Mr. Herbst loomed over her as she sat by the typewriter in the basement office. He held her story between his thumb and forefinger.

"What's wrong with it?"

"We don't publish things like this."

Lena asked which part of the story he didn't like.

"The whole thing."

She asked him to point out which part was inaccurate. Did he enjoy the food? Of course not. Teachers had their own lunchroom.

"That's not the point, Lena. The paper isn't here to criticize the school. We don't air dirty laundry, if that's what it is."

Her father defended Russia, always and adamantly. He was never wrong, even when he contradicted what he said the week before; Ida was right only when she agreed with him.

"What's it for?" she asked.

"For you to learn about how to put together a newspaper and what it means to be a journalist."

Lena convinced the rest of the staff that there was a difference between an advisor and a censor. They wouldn't write another story until Mr. Herbst relented. He didn't need to say any more. His silence defeated them. Without comment from the advisor or anyone in administration, since the students didn't submit more articles for scrutiny, no further issues of the paper appeared that term. The following year other students voted for Lena to become assistant editor. Herbst vetoed the choice. Lena and three others quit. The paper continued and the rest of the student body paid no attention. Herbst was right: no one cared what the paper printed; no one expected to be informed; a monthly paper couldn't deliver information in a timely manner; the paper was another club, a school project to provide the essential skills of citizenship.

That winter Lena told her mother that she had made a choice that would deny her a diploma.

"I'm not going to let you do it," Ida said. "You're going to college."

Lena threw her green wool coat over the back of the couch.

"I won't sign it."

She unpacked her school bag and sat at the kitchen table to do her homework.

"Don't cut off your nose to spite your face," her mother said. "This is foolish. Don't do this to me."

Lena pushed the notebook aside. "I'm just standing up for what's right. I'm not foolish. It is the oath that is stupid. You know it."

"I signed it."

"Did Daddy?"

"We never talked about it. Everybody signed it. He went to college, so he must have."

"You shouldn't have signed it. How could you sign something you didn't believe? It's cowardly."

"It is stupid. But it is even more stupid not to sign it, not cowardly. You're going to college. Not to go is stupid."

"What's the point of it? If I'm not loyal, I'll sign to hide. And if I am loyal, signing my name doesn't matter."

"The point is, you're going to college. When Hunter finds out that you didn't get your diploma, that's it. Then what?"

"So I won't go to college."

"Yes, you will."

"The vice-principal said that refusing to sign means that I have bad character. I told him that if I signed, that's when my character would be bad."

"Don't tell me about your character. What good's your character if you don't go? You'll sign it."

" 'Not a step back.' I heard Daddy say many times," Lena said. "I'm not going to take a step back."

"You're going to sign it. No more discussion."

Surprised by her mother's strength, Lena said little the rest of the weekend. There had never been a question but that she would go to college. As an all-girls school, Hunter College appealed to her and for months she imagined what it would be like to be surrounded by other smart young women. Without a diploma, the vice-principal told her when she was called into his office after she said to her homeroom teacher she wasn't going to sign the loyalty oath, Hunter College wouldn't take her. No city college would and only tuition-free city colleges were a possibility for her. No other colleges had ever been considered, no other applications had been filed.

Lena thought she had made her point. The school knew her position. Further protest on her part wouldn't move the system and martyrs were not part of Jewish consciousness. So she signed. Regret set in when, that spring, the loyalty oath was abolished by the state. Lena now found a new sympathy for her father. Signing wasn't craven but bad timing; progress didn't run in straight lines. Courage came in measured drops as well as dollops. But she didn't have to sign and she knew that she had failed herself and she wouldn't do that again.

Lena was class valedictorian and gave the graduation speech at Lincoln High. Ida, proudly seated a row behind the school officials, was as shocked as anyone when Lena, after thanking her fellow students and saying how proud she was to be able to finally address her them, she denounced the Cold War, called for unilateral nuclear disarmament and, invoking the school's namesake as she looked at the vice-principal with her hazel eyes, rallied students to the cause of racial desegregation "like the brave volunteers of the Lincoln Brigade in our father's generation who fought against the fascists in Spain." Students stood on their wooden seats chanting 'Not a step back! Not a step back!' under Lena's urging. As the principal stepped to the podium to wrest the microphone from Lena, she began her Woodie Guthrie imitation: "This land is your land,/ This land is my land/ From California to the New York Island."

"Let her speak!" a student shouted.

"Leave her alone!"

"I will now present diplomas," the principal continued, "to some of you who are deserving."

The auditorium filled with hisses.

Lena continued to sing without the microphone.

"If you don't stop immediately, I'll cancel this graduation ceremony," the principal shouted. "I will not hand out diplomas to unruly demons."

"Not a step back! Not a step back!" could be heard.

"That's enough."

The chant continued.

"That's it. Go home, everyone. Go home. I hereby suspend this exercise."

The vice-principal, who had been seated on the dais with other school officials, took Lena by the arm and pulled her from the stage. Her flushed face erased her freckles. "I roamed and I rambled / And I followed my footsteps?/

To the sparkling sands of her diamond deserts" —she continued to sing above the commotion.

Ida ran to the aisle with the graduation program rolled into a baton. She hit the vice-principal on the shoulder.

"Take your hands off my daughter!"

"Big Red," someone shouted.

The principal told the students they would have to return to school that afternoon to get their diplomas. It was uncertain that the chorus of jeers that followed were for the principal or for Lena.

"Go home. Now!" he continued. "Dismissed! Go home. Go home."

The principal sputtered his directive as relatives and students milled about. Some students ran down the aisles, stood on seats, tore the program and threw it into the air like confetti.

Slowly the auditorium emptied, students confused and uncertain about what had just happened and whether they were graduates now, next week or ever.

The Rooster
Gives Way to the Hen

~~~~~~~~~~

DURING KWAMBOKA'S YEARS AT the Royal College of Nairobi, students debated the future of the soon-to-be independent nation.

"They stole our land. We need to take it back."

"Slowly, brother, slowly. They'll go in time. But for now we need their expertise. *Wazungu* have a place."

"They need to be put in their place."

They debated the place of religion in the new society: Christianity as salvation; Christianity as a curse on tribal values; African Christianity.

They argued who would rule, how they would rule: African elders; British law; customary. They debated about those who had taken to the forests to fight and those who stayed behind: Mau Mau as freedom fighters; Mau Mau as terrorists. What was to become of the Home Guard?

Independence was coming. But then what? A single nation with a strong central government or regions each with its own president? What about those who weren't Luo or Kikuyu, then what? Who would represent the interests of the smaller tribes?

And the land: Who did it belong to—the government, individuals, the tribe or clan? Should there be title deeds for individual ownership or should they follow tribal customs and put things back as they were before contaminating by the Europeans?

Justice looked different from each hilltop.

Kwamboka listened and said little. Her concerns were about her mother's ability to support herself at the farm after her father's death. According to custom Cecilia was expected to marry a brother of her late husband. Kwamboka's father was one four boys. Tradition excluded the older brothers as levirs. Her father's junior was conscripted by the British as part of the forces in the East African campaign in WWII and died at the Battle of Gondar.

Cecilia rebuffed the pressure to become a second—or in one instance, a third—wife and leave her farm. The life of a junior wife was seldom a good one. She would rather rely upon her own efforts than be directed by both a husband and a co-wife. Her brothers-in-law allowed Cecilia to stay on their late brother's farm.

When Cecilia refused to become a co-wife and then a cow died on that farm, she was suspected of witchcraft. Cecilia's strength of character and self-effacing demeanor helped stave off the slanderous charges against her.

Another allegation surfaced when a rebuffed suitor died in a road accident. And yet once more when lightning struck the house of another man who wanted her in marriage and killed him.

"No one dies without carrying someone on his back," the dead man's brother said, quoting a Kisii proverb, and pointed to her as the cause of the death. This accusation of witchcraft disappeared for the final time only when the deceased's wife told others in the marketplace that she never wanted a co-wife, it was her husband's wishes. Neighbors concluded that his ancestors had punished him, not a witch. With no other misfortunes befalling their location, Cecilia and her daughter were finally left in peace. Cecilia belonged to the stone church on the hill and during the time she was being accused of witchcraft, she had sought help from the European priest. But he rebuffed her, telling her roughly that witches were of no concern of his. She needed to come to church on Sunday to receive communion, nothing more. Cecilia couldn't see the reason to come to church any longer when it was useless to protect her against vengeful neighbors and her participation faded just as did the accusations.

Fortunately for Kwamboka, the African nuns who ran the school didn't like the priest with the florid face any more than did Cecilia. The nuns knew he had no liking for Africans but did his duty to save black souls while not caring about their everyday and bodily concerns. His interaction with the nuns was confined to their ensuring his stomach never grumbled.

The nuns didn't notice that Cecilia had lapsed and, therefore, it had no effect on Kwamboka's status as a student. Kwamboka was a favorite. No one was surprised that her marks exceeded that of all the other girls—there wasn't much competition in that category. The shock was that she out-performed even the top boy in the district that year and came in tops on the national exam.

"We are very, very proud of you, dear Sarah," Sister Consolata told her.

Kwamboka bowed her head, held her hands behind her back and smiled.

"We were talking about you, Sarah." Sister Consolata encouraged Kwamboka to enter the order when she graduated. She was exactly the kind of child who would do well as a religious: kind, obedient, contemplative and willing to serve. Kwamboka had never considered such a life and it was flattering to be thought of in this way.

When she went home, Kwamboka told her mother.

"This might be a good thing," Cecilia assured Kwamboka. "You will have no worries about being taken care of."

But Kwamboka didn't want to be taken care of. She also didn't think of herself as obedient, not since she and her mother left the church. Doubts about the faith had also been gathering during the dark nights and she wondered if she any longer believed what she had been taught. Why would God kill his own son? And how could the son become the God when the old God hadn't died? Kwamboka saw two gods but was told they were the same. Just one God, Jesus Christ, the Son of God. Kwamboka also saw Christ gave privileges to some people because they were white, born like albinos. The more she thought about Christianity, the more she wondered whether her grandmother's generation had been right in rejecting the incursion of men with the book called the bible who came along with the men who had the guns and said they were for peace.

"You will make a fine teacher, Sarah," Sister Consolata continued her argument. "Our order has a school in Rome. You will be sent there to study. Some day you will become a sister like me."

Kwamboka protested. She didn't want to leave home. Not Kenya, anyway. She wanted to be close enough to see her mother. Her mother needed her to help on the farm.

"Your home will be with us. We will be your new family. You will become a bride of Christ."

She didn't want to be married to a man who she would join only in death. She wanted her own children, not everyone else's. More important to her than an eternal life was a life in this world. Kwamboka wanted some day to tell her own grandchildren the stories that she had been told. If she didn't tell them about Moraa, the ancestral heroes would be gone forever, forgotten, completely dead.

Before Europeans came to Kisii, Moraa Kwamboka lived with her husband Otenyo on the highest hill.

There were two versions of this story, identical except for a single detail. In one, Otenyo attempts Northcote's murder. In the other, it is Moraa Kwamboka.

From the hilltop Moraa Kwamboka could see the great lake. It was from this lake we first came.

Some say Moraa Kwamboka was a prophet. This meant she could see what was yet to be. As a little girl, people would listen to her talk about far away places. As a young woman she learned the secrets of the earth. From the tree in the forest she made medicine for headaches; from herbs in a field she made medicine for fevers. She knew the secrets to make barren women bear children.

Moraa Kwamboka was murdered by the abasongo. They killed her and here is why:

When she was a girl, Moraa Kwamboka heard the great prophet Sakawa. He said that one day giant babies with sticks of fire would come to our hills. Out of these sticks would fly pieces of iron that would sting worse than a thousand bees and kill you quicker. These ogres would have skin the color of ash and cover their bodies with things we had never seen before. The giants would have the tempers of babies and minds of witches. He said this and then disappeared.

Warriors came one day and took our cattle. What were we to do against their firesticks? Hippo hides didn't stop bullets, nothing did.

A man, his name was Northcote, was their chief and he built a boma between two streams. Men of wealth said the Abagusii should join with them against the Luo and the Kipsigis and the Maasai. Moraa said no. Northcote will take everything from us. He cannot be an ally.

Moraa was right. The abasongo could never be allies. They couldn't be trusted. He said there was a new tax on every hut and that the tax had to be paid in shilingi. Cows and goats and sheep were sold to pay the new tax. This was bitter to swallow.

One day Northcote took cattle away from Otenyo's home. Moraa told the young men, 'You are like women. You don't care your cattle are being taken away.'

She took a spear from one of the young men. Northcote was sitting on a large white animal we had never seen before. Moraa threw the spear. Northcote fell to the ground. He had a deep wound in his back. She threw the spear so hard it stuck in a tree.

This is the true story of Moraa. Others say that it was Otenyo who threw the spear. No one believed a woman could do what Moraa did. But it was Moraa Kwamboka.

It was Moraa Kwamboka, the one after whom you are named.

May you honor her with your own deeds.

It took two years for the college to decide on Kwamboka's application. They weren't sure about taking a female and one from a distant district at that. During her wait, she taught in a self-help primary school in a mud building with a grass thatch roof. Parents paid her for each day she taught their children. It was enough for her to buy dried fish, passion fruit, soap and kerosene.

Kwamboka walked for an hour to reach the school on the other side of the hill. At the end of the year she bought a used bicycle in Kisii Town and taught herself to ride, upsetting parents who thought that no woman, no less a woman teacher, should be permitted to ride. Several parents removed their children from her class, but others didn't mind. If she wanted to ride a bicycle, what was wrong with that? There was no tradition forbidding a woman from riding a bicycle, so why create one?

Many days Kwamboka conducted her class outdoors where she used a portable blackboard purchased with funds contributed by parents. She recited poetry to her students, poems she had copied from magazines she had once read in the nuns' home, and had her pupils repeat it line by line until they, too, memorized Kipling—"If you can keep your head when all about you/ Are losing theirs and blaming it on you"—and Henley—"I am the master of my fate:/ I am the captain of my soul"—not that any child understood the meaning. No matter. It was the words rolling in the mouth and the delight the children took in repeating it back, shouting out each word in unison.

She knew that she was the first female from her location to have left Kisii not for marriage but for school, one of the first Kisiis to receive higher education, an unmarried woman in the distant city.

〰〰〰〰〰〰〰

AS ONE OF A HANDFUL OF FEMALES at the college, after attempts to make herself heard, Kwamboka stood silent on the sidelines listening to the puffed up debates by strutting roosters. Women were for kitchens, women were for children, women for hospital care. And since Kisii had no forest fighters and the British let them keep their land, as a Kisii woman she was less than useless.

Kwamboka's interest in folklore was considered retrogressive, she was told; literature should to be progressive, forward looking and making room for the African voice. Kwamboka had no warrant to speak.

The price seemed too steep to bear. Kwamboka could accept ignorance on the part of her fellow students but not humiliation. And not from professors.

"What is this, Miss Kwamboka," Titus Nganga demanded. The don held her work in one hand while pulling down his eyeglasses from his head to his nose with the other. "This is what Miss Kwamboka presents as her example of . . ."

Nganga's voice faded and she focused on the desk in front of her. She shut him out. She had heard such diatribes from him before. In class there were ridicules, out of class lecherous glances that made him run hot and her cold. The scolding was a blur. All she heard was the song sung from Kisii, a song for a newborn: "Whose land is this,/ The hills and the land by the lake,/ Whose bananas and waving millet?/ Whose land is this,/ Whose valley of bright flowers?/ Whose sun is brighter than our sun?"

"Miss Kwamboka." Nganga walked closer to her seat.

"Whose cows are these,/ Cows that bellow in contentment?/ Whose fruit is sweeter,/ Whose cows are fatter / Whose rains more quenching?"

Nganga droned on.

"Miss Kwamboka!" Nganga continued. "Everyone has to follow directions. You decide to follow your own road. Is that it?"

"I thought . . ." she began.

"Do you call this thinking?" He raised her paper above his head. "Who would call this thinking?" he said, turning to the rest of the class.

Kwamboka sang to herself: "The time has come/ The time has come/ A song I am coming." She sang: "The rooster gives way to the hen/ The rooster gives way to the hen/ A song I am coming/ Give way, give way/ Ya-ya, ya-ya."

"No, Miss Kwamboka, there is no reason for you to think about this. You were to write an essay about Kenya's future, not repeat some simple-minded drivel you hear in the bush . . ."

"Play your guitar, Moraa Kwamboka,/ I want to dance in the red dust./ Play your guitar, Moraa Kwamboka./ The hen clucked in the banana plant,/ The hen clucked in the banana plant."

" . . . I can thank you for proving me right. I suppose there is no reversing the idiocy that has infected the college. God help us all, Miss Kwamboka."

"I want my cows,/ Give me my cows./ I want my farm,?/ Give me my farm."

"Miss Kwamboka!"

She raised her eyes, just a little, to stare at Nganga.

"Give way,/ Give way."

Kwamboka looks up from her desk and stares at Nganga at belt-level, her ears stuffed with song. He stammers and takes a step back, bumping against the side of his metal desk, the legs screeching on the cement floor. His face flushes. Kwamboka continues to stare as her smile broadens.

That semester Kwamboka pledged to return to Kisii each school break to talk to the old women before those who remembered would too soon be completely dead.

Farewell Until Eternity

∿∿∿∿∿∿

*W*HILE SHE REMEMBERED precisely where she was when she heard that the president had been shot—she was in the student lounge; classes were canceled; she took the subway home—, it was the numbing dread of that week in October a year earlier that made the difference, when she believed the world was going to end and then when it didn't, concluded that no one could stop the military-industrial complex from its parade to nuclear ruin.

Mostly Lena couldn't forgive the president for the Bay of Pigs.

The assassination left its mark not by changing her but by solidifying the direction she had turned to the previous year, the only direction possible. Confrontation was senseless and expecting the government to change, to care, to bring justice to the underclass was as futile as Ahab pursuing the white whale.

Since she couldn't do good, she decided, at least she could do no harm.

What is to be done? That was Lenin's question. Her father was certain he knew and responded to the call, so he joined the Party to bring about the revolution, but he was wrong. The Party came to nothing and it made him into nothing. The Party robbed him of himself and nearly rubbed out his wife with him. What was to be done was to dive deep into the well of the self and preserve what she could in the unexplored recesses. She was nothing to the world but fodder for another's ambitions, but she was everything to herself.

Cultivate your own garden. That was Voltaire's advice and it seemed right.

That week in October she could think only of Sartre. Not really think but feel the existential despair, the sickness. There was no thinking that week, only being and nothingness.

"I am going to outlive myself. Eat, sleep, sleep, eat. Exist slowly, softly, like these trees, like a puddle of water, like the red bench in the streetcar." That's what Sartre wrote.

She didn't know that she would outlive herself. Sartre had the solace of slowness and softness. But there is nothing slow or soft when there is nothingness. There are no trees, no puddles, no red benches anywhere, no streetcars.

The only cure for nothingness is nothingness. The nothingness of spaces in Japanese paintings, the blankness surrounding the line, the emptiness that illuminates one brushstroke.

Monday October 22nd the president addressed the American public on radio and television: Soviet ships headed to Cuba, the president warning them to turn back, the threat of nuclear retaliation a certainty as the ships continued across the waters to the cordon.

Kennedy represented Cuba as a prison nation and the Soviet Union as imperialist, but she knew that Castro was a liberator, America the imperialist, and Kennedy an impersonator of freedom. And she was certain that Khrushchev wouldn't back down to the American bullyboys; that Kennedy would support the Pentagon brass; that generals on both sides would get their chance to do what they were trained to do, each ready for a fitting reply to the aggressor. By the end of the week, nuclear missiles would be launched from both sides.

Twenty ships continued. American forces were put on alert. Cuba mobilized its troops. And the ships continued. America prepares to turn them back. The ships continued.

Cuba called on governments of the world to prevent the U.S. from unleashing thermonuclear war.

Who was right? If her father were alive, it would matter to him. A week ago, it would have mattered to Lena, too, but no longer. They were all insane, these men. What did it matter when nothing is left, when everything disappears? Life was all that mattered. But once the missiles left their silos, when the earth no longer existed, there won't even be a worm to care.

The Soviet ships would meet the American blockade two days later. Lena called her friend on Wednesday morning.

"Please meet me," Lena pleaded with Ellen.

Although Lena absorbed herself in literature, she seldom wrote herself, so she was surprised when years later she uncovered what she thinks must have been a diary entry of sorts:

Ellen tried to assure me. She said nothing will happen.

We walked down the street. The sun brightened the cloudy sky. We walked into the Square to watch pigeons gurgle over breadcrumbs scattered by old men huddled in worn overcoats. The pigeons bobbed their heads. They fluttered their wings when pushed aside.

We left the park and walked into the wind blowing in from the river and pushed on up the street in the shadow of the hospital. Ellen grabbed my hand.

I told her I can't leave her. Again she told me that nothing would happen.

Nothing she said helped. I couldn't stop worrying. I didn't believe everything would be alright. Our lives were splitting apart.

I thought being with Ellen would be enough. She kept me from losing my mind. Everything was gray, overcast navy blue, charcoal dust.

I couldn't stand still. I was being sucked into a maelstrom and whirled about helpless and scattered. Broad lines narrowing towards the bottom. A knot of ink-black spots.

We looked at the river. Seagulls glided above the ice blue water.

I told her I was cold. She said there was nowhere to go. Then I knew she was as scared as me.

I couldn't take it any more. I was being crushed.

We sat in the hospital. It was warm. Leather chairs stood against the tan wall. The chairs were empty. Not visiting hours.

She sat on the edge of the chair. She stared at me. Her hair hung limply.

She began, she stopped. She said something. I can't remember what.

The ashtrays on the table were filled with crushed cigarette butts. I blew ashes off the table. I said there but for the grace of God go we.

Again she said, It's not that bad. I couldn't tell her what was on my mind. This was irrationality compounded by insanity.

We sat in the lobby for a long time. We watched doctors and nurses walk by. The realm of the sick and the dead while outside, somewhere in the Caribbean and in cement silos in wheat fields, the healthy world was nearing its end.

Sterilized inside. Never-ending darkness of nowhere.

I said that if we survive we need to go away somewhere far. Australia. She laughed and said, New Zealand.

I don't know who said what. Both together. Maybe not at all. It didn't matter. The walls closed in.

The world didn't end. Maybe it will some other time.

The invisible juggernaut may start along its path of annihilation again. But these thoughts are imponderable.

Soviet ships continued to sail to Cuba, then turned back.

"There is no class warfare, Daddy!" she screamed. "There is only warfare warfare. Marx was wrong. There is no future. The struggle's over."

Her dead father stuffed his ears with wax. Her mother got promoted to an office job at the tea-packing factory.

More than ever, Lena found solace in books. She had no patience for tendentious arguments in the student cafeteria or the splitting and splitting again over the nuances of Marxist theory. She often took the train downtown to walk the aisles of the Strand, where she discovered Marquis de Sade and Radclyffe Hall in the endless aisles of used books. She read the *Kama Sutra* and Whitman.

Lena couldn't read fast enough to pacify her hunger.

Ellen told her how she revived her dying grandmother by sneaking into her hospital room a forbidden meal of macrobiotic foods and wanted to try it herself with Lena, but Lena rejected the diet for herself, preferring pints of strong coffee and cigarettes.

The stunning event of the president's assassination the following year was the last paragraph in the prologue for the life she had already chosen. Justice couldn't be won through action. She had come to accept Plato's notion that justice means minding your own business and not meddling in another's concerns.

Ellen put her signature on the Campaign for Nuclear Disarmament petition; Lena refused to sign. It was a waste of time, she said.

"Paper against bombs? It doesn't change the material facts. It's false consciousness," and as soon as she uttered the phrase, she wanted to take it back.

She knew the metaphors, the allusions, the psychological insights, the criticisms and critiques, the tricks of rhetoric. What else was college for but a search for the truth, a journey in self-discovery?

No one changes the world, she thought. The best you can do is to prevent the world from changing you.

Know yourself.

Village coffeehouses became her weekend university where in a haze of smoke she listened to poets that were frivolous, profound, absurd, satirical, howling, bellowing, gesticulating, lyrical or crude, hating and loving. In the summer she heard folksingers on streets, but she didn't frequent their coffee houses or bars. She learned to play a passable game of chess by watching players in the park. She tried filtered and straight cigarettes and intermixed tobacco with marijuana and liked wine from bottles wrapped in straw.

"I love men, not for what unites them," she quotes Apollinaire as they watch the players racing up and down hot asphalt on the 4th Street basketball court, "but for what divides them, and I want to know most of all what gnaws at their hearts.' Do you know, Ellen?"

"Me? I wish I had gone to school where there were boys. It would be nice to have them around. I miss it. And you?"

"I don't know. I like Hunter."

"Me, too. Don't get me wrong. But just look at them," Ellen said as she curled her fingers around the chain link fence. Shirts against skins. The sweat of racing player.

Lena no longer cut her hair; it reached as far as her shoulder blades. When she met new people, she introduced herself as Lena. Only high school friends now called her Big Red and commuting to Hunter on the East Side meant that she spent little time in Brighton Beach. Her neighborhood friends fell away, so she seldom heard herself called by that name. Manhattan reeled her in by presenting to her the possibilities that had been stoked by her imagination.

Since Lena and Ellen majored in different subjects, they took few classes together. They seldom saw each other during the week. The weekends were different. They met up in the Village together nearly every Saturday night, after Lena finished her cashier's job at Woolworth's. She took the subway from Brooklyn. Ellen had the easier trip from the Upper West Side. The ride home at night was too dangerous, so she stayed Saturday nights on the couch at Ellen's apartment.

At the movie, Lena thrills to the opening as a man strops a razor. He steps through a door, stands behind a woman and there is a close-up of the face of a woman who stares straight ahead, her eye held open by the man standing behind her. The razor slices through her eyeball.

"I don't like cruelty," Ellen said.

"It's a dream. Dreams are like that, aren't they?"

"Yours are?"

"Nightmares. Yes."

"But it wasn't a nightmare. She seemed almost to like it."

"That's what makes it thrilling."

"Not for me. It's what makes it repulsive."

Since first hearing about Happenings, Lena wanted to see for herself how the walls between performance and audience can be broken apart, how structure and spontaneity can mix, how sense can be made out of absurdity. The events were word of mouth and she never knew when they would take place, as they were never announced beforehand. A classmate told Lena that there was one this weekend and she gave her the time and address. Ellen was less eager than Lena to go.

"What do you think it will be like?"

"That's the point. No one knows, not until you get there. And then maybe you don't know."

"I prefer a movie. Let's go there."

"I want to see what a Happening is. We can always go see a movie. But we're lucky we know about this one."

Lena assured Ellen that they would leave if she didn't like the event.

"Let's give it a shot."

The metal door to the building at the corner of Great Jones Street was locked. They rang the bell. No reply. They looked at the address they had been given. They were in the right place.

"Nine o'clock?"

"That's what she said."

Lena pressed the buzzer in shorts bursts, then pushed down hard with her thumb.

They backed up to the curb and looked up at the large window facing Broadway. Lights were on in the loft. There was movement. Someone leaned against the window.

Lena tossed a pebble at the window.

Another.

Another.

A buzzer rang them in. They walked up a darkened staircase and into a large room that had been converted from a warehouse into an apartment. A haze of marijuana and cigarette smoke drifted up to the high ceiling.

Aside from a few lamps and mattresses, the room lacked furniture. Rubber tires filled the center of the loft's floor. Stepping from one tire to another, people crisscrossed the room. In one corner, a man wearing a white shirt and tie played a penny whistle while sitting on the windowsill sat another squeezing a concertina. Against the wall stood a person wrapped in tin foil.

Lena and Ellen watched the coordinated chaos, the movement and the stillness like splattered paint drying on a canvas.

The lights went out, the room illuminated solely from the Broadway street lamps. The music stopped. Lena's breath grew shallow. She hated the smell of old rubber and smoke. In what seemed like forever, they remained in the twilight. Their Hunter friend walked beside Ellen, took her face in her hands, and gently applied rouge on her cheeks and black lipstick on her lips.

The lights returned. Lena walked to the window to get fresh air. Ellen let her friend finish, then signaled Lena and the two walked to the far end of the room where a small group of men and women had gathered in a circle. A handheld drum, a recorder and tambourine sounded a heartbeat. A man took off his jacket, then his tie. He removed his shirt and trousers. Others followed his lead. Lena pulled her dress over her head. Ellen watched Lena and did the same. Shoes, socks and stockings were thrown onto the discarded clothes.

Men lowered their pants. Women unhooked their bras.

Underwear fell to their feet.

Lena had never been naked in front of anyone. She had never seen anyone naked before.

The group got on their knees and leaned back on their heels.

Lena glanced at the people around her. This was different than drawings she had seen in books, different than what she had imagined. Even in the dim light she found herself startled by the sight. She tried not to look at what she wanted to see.

The group leader incanted, "Farewell until eternity . . ."

"Farewell until eternity . . ." the group repeated.

"Where you and I shall not find ourselves together."

51

"Where you and I shall not find ourselves together."

The man next to her reached for her hand. Lena withdrew it and placed her hand on her own stomach. She felt his fingertips stroking the inside of her thigh. She turned her head. His head was straight ahead, his eyes closed. For the first time she saw what she only before imagined. With her right hand she sought Ellen's left. She quickly turned back and drew Ellen's hand to her mouth as she felt a familiar rush of heat in her face and dampness between her legs.

She placed Ellen's hand on her cheek, then bit her friend's knuckle. Ellen pulled her hand away.

In the taxi to Ellen's apartment that night the two sat silently on opposite sides of the cab. As usual, Lena slept in the living room. They hadn't exchanged a word since leaving the loft.

The next morning Ellen's father asked, "What did you two girls do last night?"

Lena waited for Ellen to reply.

"Not much," Ellen finally said.

"Did you take in a picture?"

"It didn't work out."

"It was a beautiful night. Did you walk around?" her mother asked.

"Yes, you know, we just walked around. Like that."

For the next two years, until Lena graduated from college, Ida thought that her daughter had stayed with Ellen each Saturday. But after the night of the first Happening, Lena rarely saw Ellen. She couldn't recall all the pads where she crashed but there was always somewhere to go, even as she couldn't always remember with whom.

The Kisumu Train

~~~~~~~~~~
~~~~~~~~~~

THE KISII MUNICIPAL HOSPITAL treated Sarah Kwamboka and Dexter Conway the same week for life threatening injuries that each had sustained in separate incidents. She had been brought there to stanch internal bleeding from an accident; Conway had suffered a knife wound.

~~~~~~~~~~
~~~~~~~~~~

KWAMBOKA HAD BEEN ABOARD the holiday children's train from Nairobi-Kampala when it careened from a bridge into a ravine in the middle of the night. Three secondary school students on their way to their parents' homes in the Rift Valley and further west, in Uganda, died.

"*Ning'o?*"

"*Nachire aa*, Maranga."

Maranga now recognized his brother's hushed voice. He rose from his bed to open the door. His brother scuttled in from the dark night.

Maranga, Conway's house servant, lived in a shed on the edge of the property next to a cypress hedge, a one-room wooden building with no windows. A lemon tree grew in front. Conway's house, provided by the government in the civil servants quarters, stood on cinderblocks twenty yards away, near the gray-barked eucalyptus tree and vegetable patch.

Maranga didn't know how Makori supported himself in the city. He never talked about his work. He never mentioned friends or where he lived. He told murky stories that created an air of unreality. But Maranga, never having been to Nairobi himself, thought that perhaps the stories were true.

The city was a fantastic place, distant and mythical, where buildings were higher than trees. But since the only time Makori returned to Kisii was to request money, Maranga remained skeptical about the touted exploits.

"*Soa*," Maranga responded. Makori entered the room.

The two sat around a kerosene lantern while Maranga prepared a kettle of tea.

"I have to ask you," Makori began. "I am getting married soon."

"This is news. I know nothing about it."

"I am just now making plans."

It was money, again, Maranga thought. What is the bride price for a city woman? Certainly more than what it was in Kisii. This could be a big sum. Maranga had never turned down Makori's requests; it was an obligation to give when asked. That is what family is for. But how much did Makori want? His salary from Conway was fair, but it wasn't large. Everything he made he gave to his wife, Bosibori, to take care of their farm. The farm only had a milk cow and a few goats, the rest going to feed the family, school fees and books. Bosibori referred to her brother-in-law as Mkora, Swahili for 'thief.'

Makori's request, though, wasn't about his marriage.

"This woman, Kwamboka, she needs to stay with you. She is hurt. She was on that train yesterday."

Maranga felt his stomach sink.

"What are you asking?"

"There's nowhere else for her to go. She needs a place to get better."

"I can't have her here," he protested weakly.

"She has to stay," Makori persisted.

"What you're asking isn't right. Please don't."

"For a short while. Until she can get better."

"This isn't a place for her. Look. This is one room. You can see what this is. I am married."

"Where else, Maranga?"

"Why doesn't she go . . .?"

"She is too well known to go anywhere, brother. Wanted Number One. That's her. No one must know where she is. You can hide her in secret."

Why hadn't Maranga heard about this woman before if she was so prominent? Surely, there would be rumors about a wanted woman from Kisii.

Makori said that it was dangerous if anyone should find out where Kwamboka was. She had to be hidden. He implied that she, like himself, was part of a banned organization and wanted by the police. This made no sense to Maranga. As far as he knew, there were no more subversive organizations. Independence would arrive next year; the British were leaving; Mau Mau laid down their weapons and had come out from the bamboo forests. What was Makori talking about? He had talked always nonsense, even when he wasn't drunk. But there were so many things changing, so many new things that he knew nothing about that perhaps Makori was telling the truth.

In any case, there was no point in arguing with Makori or even attempting to get more information from him.

Maranga's shoulders dropped. What his brother was requesting was unreasonable. A married man didn't live under the same roof with an unmarried woman, yet he couldn't deny him.

"Bosibori won't find out," Makori jokingly reassured his brother. "I won't tell. She will be better soon. Then she can go. It will remain a secret. Tell me, brother," he said sternly. "Where will she go if you don't take her?"

Makori should not ask this question, Maranga thought. It wasn't for him to answer. She wasn't his responsibility.

Why burden him with this injured woman, even if she was his brother's his wife-to-be? There were many clinics in Nairobi to treat her and certainly hiding her amongst the many houses in the city must be easier than keeping her in Kisii Town where few things remained secret for very long.

Makori ignored Maranga's discomfort. He told him to meet the bus from Kericho the next morning. His fiancé will be on it. When Maranga asked how he would recognize Kwamboka, Makori laughed.

"You'll know."

"How long?" he asked again.

"She will be better soon. And I'll be back. In a few days. Maranga, listen to me." He leaned into his brother. "Don't tell anyone I've been here."

Dogs barked as Makori left the compound and headed in the dark down the footpath towards the copse by the river.

The following morning Maranga went to the bus stage to collect his unwanted visitor. He leaned against a post of the loggia of the hardware shop as he waited for the bus to arrive. He was thankful it was Sunday afternoon and the streets were nearly deserted. The Kericho-Kisii bus pulled in. A woman stumbled on the steps and was helped to her feet by a fellow passenger. Maranga let her stand there until everyone was gone. He spoke to her quickly and he hoped she understood him, as she stood mute, her face swollen, her dress torn and muddy.

"Follow me."

Maranga slowly walked up the incline past the petrol station, turned on the road past the D.C.'s office and then down the red dirt road lined with cypress hedges. He never turned to see if she were following. When they arrived at his house, her clothes were soaked with the sweat of sun and fever.

SCHOOL TRAINS scheduled during school holidays, until that year, were reserved for white students only. All of Kwamboka's trips from college to home were by bus. Since her mother's death, she came home to visit friends.

Now that the racial barrier had been lifted and she would have liked the experience of riding a train, the cost of a ticket was beyond her reach. She barely had enough to eat as a college student. Perhaps if the fare had been the same twenty-five shillings that it was for younger students, she may have considered it. But there were no concessions made for college students. In addition, the nearest stop to Kisii was at the end of the line, in Kisumu, still 70 miles from home. A bus was cheaper and occasionally quicker.

On the first day of the month-long school break in December, Kwamboka boarded a bus downtown in Nairobi, sat for more than an hour leaning against the window as it filled with additional passengers and the roof piled high with their belonging and items they were bringing home as gifts. The bus finally pulled out of the bay but went less than a 100 feet before it stopped for petrol. When its tank was full and the tires checked, the driver turned the key but the engine coughed and sputtered. It wouldn't start. Passengers debarked and milled around the disabled bus, the men offering advice. After much coming and going by a multitude of people who inspected the bus and tinkered with the motor, using wrenches and hammers, a conductor announced that the passengers would have to board another bus, which would be arriving sometime soon.

Kwamboka stood beside the bus as cartons of stainless steel pots and pans and bundles of clothes, new and used, were lowered from the roof to disgruntled passengers who caught the packages as they were thrown. As Kwamboka bent to get her bundle, she saw a twenty-shilling note in the dust. She didn't know bills were issued in such large denominations. She picked it up and looked around. She quickly put it into her skirt pocket. Had anyone seen her? Kwamboka decided not to wait for another bus and instead walked several blocks to the train station. Yes, she was told, there was a children's train leaving later. Yes, she was told, she could purchase a ticket. Hesitantly she handed her twenty-shilling note to the ticket clerk. The clerk looked at her skeptically. What would she say if he asked where she had gotten it? Kwamboka was ready to run. The clerk passed the ticket to her. Kwamboka took her kit, placed it on the wooden bench in the waiting room and used it as a neck rest and waited for the departure.

Kwamboka stared out the window as the train left Nairobi but the sun set even before they descended into the Rift Valley. She stayed awake until Nakuru and then fell asleep after the steam train chugged and ascended the Mau Escarpment. She woke briefly at each stop on the way to the city on Lake Victoria. The last she remembers hearing was the announcement for Fort Ternan, a whistle blast, then a loud noise in the dark.

The train had plunged into the ravine around Koru, before reaching Chemilil. She didn't know how he had found her. She had vague recollections of someone sitting with her on a bus, then being left by him and another person taking charge. She vaguely remembers arriving in Kisii and being taken to a shed by someone she didn't know.

Her condition at Maranga's house fluctuated the next couple of days. There were periods when she was conscious and in her hallucinations begged to see her mother but was unable say where she came from. Maranga wasn't inclined to remove her from the house until she had completely recovered. He was afraid he would be accused of mistreating her.

One moment she was lucid and the next couldn't explain much. When Maranga told her that she had been brought by his brother to the house, she told him that she wasn't engaged to him. She knew him but only casually, in Nairobi. Most Abagusii knew one another in the city and she thinks she remembers meeting him at a party one time.

Maranga gathered courage enough to ask, "Why does he want to hide you here?"

"I'm not hiding from anyone. There's no one to hide from. What are you talking about?"

"Makori told me you had to stay here. It was too dangerous for you elsewhere. People were looking for you."

"Why would he say such a thing? No one is looking for me."

"Makori said so."

"He is peculiar," she said.

She had nothing to do with violence and said once again that she wasn't engaged to his brother. As Maranga listened to the conflicting stories, he thought that Makori probably told the story to manipulate Kwamboka into marrying him. Once it became known that she had stayed with a married man, the shame would make her an unacceptable wife to many others. It would be his chance to marry an educated woman.

Kwamboka took a turn for the worse. Her fever rose and she couldn't speak. It became clear to Maranga that she would die if he didn't bring her to the hospital in town. Her bleeding had become uncontrollable.

Doctors there ordered a transfusion, but no blood type in the bank matched hers. She would have died if Maranga hadn't overcome his fear of having his blood taken. He was afraid of *mumiani* but he would have been more afraid of what would happen if she died.

WHILE KWAMBOKA WAS BEING SEQUESTERED in the shed in his garden, Conway was at Maranga's farm on the other side of the district. In his many years as a surveyor in the colonial civil service Conway had never visited an African home other than on an official call. Now he was at Maranga's *shamba*. With independence looming, Conway thought he was through with Kisii and Africa and had made peace with returning to England, a place that hadn't been his home for his entire adult years.

Conway knew nowhere but Kisii. He had been placed there when he arrived and it seemed as though the colonial office had forgotten about him. Others were shifted about the country, but he stayed put, happy to be left alone with his instruments and papers. Conway found comfort in the lonely life he had carved out for himself. Although he belonged to the Kisii Sports Club, as did every European in town, he preferred the company of his dog, a Rhodesian Ridgeback, and found consolation in the silent visits made by a woman when he stayed in his work cabin on the Mara plains south of the Kisii highlands. At the end of the day in the border country where baboons out-numbered humans, he would lay in his cot, the hurricane lamp extinguished for the night. She opened the glass doors to the house, dropped her leather skirt next to his bed, removed her cotton top and beaded necklace and placed herself on top of his naked body. She smelled deeply of charcoal and cows and dung. Conway filled his lungs with the smell of her. He ran his hands over her oiled skin, over her shaven head.

After he fell asleep, when the sky was studded with stars and there was a low whistle in the fever trees, she took money from his wallet and walked into the night, an act repeated over many years.

Some Europeans indulged Conway's withdrawal from their circle, while some loathed what they perceived as his scornful dismissal.

But he wasn't going to return to England, after all. He had been called into governor's office in Nairobi and was told that they wanted him to stay on, to represent their interests in Kisii. The young official who spoke to him never explained what the British interests might be. Surprising himself, Conway was intrigued by the offer. There was nothing for him in England. Kisii was all he knew.

The official explained that Conway was the only Brit who spoke Gusii and it was important to have someone at the station that could understand the changing conditions.

"Let me be straight with you, man," the officer said. "The others are too set in their ways. When the D.C. was here just last month he said to me he couldn't understand how Africans could sit down with their rumps still raw from where their tails have fallen off. I thought he was joking but he went on." The officer in shirt and tie paused. "I understand there still isn't an African in the sports club."

"God knows why they would want to join," Conway responded.

Conway had been sure that his time in Kenya was up like all the other expats. He didn't know where he would go, but remaining in the new nation didn't seem right. This never should have been a white man's land; he was happy to see the sun set on the Empire. But now, listening to the young officer, he was encouraged that things could be different. Perhaps it was possible for him to do some good, not simply use the country as his refuge. Conway saw this as now paying back what had been given to him. Unlike some others in the service who viewed their work as a call of duty, Conway disdained the idea of "bringing civilization" to the unlit corners of the world. For years he merely wanted to do no harm, to be nothing more than a breeze blowing across the grass. He had found a place in a quiet corner of Africa and kept his distance from his own white tribe. A dog and a nameless woman were all the company he needed.

Staying on in Kenya must mean something more than being a gentle breeze, he now thought. The request flattered him and had stirred in him a sense of responsibility, arousing a desire to work as an equal with those who rightly owned the land. He had something to offer—a bridge between two worlds. He came up with a different metaphor: a scar stitching together a wound, a connective tissue.

Never before had Conway had a purpose other than leaving things alone. His new resolve required that he take a first step as a gesture of humility. There needed to be a fresh beginning. How could he have known so little about the life around him? He spoke their language with words but he didn't know the wordless language that guided their daily rhythms. All the years in isolation, a smug self-pity, a not-knowing grown from selfish ignorance struck him as worse than the attitudes of his counterparts. He had been no more than a parasite.

Conway was ignorant of Maranga's life apart from the work as a house servant. He always wanted to treat Maranga fairly. The monthly salary he gave him was above the going wage for a house servant and he gave him a little extra at the beginning of the year for the school fees for his children. Each Christmas he bought a gift for the house at the farm—a table, a transistor radio, a sack of rice if the price had gotten too steep. This was justice but not a relationship. Both Conway and Maranga adhered to the line separating work from friendship. Neither entertaining the possibility that something more satisfying was possible.

Maranga's wife, his children? Conway inquired after them when Maranga returned to work after a visit to the *shamba*. He knew their names, he knew about their progress at school, he knew about their health, but he didn't know them. Aside from a photo taken in town at the photography studio, Conway didn't know what they look liked. He didn't want to intrude on Maranga's private life, he told himself, but that wasn't it. He, too, was part of the colonial mentality. He had unwittingly accepted its ground rules and now could see the hypocrisy he had lived.

This had to change. Since his stay in Kisii was extended and the country would be starting fresh, Conway felt that the time was right to go to the Maranga's compound to begin his sentimental education. On his way back from Nairobi, he stopped at the farm.

"*Nasoire aa,*" Conway announces himself.

A woman looks up.

"*Nao tore soa,*" she responds reluctantly.

"Mama Bosibori, I am Dexter Conway," he says to the tall woman who stands in front of the mud house with a corrugated metal roof. She wears a high-neck floral patterned dress and faded headscarf. Strands of a shell necklace hang to her breasts.

She extends her hand.

"Your husband Joseph works for me in Kisii Town."

"Yes, I know," she says.

Conway feels foolish. Of course, she would know.

"*Ee, soa,*" she welcomes him. She gestures to a wooden stool near the door. "*Karanza.*" Conway sits.

Bosibori bends over a little girl who was clutching her dress in her fist. The girl runs down the footpath to the compound on the other side of the hedge. She returns later with a two slices of bread.

"Mama," Conway begins. "I have come to you because I have lived here for fifteen years and I have never visited you before. I don't want to be a stranger any longer. I would be honored if you would accept me as your guest for the night. Soon you will come and visit with me at my place and I will make tea for you."

"Yes. You can stay in that house over there," she says. "Grace, take *bwana* to your small father's house," referring to Makori's empty, one room house that Makori used for the rare visits he made home.

The girl takes Conway's suitcase and places it on her head as she leads him across the lawn, down an incline to a house in disrepair. The thatch needs replacing; blue paint peels from a shutter that hangs from a single hinge. Goat and chicken droppings litter the entrance to the house. The smell of must hangs heavy. Pages torn from magazines and old calendars cover the walls. Over the bed is a photo of a white woman in a bathing suit who offers a cigarette to a man up to his chest in the ocean, and in another poster there is a black woman extolling the virtues of a skin lightening cream.

The eldest daughter asks Bosibori why they are preparing goat and rice for a white man.

"It's an honor to have him in our home.

"*Omosongo* don't deserve to be honored."

"He has been good to your father. You be good to him. Every stranger who visits is a guest."

"Europeans aren't strangers. They are thieves."

"Not this one, Joyce. And you, Paul," she says to her son, "when he is here tonight, ask him to get a scholarship for you. He can do that."

Paul had never spoken to a white man before. How do you address an *omosongo*?

"I won't . . ."

"We have better things to do than slaughter a goat for him," Joyce says.

"This is the decent thing to do."

"There's nothing decent about him."

"We do this because *we* are decent. Joyce, you are sounding like an *omosongo*." Bosibori stiffens. "That's all. No more talk. Go help your little sister."

"How do I ask him?" Paul wants to know. "What do I say?"

"Tell him you like school, that you're a good student, a good boy. Then ask him to help. Think of him like a relative," Bosibori explains. "He knows how to get a scholarship."

She adds a pinch of salt to the vegetable stew.

A small crowd gathered at the homestead after sunset to welcome the guest. The smell of roasted goat wafted with the smoke from the cooking fire. When Conway spoke in Gusii, he elicited laughs, not because of his accent but because no one had ever heard their own language tumble from the mouth of an *omosongo*.

Paul sat uncomfortably next to Conway throughout the night but didn't exchange a word with him. Joyce remained in the cooking house. The location chief happily consumed the roasted meat and vegetables that had been prepared for the guests. Along with others, Conway drank millet beer through a long straw from the clay pot that was placed in the center of the circle. Guests were served rice, bread, beans, Fanta and Coke.

A guest asked Conway if he was a friend of Jim Reeves, the singer whose voice they heard from the phonograph.

"Who?" Conway responded, never having listened to popular music since arriving in Kisii.

The song played over and over: "Put your sweet lips a little closer to the phone/ Let's pretend that we're together all alone/ I'll tell the man to turn the jukebox way down low/ And you can tell your friend there with you / He'll have to go."

Conway's eyes grew heavy and asked to go to his quarters for the night.

"Paul, take our guest back to your little father's house."

Paul held a candleholder made from the bottom of a tin can as Conway followed him in the pitch-dark night. Conway climbed onto the narrow bed with a straw mattress. He covered himself with a woolen blanket. His eyes closed and his breathing grew deeper. He listened to the sounds from the house across the compound.

The door opened.

"*Ning'o?*" Conway asked under his breath.

Something dropped to the floor; a weight pressed down on top of him. Everything smelled of soot and dung. He filled his lungs with the aroma. He ran his hands over oiled skin, over a shaven head. A sharp pain pierced his groin and he gasped.

A dog barked as the figure disappeared into the dark.

Conway dipped his finger in the dripping liquid as it ran down the inside of his thigh.

Shape-up

~~~~~~~~

*T*HE BROKEN DRIVER'S window of the family's Starchief made Junius cry. The radio was ripped from the dashboard and a hole remained where he had often listened to music while sitting beside a girl on a summer night, not cruising— he had no license—, but parked far from the street light, helping a hand unzip his pants, then him unhooking; fingers and lips, sucking, licking, biting and scratching, not yet finding the line between pleasure and pain.

No car survived the streets. Chrome was stripped from the body and tires stolen. Dents and bangs went unrepaired. Trunks were pried open, hoods ripped off. One October, the Starchief was sold. Carl's work at the wharves was so sporadic, they could no longer afford to keep it. Not only did the morning shape-up cause feelings of a shameful past, with men standing around the foreman in a circle, waiting to be picked for a day's labor, but with Tough Tony in charge, work, which had always been difficult with blacks chosen last and given the most difficult jobs in the hold, fewer and fewer black stevedores found labor at all. Petitions to the State Commission Against Discrimination did little good. What could be expected when there were no black union representatives at the District level? Working with the NAACP or A. Philip Randolph to change the practices of the union didn't sit well with some black dockworkers who were willing to obtain employment, any employment, whatever the terms or conditions. They needed money for their families today and the hell with the promises about the future or appeals to dignity. Save the prayers and soul saving for church; they wanted a paycheck now.

Carl had been a union member since the war and wasn't ready to quit the cause.

〜〜〜〜〜〜〜
〜〜〜〜〜〜〜

CARL JOINED THE MILITARY AND TRAINED at Montford Point, the black Marine camp separated from Camp Lejeune, in Virginia, the primary base from which they were barred unless accompanied by a white Marine. After basic training, Carl was sent to the South Pacific to work as a stevedore with the 11th Depot. On the way to the West Coast for deployment to the Asian Theater, their troop train made a stop at Atlanta for breakfast. Carl and his company sat the waiting room until they could determine where to eat. They were soon accosted by the Military Police.

"This waiting room is for whites only," an MP told them. "Your waiting room is over there." He pointed to a sign that said 'Colored.'

The Marines didn't budge.

"We sit where we want," the Marine from Philadelphia said.

"Move."

A crowd gathered around the white MPs and black Marines who found one seat as good as any other and where they were sitting was fine. In Virginia, they had not left their base. Then they were recruits, now they were Marines. It didn't matter that they were stevedores. More importantly, they were part of America's military elite.

The commander of the troop train intervened. He took the MPs aside, then returned to the black Marines and informed them where they could get their food.

After this incident, Carl's unit was given warnings about Jim Crow laws. Their next stop was in Big Springs, Texas. When they stepped off the train, they ignored the lecture. They were Marines on their way to combat; they were

Americans on the way to fight for democracy. So they shot billiards at the pool hall and had sandwiches at the soda fountain. Big Springs residents expressed curiosity about blacks in Marine uniforms, but they were courteous and encouraging, not hostile.

The final stop in the US before boarding the ships for the Pacific was Camp Elliott, across the bay from San Diego. The small city of Coronado, Carl found, was as hostile to the black Marines as Atlanta had been. The Marines of the 11th Depot were in no mood to be told where to sit. When they attended a concert at an outdoor stadium, Carl was the first to refuse to take a seat in the bleachers. He sat near the stage. Several buddies joined him there. Others stood in the aisles, squatting on the steps.

"Niggers in the back!"

"Up your ass!" one Marine shouted back.

They were ready to fight but thought better of it. They wanted to get to the war zone, not spend time in the brig in California. When their commander heard of the incident in Coronado, instead of punishment he gave them liberty for several days to go across the bay to San Diego, the last time many would set foot on US soil.

Carl never talked about the war. Although the 11th Depot Company was designed to off load supplies to combat Marines, they often found themselves in the midst of battle. They drove LSTs and Ducks onto beachheads, carried supplies to Marines in foxholes, carried wounded soldiers to safety and stayed with them until they were evacuated. One time Junius had found a letter carefully folded in a box on his father's side of the bedroom closet. It was from General Vandegrift who commended his unit for its "whole hearted cooperation and untiring efforts" which "demonstrated in every respect" that they "appreciate the privilege of wearing a Marine uniform and serving with Marines in combat. You are a marine, period."

The box also contained a Purple Heart. Junius knew never to ask how his father had been wounded and whether he had ever killed anyone.

On the Brooklyn docks, Carl had been a foreman, but when his union failed to prevent the merger of Local 968 with Tough Tony's Local 1814, Carl was removed from office in the union. He joined the newly formed Unity Ticket as an alternative to 1814. Union thugs broke into Clyde Blue's home as Carl and others were meeting. Carl's eye was blackened. Junius thought his father deserved another Purple Heart.

Now Carl had to shape-up with a gang like other black stevedores from the South and Caribbean who had always worked as casual labor, not as union workers. He went from Brooklyn to Manhattan looking for work, and when things were especially bad, New Jersey. What work he got was unloading the dirtiest cargo. No blacks were hired as watchmen, checkers or forklift drivers, all skills he had developed in the Marines. All that was available were mule jobs in the hold.

Carl and Susan decided to rent out the basement as an apartment. Maybe they would look at Long Island again. Carl submitted several applications to Grumman, Fairchild and a dozen other facilities. None responded. There was no place for a former Marine who had spent the last eighteen years deep in ships' bottoms. In the privacy of his own thoughts, Carl regretted that he hadn't taken advantage of the G.I. Bill and gone to college. But now even a G.I. mortgage wouldn't be enough to make it feasible for them to move.

The Cassels remained in Weeksville as change washed away the final remnants of its identity. Within a few years the surrounding neighborhoods had been transformed. It was as though a plug had been pulled; Italians, Irish and Jews disappeared. Bedford-Stuyvesant was now Brooklyn's

Little Harlem. Houses on their street were boarded up, a fire burned down the nearby broom factory, they set traps for rats near the stoop where they put the garbage cans. The roller rink closed, the bowling alley was shut, city pools didn't re-open.

There had been rough neighborhoods and gangs as long as Junius remembered. He made a zip gun—take a cap gun, file down the hammer, tie it up with a rubber band, pull back on the rubber band and shoot a bullet. There were white gangs, black and Puerto Rican gangs. Junius knew where to go, what to avoid, whom to stand up to and when to run away. There was an abandoned train tunnel where gang members beat and tied people. There were fights with sticks, bats, clubs, bottles, switch blades and zip guns, which were as likely to blow up in your hand as put a hole in someone. This was hit and run fighting, bricks thrown from roofs, a stabbing with an umbrella. You were never attacked if you were with your girlfriend.

In the three years Junius attended high school, street violence changed. No longer governed by rituals and honor, chaos reigned. No one was immune; there were no safe havens. Zip guns were things of the past, replaced by midnight specials.

Carl's old wound grew worse. He was lucky to find sporadic employment with the Urban League, a messenger for a law office, driving a cab, cleaning stables, a night watchman, an auto mechanic's assistant. His limp became more pronounced. Without Susan's income and the basement rental, which now had been subdivided into two apartments, they couldn't survive.

〰〰〰〰〰〰
〰〰〰〰〰〰

MARVIN SUGGESTED THEY CHANGE the name of The Sparrows, those little brown and white birds, when Sal Lo

Bianco, their fourth member suddenly moved away. They didn't know where his family went and they lost touch with him.

"The Blackbirds, you know, something completely black."

"Never more," Junius retorted. "Quote the Raven."

The friends began to riff on the only poem they all liked reading in junior high school.

"Let us ponder weak and weary."

"Over many a quaint and curious volume of forgotten lore."

"Truly your forgiveness I implore."

They snapped their fingers and repeated the lines two more times.

No matter about the car. Junius wouldn't dare sit in it anyway. There were safer places, away from the shootings, the drugs. School, for instance, in Manhattan, where his parents insisted he attend. They wouldn't let him go to the local high school. Junius didn't object to their suggestion, though there were other schools that appealed to him more. Marvin already was attending the High School of Music and Art, in Manhattan, an hour's subway ride away.

"We'll find better singers at my school. We'll cut a record. Connections. It'll open the scene to us, Junius. It's in the City. Everything is there."

But there was no basketball team at M&A. He could always sing, but he could only play ball in school. They couldn't use the park courts any longer; the hoops were torn away and the parks had been taken over by gangs and drug dealers.

"Do you want to sing or play ball?" Marvin asked.

"Both."

"You gotta choose."

Eldon thought Junius should go to Boys High, with him. They both were nearly six feet tall and they were nearly unbeatable on two-on-two against boys their own age.

"You're good enough for varsity," he said. "We'll start in our sophomore year."

Junius thought about the recent two undefeated seasons at Boys and the city championship.

"You're as good as the Hawk. It's your ticket to college."

"Yeah, sure."

"We'll continue singing. It doesn't have to be one or the other. You can do both."

"If I play ball at Boys, it's singing in the showers. That's not what I want."

"The trestle's not going anywhere. We can always sing there."

When he received notice that he had passed the audition for Music and Art High School, to his parents' relief, Junius accepted. Marvin was right and Eldon wrong. He couldn't do both, not the way he wanted. There would be no time left to practice and perfect his ball game, not after the long commute each day to Manhattan, the rehearsals and practices and homework.

Over the next three years, Eldon's game exceeded even his own expectations. He was All-City and All-American, another star from Brooklyn in the basketball firmament. The point shaving scandal from two years before that snared Connie Hawkins hung over the school and the team. Big-time colleges were leery of taking another player from Boys. Still several small-time colleges recruited him. He was too good for everyone to pass by. Small programs would invest little and hope for a great return. Eldon's problem was which college to choose.

"Palm trees. I want a place where there are coconuts on the ground."

Offers came from colleges in states he never heard of, none of which had palms. Eldon didn't know much about geography. The time they went to Coney Island and rode the Wonder Wheel Eldon marveled at the view from 150 feet up as the car they were riding rocked back and forth on its track.

"Man, you can see Europe from here!"

"That's Staten Island," Marvin told him. "That's a bridge there. There's no bridge big enough to connect New York with Europe."

Junius was less successful in convincing Eldon that Brooklyn was on Long Island.

"I didn't cross over any water when I went out there," Junius explained, "so we must be on the same island."

O.K., that was Staten Island across the water, he admitted, but Brooklyn wasn't part of the Island. If it were it wouldn't be called Brooklyn but Brooklyn Island.

Eldon finally selected the college by how it sounded: 'Wichita.' And that's where he went.

Junius's future was less clear. The more he had performed at school the more he wanted to be part of the entertainment world. Music and Art filled him with song and lyrics and rhythms and he lived a kind of life five days a week that appealed straight to his bones. He listened to music he had never heard before, he learned songs that were foreign to him and discovered that his voice could do more than doo-wop and he could do more than shuffle his feet and snap his fingers.

His high school years were better than he had hoped, more than what Marvin had promised. He wanted his life to continue the way it had been for the last three years at M&A.

Junius didn't see the point of going to college. For Eldon it was the ticket for stardom. But a degree didn't get a record contract or make you a better singer. At college you weren't surrounded by talented people or with those who had connections to the music business. Whatever he was to become, as far as Junius was concerned, college would be of no use.

"I missed my chance," his father said. "I'm not going to let you mess up."

"Where am I going to go?"

"Brooklyn or CCNY. They're fine."

"If you want to be an engineer or accountant."

"You want to be famous."

"I want to sing."

"No one's stopping you from singing. But go to college. You'll have something to fall back on if your singing doesn't work out."

"It'll work out."

"You're not going to work in a ship's hold. You're not going to be nobody's nigger."

Carl was beginning to tremble. He rubbed his sore knee.

The only thing Susan said that morning was, "Do you want Brooklyn or City College?"

Eldon wasn't going to get his palm trees but instead cornfields in Kansas; Junius planned on taking the A train to 125th St. to CCNY in Harlem; and Marvin had gotten a part in a small production in a theater in Greenwich Village.

This was their last summer together and they knew it. The Sparrows would continue, Junius was certain, but it wouldn't be with Eldon and Marvin. Junius felt as though his life had been put on hold, a car revving its engine while at a stop light.

But they could still sing until September. Or at least August, when Eldon would be leaving for the long bus ride to Kansas.

"Wichita. It sounds so sweet, Wichita," Eldon repeated.

Marvin wrote a song about Eldon's leaving for the prairie and his high-flying moves while The Sparrows practiced in Junius's upstairs bedroom. They were better than ever. Not since Sal had moved had they thought about him, but now they wished he were with them for their last performance. It wasn't his fault that his parents fled and deserted the neighborhood.

Junius saw Marvin rolling a reefer. "Not here," he said. "Not in the house. My Mom can smell that stuff from a mile away."

Susan could smell it on Junius's clothes when he was near someone smoking pot, a common thing at his school. He insisted that he didn't do drugs and she believed him.

Eldon took it from Marvin and put it in his pocket.

They knew what was happening in Harlem. It was in all the papers, front page, and all day on radio. Junius could hear the radio downstairs in the kitchen, but his parents didn't talk about the riots, not for the first three days. The Sparrows knew that hundreds of people had protested the shooting death by the police of a junior high school student and things had gotten very bad. The rumor was that a bomb had been thrown and a policeman had been killed. Entire blocks of stores were looted and burned. A rioter had also died.

Eldon suggested they go to see for themselves.

"It's not right what they did. We've got to defend ourselves. They just can't go around killing kids. It's like Birmingham."

Eldon was serious. They had seen Eldon draw his switchblade in the schoolyard.

"They're going to get us next." He took a piece of paper out of his pocket.

"Don't be stupid," Marvin said.

"You're the one who said it. Didn't you give me Malcolm's words last week?"

"That's a speech. It's like a play, you know, to get you to think. It's to get people's attention."

" 'By any means necessary.' You just want to stand here like a fool while they beat the shit out of you?"

"What do you think you're going to do against the pigs? Southern crackers got nothing on New York's."

He and Junius wanted to practice the new song.

"We're doing this for you, Eldon. Why do you want to get yourself hurt? You got something going."

"From the top," Junius said.

"So we're just going to sing, as though nothing's happening? We're going to let killer cops go free?"

Eventually Eldon cooled down and the trio continued to practice throughout the blistering hot weekend while the riot escalated. There were speeches on street corners in their neighborhood that attracted larger crowds each day.

On Monday they were ready to sing under the railroad viaduct.

Susan asked Junius to stay inside. There was a demonstration planned on Nostrand Avenue, she told him.

"It's called by CORE," Carl said, pushing his coffee cup to the center of the table. "I like what they stand for, but not these new hotheads that have taken over. They're asking for trouble." He spoke slowly, lowering his voice as if talking to himself. Carl had wanted Junius to go with him to Washington the summer before. "They don't have a dream, Junius. They're just eaten by anger." Junius and his father had also disagreed over the school boycott in February and made clear to Junius that he was never to participate in such an action. He said people died for the right to go to school. There was never a good reason to stay home. "It'll only lead to more violence," he said, referring to the CORE rally scheduled that day. "There's been enough violence." He paused. "Things are moving in our direction, Junius, you can count on it. We don't need any more deaths to prove it."

"The only dead people I see are us," Junius responded quietly.

"Believe me, non-violence is the right way. Organize. The courts. You be more . . ." Carl couldn't continue. The pain dug deep.

"You took up a gun . . ."

"Please, Junius," Susan pleaded and Junius stopped.

"I'm meeting Eldon and Marvin. It's far from Nostrand. You know, to our 'studio.' To sing. I'm not going near Nostrand. We're under the railroad, this side of Atlantic."

"I can't order you, Junius." Carl looked at his son.

"It's probably our last performance together. Everyone's going to be there."

"Stay home today," Susan said one more time.

Carl worried about his son's indifference; Susan worried about his safety.

The Sparrows met later that afternoon at their usual rendezvous, under the trestle. They placed their caps and jackets on the ground as they rehearsed. Trains streamed overhead every half-hour, the clacking of the wheels absorbed by the steel girders. They planned on a mix of songs, some new ones taken from the tops charts and ones they had perfected over the last few years.

Their songs included "Under the Boardwalk," "Mercy, Mercy." They had fought over whether to add "Can't Buy Me Love" to their list.

"I don't want to sing no white boy music," Eldon insisted.

Junius and Marvin agreed but argued that good music was good music. At school he enjoyed Bach's choral music. The protest folk music in the Village appealed to him.

"It depends on how it's done," he told Eldon and they were going to do it even better than the Beatles. Eldon relented and "Can't Buy Me Love" stayed.

The rest of the songs were from their repertoire: "Duke of Earl" and "Twistin' the Night Away." Their favorite was "Earth Angel." They wanted to close with "See You in September," and then, when everyone insisted on one more number, they would encore with their original song "We'll Sing Forever," the send-off tribute to Eldon and their final one as the Sparrows.

They put on their jackets and waited for their friends to arrive. But no one showed up, not one.

While they waited for the crowd to materialize, they sang, "Dogs begin to bark now,/ And the hounds begin to howl/ Watch out stray cat,/ The little red rooster's on the prowl."

Eldon bayed and they laughed at the way they sounded in the dark.

Nearby smoke billowed over a rooftop. Police cars sped by, sirens echoing off walls, interfering with their close harmonies. They laughed as flashing red lights made their venue into a nightclub stage. Paddy wagons and fire trucks raced by.

A teenager ran under the tracks from the north side, shoved Marvin aside, tripped, scuffled to his feet and then ran out the south end. Marvin rubbed the back of his head, which had hit the pillar behind him. Two patrolmen with drawn pistols turned down the street.

The Sparrows backed away to let them go by.

One cop stopped, took his baton and with a wide swing hit Eldon on his right forearm. As he lifted it for another swing, Eldon and Marvin scattered out from under the overhead tracks and disappeared down a side street.

The cop looked at Junius who raised his hands above his head. The second officer snapped cuffs on Junius's wrists and walked him to a paddy wagon at the corner. Within a half-hour the patrol wagon was filled with black teenagers and men and one female. Junius knew a few from the neighborhood.

When he was bailed out of the Brooklyn House of Detention the next morning, Susan told him, "You're charged with assaulting a police officer."

"Also resisting arrest. And possessing marijuana," Carl added.

"We were just singing. I swear. We weren't doing anything else. I didn't do any of that. I don't use drugs. I swear to you."

"I asked you to stay home."

"We weren't doing anything. I swear. Just singing."

"You did what I told you if you ever met the police? You didn't give them no lip, did you? You were polite?"

Junius nodded his head in agreement.

"Who do you think a *jury* will believe? You or the police?" Carl asked rhetorically.

"That doesn't mean I'm not telling the truth. I'm telling you what happened."

"I'm not the jury, son."

Susan sat next to Junius and put her arm around his shoulder.

"Eldon got hit," Junius whispered, fighting back tears. "He wasn't doing anything d. They just hit him."

"Bad?"

"I don't think so. He and Marvin ran."

"They were arrested with you?"

Junius shrugged his shoulders.

"I don't know where they are."

"Call Tom," Susan urged her husband. "He'll know what we should do."

"This isn't good, son."

Junius's stomach cramped and he vomited.

〰〰〰〰〰
〰〰〰〰〰

SOON AFTER THE SUMMER RIOTS, Junius walked through the marble doorway decorated with carved cannons, cannonballs and spears at the fortress of a building at 39 Whitehall Street. Most of the day he stood in the Army Center in snaking lines on the iron steps, stepping into one room after another, answering questions, told to drop his shorts—turn right, cough; turn the other way, cough—, taking tests and filling forms. Before the week was out, he was sworn in, put on a bus for Fort Dix, had his head shaved, his civilian clothes taken away, given a rifle and told that at the end of the eight weeks he would be a professional killer.

"Do you understand me?" the sergeant shouted.

"Yes, sir."

"What did you say?"

"Yes, sir!"

The drill sergeant would get them to shape up before they ship out.

As Junius fell asleep on the bottom bunk in the wooden barracks during Basic Training, he would sing to himself. In the morning shower, while field stripping his rifle, wherever he could, he would sing the summer's hit song: "Callin' out around the world/ Are you ready for a brand new beat?/ Summer's here and the time is right/ For dancing in the street."

"You like singing, soldier?" Sgt. Torres looked Junius in the eye and stood inches from his face. Junius could feel his spittle. The company had just returned to the barracks after a day at the rifle range.

"Yes, sir."

"What did you say?"

"Yes, sir!"

"You're fucking 'A,' Numbnuts. From now on you're going to take your sorry singing ass and teach all the fucking girls to sing."

Junius smiled.

"You smiling?"

Junius knew whatever answer he gave would be unacceptable. Once he had answered, "I thought . . .", which was responded to with, "You're not paid to think, soldier."

"Yes, sir! No, sir." It didn't matter which sir, up/ down, right/ left sir, whatever you say sir and it was never loud or quick enough.

"No fucking with me, you cocksucker, son of a bitch mother fucker. Get down," the drill sergeant pointed to the ground, "and give me ten!"

It took Junius a minute to do the last two pushups, as Torres stood over him and continued to growl out what Junius was certain were expletives in some language known only to the sergeant.

For rest of Basic Training, after chinning at the bar in the quadrangle in front of the mess hall, Torres had Junius lead the squad in the bunny hop—forward, back, forward, forward, forward—as they entered for the evening meal. The other squads in the company watched and laughed as Junius and the others jumped forward and back, then forward, one, two, three.

Was this another humiliation, like the toilet seats without stalls in the middle of the latrine, designed to break civilians down into grunts, men who wouldn't hesitate to kill another? What the streets had accomplished, the army would complete.

Torres ordered musicians to return to the post with their instruments after their first weekend pass.

Was this another of Torres's sadistic jokes?

For the next four weeks, Junius led the platoon's makeshift band of bass drum, trumpets and flute whenever and wherever they cadence marched, through piney woods, white dust trails, across logs tossed over creeks, on the parade grounds, to the rifle range. He used standard calls and also made up dozens of his own.

> I don't know but I've been told
>
> Russian pussy is mighty cold
>
> Sound off, one two
>
> Sound off, three four
>
> Cadence count
>
> One, two, three, four
>
> One, two—three, four
>
> Lulu has an uncle, whoa

Her uncle's name is Chuck

Every time he's at her house

She'd always want to

Bang bang Lulu

Lulu has gone away

Bang bang Lulu

Lulu is here to stay

Cadence count

One, two, three, four

One, two—three-four

Looked right up

And what did I see

A three striped bird

Right shittin' on me

Sound off, one, two

Sound off, three, four

Cadence count

One, two, three, four

One, two—three-four

The last cadence count led to several days of KP where he rose before the 5 o'clock reveille to peel potatoes, scrub pots, clean garbage pails, straighten shelves in walk-in refrigerator and polish the tile mess hall floor with a buffing machine that bucked around with a mind of its own. Each night he returned to the barracks at lights off.

At the end of Basic Training recruits received their deployment as readymade soldiers.

Torres gave Junius his letter.

"You like music so much, I like you, too. I put in a good word for my favorite recruit," Torres bellowed, the last time Junius would have to listen to the equine snort.

Junius was assigned to recruiting and publicity and was to report in two weeks to Fort Slocum in New Rochelle, New York. Junius had no idea where that was. But he was sure that he wouldn't be boarding a plane for Europe or a train for California or a ship to Panama. At the end of Basic Training, he would figure out how to get from Bedford-Stuyvesant to his new home.

On the last day of Basic Training, without the drill sergeant's permission and to the delight of the Company Commander, Junius gathered the band outside the barracks to lead the company in a call and response: "They're dancing in New Jersey/ Down in New Orleans/In little old Ft. Dix/ All we need is music, sweet music/ Dancing in the pines."

Welcome Hard Times

~~~~~~~~~
~~~~~~~~~

MOST MORNINGS LENA AWAKES in another rat-infested apartment with someone whose name she can't remember. Neither can she remember what or how much she drank or ingested.

Since graduation from Hunter College Lena had been working in bookstores in the Village, gladly accepting minimum wage for the opportunity to indulge her reading habits. She took pleasure in steering customers to titles she thought were the most useful and finding new titles on her own. She moved from one bookstore to another when she finished the books that interested her and when she knew most of the customers, specialists in specialized bookstores—musicians, poets and writers, political radicals, each to their own, engaged, posturing, passionate and, to Lena, finally boring. When she knew everyone who came in and anticipated every argument that ensued and could mouth every position stated, she moved on.

Lena stayed longest at the Oscar Wilde Bookshop, reading about lives she scarcely knew existed and meeting both men and women who openly expressed affection for the same sex, where she helped edit the Hymnal, a monthly newsletter for homosexuals and lesbians. Gay New York and New Jersey license plates were also for sale, as were trinkets, buttons and posters. Lena listened to discussions about gay pride, a new idea for her, and she wondered whether it wasn't another example of the white community appropriating something essential from the black. 'Black pride,' yes, but 'gay pride?' She wasn't fully persuaded.

"If you believe in yourself," Rodwell said more than once, "you can make anything happen."

Lena had left her mother's Brooklyn apartment after graduation from college but didn't want a place of her own with the burden of leases where she would be beholden to landlords. A few items that could be packed into a bag was all she needed and therefore, all she wanted. She admired the hobos on the railroad tracks that Woody and Seeger sang about, not homeowners in their ticky-tacky tracts. She moved around the city, from apartment to apartment, crashing with those she met while leading them to her new favorite books, leaving petty cash when her stay extended for more than a day.

The vagabond life of the body electric.

Despite Lena's growing assurance that consciousness, not politics, changed the world, the war could not be avoided. Protests, rallies, marches, leaflets, newspapers, TV, music, anti-draft riots—there was nowhere for her to turn.

At Oscar Wilde, Lena saw an ad for an audition for what was called a psychedelic, nude burlesque troupe, at the Mayfair Theatre.

"Why not try out?" Rodwell encouraged her. "Look, I know you need some money. You don't have enough for rent, but I can't pay you any more than I am. Not even for the work on the newsletter."

"It's OK. I like it here."

"Then, goddam it, show up when you're supposed to."

"I have enough to live on."

"Like shit you do. You're just bumming around."

"I like it this way."

"I'm not going to fire you if you take the other work. It's probably nighttime any way. You can work days here. You're doing a good job, even though I need you to be more dependable," Rodwell said. "You can earn some extra money. I think you can use it."

It amused Lena that men would pay to see naked women.

"Go ahead," Rodwell encouraged her. "You just might like it." Rodwell was circumspect about Lena's private life and she was surprised that he took an interest in her. If he knew that she slept with men, he would probably fire her. She wasn't sure if Rodwell were teasing or goading her.

Not beautiful and not a good dancer, Lena was hesitant about auditioning, unsure whether she would be accepted. But she would audition, not because she wanted the money, she thought, but if her body were electric, then men should pay for the charge they got, even if they weren't plugged in.

A stanza of a poem by Delmore Schwartz, who she had met many times in various bookstores, came into mind: "Twenty-eight naked young women bathed by the shores/ Or near the bank of a woodland lake/ Twenty-eight girls and all of them comely/ Worthy of Mack Sennett's camera and Florenz Ziegfield's/ Foolish Follies."

"Do you think anyone is going to be looking at your face?" Rodwell asked. "As Bloom says, it's 'the plump mellow yellow smellow melons of her rump, on each plump melonous hemisphere, in their mellow yellow furrow.' "

"Who?"

"Leopold Bloom."

"Joyce?"

"Of course. *Ulysses.*"

Lena parried: "Electrical banana/ Is gonna be a sudden craze/ Electrical banana/ Is bound to be the very next phase."

"The Beatles?"

"No, Donovan," she said. "Mellow Yellow."

"He took it from Joyce, then."

"Maybe. But if it feels good, it is good, that's the important thing."

Rodwell didn't look closely at the lesbian literature in his store, so Lena was certain he had no idea that she was referring to her new purchase she toted in her knitted handbag.

"Sure, sure," Rodwell said impatiently. "But not theft. It doesn't matter how you feel."

"Capitalist."

"I have to pay the rent."

"No you don't."

"I still have to buy books. I don't publish them. Where else will you to get such an education? No library will support these authors. They're as underground as underground gets. What does Mao say about this in the *Little Red Book*? That book's for sale, too, isn't it?"

"I'm no Maoist," Lena replied lightly, splitting ideological hairs that held no interest to Rodwell.

Rodwell put an end to the conversation.

"Take off your clothes and get paid to have them leer," was his final advice. He straightened the pile of small pins of cops, construction workers and cowboys with mermaid bottoms that were displayed behind the cash register.

The press was invited to the try-outs for Art Steuer's psychedelic vaudeville. The director wore a "Dick Gregory for President" button pinned to his gray collarless suit jacket, white buck shoes and around his neck hung an American flag tie. The theater smelled from the sticky scent of patchouli-laced incense.

"Greetings, dear friend," Steuer says to each reporter as he places pink carnations behind their ears.

"Flowers to the People!" he shouts with a raised fist.

Flowers are also strewn on the theater seats and are tied neatly to microphones on the stage.

Lena and four others walk out in front of the curtain. As Burning Bush pounds out its beat behind the lead singer—"Have you seen my new pet beaver/ Her eyes the color of plasticine/ Soft like jelly/ She melts when exposed to heat"—the young women take off their clothes as they twirl and swoop in front of the snickering reporters. Lena tosses all her clothes at Steuer, then struts to the reporter from the Daily News, takes the carnation from behind his ear, returns to the stage and gives it to another dancer to place between her teeth.

"Ladies and gentlemen of the press, today you witness the revival of a great American folk art brought up to date. Behold the new Sally Rands! The Hippie Strippies" The band played and the women more or less danced. "And now for the first topless camerawoman," Steuer announces.

From stage left a large, naked woman appears holding a 35mm camera with a telephoto lens tethered to a gold lame G-string. She turns the camera on the press corps.

Lena reads the story in The Village Voice the next day. "None of them had maxi stripper bodies; all were young, cool, and mini-chested, with very plain faces. The only pretty girls in the theatre were the camera assistants, and they kept their clothes on," the reporter wrote.

The article also mentioned that the strippers were going to do a naked radio show.

"No money," Steuer tells her when he reaches her on the phone at the bookshop. "We're doing this for the people."

"Not me. I'm not taking my clothes off again. It's too damn cold."

"This time you'll be in a studio. We need to get the word out about the protest at the convention. So there's this warm-up at Grand Central. Come on, you'll be good. All the girls will be there."

Lena's faith in social change hadn't been totally extinguished. The least she could do was advertise the rally on the alternative radio station. Being an announcer wasn't enough; anyone can read a script. She needed to challenge herself to discover where her inner self resided, if she had a core on which everything else could rest.

In the interview on WBAI, Lena, not just topless but naked when she spoke on the air, encouraged listeners to join the spring mating to celebrate the Spring Equinox at Grand Central Station, to start at midnight and continue until they "yip up the sun." Reading from the flier in her hand, she told listeners to "bring bells, flowers, beads, kazoos, music, FM radios ['listen to WBAI,' she added on her own] pillows, eats, love and peace."

Rock stations in the New York area picked up the story about the demonstration at Grand Central.

Lena returns somewhere with someone and takes something she's never seen before.

"Let's spend the night together," she said.

"Now I need you more than ever," anonymous (maybe Lena never asked for his or her name or perhaps she heard it or couldn't remember) replied.

"I'm so strong I can't disguise," Lena continued to riff and floats to the sky, molting like a snake, her mind racing down blinding alleyways. She follows the *Kama Sutra's* instructions: bite the sides, press outside, press inside, kiss, rub, suck a mango fruit, swallow up. She popped pills, smoked pot, ate mushrooms, dropped acid—anything but needles; she hated being stuck—or maybe it was something else that night.

Her body was Eros in revolt against civilization, her body against the body politic.

The smell of others' bodies clung to her, their sour breath coating the roof of her mouth. Her clothes smelled of strangers when she returned to the bookstore two days later and read the story in the Village Voice.

> Last year the name of the game was the "Be-In," this year it looks like "Yip-In." At midnight on Friday, March 22, the yippies will have a Yip-In in Grand Central Station. At least a thousand flowered, belled, beaded, and body-painted people are expected. Smart yippies will bring blankets and pillows to sit on. If you want to wear a costume but don't own one, you can get one free at the Free School, 20 East 14th Street.

> There are 25 entrances into Grand Central, so if you find one blocked or closed, the yippies advise to keep trying.

> All this activity is to raise money and attract publicity for the yippies' August demonstration in Chicago at what they affectionately call the Democratic Death Convention.

The newspaper underestimated the turnout—it wasn't 1,000 but 6,000 who showed up at Grand Central Station, causing mayhem. Lena was too wasted to get out of bed to join the protest.

"It was the most extraordinary display of unprovoked police brutality I've seen outside of Mississippi. The police reacted enthusiastically to the prospect of being unleashed," a witness said.

She hated herself for missing the protest. The Yippies were a new kind of politics, one that she could favor because it didn't take itself seriously. Anarchism and satire—that made sense in going against the machine. But what good would it do to get her head bashed? Nothing was going to change, even by jokesters. Be there, stand up. But it was futile, all politics was beside the point.

Change yourself before your change the world.

"You're a wreck," he said.

She pursed her lips dismissively.

"I can't have you like this. I have to be able to depend on you."

"How bourgeois."

"I have to know you're going to show up."

"I'm here."

"When you show up."

"I'll tell you when I find out."

"God, Lena. Enough. Take some time off. Go home."

"Easy for you to say. You have one."

Lena steadied herself on a stool and leaned on the counter while Rodwell arranged the titles in alphabetical order by author's name, divided male and female, creating a new world on Mercer Street.

"Truth is power," he said as he returned to the counter. "And the truth is that you're killing yourself."

"The truth is I want to be left alone."

"Truth is the greatest good. For your own good, Lena, for your own good, I'm telling you."

"You hate women, don't you?" she declared.

"No, I love men. But you, Lena, what I see is you hate yourself. You know what Wilde said? 'To love oneself is the beginning of a lifelong romance.' "

"I don't believe in romance."

"What do you believe in? Tell me, Lena. I want to know because I see you don't believe in anything."

Lena looked at the handsome man, his thick hair covering his head like a fur hat that swept over his ears, a thin turtleneck under his white shirt. She wanted to go home with him but knew its impossibility.

"Fuck yourself, Rodwell." She corrected herself. "No. Me. Fuck me." She steadied herself against the back wall as she stood to leave.

Outside, tinkling of thumb cymbals, flowers, and an Indian drum. She takes a proffered card and drops it into her handbag. Spinning around her, holding out a flower for her to take, swirling saffron robes: "hare krishna, hare krishna/ krishna krishna, hare hare/ hare rama hare rama/ rama rama hare hare."

"Fuck all of you," she says under her breath.

She returns to the bookstore. Rodwell turns from arranging books on the wall when he hears the door open. He watches Lena as she walks behind the counter and dials the phone on the wall.

"Can I talk to Ellen?"

"Who is this?"

"Lena."

"Ellen's not here," the voice replied sharply.

"I need to talk to her."

"I'll tell her you called."

"When will she be in?"

"Good-by, Lena."

"Yeah, you too."

She asked Rodwell if she could sleep in the office. Instead, he called a friend who took her to his apartment on Riverside Drive. She's shown the guest room. The lamp is shaped like a phallus, a chandelier made from pawnshop balls hangs over the dining room table; matched placemats and dishes, neatly folded napkins and phallic faucets make Lena laugh. When she wakes the next morning, she empties the contents of her shoulder bag onto the floor.

"Keep calm. Chant Hare Krishna."

The cherubic androgynous child on the card she had been given looks at Lena, calm, lips nearing a flute, eyes lined with kohl. She wears a bejeweled red turban and on her lap a white cow longingly rests its head.

The street chanters weren't calm or serene, Lena thought, but more like giddy children. Lena puts the card down and picks up a leaflet she had taken from a coffee shop weeks before.

"Rise up and abandon the creeping meatball!" the Yippie flier proclaims. "Drop out, leave school, run away from home, form your own community."

She looks at the Hare Krishna card again and, to her relief, she falls into the green haven of grass and powder blue sky she sees behind the psychedelic goddess.

She leaves without thanking Rodwell's friend and for the next two nights sleeps on a park bench.

To start afresh, to begin again. She remembers the dog-eared page and the passage from *The Grapes of Wrath*: "This land, this red land, is us; and the flood years and the dust years and the drought years are us. We can't start again."

Steinbeck's wrong, Lena argues. You can start again. He says so himself in the same paragraph. "And some day—the armies of bitterness will all be going the same way. And they'll all walk together, and there'll be a dead terror from it."

That's what attracted her to the East Village apartment when her head has cleared, someplace where she could find others to walk together, the same way, not to the stillborn dream of the land of oranges and sun the Oakies sought but that of a new body promised by Whitman and Wilde. Unlike the apartment overlooking the Hudson where everything was arranged, fussed over and admired, here in this tenement was a riot against beauty. The room smelled of sweat and food and smoke. On the walls were posters of triumphant Soviet heroes, a stoic Che Guevara, and on the table a plaster bust of Chairman Mao presided over the revolution.

Share a meal, share a mattress, share a joint. But the pronouncements, the declamations, the denunciations— "grab stones, bombs, knives, whatever you can find"—drove into her softened brain. She stayed only until she could find another place that promised more than hammers and golden stars.

The doe-eyed goddess beckoned, promising calm; carefully laid napkins promised ordered beauty. She yearned for release.

Lena spent hours in the Strand Bookstore, wandering the endless aisles of used books. She attended experimental plays at the Judson Poets' Theater. It was there that she found herself returning, to watch Monday night dance and exhibits by Village artists. She moved into a space with an artist in a refurbished office in a church, an area also used by counselors for drug users and women seeking abortions.

Her roommate encouraged Lena to attend a Sunday service. Not all religion was degenerate, she said to Lena. "Just look at where we live."

The sermon centered on decriminalizing prostitution and concluded with quote from Jerome about poverty, He then issued a challenge: "These words are the essence of the Sermon on the Mount. They can and must be lived today. The golden rule is the essence of selfless living. Meeting friends is great, but there are other young people who would like to gather and seek and live the life of active love. Can't we do more than talk? While pondering these questions an idea took root. A community of our own. We invite you to join us on our quest."

Before the week was out, Lena joined the excursion north, the possibility of living away from the choking city appealing to her as much as a new beginning. As she boarded the VW kombi to take its emigrants to Vermont, she stowed a satchel containing all she owned under her seat. What was she doing? She didn't accept Jesus as her savior; she didn't even believe in God. She didn't believe in anything any longer, only the desire to find calm. Perhaps she could find what she sought without the faith that others thought it required.

The pink kombi with a pig's nose between the headlights and inflatable pink ears on the roof lumbered up the secondary highways and buried itself in the summering mountains, an odyssey to build a new nation by breaking the land again, vowing to live free or die, turning their backs on the old world to greet a new dawn. She says aloud: "He who binds to himself a joy/ Does the winged life destroy."

A muddy commune-in-the-making awaits the recruits. Other vans full of pilgrims and seekers followed and by summer there were more than twenty at the commune called The Brothers House.

The Manhattan church owned the deed to the property but turned operations over to those who lived there vowing not to interfere. Governance was from the bottom up. The only stipulations were that communards must be non-violent and had to live as best they understood a life reflecting that of early Christianity. This meant that the commune was self-governing on the basis of consensus and that there would be no financial support from the mother church. They would have to be self-sufficient, tilling the land, planting and weeding, milking the dairy cows. No money would exchange hands. No one would have more than another. They never uttered it, but Lena knew, "From each according to his abilities, to each according to his needs." She had heard it countless times as a child. Now she could live it.

Theology was never discussed, prayers gave way to meditation, worship service became silent meetings, and references to the bible grew increasingly rare.

There was no time to read, a difficult transition for Lena to make. There were no newspapers. They seldom listened to the transistor radio. The mountains made television reception all but impossible—it didn't matter, there was no electricity. The war intruded on their daily existence only when a young man fleeing the draft or a scarred veteran from Vietnam arrived. News of the world came word of mouth through contact with other communes. Some stories were too exaggerated to be true, but everyone knew that anything was possible. The country was at war not only in Vietnam but in the streets of America's cites and on its campuses.

While dedicated to "God's law, not Man's law," interpretations of the law drifted month to month. Eventually tolerance triumphed over literalness. It was settled: what God didn't forbid was permitted.

The theological concerns held by a few were finally subsumed under the rhetoric of the mystical body, a state achieved by the liberation of sexual pleasure.

"Politics is nothing more than reorganizing the theater," declaimed the man with the long beard and hair tumbling over his shoulders. He continued, paraphrasing *Love's Body*, which was passed around as the new manifesto of transformation. "Through the body, not our minds, we become part of the band of holy fools who will make the new world. We have fallen from grace, sister, and will return to ourselves through the innocence of our natural instincts. We are nothing but our bodies. Pleasure is God. God is pleasure. We are all God."

She refused to sleep with him but not others.

The commune adopted the motto 'Love Life' and they did, in all its forms and permutations and possibilities. With every nail Lena placed in the house she built on the hillside, she felt liberated from her self. In every pot scrubbed she saw reflected her own of cleanliness. She was starting over.

Lena was the first to object to the commune's name.

"Shouldn't it be The Brothers and Sisters House?"

While no one argued against her bid for sexual equality, reaching a decision was a lengthy process. As the discussion continued for several nights around the dining table and after they sat around the floor of the one finished room in the house trying to reach consensus, a carpenter had built a signboard and placed it at the bottom of the hill where the commune's track met the state road.

Welcome Hard Times, he boldly painted in white paint, putting an end to the conversation.

Welcome Hard Times was joined by a dozen other communes that year of new beginnings, false starts and modest successes in Vermont, the year of assassins and despair.

Lena helped complete construction of the house the following summer; she milked cows and learned which vegetables grew best in the New England soil. Lena's cardinal red hair had cooled to red gold and now reached halfway to her waist and for the first time she had calluses on her hands. She wore hats during the day to protect her pale skin from burning.

Demands lessened on the commune as work became more efficient, allowing Lena, for the first time since arriving, to read again. In her spare time, she went to the bookstore in the village a walk away that had been opened by two psychology professors from Boston. She had no money to buy books, so she swept and straightened the store in return for the privilege of treating the shop as her library. She made suggestions and became their literary mentor.

While water was still pumped from the well at Welcome Hard Times, there now was electricity from a generator. The night that a band from a nearby commune plugged in their instruments, the wires sparked. Flames engulfed the house and it collapsed into smoke and ash.

Welcome Hard Times was gone. Members scattered to other communes—political, spiritual, lesbian, anarchic, prankster, escapist, back-to-the-land organic farming. Lena chose to move into the rear room in the bookstore in Allens Corner. Not having to be with people all the time, not having to share everything, having a space that was her own and not having to justify every thought and wish helped sooth her soul. She opened the store at 10 and often didn't see the first customer of the day for hours. Once again she devoured books and magazines. Nights were alone at the potbelly stove. She bought a transistor radio. On clear nights she could hear stations from Boston, New York and occasionally from Toronto.

When the owners decided to return to Boston to open an art movie theater, they left Lena alone to manage the shop. Members of her commune had scattered, many leaving for a more benign climate in Arkansas or New Mexico. Lena decided to remain in Vermont. There she reads a new translation of a Pablo Neruda poem. She clips it from the journal and puts it into her handbag. She carried it with her for years.

"If you ask me where I have been / I have to say 'it happens.'/ I have to speak of ground darkened by stones,/ of the river that enduring destroys itself:/ I know only the things that birds lose, / the sea left behind, or my tearful sister. / Why so many regions, why does one day /attach to another? Why does a black night / accumulate in one's mouth? Why the dead?"

Why Is This Night Different?

~~~~~~~~

IN NO CONDITION TO RETURN to the university, Kwamboka visited Conway's home while she recuperated, often remaining for dinner and on Sunday afternoons sitting with him near the towering eucalyptus.

Until he met Kwamboka, Conway's only pleasure had been with his compass and chains, level and transit, his only friend the Ridgeback, but with Kwamboka he began to understand the difference between contentment and joy. Even unlocking painful memories as he told her about his suffering at the hands of an uncle brought a satisfaction he had never known. Over the next three months, he revealed everything to Kwamboka, except the shame he felt for the silent visits with the woman on the savannah. She listened, keeping a respectful distance between them, never having heard a European speak before except to give orders. She had never known a man before who only wanted to talk.

The assault on Conway and the train accident on the children's train were unresolved. The investigation into the train wreck was dropped by the newly independent government the following year; Makori, the prime suspect in the stabbing, had vanished, although there were rumors that he was the homeless person whose bones were picked by vultures on the shores of Lake Victoria.

Conway wished Kwamboka would stay but he wouldn't make such a request. Instead, he encouraged her to finish her degree and a half year later she moved back to Nairobi. After completing her studies, she began her graduate school. She didn't return to Kisii again and, after a flurry of letters, they lost contact with one another.

Two years later, certain he was a nullity in this is a black man's land, Conway retired and moved to Nairobi. No one wanted a remainder, a leftover. It seemed as though the Kenyan and British government agreed. No one protested his going. Rather than being the bridge he had hoped to be, he was far less. Africans, Americans, Icelanders—they were all welcome, anyone but a Brit from colonial days who couldn't find his way home. When the government put in place new immigration law that banned non-Kenyans from owning shops or trading in municipal markets, its Indian population had to choose between taking Kenyan citizenship or obtaining British passports. Within months, tens of thousands fled the country, thereby allowing Conway to purchase a house on a large plot, behind a cypress hedge that muffled the sound of people on the road walking to work or to look for work downtown. He could sit on the verandah with his morning tea, afternoon White Cap and evening gin and tonic listening to music on a phonograph and news on the shortwave.

The expansiveness of the house also brought with it a new sense of loneliness. It was too much for him alone.

Kwamboka was living in a single room in the graduate dormitory, having completed her Masters degree and now begun on a new round of course work for her doctorate. As had been the case before, there were few other females to befriend and the attitude of the males, if anything, had become worse. They saw themselves as the presumptive heirs to newly acquired African power and they were preening and clucking as though they already were government ministers.

When Conway spotted her at a coffee shop, she all too happy to accept his entreaties to meet him. They had coffee one morning at the New Stanley; they met for Indian food at lunchtime; they had afternoon tea on Biashara Street. Some things were new to them both: cinema, visits to the museum and arboretum. They ate sandwiches in Jivanjee Gardens on a bench shaded by lavender-hued jacaranda trees.

Kwamboka became less self-conscious about being seen with a white man. She took pleasure when a fellow student saw her with Conway, imagining what must have been going through his mind—sleeping her way to the top, a mixture of admiration and disdain.

They weren't the only ones like them. As they became more social, they found other mixed-race couples and occasionally they would take in a show at the theater with Berrycloth and his wife. Neither of them knew how to put on a dinner party.

Sitting at a table in his garden listening to mourning doves in the wild chestnut tree, not knowing how else to present it and perhaps not certain about it himself, Conway said, "Look at all the money you could save. No charge, of course," he added, anticipating what he thought her next question would be.

What was he suggesting? In spite of the years she has known him, he was still a mystery to her. It didn't seem possible to ever understand what Europeans were after.

"I meant no offense," he stumbled, waiting for her reply. "Forgive me for my insensitivity."

Kwamboka folded her hands on her lap and brushed the scone crumbs the top of her skirt.

"What are you saying?" she asked after a long silence. "Tell me. Why do you want me in your house?"

"I'm truly sorry, Kwamboka."

Kwamboka's furrows softened.

"So many reasons, Kwamboka," he began as he pushed his coffee cup towards the center of the table. "But it all boils down to this: I would like the privilege of your company. You make life easier for me."

"That's too much to ask. I'm not here to take care of you." She didn't mean it to be this harsh.

"It's something else completely, Kwamboka. I'm trying to say that without friends life isn't worth living. I see that. It took me a long time. But I see it."

"Yes. But I am not a nursemaid."

"It's your friendship that I desire." He wiped the the corner of his mouth with the napkin. "Let me ask you," he challenged, "why not live here? Am I so bad?"

Kwamboka's eyes closed. She breathed deeply and tried to put what was happening to her into perspective but there was no frame in which to put it. The age, the color.

"No. Not a bad man at all," she said shaking her head. "Different, that's all. I've never known a European before, one who wasn't a teacher of mine."

"Are you afraid?"

"Yes, a little."

"Well, we've really cocked up, haven't we Europeans? Will we ever get it straightened out?" Conway said softly. "Some more coffee?"

She held out her cup.

"There's a room for you, if you want it, Kwamboka. It will always be there for you."

~~~~~~

CASEMENT WINDOWS opened onto a garden of bougainvillea, a ceiling fan spun lazily and the hardwood floors were polished to gleaming perfection. During the dry season, Kwamboka often walked to the university to do research or meet with her doctoral advisor. Weekends she devoted to writing. Although her proposal for her dissertation hadn't yet been approved, she continued her research into Kisii folklore. Throughout the year Kwamboka traveled to Kisii to do her fieldwork.

After dinner Conway would sit near the fireplace or on the verandah in warmer weather to read a book he had purchased from a downtown bookstore.

"I'm making two versions for each tale," she explained one cold night. "There are the originals, as best as I can get them. I try to make sure they're accurate but I don't take dictation. Sometimes I wish I had gone to secretarial school."

"Let me buy you a portable tape recorder."

She refused, saying that it would probably interfere with the flow of things. She would rather listen carefully.

"After I hear a story, I try to find another old woman who will tell it again. There's always some small difference."

"Two sets, then?"

"Sometimes I prefer one version. It seems more authentic to me, less influenced by European folk stories. Or I may rewrite it, taking a little from each. All this is only the first set, what I call the authentic or original tale. It's the oral telling. I write this in Gusii. But the second version is a re-writing and I do this in English. The original tales are what I'm doing for my degree. When I'm done it will sit on the shelf with other dissertations. It's good for an historic record. For historians. But what good is it if children don't read them? They need them in English."

One evening she offered to read one story, in all three iterations, to Conway. During the course of the first telling, Conway asked for the translation of some of the more esoteric Gusii words.

Skunk's and Hare's mothers were glad to get them out of their houses. Skunk enjoyed wrestling while Hare liked playing tricks.

One day Hare said, "Our mothers are always telling us what to do. I think we need to put a stop to that. Tonight I will beat my mother and you will beat yours. I will hit my mother first, so you know that I am serious. Then you hit yours."

That night Skunk heard whacks and cries coming from Hare's home.

Skunk waited for Mother Skunk to return. When the door opened, Skunk raised a stick but before it could land a blow, Mother Skunk threw the stick out the window.

The next morning Hare gave one look at Skunk and burst into laughter. Skunk now was black on the underside with a white tail and stripes running down its back.

Skunk told Hare what happened.

"You mean you really tried to beat your mother?" Hare explained the whole thing had been a joke. He had made the noises himself by hitting a mat. Mother Hare cried out because she was in on the trick. He would never hurt Mother.

When Skunk went home that day, Mother Skunk wouldn't let him in.

"Don't you ever come back!" she shouted.

With that Skunk let out the worst, most foul smell ever. Skunk then ran off and dug a hole. Until this day Skunk lives alone and only comes out at night, too ashamed to be seen or be near anyone.

"Have you thought about publishing the stories?"

"Some. The school market is growing and a few publishers are now printing folktales from different tribes. There's nothing from Kisii yet. But first I need to finish my dissertation."

"I like what you have," Conway said. "It does keep the spirit of the original. I think it will be published."

Kwamboka looked at Conway affectionately.

"What? What is it, Kwamboka?"

"Your skin," she chuckled. "Your red skin. It is funny."

"Yes, like being a giant baby," he said. "I know that story about the arrival of Europeans in Kisii and you thinking that since we're the color of babies, we must be . . ." He stopped. "How did you translate one of the words? Ogres was it?"

"Not that, Dexter. Babies. Giant babies. But babies are harmless."

"And we were hardly that."

"No, no. It's not that that I mean. They were heartless, yes, but you.. Not you. You are different."

"Then what's funny?"

"It is that after all the years you've lived in Africa that I think your skin should no longer be so red. You should be at least a little darker. Not like me, of course."

"My skin burns in the sun. I just peel. I can never get dark."

She leaned across the table and stroked his forearm with her fingertips.

"If you had a child," she asked, "what color would it be?"

"What?"

"Would your baby be dark because it was *born* in Africa?"

Conway didn't know if she was serious, but he took the question at face value.

"That's not how it works. A European could spend his entire life in the tropics but if he's fair-skinned, so will the baby. If the mother's also fair, that is."

"So people don't change?"

"As we say in English, a leopard doesn't change its spots."

Kwamboka held his hand.

"I heard it in school, from the nuns. 'Can the Ethiopian change his skin, or the leopard its spots? Then may ye also do good that are accustomed to do evil.' But you're not evil, Dexter. You are good man, Dexter, a good man."

"For an *mzungu*, you mean."

"What you are on the outside isn't what you are on the inside."

She put his hand on her cheek.

"Look at you," she said. "Your face." She laughed. "It has turned like a ripe tomato. You see. You can change, right in front of me."

"Then I'm like a chameleon," Conway said in embarrassment.

"Like a man," Kwamboka responded. She pulled her chair next to him and put her hand on his forehead. "You're warm, Dexter."

"It's the fire," he said as he leaned into her.

And it was like that for many evenings, Kwamboka reading, Conway commenting on her stories, the logs crackling in the fireplace, and nights together under a wool blanket.

Kwamboka's frustration with the university was dispiriting as her advisor still hadn't approved her dissertation proposal. With every submission he had new objections. It felt as though there was no way to please him. There seemed to be no limit on how long she could be strung along.

Although Kwamboka and Conway never as much as held hands in public or seemed anything more than just friends, they were part of a group of African-European couples who would often meet each other in hotel bars for afternoon tea. One day Kwamboka mentioned her folktales to Tom Berrycloth.

Berrycloth, who had been an Assistant District Officer during the colonial era and had been openly critical of British treatment of political prisoners during the Emergency, started his own book company in an office on Muindi Mbingu Street, publishing both biographies of former freedom fighters and children's books.

"Good that you mentioned that. I'm developing a line of folktales from different parts of the country. Something from Kisii would make a nice addition to the series. I think the government would be interested in adopting it for the primary grades."

"Even stories from Kisii? I thought Europe-centric books were being replaced by books by Kikuyus."

"Well, of course. Most school children are Kikuyu, so that's where the market is. But there's room for other tribes to be represented. I'm willing to take a chance on it. We'll take on all the expenses of publication and you'll receive royalties based on total sales. By the way," Berrycloth said, changing the subject. "if you and Dexter are free this week, Gideon—you remember the chap from Israel?—well Gideon has invited a few of us for a Passover service."

At the house, Kwamboka asked Conway about Passover.

"A Jewish holiday."

"Gideon's a Jew?"

"He is from Israel."

"Yes, of course. But I didn't think he was a Jew."

"What did you think he was?"

"I don't know. I just never thought about it. He doesn't look like a Jew. He doesn't have a beard. I never met a Jew before."

"No. None in Kisii. But what did you think they looked like?"

Kwamboka shook her head.

"They're Christ killers. That's what the nuns said and I never thought about it again. I guess . . . I don't know. Like the pictures in the books the nuns gave me I read at school. I thought Jews had long beards. Big noses."

While the Hebrew Congregation stood just two blocks from the college campus, Kwamboka gave less thought to the synagogue than she did to the mosques and Hindu temples found throughout Nairobi. The synagogue could as easily have been a warehouse in Kwamboka's mind. That there were Jews in Kenya came as a great surprise to her, but more so was Conway's comment, "Jesus was a Jew, you know."

"Then why doesn't he look like one?"

Conway never teased. So he must be telling her the truth about Jesus, Kwamboka thought. This didn't make sense. If Jesus was a Jew and was the Son of God, then God must also a Jew. If God and his Son were Jews, why did the Church condemn them to hell?

"When?" Kwamboka asked. "When did Berrycloth say this Jewish thing taking place?"

"What difference does it make when it is?"

"We are going, aren't we?"

"Why would we go? Why would you want to do that? You're not interested in Jews are you?"

"I'm not interested, but I'm not uninterested, either. I'd like to know more about Israel and the whole thing sound intriguing. How did that small country defeat all the Arabs last year? A war that was over in just six days. Don't you think it was amazing?"

"Not any more than you defeating the British Empire. You had spears. The Israelis had planes."

"Yes. But we took more than fifty years. Maybe we have something to learn from one another."

The meal was at the home of Daniel and Betty Cohen, whose families were amongst Nairobi's first white settlers and founders of the Nairobi Hebrew Congregation. They owned several successful business enterprises around the country. In addition to their three grown children, their wives and four granddaughters and one grandson, there was another Israeli and his wife, Gideon and his African girlfriend and a few other local couples.

One of the Cohen's grown sons, a young man in his twenties, guided the non-Jews throughout the three hour-long service, a celebration punctuated with conversation, argumentations, songs and laughter.

"On this night," Daniel Cohen began, "each person should see himself as going out of Egypt. We recount the story of the Jewish people's plight in Egypt and recall their suffering and persecution. We are with them as God sends the ten plagues to punish Pharaoh and then follow as the Jewish people leave Egypt and cross the Red Sea to freedom's land."

Each adult at the table took turns reading from the book describing the Jews' deliverance from slavery. With each sip taken at the prescribed times through the meal Kwamboka increasingly enjoyed the sweet red wine. She ate tasteless unleavened bread even as it crumbled in her hand, savored the paste of fruits and nuts, dipped a cooked potato into salt water and nibbled on a hardboiled egg until she finished it.

Kwamboka knew the story of Moses and the exodus from Egypt. What she didn't know was that the story was told and retold each year in this manner. Here was a tradition passed down in both an oral and written form that has survived for more than two thousand years. She thought about her collection of Kisii folktales and her transformations of them and became more convinced than ever that she needed to preserve them in ways that could be of use while at the same time keeping their essence.

"Next year in Jerusalem," the Jews recited to end the service. "Next year in Jerusalem."

The other Israeli introduced himself to Kwamboka. He worked for Mashav, he said, Israel's agency for international development.

"My name is Dani Sassoon," he said.

"My name is Kwamboka."

He held out his hand. Kwamboka hesitates in taking it.

"Is this your first time to a *seder*?"

"A what?"

"A Passover meal."

"I've never met a Jew before."

"You know Gideon."

"I didn't know he was a Jew."

Sassoon quickly overcame his discomfort.

"No, no. Why should you? We Jews are a small number here in Nairobi. I bet you didn't know that Nairobi once had a Jewish mayor. That's Issy Somen over there."

Before independence, she learned. That wasn't a good mark for Jews as far as she was concerned.

"Well, I hope this was a good introduction to we Jews. What did you think?"

"Do children always participate like this?" she asked.

"Oh, yes. It's always the youngest son who asks the four questions. If the family doesn't have a son, we buy one for the night." Sassoon saw the horror on Kwamboka's face. "I'm making a joke. If there are no children, anyone can ask."

"A girl."

"Of course, a girl, too."

Kwamboka said she enjoyed the singing. She remained quiet about the food.

"What exactly are you doing here? What kind of aid are you bringing?"

"I'm a physician," Sassoon explained. "I'm working with nurses to provide vaccinations against childhood diseases. Measles and mumps. Kwamboka you said? Did I pronounce it right?"

"Kwamboka."

"Where are you from?"

"I live in Nairobi."

"You were born here?"

"No," she said. "Kisii."

He shrugged his shoulders.

In the west, near Lake Victoria, she told him.

"I have heard about the lake. It is famous. But I have only been as far as Nyeri."

"That's in another direction."

"The lake must be beautiful."

It's a lake, Kwamboka thought to herself. Water with fish in it.

"Perhaps the next round we will be able to extend the program to your home area. It's a six-month program, so I return to Tel Aviv next month. I don't know if I'll be back myself, but Israel wants to continue with it."

She continued to chat with the man, the only man along with Gideon without a jacket, whose shirt was open at the neck. The conversation grew easier for Kwamboka as she grew accustomed to his style. She wasn't certain why she offered this information, but she told him about the lack of support from the university.

"Few see the value in what I do," she said. She withheld her opinion about her advisor being a Kikuyu. "But tonight was a great thing for me. Putting down your past on the page is very important to witness."

"Have you thought of continuing your studies elsewhere?" Sassoon asked.

That possibility never occurred to her.

"If you would consider going abroad, I believe I can facilitate it. When I return home and, if you would like, I can make connections for you."

Without thinking, Kwamboka replied, "Thank you, but this wouldn't be possible for me."

"And why?" Sassoon wasn't going to let her off easily. "What you want to do is good. And you say you can't do it very well where you are. So why won't you go for a short while somewhere else? Isn't that a good thing?"

Kwamboka didn't know what to say. Before the lightning fast war, she wasn't even sure she knew where Israel was.

"If you like, Kwamboka, let me know."

What would it mean to leave Kenya? Would she have to take more courses, would she be the only African? She spoke Gusii, Swahili and English and now she would have to learn yet another language.

As they lay side-by-side, Conway asked Kwamboka, "Have you thought about talking further with that fellow from Israel? What was his name?

"Sassoon. Why would I do that?"

"There may be something there. I think you may be right about your committee. It may be a hopeless cause."

"I think there is more to what he didn't say," Kwamboka responded.

"Meaning what?"

"Like all the others. No one gives you something for nothing. No man."

"He and his wife looked happy."

"Come on,"

"He was representing his government. Israel wants good relations with Kenya. Nothing more. Nothing personal in what he's offering, I'd say." Conway stopped himself short. Then, "*All* the others? Me, too, Kwamboka?"

No, she thought. Conway didn't demand anything from her. That made it even more difficult for her. His needs were mute and deeper than she could plumb. They lay next to each other in the dark. As she put her hand on his cheek he withdraw into himself like a sensitive plant whose leaves fold inward when touched.

"I think you should go, Kwamboka. If you can leave, take it. There isn't much for you here."

She removed the blanket from him and removed her nightgown. She leaned over Conway and unbuttoned his pajama top. She slid it from his shoulders.

"Go," he said.

Kwamboka placed her body on top of his, pinning him under her weight and she felt him become discarnate under her until he disappeared completely.

Blue Spade

*T*ORRES INTIMATED that he was responsible for Junius's assignment, mocking him as though a posting to Ft. Slocum was a punishment. For Junius, being a soldier was his punishment. Although Basic Training had turned into a lark, Junius hated the regimentation, the mindlessness, the sadism of drill instructors and a few of his fellow soldiers. Initially bitter about being shut out of college, his consolation was that everyone sooner or later would have to serve. Eventually the draft would scoop up every male, shear them and train them to be killers. The military was better than prison. Now he thought that if he were going to spend the next three years in uniform, at least it could be far from New York.

During the last week at Ft. Dix, orders were handed out: his bunkmate was headed for Alaska and another in his platoon received orders for Germany. Many were deployed to Vietnam.

WHEN JUNIUS HADN'T RETURNED HOME by midnight, Carl and Susan's concern became worry. They didn't want to wait any longer. They went looking for him in the roiling streets filled with police, burning buildings and mobs. They still hadn't found him by sunrise.

Finally they received a call from the Brooklyn House of Detention.

Carl called Jones.

"First, we need to get him home," the assemblyman advised.

The Cassels posted bail, then negotiated their way through the crowded lobby in the jail that was filled with the relatives and friends of the hundreds who had been arrested that night. The Cassels were sent to the wrong desk, then given incorrect papers to fill out, needed to redo the forms when they had put information on the wrong line, then waited two more hours before Junius walked out into Carl's custody in the late afternoon, his skin ashen and his face drawn from a sleepless night.

The following day they met with Jones at his storefront office on Fulton Street. The desk was covered with papers, the walls filled with heavy books and law journals. Photos of Jones with judges and politicians competed for cramped space.

"Thank you for seeing us, Tom," Susan said.

"Please," he said, pointing to the worn couch by the window. "Excuse the mess. I'm packing my belongings for my new office."

"Congratulations, Tom," Carl said. "Or should I say, Judge."

Junius continued to stand.

"Not yet. I'm not sworn in yet. And I want you to meet Miss Chisolm. She'll be taking my place in Albany. I asked her here." He turned to Junius. "Are you all right, son?"

"Yes, sir," Junius said. His hands trembled and he needed to lean against the couch to keep himself from collapsing.

Jones removed his glasses and put them on top of a book sitting on his desk. "Can I get you a drink of water?"

"No, sir."

"Sit down, Junius," Susan ordered sharply. She moved to make room for him.

Junius slumped into a chair next to the dark wooden desk.

"Sit up straight, Junius," Susan said.

"Did anyone hurt you?" Jones asked him.

"No, sir."

"I understand this is hard for you, young man," Jones said.

"I didn't do anything, sir," Junius replied.

"I believe you, son. Why don't you tell me what happened."

Over the next half-hour, with patient questioning by Jones, Junius related what happened that night.

"I'll see what I can do, Carl. The least I can do is to get the most serious charges dropped. Then we'll see."

"What happens then? I'm afraid for my son, Tom," Carl said.

"We're going to make this right. This can't continue like this. The police are out of hand. We see it in Mississippi. We need to put a stop to what they're doing to our people."

Carl and Susan sat silently.

"I don't have much money, Tom," Carl finally said. "Work hasn't been good lately."

Jones stood and looked out the window. Plumes of smoke rose from the smoldering buildings.

"Don't worry, Carl," he said. "Junius didn't do anything. I want to take this case. I'm going to do everything in my power to stop this mistreatment."

Jones met with the assistant district attorney and the head of the local draft board, brokered a deal and charges against Junius were dismissed. Jones had been promised the file of Junius's arrest would remain in the bottom of a drawer as long as he wasn't arrested again.

"My God, Susan. This is a bargain with the devil," Carl said when Jones explained the deal to him.

"It's the best that Tom can do, I'm sure. Maybe it wouldn't be so bad for Junius to be in the army."

"No, Susan. If he joins the army, Junius will never go to college."

Junius listened from the other room as his parents debated the condition for the charges being dropped.

"Do you want a trial for our son, Carl? What do you think his chances are in front of a bunch of people who see us as animals? He can either take his chances in front of a jury and wind up in prison or go to the army. Do you really think they'll take his word over a police officer?"

"No."

"I think Tom got the deal because he didn't think he'd win if it got to court."

"He needs to go to college, Susan. This would be the biggest mistake in his life to walk away from it."

"If college is really for him, he can go when he gets out."

"Look at me, son" Carl said. "Look where I've wound up. I can't even get a shift these days."

"Times are different."

"Maybe so. But the army's not." Carl began to shake, the way he did when the memories resurfaced.

Susan knew Carl was no longer talking about Junius and college.

"If he goes to college," he continued, "he'll be deferred at least until he's graduated. By then maybe the war will be over."

"But that's not the bargain," she said gently. She tried to calm Carl's trembling hand by putting hers on top of his. "It's not whether he goes to the army or not. It's about whether he goes to jail or not."

"Susan, you don't know . . ." His voice trailed off. "Did Althea tell you about the letter she got from her son? Bobby talked about it to me. And it's not just their boy. There's lots of boys going off to this Vietnam. The war's shit, Susan, not like my time. It's no damn good."

"You did your duty."

"This ain't duty, Susan. This is different. No Negro should be fighting in Indo-China. This is a white man's war. Protecting oil and things like that, not stopping fascists. I don't want my son dying for this. I've done enough fighting for all of us."

A sorrow overtook Susan's face. She had never seen Carl so tired.

"But what's the choice? Do we really have one?"

Carl closed his eyes and rocked slightly. He rubbed his hand hard against his chin.

"I don't know, Susan. I just don't know."

"Junius," Susan called. "Come here."

They presented the situation to their son.

Although the war was front page in every newspaper and the lead in evening newscasts, Junius hadn't given much thought to it. Some students at school talked about Malcolm X's denunciation of the war, but he paid no attention to politics and what little he knew about Malcolm X he didn't like. The white kids at Music and Art had never given him trouble. Music drew them all together; race never kept them apart. The school's hierarchy was based on talent, not race.

Junius knew for certain that someday he would be drafted and he would go, but the military was a distant thought, no more real than marriage or old age. He pictured himself on stage in a sparkling maroon jacket, bow tie and purple shoes with hair picked out into a large, soft ball. With more difficulty, he imagined combat boots and a rifle.

"If I don't go to college, it's OK. I really don't want to go," he added.

"But do you know what the army's like?"

"I have to go sooner or later, don't I?" Junius asked. "You did it, Daddy. So can I."

"This is different."

The Cassels called Jones to tell him that Junius would accept the deal. What they didn't know was how far Jones' influence reached. Not only were the charges dropped against Junius, but Jones had also arranged for Junius to be in a non-combat unit that would be stationed stateside. Junius was to be sent the Defense Information School where he would receive training in publicity for recruitment purposes.

Junius had two week's home before reporting to Ft. Slocum and was surprised to find that in the eight weeks he hadn't been home his father now spoke with a slur, and wobbled as he walked, even with a cane. Climbing the stairs in the rowhouse exhausted him, so most of the day he sat in his room on the second floor reading the newspaper, listening to the radio and watching the Huntley-Brinkley Report on TV. Susan wondered if it wasn't the thousands of troops being sent to Indochina that had brought on Carl's stroke.

Susan now took a bus to her job as a sales clerk in a clothing store in downtown Brooklyn and left Carl alone during the day because he insisted that he didn't need a nursemaid. The Cassels had put the house on the market when Junius entered the army, but there were no buyers. Theirs was one of the few houses on the street that wasn't boarded up and gutted.

During his two-week leave before reporting to Ft. Slocum, Carl insisted that Junius not wear his uniform as long as he was at home and Junius complied when he went out to meet his neighborhood friends. They told him that Eldon had left for Kansas in early August.

"But he was on the streets last week," Marvin explained. "The coach was going to sit him on the bench, have the white guys start."

"Freshmen don't usually start."

"But you know Eldon. Do you think that any of them could be better?"

"So he left?"

"Yeah, he came home. But I don't know where he's gone to. No one's seen him since."

Another day Junius took the A train with Marvin who had an audition for a pilot sitcom about an African American family. At Hubert's Flea Circus they argued about whether the tiny bugs were really pulling chariots on thin wires; they stopped at a peep show and when the audition was finished, spent a hour in the Colony Records store.

"What are you going to do about the army?"

"Me, they won't take me. I'll tell them I got flat feet."

"There's plenty with flat feet."

"I'll tell them I'm queer. They'll believe that."

At the end of two weeks at home, Junius put on his uniform, slung his duffel bag over his shoulder and boarded the subway, making several changes until the final stop in the Bronx. From there he took a taxi to the ferry slip in New Rochelle, finally arriving at the post on David's Island.

The base wasn't at all like Ft. Dix: no wooden barracks or barracks of any sort, just a small island with lawns and a few trees between brick buildings, the Victorian mansion of the General's House, children's playgrounds, open fields sloping to the tree-lined water's edge, a place more like a campus than a military facility. At Ft. Slocum, the routines that Junius had become to believe defined the military were absent. There was no command revelry or mandatory lights out. Rank mattered little. It was as though the Chaplains School, which had been on the base before the Defense Information School moved in, had left its compassionate personality on the island itself.

Junius had been sent to be trained in radio and TV broadcasting, recruiting and publicity, the sector responsible for writing, publishing and broadcasting materials that would foster the image of the army. There he taped and edited radio and TV shows. Whereas previously he avoided the news, he now found himself immersed in it, how to report it, how to reformulate it, what to leave out, how not to say what the government didn't want said and say what they did even when the facts didn't support it.

It wasn't clear to Junius whether he was being trained for. One thing was certain—he wasn't at Ft. Slocum because of his singing voice.

Mornings were spent in classrooms, while the remainder of the day he was engaged in hands-on instruction in the base's audio studio.

"Do I have your permission to stay here, Sarge?" he asked at the end of the class. "I'd like to really learn this stuff. This is new to me and I would like to get it down pat before school's out."

"Like homework, soldier?"

"Yes, sir."

"You're responsible if anything is missing, you understand, Cassel?"

"That's OK."

"If anything's missing, it comes out of your pay, you understand that private?"

"Sure, Sarge."

Junius stayed at the end of each day, often bringing his dinner back to the studio with him. What Junius really wanted the studio for was to use the recording equipment to tape himself: as Smokey Robinson, Marvin Gaye, Wilson Pickett, James Brown. As he played back the tapes, he could now hear himself as others heard him and he sang the songs over and over, recording and dubbing over his own voice as backup. Each night he ended with "I'm gonna wait 'til the midnight hour/ That's when my love comes tumbling down/ I'm gonna wait 'til the midnight hour/ When there's no one else around."

Despite uniforms and saluting, after Basic Training life at Ft. Slocum hardly seemed burdensome, particularly as Junius mastered new skills. The multiple dials and numerous levers on the console, the oscillators, compressors and equalizers behind the plate glass window made him feel as though he were on the deck of a spaceship. He enjoyed wearing headphones and using hand signals to those on the other side of the sound booth.

There were no other performers at Ft. Slocum, so the time was his alone. And while his pass allowed him to come and go freely from the base, he didn't go home for a month, instead calling from the public phone outside the classroom.

Junius's assignment to Ft. Slocum lasted two months, enough time for him to be given all the requisite licenses required by the army to use the various pieces of equipment, from a movie projector to the mixers. Perhaps, Junius thought, now that he had graduated from the training program, he might be stationed abroad and see the world after all.

The army had other plans. He wouldn't be going to Europe or even as far as New Jersey. Instead, he was being attached to the 26th Army Band at Ft. Wadsworth, on Staten Island.

〰〰〰〰〰

"WELCOME TO THE BLUE SPADES, Cassel" the personnel clerk said, as Junius handed him his orders. Fresh off the ferry from Lower Manhattan and a short bus ride, Junius found the administration building in the shadow of the Verrazano Bridge.

Junius looked puzzled.

"Our nickname," he said, pointing to the plaque on the wall behind him. "That's what we're called, Blue Spaders."

It looked more like an arrow, a blue flint, to Junius.

"OK. Here's what you need. Fill out the papers, then you can report over to the practice room in Building C. You'll find some guys there." The clerk looked at Junius. "Shit, we were told to take you. But we don't know what to do with you, Cassel. No instrument. We got no singers. But, shit, man, this is the army." He handed Junius a ream of papers. "Everything in duplicate. Where it asks about your instrument, just leave it blank. Maybe we can find a goddam kazoo for you. But what the fuck. Here. Take this. Sew the patch on. Don't worry about your fatigues. Class A's is the working uniform. That's what we wear around here. You won't hardly need your fatigues."

Junius found the practice room. A dozen soldiers chatted as they cleaned their musical instruments. A corporal was bent over a bowl disassembling his trombone and placing the slides and the bell into the tub of warm water.

"What's this?" he asked as he looked up at Junius who had now entered the room.

Everyone turned to the newcomer.

"I've been told to come here. I'm Junius Cassel. I finished training at DIS. This is my new unit."

"DIS?"

"Defense Information School."

"Don't know what that is," the trombonist said.

"At Ft. Slocum."

"Never heard of it. In Mississippi," the corporal challenged.

A few snickered.

"The Bronx."

"Right. I'm going to believe that."

"What's your instrument?" another asked.

"My voice," Junius said. "I've been told you don't for a singers in the band, though."

"You're fucking A-right about that," the trombonist said.

"So what are you here for?" a trumpeter asked. Larry Seagal was running a brass saver brush through the valve casing.

"I was sent here. What the hell else do *I* know."

"The army fucks up again," another musician said.

"No, no. Now we are real spades," the trombonist remarked, placing the pieces of his instrument on a towel beside the bucket. "Blue Spades, here he come!" He began to hum, then sang, "What did I do to be so black and blue?' and laughed aloud. "No more blue. No more blue, Now we can call ourselves the *Black* and Blue Spades."

With the instinct to act without thinking that he had learned in Basic Training, Junius ran across the room, grabbed the corporal from behind and shoved him against the wall, banging the musician's head against the stone.

"Hey, you crazy or something?" one musician said.

A few rose to their feet.

"What the fuck did you say, mother fucker?"

Junius was pulled off the corporal.

"I'm just saying, that's all. No reason to take offense. I thought you'd know the Waller song."

"Shut up, Wayne," Seagal demanded.

"Can't he take a joke?"

"Forget about him, man. Wayne's a schmuck," Larry said to Junius. "The guy's a fucking joke. He plays his trombone through his ass." He turned to the trombonist. "Man, you're one stupid fuck. You leave the kid alone or I'll tear your lips from your face and shove them up your ass."

The incident wasn't dropped, despite Larry warning Wayne about reporting it. Junius was called into Mr. Flores office by the end of the day.

"Pvt. Cassel," the warrant office said looking at the paper on his desk. "At ease."

Junius placed his feet apart and his hands behind his back.

"You just get here and you already fuck up. This isn't starting so good for you, private. I could transfer your ass you right out here now and send you to Nam."

"You just get here and already you're a screw-up. I have a report on you. But you tell me what happened." Junius related the incident. "Private, Corporal Marsh isn't the last asshole you're going to meet. But I'm not going to let you fuck up this band. You understand me, private?"

"Yes, sir."

"This is the last time you're in here for this shit. The next time it's Article 15 and you're out of here, private. I'm not sure who assigned you here and I'm not going to keep your sorry ass if you are reported one more time. No one's going to fuck with my band, you understand?"

For the next week Junius was assigned to keeping track of inventory, updating files, and checking instruments in and out of the instrument repair room in the basement of a century-old stone building. The smell of mold reminded him of the dank subway tunnels, the urine soaked alleyways in the projects.

Until he could learn to play something useful for a marching band, he joined them by tapping on a musical triangle just as he had done in third grade. The company clerk issued him a glockenspiel and after a few months of mentoring by Larry, who also played the xylophone, when the band assembled for a parade, Junius marched with them, his instrument mounted in a snare harness. He wrapped the mallets with cotton to dampen the sound, then tapped the metal tubes lightly so not to disturb the soldiers marching around him.

Larry, several years older than Junius, liked him and when he discovered how well he could sing, whenever they got off base on Wednesdays, he took him to Roseland. The gathering of musicians looking for gigs reminded Junius of his father's shape-ups, trolling for a job and waiting to get picked. But he didn't mind; he almost always came away with work since Larry, as one of the top trumpeters in the city, was in demand and insisted that bandleaders take Junius as the singer. Being black had become an asset, Junius discovered, as rhythm and blues and doo-wop were part of the pop charts. There was a double-advantage for Junius: he got to sing and, for the first time, got paid.

Only once did Junius's work with Larry not go well, at a wedding. After signing "I Can't Get No Satisfaction," with the moves of James Brown, the father of the bride rushed to the bandstand in a rage, demanding that Larry get rid of that *schwartze*.

"Get him out of here!"

"Who?"

"The *schwartze*. Get that animal out of here."

"You want him out? You'll get him out. And me, too. Let's go, Junius. Let the prick lead the band himself." Larry packed up his trumpet, left the bandstand and drove Junius home. Neither got paid that night.

"Shit, man" he said as he pulled up in front of the Junius's rowhouse. "This is where you live? It's like the street's been bombed."

Junius said nothing.

"Listen. Why don't you come back to my place? There's a spare room you can have."

He wouldn't say that he lived with his parents. But a few months later when Carl died and soon after Susan abandoned the house to move in with Carl's cousins in Buffalo, Junius stayed with Larry on the weekends in Kew Gardens, in Queens, an all-white leafy neighborhood with large single family houses surrounded by well-kept lawns. Mothers held their children's hands in the playground when Junius sat on a bench; in the grocery store women clutched purses close to their chests as he shopped. He was followed in the neighborhood record store.

As the war deepened, Larry's views about America's involvement grew trenchant. He was disillusioned with government lies. Junius was surprised Larry had ever thought differently. But while Larry signed petitions, marched in protest demonstrations, added his name to ads denouncing America's involvement in Vietnam, Junius didn't join him. These protests were the white man's cause, led by whites who wanted to save their own skins. Cities were burning, black men being killed on American streets— that was the problem, a domestic race war and where were the white boys now? The civil rights cause had been abandoned for the right not to be killed in war.

"What about Ali? He wouldn't be drafted."

"What about him?" Junius responded with a rhetorical challenge. All Junius knew was that he was a boxer who changed his name when he became a Black Muslim and was in trouble with the government. What else was new?

Larry and Junius no longer talked about Vietnam or their views of the peace movement or race. Junius avoided talking about Black Power, something Larry was eager to discuss, not because Junius wanted to preserve the relationship but because he didn't know what he thought of it. The further removed from Basic Training he became, the more Junius was glad for having learned how to defend himself and use a gun.

"Black men are dying in the war, too, Junius, not just white boys, you know that."

Larry did convince Junius to add his name to one ad taken out in the *New York Times*. Larry's name was listed with his rank, while Junius's name appeared without his.

Soon after the full-page ad appeared and several band members marched in a protest rally wearing their uniforms, duty hours were extended. Class A's were replaced by fatigues as the duty uniform, reveille was instituted; mandatory practices were held on Saturdays, and civilian club dates were strongly discouraged.

"Tighten your belts, men," the warrant officer admonished. "Accept it. This additional training will contribute to our band's mission. By doing this, you'll eventually return to your former status."

Larry was reduced a grade. The following month he received orders to report to a base in Texas. Three months after Larry's transfer, Junius received a brief letter from Larry, telling Junius he was in Vietnam. Junius replied telling him about the musicians he had heard play in the City. That was the final correspondence between them.

Junius remained with the 26th Army Band, shuttling between Ft. Wadsworth and Ft. Hamilton on the mammoth bridge spanning the Narrows, until his honorable discharge. He didn't protest against the war again, although he had come to loath it and if ordered to serve in Vietnam, he was prepared to desert.

Your Heart Will Be on Fire

FOR THE FIRST TIME since her college days, Lena begins a poem of her own, a full day's labor of joy. She sits at the library carrel with a green-shaded light and writes, "My mother's name is Anna/ I was born in forty-two/ In the middle of our war/ Shining she found me/waiting in blue air/ With a bear's tongue / she licks me to deep flame."

Lena pulls the chain on the lamp and the light clicks off. She crumples the paper and throws it in the trash bin under her desk.

Lena's muse had been primed by the Russian poets, Anna Akhmatova most of all, a woman as courageous as the Night Witches her father had gloated about. "Half harlot, half nun," she was called.

What is it to be this woman Anna, condemned for being "preoccupied with female concerns," who wrote, "You will hear thunder and remember me,/ And think: she wanted storms. The rim/ Of the sky will be the/ colour of hard crimson,/ And your heart, as it was then, will be on fire." What is it like to be you, Anna, your lover never to return from the Gulag, you, giving courage to those who stood on line for bread?

Lena first read Akhmatova's poetry in the Russian literature class she was taking and when she found in an art magazine her cubist portrait, Lena cut out the page in the back of the bookstore, pasted it on black cardboard and hung it on the wall of her basement apartment.

The more she reads, the more she learns what had been kept secret from her. More confused than certain, she searches for Henry and for Ida in the dust the poets have churned up. How can her parents have given so much away? Is it possible that they didn't know? She despised her father for his cravenness, the only courage shown by Ida who scrubbed every trace of him from the apartment and refused to visit his grave. Lena wonders which woman suffered more.

Lena had come to the Bread Loaf campus to be near those whose lives were lived in words. Because the conference only accepted published writers she took work in the kitchen as a dishwasher. Her enthusiasm for the writers' conference drained quickly, though, as she saw that many writers were as devoted to their craft as Henry had been to the Party, possessing the vicious talent of not seeing the person before them. These lovers of words were lovers of themselves, but the service-staff of housekeepers, grounds keepers, waiters, maintenance crew and dishwashers—they existed only in creative imaginations. The demarcation between writers and service-staff was as wide as the gap between worker and owner, Party leader and follower.

Wood shingled buildings lay about the grounds. Her cabin with a fieldstone fireplace and furniture that smelled of burnt wood calmed her. At night, she sat in an Adirondack chair on the porch and fell asleep with the curtain thrown wide and under a cotton blanket, a book on her stomach.

The Bread Loaf campus closed at the beginning of the fall semester, but Lena wanted to remain in Middlebury. The village appealed to her, with the countryside only a stroll away. But the main reason she stayed was the access she had to the library. She thirsted to make up for the parlous times at the commune. Finding employment at the college library was easy and while the pay was low, she could take six credits a semester tuition-free.

When the college opened an overseas program, in Moscow, no one had asked her opinion, but she did have many things to say to whomever would listen. Didn't they read what they had in their own library? Pick up Nadezhda Mandelstam's *Hope Against Hope*, the memoir depicting her and her husband's tortured life in Stalin's time. How could the college lend itself to a country that had committed unspeakable things against its own artists? The new Soviet constitution—didn't anyone bother to read it?—reaffirmed "the aims of the dictatorship." The freedom now granted to artists under the Krushchev thaw was a sham and would reversed under the next dictator. Let these professors see how long they would last there. She ticked off the books in her literature classes that couldn't be read in the Soviet Union.

Lena acquired the reputation as a reactionary, an unfair characterization, she thought. 'Don't trust anyone over 30.' She had hurled the slogan herself. Now the epithet weighed as heavily as if a placard had been hung around the neck denouncing her as an enemy of the proletariat. Had she, Lena wondered, crossed the generational divide to discover the shallowness of the mantra?

Despite the allure of contemplation and Arcadian surroundings, Lena knew she belonged to New York.

There were no illusions about the place she was returning to. New York was a hellhole. But hadn't Leningrad also teetered on the brink? Akhmatova had spent seventeen months waiting on queues to visit political prisoners. On one line a woman recognized her and whispered, "Could anyone ever describe this?' And Akhmatova answers, "I can." And she did.

Lena needs to bear witness. Solipsism is a secular sin.

〰〰〰〰〰
〰〰〰〰〰

LENA MAKES A PHONE CALL AS soon as she returns to New York.

"Junius Cassel?"

"Yes."

She thinks he recognizes the voice.

"This is Lena Morrell."

"Who?"

"Remember, we met last year in Middlebury?"

He hesitated.

"Last year, you were in Middlebury with the Down City Slide?" she said, a little unsure that she had the right person.

"Yeah. We played a few places. Where's Middlebury?"

"Vermont. New England. You were at the Iron Horse Café. A few blocks from the campus. You were there for two nights."

"Oh, yeah. I brought up one of my groups."

Was she remembering right? It was him that she had slept with. She couldn't forget his name. Junius.

"Your name is Junius?" she asked when the met.

"Yes."

Lena let out a small laugh.

"You think my name is funny?" Junius was irritated. He rejected all the nicknames his friends tried to pin on him, insisting on the use of his full name.

"It's this coincidence. That's what's funny. The only movie I ever went to see with my mother was Spartacus. Did you see it?"

"No."

"My father wouldn't allow me to go to movies. He was dead when time the movie came out. If he were alive at the time, this is probably the only movie he would taken me to see himself."

Junius asked, "Do you want a beer?"

"Sure" She drank the Budweiser from a plastic cup. "Spartacus was about a slave revolt in ancient Rome. Dalton Trumbo wrote the screenplay." Junius nodded his head as though he understood. "It was from a book by Howard Fast. Both writers had both been blacklisted and now here was this big movie from Hollywood."

"I know so something about blacklisting," Junius interjected.

"Maybe."

"But what's so funny?"

"A group of communists in Germany, before the Nazis took over, called themselves the Spartacus League. One of the leaders was Rosa Luxemburg. She signed her pamphlets 'Junius' as her cover." She laughed again, this time more loudly. "So you see, my parents would have approved of you."

Junius showed his skepticism with a dismissive hand movement.

"Well," she added, "it at least it would have presented them with a dilemma. Which is more important: that you're a fellow traveler or that you're black?"

"You were the white chick with the red hair, right?"

Would she describe him as the black man who was bald?

"You said that if I was ever in the city I should give you a call. You gave me your phone number. Remember?"

The night Junius left, he wrote his phone number on a napkin, which Lena then used as a bookmark in a Gwendolyn Brooks poetry collection. She didn't know why she had looked at that book again but now that she had she didn't hesitate to call. She needed a place to crash.

"Yeah, well. What?"

Lena grew irritated. But why should he remember her? He's probably been with more women than books she has read.

"Sorry to bother you, Junius. I mean, I guess you're seeing someone now." How reactionary, she thought. She tried to find her way through the morass of fractured communication.

"I'm always seeing someone."

"A steady."

"That's my business."

"Yeah, I know. I'm just . . ."

"That was a good night." His tone changed. Junius continued, "The band was hot that night. So were you. It went over well with a white audience. It was my first time to Vermont, you know."

"So," she said, "I'd like to see you again. Perform."

"I'm not doing that any more."

"Oh."

"I'm managing now. I came up with one of my groups to see what they were like on the road. I just sat in on part of the set. Do you want to book one of my groups?"

"I don't do bookings. I worked in the library. Besides, I'm not there anymore. I left."

"The library?"

"The college. I worked in the college library."

"Where are you at now?"

"That's my business."

Junius laughed.

"You don't want to see me? That's OK," she said.

Junius was used to making the first moves, leading the dance. He had a suitcase of opening lines. No woman had ever initiated a phone call to him before. 'Man-haters' is the way his friends described such women. But he had met the Chisholm woman in Jones's office and she was often in the news with her bluntness. And the next mayor of the city may be the loud, funny-looking lady with the big hat—she couldn't be a bulldyker; wasn't she married with children?

Junius tried to remember more details of that night in Vermont but could recall only snow and a languid conversation with a woman with the long red hair that ended as it always did.

"No. I'd like to see you. Do you know Patsy's?" he asked, pulled in by her forthrightness. "We can meet there."

Lena didn't want to show her ignorance. When she hung up, she found an ad for Patsy's Pizzeria in the Manhattan Yellow Pages. She took the subway to 125th Street and walked downtown a few blocks and then over the First Avenue. She couldn't avoid the garbage and needles in the street. How foolish she had been to accept Junius's invitation. As the only white person and single woman in the East Harlem pizzeria, she became increasingly uncomfortable as she waited for Junius. She read the menu several times, sipped a cup of cola and wiped the Formica tabletop clean with the paper napkin. Had he been joking? Maybe she had been too eager in arriving early. But there was nowhere else to go.

"Lena," Junius says. As he enters the room he removes his aluminum-rimmed sunglasses, places his leather jacket on the back of an empty and sits down opposite her. He is wearing a tailored shirt open half-way down his chest, revealing a wisp of hair. A floppy cap sits tightly on his head.

Her initial discomfit turned to antagonism. She slid her foot firmly into her slip-on clogs.

"I was about the leave," she said.

"Don't you like it? What's wrong? Patsy's the best pizza around. Want a beer?"

"I've been here for an hour."

"Look, I was at the Patsy's downtown, the restaurant. That's what I meant. When you didn't show up, I thought you probably thought I meant the place up here. So I gave it a shot and came up here. I didn't know you'd prefer pizza to Italian."

"Yeah, sure. I got things to do, too," she said standing to leave, not believing his story.

"Hey, wait, Lena. I mean, like, if you want to go, OK, but why not stay? You're already here."

"Well, I'm glad to see you, too," she retorted.

"Look. If you don't believe me, let's go downtown to the other place. They'll vouch that was I there. Unless you want to stay here."

Lena didn't know what she wanted. But she knew wasn't going to walk the darkened streets now that night had fallen.

"Just take me to the subway."

"No, no. Come on. I have my car outside. You'll like the other place. You didn't eat yet, right? I go there often."

Junius's sunburst yellow sports car was parked outside. He handed a five-dollar bill to the teenager standing next to it.

"I brought it back from Japan," he said as they drove down the Harlem River Drive. "What do you think?"

Why did she care about a car, especially one as flashy as this one? Her stomach growled.

At Patsy's the conversation over clams and white wine was about music and books, life on the commune and Junius's business ventures and a recent trip abroad to sign a Japanese group, but not about sex, which they both knew would be how the night would end. Sitting across from Junius the desire for the warmth of another's body welled up in her. Continuous couplings had lost their savor before moving out of the commune. She longed to feel another's skin, the last being Junius's. She yearned to be held and feel the hands and lips of just one person on hers. Touch me, she thought.

She stayed with Junius at his apartment for several weeks because there was nowhere better to go, then it became that there was nowhere else she wanted to go. How strange, Lena thought. Once again she felt the weightlessness of not thinking but this time it was accompanied by a fullness of being. She had known the realm of the senses before, but never this way with a man.

And she read him poetry: "I give you my love more precious than money,/ I give you myself before preaching or law;/ Will you give me yourself?/ Will you come travel with me?"

Whitman, then Thomas, the Russians, and all her loves, reading aloud to him, reciting from memory, bringing home purchased books, borrowed books, dog-eared books, keeping for herself alone poets of different loves. Would he come on these journeys with her?

She recited for Junius a Rumi line, "The way you make love is the way God will be with you."

The Persian had it right: Junius hadn't fallen in love but had constructed over several months love with the steadfastness of a master builder. And for the first time she felt something more than spasms and oblivion. She allowed herself to be shaped by his music and when he sang she was consumed in the way poems set her heart on fire. Unlike the pretensions she had come to expect from poets, Junius lacked the cynicism that she had come to loath at Welcome Hard Times. His joy, his sincerity calmed her and now she was filled with melody and lyrics and all she could see was his face and dark eyes.

Junius played music for her, had her listen to singers she never heard of, music she never listened to before. His knowledge of music was as deep as hers was of poetry.

Sounds enveloped both. Just as she was swimming in words and beats, he was immersed in notes and beats. They explored each other's territory intrepidly.

Junius told her about Larry.

"I think about him every time I see one of these guys on the street, you know, squeegemen at the lights, when they clean the windshield. And I also wonder what's happened to my other friends. It's so sad, really, not knowing what happened to him. Dead or running the streets. So many vets like this. Maybe I'll catch up with one of them one day. But I don't think so. I think they're gone, one way or the other. I was just lucky, pure fucking lucky, to remain stateside."

The last time Junius sang in public was at Middlebury, but the two of them developed a game of trading a song for a poem—one Larkin "At last you yielded up the album, which/once open, sent me distracted" for one Wonder "If we don't change the world will soon be over/Living just enough, just enough for the city." Junius chose music that picked up on a word, a theme, a mood, an image or the rhythm that reflected Lena's choice in a poem. Lena found a poem that responded to Junius's musical call. He brought LPs and tapes to their West 95th Street apartment.

"I'm going up to the Bronx. Come along." He said that a former warlord, who now called himself Afrika Bambaata, was bringing the gangs off the streets by creating music, art and dance venues. "B-boying," Junius said. "Breakboys. I haven't seen it for myself or heard it yet. But I've been told I should check them out. It's fresh. A different sound and a new style of dance. The guy's organized a park jam."

This was Lena's first time in the Bronx since her father's funeral. After parking the car and giving a teenager $10 to watch it until they returned ("There's another ten when I get back.") Junius stayed close as they walked past junkies and cars without wheels hoisted on bricks. Apartment buildings were empty hulks; the smell of smoke hung in the air.

They followed the thumping beat to the schoolyard where they found the b-boys and the deejay. Here the gangs had put down their guns and under basketball backboards that no longer had hoops, behind fences that were ripped apart to make new entryways, they moved to music that was pumped from an amplifier that stood in front of a man with a shirt decorated with an outline of Africa. He controlled the records on his turntable. One after another, teenagers approached a large piece of cardboard spread on the ground. They twirled and spun on their heads, leaped and kicked as if they were in a kung-fu movie.

Junius listened intently and watched the b-boys doing their moves. Lena could sense his calculating, sizing up the business possibilities.

"Hey, man, welcome to the Zulu Nation," the djay said. He wore a goatee and ski goggles are pushed up on his head. He ignored Lena. "This is DJ Cowboy and Mr. Biggs." He pointed out Queen Kenya, Pow Wow, and Kool DJ Red Alert. "This here's Disco King Mario. You picked a good night, my man. DJ Kool Herc is here, too."

Lena remained silent throughout the night as she and Junius watched the deejay play snippets of music from two turntables and a mixer contained in a box called 'the coffin.' There was no complete melody—sometimes there was no melody at all—but instrumental breaks from James Brown, disco tunes and funk strung together in a continuous loop of thumping dance beats, with stuttered riffs, no singing, scratches Bam Bam called shigi-shigi, pieces of melodies that flowed into one another and scat-style rhyming. B-boys performed while graffiti was being spray-painted on a brick wall.

"This is dark matter moving at the speed of light," Bam Bam told Junius. "We're dancing towards paradise. It's love power. Black love power. It's the New York Nation, the DC Nation, the French Nation, the China Nation. It's the Warrior Nation of Love. The Sonic Nation. This is funk funk, deep funk, soul, disco, rip rap, way down deep, dig."

The other deejay, across the room, responded, "Rock on, my mellow" and "Keep on, rock steady, b-boys and b-girls. To the beat, y'all, you don't stop now, y'all hear," as the tracks moved seamlessly from one song to another.

When another DJ took over, Bambaataa talked to Junius about how he left the violence of gangs to provide a lifeline to kids through music, dance and art. This belonged to them, a creation out of the ashes, he explained.

"Hope against hope," he said.

How curious, Lena thought, that he uses the same phrase as Mandelstam used in her memoir. Is this what Leningrad was like during the war? Is this what it's like to live where words are more precious than bread?

With the music as loud as the psychedelic rock Lena had once listened and danced to, Junius began to dance with her. A pulsing light illuminated Junius's damp head; Lena sweated under her long, auburn hair. She wanted to lose herself in the music, to blot out her surroundings, but couldn't. She felt the pounding in her temples. Lena signaled to Junius that she wanted to go.

Bambaataa directed a crewmember to take them to their car. As they walked down the unlit, deserted street, Lena pressed close to Junius. She held her breath and felt some relief when she saw the teenager leaning against the yellow car. Junius took out another bill and handed it to the teenager. Junius opened the door for Lena.

The escort leaned into the open window on Junius's side, his gold necklace banging against the car's door, his grillwork covered all his upper teeth. With a wide smile he said, "Nice bitch you got."

Without thinking Lena turns and leans and screams, "Fuck you, you pig!"

Junius pushes Lena back to her side and rolls up his window as the man steps back. Junius turns the key hard in the ignition. The crewmember smiles and waves to them as they leave.

Shaken, Lena asks, "What would you have done if the car hadn't started?"

Junius motions to the glove compartment.

"Open it," he says.

There is a pistol wrapped in a hand towel.

"Nothing was going to happen," he said. "He's ignorant. That's all."

"Ignorant? What, are you defending him? No one calls me a bitch."

"It's just a word used on the street."

"It's not just a word. Nothing's just a word. You of all people should know that."

"What I'm saying is that I've learned to pick my fights."

"I'm not worth fighting for? Is that what you're saying?"

"You know that's not what I'm saying, Lena."

He didn't attempt to explain himself.

But Lena knew he was right. It wasn't that she felt that Junius was like every other man who took on the mantle of privilege. It was worse: she wished Junius had done something to make her feel protected.

"That was really interesting," Junius said when they returned to the apartment, "really very good. I think I can work out something here."

"I hated it."

Junius laughed.

"Good for business?"

"The place was shit. I'm not saying I liked the music much, either. But there's something happening . . ."

"A bitch?" she interrupted. "Is that because I'm white?"

"Because you're a woman. You could be black and it would be the same. It's just a term . . ." He stopped himself. This wasn't going to get far with Lena.

In music, Lena had learned from Junius, it is called a grace note, non-essential to the melody. Perhaps for Junius the word was that, she thought. But for her it was part of the score.

"He can't understand how we could be together."

"You mean a black man with a white woman."

Junius laughed again.

"What? What's so funny?"

"When I was coming up, my parents had some records that I wasn't supposed to listen to. But I listened anyway. I remember this from an old record album. A black guy dies and pulls up to the pearly gates. 'What do you want?' 'I'm Sam Jones,' he says. St. Peter looks in his book. 'You ain't in here.' 'I'm the cat that married that white girl in Mississippi.' St Peter says, 'How long ago has that been?' Jones says, 'About five minutes ago.' "

"Is that what this is? Mississippi?"

Junius walks to the kitchen and returns with two beers.

"You got to love what they're doing. The DJs are playing with rhythms and words. How can't you love their street names? It's poetry, isn't it? They're better at this than I ever was, making music. They don't know anything about singing; there's no melody. It's all raw. They're making up this shit that's never been done before. But they're not going to get anywhere without connection. I think I can help them."

He stopped, then he added what he thought would win her over.

"How can you not love their names? It's pure poetry—Grand Master Flash, P-Body, JoJo, Casanova Fly. This is the next generation coming up and they're doing it with words and music. It's what I was doing when I was a teenager. But he's doing this not for himself but for all the kids. There's something beautiful about it. He's bringing them back to church, in a way, isn't he?"

Junius begins talking, then singing a spiritual from church.

" 'Turn away, turn away, turn away from sin,' " he sings. "That's what he's doing there, don't you see? He's getting the kids to turn away from sin through the music."

Lena wasn't convinced. Being called a bitch wasn't turning away from sin and Junius not seeing the violence done to her was wasn't a turning but a tolerating.

Maybe it was his being a Christian, she thought; perhaps she was more Jewish than she imagined. Where he saw the brokenness on the road to redemption, she saw the need to stand up against oppressors.

For the first time since they lived together, in bed that night Lena turned her back to Junius. She said nothing.

"I'm sorry," he said as he listened to her breathing growing deeper. "I should know better."

She was already asleep.

Not Now

~~~~~~~~
~~~~~~~~

*I*T SEEMED TO KWAMBOKA that it drizzled almost every day that spring. Before leaving Kenya she looked forward to winter so she could feel for herself what snow felt like. But in London it was only a dusting of flurries in December. Dampness and drear persisted longer than she thought possible. In winter she wore woolen coats and rubber boots, gloves and neck warmers but there was no snow, only constant and tedious dampness. It was slightly warmer in May but not much. Heavy jackets were put away, but she still used the space heater in her flat and welcomed a cup of hot tea. Londoners said the past winter was milder than usual. But here it was spring and it was cold, wet and dull.

She couldn't imagine getting used to living without the warmth of the sun. At home there were two seasons—wet and dry, but England offered only one, unpleasant season. She would never get used to the perpetually gray skies, the dampness that never left her bones. Kwamboka longed for stronger weather, the heat of the sun on her skin, a place of brighter skies, hail storms and lightning.

Finding another black face, eating *ugali* and *wimbi*, drinking orange soda and speaking her mother tongue was all but impossible.

Five years was enough.

She absent-mindedly traced her name on mist on the inside of the telephone kiosk's windowpane. She smiled when she saw that she had appended her newly acquired title. Dr. Kwamboka, she thought. 'How do you do? I'm Dr. Kwamboka. Dr. Kwamboka to you,' she said in an imaginary interchange with a former teacher. 'Yes, you can go back to your farm. I'll be teaching this class from now on.' No apology would be accepted. He deserved the company of his cows. They would have a thing or two to teach him.

Kwamboka waited for the operator to make the connection. The telephone rang. She couldn't wait to tell Dexter that she was coming home. Even as a doctoral student, she was able to save enough money for the ticket home without needing to borrow.

She thought about Dani Sassoon.

"I can get you a place in Tel Aviv," he told her. "In social work."

"I want to be a teacher."

"Let me try. I'll see what I can do."

He called again.

"Social work is the only possibility in Israel. But I think I can secure a place for you in England."

Sassoon assured her that there were no strings attached. The Israeli government was providing her with a full scholarship. They would even pay for the application fee.

"An educated Kenya is good for everyone," he said, explaining his government's interest in providing her with the scholarship.

Maybe a desert in the Middle East would have been preferable.

A click on the other end. Someone had picked up the phone.

"Hello. Hello," she shouted into the receiver.

The line crackled. A voice on the other end faded in and out like the signals on Kwamboka's shortwave radio.

"Who is this? *Nani huyo? Nani huyo?*"

"Sarah Kwamboka. I am calling from England. Is Mr. Conway there?"

"Wait. I'll get *bwana.*"

Now no one was on the line. Perhaps they had been disconnected. But there was no dial tone.

"Yes? Who is this?" a weak voice asked.

"It's me, Dexter. Sarah."

"How the hell are you?" Conway asked. "Where are you?"

"England," she said. "I'm still in England. I've completed my studies, Dexter. Can you believe it? I'm Dr. Sarah Kwamboka now."

"I'm so happy for you. This is a great honor. You'll wear the mantle well," he said. "What wonderful news!"

"Yes," she said. "And now I can come home."

The line went silent again.

"Dexter?"

"Yes, Kwamboka."

"I plan to be home in a few weeks. I wanted to let you know. I'm looking for a ticket now. As soon as I know when I'll be arriving, I'll call again. But I couldn't wait to share the news. "

"What did you say?"

"I've gotten my degree."

"No, no. I mean about coming back."

"As soon as I get my ticket."

Silence again. Had he hung up?

"I don't know, Sarah. Are you sure this is what you want to do?"

This was an expensive call, costing her more than she could afford. She didn't want to have a conversation with Conway or explain anything; she simply wanted to exchange the news and have him help her settle in.

"Of course. I can't wait to get back. Dexter," she continued, "I want you to talk to some people to pave the way. See if there is anything at the university."

"I don't know."

"What?"

"About your coming back. I don't know if this is a good idea."

"What?"

"I would love to see you. More than you can imagine. And I'll talk around for you. But please, this isn't a good time for you to return. It's dicey."

He paused, waiting for Kwamboka.

"Have you been following the news?" he asked. "A bomb exploded downtown."

The static grew louder, then subsided.

"Take some more time, please. Stay a while longer. The future isn't bright at the moment."

"Speak louder. I'm having difficulty hearing you."

"I can't say any more."

Activists she had known had been concerned about phone taps.

"Not now," was the last she heard him say, as the crackle grew louder. She thought he said something about her book of children's stories and then there was silence.

Kwamboka picked up her *kiondo* and slowly walked back to her flat unsettled by the conversation. She unlocked her door, threw her bag on the floor and drew the curtains to the window overlooking the squalid backyard. She took a spoonful of Lyon's tea and boiled it with milk and sugar in a saucepan.

During her time in England, she had picked up snatches of news from other students or from a lecturer who mentioned something to her in passing. But in the last half-year she so desperately wanted to finish her dissertation she had cut herself off from contact with the larger world.

She heard that the university in Nairobi had appointed a

female department chair, a woman with her doctorate from an American university. Kwamboka thought that maybe she had been appointed dean. But that would have been too much to hope and she set it aside. But it was that bit of news, however incomplete, that caused her to double-down in putting the finishing touches on her work on her dissertation: "Intertextuality: The Influence of European Fairy Tales Upon Traditional Stories of the Gusii." The text would be bound in a non-descript black cover and deposited in the bowels of the library where, she was sure, it would remain forever unread. She would have one copy for herself that she would keep like a trophy, useless except for the memories it elicited. But that was the price of getting her doctorate. The degree, her advisor had said, was like getting a union card needed for employment.

As a girl in Kisii, she had been kept in an unlit mud house for days so she could be transformed from a girl to a woman; this time she had been hidden away in stone buildings in the final rite into adulthood in the world of academia. She was a doctor. Dr. Sarah Kwamboka. She would soon be teaching others how to be teachers.

As she mulled the thought that she had wasted time on her dissertation, one of the stories in her collection of folktales came to mind.

Monkey lived in the jungle that lined the river, scampered up trees and swung from vines. As Monkey ate fruits gathered from the forest, bits fell into the water below its perch. Small fish immediately swam over and ate the shreds and seeds.

Every so often Monkey, grasping more food than it could hold, let a whole fruit tumble from it hands. Hearing the splash, Crocodile would swim over to enjoy the treat.

After happening several times, Crocodile devised a plan. When it saw Monkey in a tree overhanging the river, it circled until a fruit fell, then thanked Monkey.

"I can't climb trees myself," Crocodile said to Monkey, "but mango is certainly good. So I have you to thank for introducing me to this most delectable morsel."

Flattered by Crocodile's big and kind words, every day Monkey tossed a mango, banana or papaya into the water for his newfound friend.

"You are so wonderful, dear Monkey," Crocodile said. "I want to bring you home to meet my family, so they too can see how great you are."

"I would like that very much," Monkey said. "But I don't know how to swim. How will I get there?"

"No problem. Just jump on my back and I'll take you."

Not hesitating a moment, Monkey dropped from the tree onto Crocodile and floated down the river. Crocodile's mouth watered as it felt Monkey on its scaly back. Finally, unable to contain itself any longer, Crocodile snorted: "Now I can eat you. And most especially I look forward to tasting your heart."

An evil laugh followed.

"My heart?" Monkey screeched. Its heart beat so furiously Monkey thought it would burst through its chest.

"Yes, your heart. I can taste it already."

Monkey crawled over to the top of Crocodile's head and looked down into its eyes.

"Why didn't you tell me that's what you wanted? I left my heart in the treetop for safekeeping. I never travel with my heart. It's too precious."

Crocodile stopped paddling.

"But we are good friends, aren't we?" Monkey continued. "If only I knew that it was my heart you wanted, I would have brought it along. But all isn't lost. Just bring me back and I'll get it for you."

So Crocodile brought Monkey back to the shore where he jumped onto a low-hanging tree.

Here is the riddle: Who was stupider—Monkey for going with Crocodile in the first place or Crocodile for believing Monkey had actually left its heart behind? Some think it was Crocodile because how could anyone think that Monkey could live without a heart, while others think it Monkey because he was foolish to believe in false flattery.

〰〰〰〰〰〰〰

SHE COULD MAKE GOOD USE of her new title. Provided she could get an appointment, there would now be an income from the university. Let others have their fights in Parliament and make their deals in posh hotels, let them grab the land that had once been grabbed from them. She wanted to pave the way to the future by educating educators.

Conway's warning remained with her and she would take it under advisement, but the desire to return, whatever the risks, drew her to the International Conference of Social Research in Africa. She would pass around her résumé in hopes of attracting the attention of one of the universities in East Africa. She would even consider taking a position in Nigeria or Ghana, anywhere to be closer to home.

Most delegates to the conference came from Europe. None were from Africa. The first offer came from a medium-sized aging from Michigan State University who spoke with an accent she hadn't heard before and found difficult to understand.

"We're the largest and the best," Professor Hooker explained, trying to persuade Kwamboka to join the faculty.

"Where is it?" she asked.

"In the middle of the United States," he said. "Not as beautiful as Kenya, I grant you that, but our research facilities can't be beat. We specialize in African studies—I guess I don't need to say that. We are building something new and important."

"Do you have a teachers' program?" she asked.

"Our African Studies Center covers a lot of territory. We have linguists, historians (that's my field), anthropologists and other disciplines. You'd be a great, great addition."

She hadn't considered America.

"I want to teach in Africa."

"You can do that. I also am an adjunct professor at the University of Malawi. Once you are part of the faculty I'll help you get a part-time appointment in East Africa. I have the connections for all that."

She told him about her dissertation. Hooker assured her she could teach African literature while she pursued her own interests. But Hooker was too insistent. Perhaps this is what all Americans were like, she thought, and she didn't like.

"Let me think about it," Kwamboka said, hoping to find another university looking for someone in her field. Towards the end of the afternoon, the task seemed hopeless.

She received one other offer, from another American, a black man with glasses, who spotted Kwamboka as the room thinned out. Kwamboka had heard about black Americans; she had seen one at the University of London but never spoke to him. Kwamboka couldn't help but stare at this American professor, his hair picked out six inches in a massive and soft ball, nothing like anything she had seen in Kenya everyone's hair was closely cropped.

"So what do you think, Sarah?" he said.

"I'm taken aback," she said, touching her chest with her right hand.

"Why not you? You're what we're looking for right now. I came to the conference hoping to find someone like you. And here you are. We can say that we are both lucky."

He bought her a glass a white wine, which Kwamboka found undrinkable, and a couple of small fried breads, much like that which she knew from home.

"In truth we want a woman right now. Take a look around, Kwamboka. You are the only woman here. Did you notice? The only one. Women in this field are scarcer than hen's teeth."

"It's not that I'm African?"

"Yes, of course that. A woman and an African." He laughed. "Two for the price of one, so to speak. An African woman. We can meet two goals at one time."

Kwamboka didn't find it amusing, but her spirits were worn thin. If she couldn't find a position here, there was no hope. Prof. Johnson was off-putting, like Hooker, but less so. If she didn't consider this possibility, what was left?

"In truth, I am hoping to find a position in Africa. To be close to home."

"I wish you luck, Sarah," he said as he leaned closer to read the name on her nametag again. "But if you do change you mind, let me know." He reiterated the benefits of teaching at his university.

"Does it snow all the time in New York?" she asked with a smile as Johnson rose to leave. He sat down again. More seriously she wanted to know about crime. "I heard the streets are full of gangsters."

"Not full," he joked. He saw that she didn't find it amusing. "Don't worry. I've lived there all my life and I've never been mugged."

Small comfort, Kwamboka thought.

That evening she attended a lecture given by a Kenyan poet whose name she recognized not for his art but for his politics. He had a coterie around him each semester, students who attended his classes more for his fiery rhetoric than for his oeuvre or insight into the nature of poetry. Newspapers featured him and for a short while, until the government shut it down, he had a column in a small newspaper. In one issue of the *Weekly Review* she found a reference to the release of a new book of his collected poetry. But Kwamboka had never met him. She looked forward to listening to him.

His presentation, in a large, dark wood lecture hall, was far from full. Although it was the capstone lecture of the conference, many participants had already left. Some preferred the pubs nearby.

"Ladies and gentlemen," the moderator began. "It is my great pleasure to introduce to you this evening one of Kenya's—indeed I should amend this to say one of Africa's—great writers. I beg your pardon. I will amend this one more time. Okech Odhiambo is one of the *world's* great writers, a treasure for us all. If not for the persistence of Eurocentrism and the cartel of the publishing industry and the hegemony which they exercise over what the public reads and the awards writers receive, he would have long ago gotten the recognition he so richly deserves."

There was enthusiastic applause, the kind a performer receives when the audience recognizes the first few bars of their favorite song. The praise continued.

"However, the sad fact of the matter is that his own government . . . "

The poet leans forward and interrupts, "It's not my government."

Applause bursts from a dozen in the audience.

"Just so," the moderator says. "Rather, he is viewed as an enemy of the state and now must reside in exile."

Kwamboka looked at the poet sitting at the dais. His army fatigue jacket was devoid of patches or signs of rank. The auditorium lights reflected off his high cheekbones. He looked older than Kwamboka had pictured but was more attractive for the wear.

As Okech listened to his introduction, he seemed to grow bored. His eyes warily scanned the audience and locked on Kwamboka's.

"You all undoubtedly know last year he was detained without charges for publishing his poetic satire about a corrupt African president, whose face was described as resembling a dog's arse. Due to a campaign, which, I am proud to say was initiated by this school, he was released. But Okech's poetry is matched only by the courage. So he found himself confined once again after he went into the slums himself to read his works directly to the masses."

Okech winced as he shifted in his seat. Kwamboka wondered how many times he had listened to such laudatory remarks. "The police kept him for a week where he was beaten and tortured, then released. He fled to Uganda and now resides in Canada."

Finally Okech rose from his seat and limped to the podium. He opened a book on the lectern and read from his epic poem about a boy orphaned after a greedy neighbor killed his father and his mother was driven to suicide by privation. The boy was forced to wander the countryside where he befriends wild beasts that form an army, which wrests control of the country from jackals wearing British army uniforms.

There was enthusiastic applause. Kwamboka pictured a face looking like a dog's arse.

Okech put the book aside and stared into the audience with steely eyes.

"I will now speak plainly. No more allegories. I won't hide what I mean to say. So all of you who are here today from the imperialist press or from the press of my dictator president take out your notepads and write down what I say."

There were nervous laughs.

"Again the fascist imperialists are spreading propaganda amongst the *wananchi*," he said in a voice barely audible in the lecture hall.

"Use the microphone, please," someone shouted.

Okech ignored the request.

"If these elements aren't wiped out, the traitors of Kenya's true revolution will destroy the political consciousness of the masses, they will steal all the land, swallow all the wealth and vomit out the people."

Kwamboka slumped in her seat. She stopped listening. She heard it all before, the rhetoric, the slogans that required no thought, the language she had briefly used herself. She could predict what he was going to say before the words tripped from his tongue. She played a game with herself, ticking them off as they were uttered: solidarity, contradiction, revolution. His gentle demeanor belied the hot slogans. At one time Kwamboka would have engaged the game. Now she found it a farce and slightly ridiculous, even more so as many in the audience reacted to the stock phrases with heavy clapping. She no longer had patience with talk she found empty.

At the end of his presentation, Okech left the stage, used a walking stick to go to the back of the room where he stood beside a table autographing copies of his latest book, essays on neo-imperialism. Kwamboka queued to buy a copy. His books were banned in Kenya. If only for academic purposes, she should have one. She handed him a copy to autograph.

"I'm Sarah Kwamboka," she introduced herself.

He gave no sign of recognition. She thought that the way he had looked at her from the stage that perhaps he remembered her from the university in Nairobi. Or that at least he would inquire about her, what she, a Kenyan woman, was doing at the conference.

She finally said to him in Swahili, "You read your poetry in Mathare Valley?"

"No. It was in Shauri Moyo and Kibera, not Mathare," he corrected in English with a smile. "Why do you speak to me in Swahili? It's another language of a master."

That was a matter that she increasingly wanted to answer in the negative.

She stepped forward as she handed him the book. It was a familiar smell on his breath—tobacco and alcohol. One eye of Okech was rheumy, they both were red. From tiredness? From his ordeal? Kwamboka turned away in embarrassment.

"I wanted to have this when I return to Kenya," she said. "I know I won't be able to get them in Kenya."

"Don't be foolish," he said. "You can buy all my books in Nairobi."

"But they . . ."

"They are available in all the bookshops downtown. But you know who frequents these shops, don't you? Tourists. Have you ever seen a Kenyan buying a book? Of course not."

Kwamboka started to say something but he continued.

"The government doesn't care that the books are sold to those who can afford them. Indeed, they point to the displays in the shop windows and they say, 'See, we are tolerant. What is this censorship you hear about?' The government is very clever. As long as my books are in English I am tolerated. If you can't read, what difference does a book make? But when I go to the people and read to them in their own language, then I am a threat and must be caged."

Kwamboka didn't like the lecture.

"When they crack down on me in Shauri Moyo, I don't need to convince anyone of what is really going on. They see for themselves with their own eyes. The government speaks its own accusations."

He shifted his weight from one foot to another. No doubt he had been injured in detention.

Okech glanced at the lanyard that hung around Kwamboka's neck.

"Do you live in London? What is it that you do?"

"I have just gotten my degree in the school of education," she found herself stumbling.

"That's nice. Congratulations. And what do you plan to do with it?"

"Teach," she said.

"Oh, a teacher. That's good. It's a difficult job. All those children. All day. I don't think I could do that myself."

She almost blurted out that she had been offered two university appointments in America.

Okech lost interest in her. He had dismissed her as unworthy of further attention. Nothing she could say would make a difference. Kwamboka vowed that she would never try to justify her actions to anyone.

He walked away from her with the contempt of indifference. She could be angry but she knew that would give him more satisfaction than it would her. She should have known from his poetry that he had been forced to live in a modern world without his spear or shield. Whatever he thought, his words would have no effect on land grabbers nor would it be of help to those crushed under the weight of greed.

Kwamboka was walking to the exit when Okech accosted her. She saw him glance at her nametag again.

"Kwamboka. I was hoping not to say goodnight to you here. I am leaving for Los Angeles tomorrow. My hotel is nearby. There is a limousine waiting. Would you like to join me for a drink?"

You've had too many already, she thought. Vulgarities raced through her mind but she could not bring herself to utter them.

She thought about Conway and tried to imagine what her life would be like in Nairobi.

On the street she saw the black American heading into the pub across the square. She followed him in and joined him.

"About your offer," she said. "You said it was in New York."

"Yes. New York University."

"Tell me more."

Beatmatching

〜〜〜〜〜
〜〜〜〜〜

AFTER DJ KOOL HERC WAS STABBED at one of his own parties, Lena refused to go with Junius to the South Bronx. For a while, Junius went alone, but Lena convinced him to stay away when she said she couldn't sleep until he got home, which was after sunrise. His assurances that he could take care of himself did nothing to assuage her fears and Junius relented. In the years that she had been back in the city, conditions had only gotten worse. She half-heartedly suggested they move upstate. But she knew that neither would leave.

With his growing reputation for promoting talent, money continued to find Junius and he enjoyed having it, although he didn't indulge in flashy purchases. He more enjoyed staying at home with Lena listening to music and having her read to him.

Junius used their West Side apartment as his office: telephone calls, preparing contracts, meeting with clients, listening to demos, conferences with lawyers and partners. He converted one of the bedrooms into a recording studio and singers were able to make demo tapes there. In the last year, Junius expanded his management company, invested in disco and hip-hop recording labels, registered several patents for recording equipment, co-owned a mid-town recording studio and made music videos for TV. During their first two years, Lena would go with Junius on his business trips. Now she mostly stayed in their apartment when he was gone.

Dozens of music newspapers and magazines competed for space in their living room with Lena's books.

"I'm worried about you, Lena," he told her.

She shared his concern; she could feel herself being too comfortable in a world of words, indifferent to the world around her. The temptation to turn inward was too familiar.

Junius broached the idea of her working. She wasn't certain about that. What would she do? She rejected his offer to use his connections to find her a job. Instead, she enrolled in a masters program in library science.

Junius gladly paid her tuition, which Lena called a loan. Junius referred to it as a gift, instead of flowers or chocolates.

"When you finish," he said. "We'll go to Japan. I know you'll love it there."

"Maybe."

"Here's something funny. In Japan the devil is black."

"Even there," she said with a hint of resignation.

"That's what I've read."

"And that doesn't bother you?"

"I've never experienced prejudice personally while I was there. Just the opposite. Schoolgirls wanted my autograph. People followed me in the street. They must have thought I was Barry White or something. It was crazy, but I liked it, where people came up to me like that. I stood out . . ."

"Like we do."

" . . . but completely safe. Without hostility."

"Did you ever think about living there?"

"You mean moving to Japan? No. I wonder how long it would be before I would become the devil."

Graduate studies came as easily to Lena as making money did to Junius. She happily attended classes, quickly finished her term papers and completed her dissertation.

Her advisor wrote a recommendation for a position at NYU and in less than two years after beginning graduate school, she had the job at the university library on Washington Square.

Lena still turned down traveling with Junius. She was happy to be surrounded by stacks of books and journals in the library, helping students and faculty track down their material.

"I travel everywhere with you—in bed."

Lena began bringing home books for Junius to read.

"I thought you would find this one interesting," she said, giving him a book on the history of the blues, another on the relationship between Italian crooners and opera.

Lena read poetry to him every night.

Junius bought her a book by Alice Walker. She kept to herself that she had already read the novel. Like her mother before her, who Lena had found as a child secreted books in her dresser, Lena didn't reveal all her habits to Junius. Folded into her winter sweaters she hid two paperbacks by Audre Lorde and a copy of *Conditions: One* magazine.

With Lena's urging, Junius visited the Schomberg Collection, the specialty section of the New York Library that focused on black history. There he read about a part of New York history he knew nothing of: a the slave market begun in 1626; the slave revolt in 1712, 13 hanged; the 1741 uprising, 18 hanged, 13 burnt at a stake, 70 exiled to the West Indies.

He found references to Weeksvlile, which, he discovered, was a free black community before the Civil War, named after James Weeks, a stevedore. He comes across a reference on the microfiche that causes him to stop turning the handle on the machine. He rubs his knuckles.

"You know, I never got excited about the roots thing. And this stuff about my African past, it's never meant anything. But this is amazing."

He takes a Tab from the refrigerator and sips the diet soda directly from the can.

"I was named after my grandfather. I've always known that, Lena. But this was incredible. I found there was a Junius active in Weeksville in the 1800s, so it maybe I got my name from him also. And the school I went to as a kid, Lena, P.S. 243, he founded that. And there are old wooden houses in an alley where I used to play. It turns out these were some of the original houses in Weeksville. And they were built on an old Indian path. All this history around me and I didn't know a damn thing."

Junius's excitement pleased Lena.

"Here is the most amazing part. His name, Lena! Junius. He was Junius Morel. Junius C. Morel. Morel, Lena. Can you believe it?"

"Really?"

"I'm not kidding, Lena. Junius Morel!"

"Not Morelowitz?"

"It's like this was meant to be. And my mother," he continued, "probably took her name from a woman who lived there who became the first female African American physician. I sometimes wondered how she got Susan. That's not a black name. There is so much, Lena. So much."

He grabbed her hand and held it gently.

"Some things are just destined to be, Lena. Our meeting each other was fate."

"I don't believe in fate," she said suppressing a giggle. "I don't believe everything is laid out for us. My father changed his name because of anti-Semitism, not because the stars were aligned. History isn't inevitable. Nothing's predetermined." Her father's arguments about historical materialism and economic determinism were churning in her head. "We make choices. Henry made a choice. That's how we got this name. We chose to be with each other. No one makes us. It isn't inevitable."

"But why did we meet? Do you think that just happened?"

"It was chance. You happened to come to Middlebury and I happened to be at the cafe that night."

"That's exactly what I mean, Lena. What are the odds of us both being there at the same time? I was never there before. It was fate," he said.

Lena stopped, then added ruefully, "You know, you make it sound like somehow my father arranged for us to meet. He changed his name so it wouldn't sound Jewish. So no one would know he was Jewish. To get a fucking job in a fucking city hospital."

"And so we could meet," Junius said quietly.

Lena's mood altered.

"And I made a choice never to think that I didn't have a choice."

"So a black man is with a white woman because he thinks it is fate and a white woman is with a black man because she thinks she made a choice."

"That means you're stuck with me, you have no choice, and I choose to be with you so that you don't have a choice."

"It's funny how fate sometimes work out to be a good thing." Junius walks to the record player, places an LP on the turntable but picks up the arm from the record before Barry White's voice comes out of the stereo speakers. "But very sad, too. The entire neighborhood wiped away, gone like those villages we burned down in Vietnam."

JUNIUS SAYS TO LENA, "I feel like we need to celebrate or something. Our being together."

"Do I have a choice?"

"Not as far as I'm concerned."

She would rather be in bed with him than in a room full of strangers, to be with him in a room lit with candles, not being assaulted by strobe lights. She wants to read to him again the poem she read the night before:

"Just as my fingers on these keys/ Make music, so the self-same sounds/ On my spirit make a music, too./ Music is feeling, then, not sound;/ And thus it is that what I feel,/ Here in this room, desiring you."

But the singing that night, the interminable flowing, wasn't going to be in bed together but at The Loft, an invitation only club in a converted warehouse. The club hosted dance parties without liquor or food sales, beatmatching mixed with songs played in their entirety, soul, disco and funk—whatever sounds and rhythms elevated the dancers in ecstasy; costumes showy and outrageous, elegant, bejeweled; straight and gay, men, women, black, white, Latino. A dancer wears white drawstring pants, his feet clad in silk slippers, the DJ twirls his red cape around his shoulders to the beat, the beat, the beat, the beat, the beat, the electrifying beat spinning, blasting from speakers.

Streamers and balloons, hanging from the ceiling, festoon the hall.

She had come with Junius to celebrate, but he runs into music producers who wanted to talk to him. Initially he rebuffs them but they insist, they need him, there was a big deal on the table, and soon Junius is gone, in an office, to discuss investing in a discothèque, one that profits artists, DJs, and club owners. Lena is left at a table; she watches the dancers. She is getting dizzy from the flashing lights. Her head bobs slightly, she stands up, her hips sway and a hand reaches out to her. Lena shakes her head and looks around for Junius. She doesn't see him. The woman motions again. Lena moves to get Junius but her hand is grabbed by the woman in the yellow dress and pink, floppy hat and is led to the floor where Lena dances, shifting her feet from one side to the other and lightly clapping her hands, the soundless sound drowned out by the electric beat. The other woman is singing to the music and Lena reads her lips: "When you're laying close to me/ There's no place I'd rather you be than with me." The woman knows the lyrics to every song played, it seems.

When the beat quickens, Lena begins to dance the way she hasn't for years, every muscle in her body undulating. The woman pulls Lena to her. Lena, her pale face flushed and her hair dank, towers over the younger woman. The woman places her hands on Lena's rear.

"Do it to me again and again/ You put me in such an awful spin, in a spin, in-uh/ I love to love you, baby," the woman in the mellow yellow dress sings. And Lena feels fingers on the keys, the desiring beauty, her green going, and she slips, whispering too quietly for anyone to hear, "Oh as I was young and easy in his mercy/Time held me green and dying/Though I sang in my chains like the sea."

The younger woman, the younger woman, my green going—Lena thinks, is felt—time holds me dying.

Junius watches Lena as he re-enters the dance space. She is with a young woman who is staring into her eyes. Lena's face flashes with the pulsating lights. She doesn't see Junius as he walks up to her. She is returning the woman's gaze. Junius can't tell if Lena can't hear him or ignores him as he says it's time to leave. She continues to dance. Although it is almost dawn, the Loft is still crowded.

Junius takes her elbow and she shakes him off. How she gets outside with Junius she doesn't know. It's chilly and overcast. It feels like snow. The blast of air sends shivers through her.

Lena doesn't remember what she had done most of the night but she doesn't deny it when Junius accuses her of getting high. The room was awash with coke and hash and weed. Lena had once called him a puritan when she found that he didn't drink anything more than wine or smoke. She told him she had tried everything but all that was behind her and she had no desire to go down that road again.

Junius said he didn't believe her.

What Lena remembers from the night is this: when they returned to the apartment, having her clothes removed and Junius pushing down on her.

What Junius remembers is this: removing her clothes and her pulling him onto her.

She remembers: "Fuck you."

He remembers: "Fuck me."

She remembers: "Help."

He remembers: "Hurt."

She remembers biting his neck.

He remembers her sucking his neck.

She remembers gulping for breath.

He remembers her gasping.

Junius wanted to know what she meant when in the car home from the club she repeated several times, "Chains like the sea."

"I said that?"

"You were mumbling. But yeah, that's what you said."

"I don't know why I would say it." She thought. "I've been thinking about getting old. Maybe that's it. I love the Thomas poem."

"You were no old woman yesterday, Lena," Junius said. "It was like you were trying to have me devour you last night. It scares me, Lena. I'm not sure you even knew who

I was or who you were with. It was as though you were someone I didn't know. As though I was . . . I don't know."

She was in no mood for remorse.

"Did you enjoy it?"

"You don't even remember."

"*Did* you enjoy it?"

"That's not the point."

"Then what is? Some things just don't have to have a point. There's no point to pleasure."

"When you can't even remember? That's not pleasure. Being wasted isn't pleasure."

"I don't know, maybe you don't care anymore, maybe all you care about is business," she said. But she knew that Junius was right. It was why she left the commune.

"Oh, God, Lena," he sighed.

She wanted to apologize to him, to somehow rub away her hurtful comment.

〰〰〰〰〰〰〰

JUNIUS SIGNED CONTRACTS WITH NEW GROUPS, spent more time in recording studios, met with video producers and TV executives; Lena worked eight hours a day at the university library and took the subway to work. She wasn't certain what had happened at the Loft, but she wavered between indifference and repulsion, offering transparently false excuses about being too tired. Junius came to bed after Lena was asleep and she was up and often out of the apartment before he was awake. She was more content than ever with her books and watching tapes of old movies.

Two months after the dance, Lena felt nauseated in the mornings. She nearly convinced herself that it was from overheated and crowded subway rides. Then she could no longer hide it from herself. She had experienced it once before and was certain. She thought about the best time to tell Junius. She chose a late Sunday afternoon, after Junius finished watching a Knicks-Bullets game.

His face gave away nothing when she told him.

"Are you scared?" he finally asked her.

"I am."

"Are you sure?"

"Yes."

"What are you afraid of?"

She didn't know.

"That I'm going to leave you?"

"That's not it."

He put his hands on Lena's face and turns it towards him. She leans away. He kisses her on her temple instead of the lips.

"It's not what we planned, is it?" he said thoughtfully. They sat quietly for a few moments.

"I never had a plan," she said.

Junius leaned into her and took her hand.

"I don't know what to do," she said. "A baby? I never thought about being a mother. I'm not suited for it."

"Me, either, Lena." He hesitates. "But something good has been put in front of us."

"This is good?"

"Yes."

"So you want the baby?"

Through her trembling, she could barely detect his hesitation.

"Yes." He smiled, his eyes saying something else. "And I want you, too. There's been a lot more scary shit than this, Lena."

Two months ago she could have sorted this out but that night at The Loft had cast light in her shadowed corners.

Junius said, "When do you want to get married?" Lightness had returned to his voice as he thought about what it would mean to be a father.

Shaken from her abstraction, Lena stiffened.

"We can go to City Hall this week."

Lena began to cry.

"No, no," she said. "Please, Junius. I need to think."

"Thinking isn't a strong point for either of us, is it? It's feeling, isn't it? What's your heart telling you, Lena?"

He put his ear on her chest.

"It's telling me many things."

"Such as, 'marry the brother.' "

"For one."

"What else?" In his mind's eye Junius sees Lena's face as she danced with the woman in the yellow dress.

"My feelings are like Plato's horses pulling in different ways. I need to figure out how to get them all going in the same direction."

They sat quietly for a long time.

"You know, I never planned—I never thought about being a father," Junius mused.

Lena turned her head up and teased, "Is this your first?"

"What?"

"Baby."

"I'll tell if you will," he joked.

She pursed her mouth and wouldn't tell.

Junius was right: it was feelings, not reason and that led her to make an appointment.

This was her choice to make. A baby wouldn't be left to chance.

At the clinic, where she sat alone and chilled, they told her that she would be able to return to work that afternoon.

Complications developed and she never made it to work. When Junius returned to the apartment, he found Lena in bed and blood soaked towels on the floor. She was pallid and weak.

"What's wrong, Lena?" he said with urgency. "We need to get you to a hospital."

"No, don't. I'll be OK."

She told him where she had been.

Stoic reserve descended on him.

"I don't know, Junius, but I needed to know why you were marrying me. Was it me or the baby?" she said to him. But she knew that wasn't the reason.

Junius said nothing as he cleaned the floor and adjusted her blankets.

"I'll be OK," she tried to assured him, insisting that he not call an ambulance.

"You should have talked to me, Lena. You should have at least talked to me."

Junius wrapped his anger in a preternatural calm.

Lena regained her strength but then the bleeding reoccurred.

"You can't stay here," he told her, as he called a hospital. Junius sat next to her in the ambulance, stroking her hair, as she was taken to St. Luke's.

"I'm sorry, Junius. I really am," she said, the siren blaring and the flashing lights illuminating her frightened face.

"You just decided to do this on your own." Junius spoke softly. "It was my child, too, Lena. What were you thinking? What were you thinking?" He stopped and looked for his words. "Or maybe you think," he said slowly, "that black men don't care for their kids, that I'm going to walk away and leave the two of you? Is that it?"

Nothing she could say would make a difference. There was nothing she could do to repair the wound.

"Is this what you think?" he asked.

No, she wanted to say. That's not it.

On a Barren Branch

~~~~~~~~~

ON THIS TRIP, the first since Candace's death, Junius wasn't interested in the upper-deck lounge where previously he had enjoyed gathering by the piano to pass the time on the long flights. This time, on his way home, he wanted to be alone.

Tokyo had always been a place for business. The restaurants and clubs were part of work. He tried to enjoy Japanese cuisine but couldn't get used to uncooked fish or, at dinners in his honor, watching live shrimp on a plate doused with alcohol. Ice cream at Dipper Dan and Suntory beer wasn't enough to make up for steaks and fries, pizza and tropical drinks.

Junius had told Candace about schoolgirls following him to get his autograph whenever he walked the streets. The summer before this trip, when they rented a house in Southampton for Candace to recuperate, they were accosted by a group of Japanese tourists on Meeting House Lane.

"You see, Candy, even here," he said as a man approached him with a piece of paper extended in his two hands. "We're the only blacks here, so they want our autograph."

This time it wasn't an autograph that was wanted.

"You know where we can find him?" the tourist asked, handing him a photograph.

"Who is this?"

"Famous sailor."

"This is from a long time ago. I don't know who this is."

The man pointed to the name under the faded photo.

"He is a black man, like you. We are looking where he is buried."

Junius shrugged.

The man bowed and left.

At the historical museum they saw the same photograph on display. A 19th century whaler from the Hamptons, Pyrrhus Concer, was famous in Japan for being the first black person to enter Japan. They found his tombstone at the graveyard at the Old North End Cemetery: "Though born a slave/ he possessed virtues/ without which kings/ are but slaves."

Previous summers Junius met with clients at their beach rental, but not this summer. With her illness, they realized how little time they spent together, just the two of them, and while they were hopeful about Candace's recovery, they didn't want to take anything for granted. Her illness made clear how often Junius came home late; Candace, too, was out, with the theater ensemble. Junius offered to cut back on his work. But Candace wouldn't give up acting; that would be giving up on life itself. At least for one month they could be alone together. In the fall she began rehearsals for a new play but dropped out before it went into production.

Candace had wanted to go with Junius on his semi-annual trips to Japan but her schedule never allowed for it. And when his associates came to New York, she seldom met them. It was always man-to-man and she had no interest in what he and his colleagues did. When they married, they had agreed that neither would question the other about where they have been or why. Now they wondered whether they had been too solicitous—"Freedom's just another word for nothing left to lose," Junius reminded them—and they both regretted what they had let slip by.

Junius thought he had gotten over his use of sleeping pills to deaden his melancholy but when he found he was too restless to read or listen to music and couldn't find a comfortable position in his seat, he turned off the reading light and took two pills with club soda.

"Anything else?" the stewardess asked, as Junius pushed his seat into the reclining position. She covered him with a blanket and gave him a pillow. "Can I get you a drink?"

Junius pulled down his eye mask, turned on his Walkman and was soon sucked into the turbid world of chemical dreams.

∿∿∿∿∿
∿∿∿∿∿

NEEDING TO GET AWAY from New York, he had arranged to meet Ito Bunta in Tokyo. As they drove through Tokyo in a Nissan President, Junius thought about the time he was accosted in Manhattan. A man with a bucket approached Junius's car as he waited at a stoplight. Junius rolled up the window and averted his gaze from the squeegee man. Waving him away would do no good. The hooded man leaned across the front of the car and squirted water on the windshield. Wiping it with his washcloth streaked the glass. He stood in front of the car.

Junius, angered, rolled down the driver's window.

"Hey," he shouted.

The man returned Junius's stare.

"Get away from my car."

A swift blow with the handle of the squeegee left spider marks on the window.

Junius stepped out, with his hand thrust in his jacket pocket, when he looked closer at the squeegee man.

"Marvin?" he asked.

The man turned his back and wobbled away.

"Marvin?"

Previous trips to Japan had been all business; meetings, dinners, club hopping and drinks, all were required to get anything done. He was the ambassador of popular American music while at the same time he searched for Japanese talent to sign with American labels. He reviewed the Original Confidence charts and watched TV shows that spotlighted new musical groups. He pursued former teen idol Kenji Sawada to sign with him. Ito Bunta, Junius's Japanese partner, arranged for Sawada and him to appear on a popular variety show. Junius agreed, hoping this would seal the deal with the star.

Eiji Masuda, the show's host, in a polyester plaid jacket, outsized bow tie, green shirt with floppy lapels and hair dyed blazing yellow, came on stage. The host chatted with the nattily dressed Sawada. Masuda turned to Junius, and through an interpreter asked, "Do you know Sarah Vaughan?"

The jazz singer's concert at the Sun Plaza Hall a few years ago had been a sensation in Japan. Junius had the album at home.

"No," Junius laughed. "America's a big country."

"Sing one of her songs, please," Masuda said.

"No, no," Junius declined. "I'm not a singer. I'm a producer. I don't sing. Thank you."

Masuda persisted. The host then turned to the audience and shouted something to them.

Junius declined several times more, but Masuda revved up the audience.

"Cassel! Cassel!" they chanted.

He didn't want to embarrass Bunta.

Junius quickly chose his favorite song from the album. He snapped his fingers, then began up-tempo, the way she did. "Pack up all my cares and woe/ Here I go, singing low/ Bye-bye blackbird/ Where somebody waits for me. . ."

He trailed off, wandering into his own country. He twisted the gold band on his finger. He continued, slowly this time, softly. "Sugar's sweet, so is she/ Bye, bye blackbird/ No one here can love and understand me/ And all the hard luck stories they all hand me/ Make my bed and light the light/ I'll arrive late tonight/ Blackbird, bye-bye."

When he finished, Masuda spoke to the audience. The comment wasn't interpreted for Junius. They laughed and the prompter waved his right hand in a circle above his head to encourage the audience to continue their applause. Masuda turned to Junius and said something to him that seemed to Junius to be in all seriousness. No one laughed.

The translator said, "He asked if you are you sure you aren't related to Sarah Vaughan."

The next morning, Ito read to Junius a critic's review.

"A big hit. He liked your singing very much. He was sure you would become a star, as soon as your album was released in Japan. He thought you are better than your sister."

"Sister?"

"He writes you are Sarah Vaughan's brother."

All other times, Junius flew home when his business was done. This time Junius had decided to stay on for a bit. There was nothing and no one in New York. Time would do the healing, he had been told, and maybe it would even be accelerated if he were somewhere he had never been before, where there were no expectations.

Ito agreed that Kyoto was a good choice for what ailed him and offered to accompany him. As a foreigner without knowledge of Japanese, he would find it difficult, Ito said. Unlike Tokyo, English was rarely spoken there; street signs were in *kanji*, not Roman letters. How would he find his away around? Where would he stay?

"I don't know, but I need to be by myself where I can just be. Alone."

"I understand. Convalescence of the soul. I have a colleague in Kyoto. He can meet you. He can be your interpreter."

"Thank you, but I need to be without anyone else."

"I understand. I think this may be a very good idea for you. You are lucky to go now. This is *sakura* season, the cherry blossom festival. It is everywhere in Japan but it is especially beautiful in Kyoto."

"I am sure it is. But a festival isn't for me."

"Oh, this is very different. No music. It isn't a show. It is something symbolic. Cherry blossoms are a special kind of beauty. You must also visit the rock garden, Ryoan-ji. Here. Let me write the name for you. Show it to anyone and they will direct you. This season is time to be reminded about the important things in life. A time to reflect on *mono no aware*. The passing of beauty."

At the airport, Ito bowed and handed Junius a small package tied neatly with a red bow.

"Take this, please. You said you don't want a guide. So I have this for you. It is a different kind of guide. It may help ease your mind."

Junius bowed in return and placed the gift in his jacket pocket. While waiting for his plane, Junius watched as many as five groups of men and women wearing what he assumed to be their company uniforms—jackets and ties for the men, skirts and blouses for the women—gathered in circles around someone who led them in chants and song, which everyone joined in enthusiastically. Then a leader would raise a pennant with a company logo and the group would file after him to the boarding gate where they left for a communal holiday. Four bridal parties also waited for departing flights, the groom in his wedding attire and the bride in her bridal kimono; families and friends snapped pictures while they waited with the couple until they, too, disappeared down the boarding ramp.

He envied the way they moved, like a school of fish. Just as he longed to be away, he wanted to be absorbed by others. Apart, a part; apart, a part, apart, a part—a heartbeat of opposites.

Shortly after departing Narita, passengers scrambled to the right side of the plane to peer at snow-capped Mt. Fuji that floated above the clouds. Junius fumbled for his camera but the before he could snap open the case, the mountain was out of view.

He continued to gaze out the window when two lightning flashes transformed the gray sky green, and he remembered sitting on the pier in Key West with Candice waiting to catch the elusive green flash. The flashes were so rare that some said they didn't exist at all. They returned each night waiting for the once-in-a life experience.

He waited with his Pentax on his lap to see the green pulses again but the plane had flown past the thunderstorm and not long after he was on a bus to Kyoto. Ito had made reservations for Junius at a *ryokan*. Junius took out Ito's hand-drawn map and showed it to the taxi driver. Bamboo rustled in a large pot beside the entrance to the two-storey wooden building, the most traditional structure on the street of houses. Junius pulled a bell rope and a slender young woman opened the door.

Junius removed his shoes and placed them amongst a jumble of footwear. He followed the woman to the reception desk.

"Cassel-sama." She bows slightly. "Welcome. We are expecting you."

Her mother would return soon. She took him to his room, one with its own bath and toilet, a squat table and cushion on a *tatami* mat. A scroll painting hung from one wall. Sliding rice paper doors opened onto a garden and pond.

He carefully unwrapped Ito's present, a book with a jacket cover of a crow sitting on a leafless branch. Junius snorted. Did he ever mention to Ito that he once was a Sparrow?

He sat on the cushion on the floor and closed his eyes and must have fallen asleep when he heard his name called. An older woman wearing a kimono held a tray on which was an iron teapot, cup and cookie. She bowed and entered the room. She placed the tray on the table and sat on her heels and poured warm tea that smelled like mown grass.

"My English not good," she apologized. "I learned from American soldier. My daughter is good to talk, not me. She learns in school."

Junius told her his father had been in an American Marine during WWII and as soon as he said it, he wished he hadn't.

She smiled when he spoke; he smiled when she spoke.

"This is a great writer," she said, gesturing towards the book on the table. "Do you like him?"

Junius said he had been given the book as a gift.

"Who is the author?" he asked.

"Basho. Very famous. You will like."

Junius thought he heard her say she will bring him dinner. She tells him she will make a special meal for him. When the teapot is drained, she leaves the room.

Junius looks at the book and opens it. Ito had given him a bi-lingual edition. On one page the poem appeared in Japanese, on the opposite an English translation. Basho, he reads, was a poet of eternal aloneness.

"There is a great beyond in the lonely raven perching on the dead branch of a tree. All things come out of an unknown abyss of mystery, and through every one of them we can have a peep into the abyss." The introduction, longer than all the poems together, said that in the sound of ripples in a pond caused by a frog the universe is found, in the abyss of loneliness there is the enjoyment of the twining of life and nature. The pursuit of material comfort and physical sensation is left behind. This is the creative principle of the universe caught in the simplicity of one bird, one tree, one brief poem.

Junius skipped the remainder of the introduction. On the left page is written—

古池蛙飛び込む水の音

"Furu ike ya/kawazu tobikomu/mizu no oto."

On the right he reads, "A pond out of time/ A frog leaps in the water/ The sound of ripples."

He reads the three lines to himself in English, then aloud, finally from memory.

The book is brief, no more than forty pages, less than twenty poems.

The last poem reads.

枯枝に烏の止まりけり秋の暮

kare eda ni/karasu no tomarikeri /aki no kure

"On a barren branch/ A lonely black bird has come to perch/ Fall dusk grows darker."

He hears his name: "Cassel-sama."

His host enters the room with a covered dish, knife and fork, a glazed teapot and napkin. She places the tray on the table.

"Here is your dinner," she says as she backs out of the room without conversation. Junius thanks her, using one of the phrases he has learned. She closes the door behind her. He slides open the garden door and looks out onto a stone lantern by a pond. He lifts the cover from the plate—a hamburger and boiled potato.

He opens the book again and returns to the preface. He reads that Basho used three principles of beauty. *Hie*: cold beauty. *Yase*: spare beauty. *Karabi*: austere beauty.

Junius pulls the garden door closed.

His host returns, removes the tray and pushes the squat table and legless chair against one wall, unfurls a sleeping mat and places on it a heavy cotton blanket.

The following morning she brings him a tray of tofu, grilled fish, miso soup and rice.

Junius strolled the streets aglow with pale buds about to burst. At Ryoan-ji he sat on a wooden porch with other silent visitors gazing at a garden of white pebbles in the middle of which fifteen rocks jutted out like islands in a sea.

Nightfall and the streets were now crowded but yet there was quiet.

The following morning everywhere was lit in a luminescent hue. Overnight the trees had opened into full bloom. Families took picnic baskets to parks where they set out blankets under the falling blossoms. Lovers stood on bridges overlooking ponds and streams. This was the festival Ito had told him about. This was the excitement: a stroll on a winding path, watching pink flowers drift to the ground.

Junius is ignored. During this festival he no longer is an object of wonderment. Other things hold their attention— cherry blossoms falling and fading, falling and fading.

Mono no aware.

The passing of things and the beauty of memory captured in the moment.

〰〰〰〰
〰〰〰〰

ON THE NEXT TO FINAL LEG of the flight home, Junius looks at the books he had bought at the English-language bookstore in Kyoto. He reads about the values of impermanence, incompletion and imperfection. To hold on to what must disappear, to expect to finish what never ends, to strive for perfection when nothing can be perfect— these are the sources of unhappiness.

A fellow passenger encouraged Junius to join him in the piano lounge. He declined. Instead he took out a book of Zen stories. He had heard the question before but never the story.

> One day Mamiya went to his teacher for help with a personal problem. The teacher responded by asking him to explain the sound of one hand clapping.
>
> Mamiya concentrated deeply but he didn't have an answer.
>
> "You are too attached to many things," his teacher said. "You are attached to food, wealth and sound of one hand clapping. It would be better if you were dead. Maybe then you would solve your problem."
>
> The next time Mamiya came to his teacher his teacher asked what he had found about the sound of one hand clapping.
>
> Mamiya put his hands to his chest, groaned and fell to the ground as if he were dead.

"I see," his teacher said. "You have taken my advice and died. Very good. But what about the sound?"

Mamiya said, "I haven't solved that yet."

"Dead men can't talk," the teacher said, ordering Mamiya to leave.

Junius watched the Rockies slide beneath him and ate little of his lunch, leaving the glass of tonic water untouched. He pulled down the window shade and pushed the button on the armrest to recline his seat. He was nearly asleep, for the first time in months without a sleeping pill, when he jolted awake.

The passenger across the aisle asked, "Are you alright?"

One More Drop

~~~~~~~~

THE UNIVERSITY PROVOST denied the union representative's charge that the disparity in pay between librarians and other faculty members was a matter of sexual discrimination. An analysis by the American Association of University Professors supported Lena's position.

In front of the university's Brown Building, strikers argued their cause and encouraged those passing by to sign the petition demanding equity.

Lena had chosen the site for the rally because of its symbolic importance. Brown Building was the site of the Shirtwaist Triangle Factory, the 1911 fire that killed 123 women and 23 men. Many were trapped on the top floors of the building, others jumped to their death.

When Lena first read about the fire and the strike—"The Uprising of Twenty Thousand"—that was led by Clara Lemlich, the organizer's name sounded familiar. Lemlich, an active member of the Communist Party, had lived in Brighton Beach, which meant that Lena's parents and Lemlich likely belonged to the same cell, although perhaps not at the same time. Lena thinks she remembers Ida referring to Lemlich and hopes that her recollection is accurate.

Lena's activity took on added dimension for her because this was the very street in which the garment workers gathered for the strike, the very sidewalk onto which bodies plummeted the following year. In front of this building Lena handed out leaflets and collected signatures.

"You teach here, don't you?" Lena asked, leaning over the shorter woman who was picking up a flier from the folding table.

"Yes, I do," the woman answered.

"I have seen you in the library. I'm Lena Morrell." She held out her hand. "Can I get you to sign the petition?"

"I'm Dr. Kwamboka. I wish you luck."

"Yes. We'll take that. Who can argue with luck? But are you going to sign?" She handed her a pen.

Kwamboka hesitated. Lena placed a leaflet in the professor's hand.

"I hope you'll support us."

Kwamboka folded the paper and placed it in her *kiondo*.

"Nice bag," Lena commented. Again she urged her to sign the petition. Lena held up a pen.

"Certainly." She quickly scrawled her signature.

When it began to rain, Lena gathered up the material and rushed to a nearby luncheonette. She rubbed her hair dry, placed a notebook on the counter and began to write. An hour later Kwamboka entered and sat at on a stool opposite her.

"Dr. Kwamboka," Lena called across the counter top. She dropped her things into her shoulder bag and moved to the stool beside Kwamboka. The waitress put a jelly doughnut on the counter. "Nice to see you again. Let me buy you a cup of coffee."

Kwamboka reluctantly agreed to a cup of tea. Lena slightly arched her brow as Kwamboka added a half-cup of milk and three teaspoons of sugar—"Kenya style," she later explained.

"Do you want something else? The prune Danish is good."

"The what?" Before Lena could answer, she continued, "No. This will do."

"So, Dr. Kwamboka, how long have you been at NYU?"

Kwamboka answered dryly, giving her the barest facts.

"You're Kenyan?" Lena responded. "There are other Africans here. If you'd like to meet them . . ."

"Not from Kenya," she said sharply.

"I only meant . . ."

"That all African are alike. We aren't."

"I don't think that's what I meant. But maybe you know better what I mean than I do."

Kwamboka put down her cup.

"Listen. Professor Kwamboka . . ."

"Kwamboka."

"OK. Dr. Kwamboka."

"Just Kwamboka. You can call me that," she said, trying to ease the tension.

"Listen, Kwamboka. Do you think we can start over? I don't know anything about Africa but I'd like to learn. Help me out."

Kwamboka wasn't certain what to make of a woman as direct as this. Circumlocution was the preferred manner at her home. But she was in the States long enough not to take offense by the forthrightness.

The following week, Lena spotted Kwamboka as she was entering Brown. She waved her over.

"I've already signed."

"Yes, I know." Lena replied. "I'm glad to see you again." She chatted a bit. "Do you want to join me for some tea with your sugar when you're finished with class?"

Missing the joke, she answered flatly, "No, thank you."

"There's a movie playing around that I'd like to see. You know, after what you said about Africa, I thought it would be a good idea. It takes place in Kenya, I think."

"Oh?"

"*Out of Africa*. Sort of like you."

"Perhaps."

Lena ignored Kwamboka's irritation.

"I thought you might want to come with me. So if you want to do something this weekend, let me know." She handed Kwamboka a piece of paper. "My phone number."

In her faculty mail box, Lena left for Kwamboka a hand-written poem —"With smoke, like masks, we cover up our faces./ A joke, a shoulder, twitch, a weary stare./ False words flare up, then fade and leave no traces./ Have I offended you, my dear?"

In Kenya friendships grow as do living things: with time, under the right circumstances. The invitation from Lena Morrell felt like eating fruit before it ripens. Everything in the States was rushed; everyone was scurrying. More than anything, though, since Kenya there was the continual feeling of disconnection. She read the poem again. It was an apology, after all. She waited three more days before calling.

"I like the poem," she said when the met. "You wrote it?"

"I'm not a poet. No. It's by a Yiddish poet."

Lena needed to explain further.

"Yiddish was the language spoken by many Jews, even after they arrived in America."

"You're a Jew?"

"Now look who is being offensive."

"What did I say that is offensive? There's nothing wrong with being a Jew. I went to a Passover service a few years ago, in Nairobi. It's a long story, but that's how I came to America."

"And some of my best friends are black," Lena responded.

"What?" Kwamboka said in puzzlement.

"Forget it. It's kind of offensive and hard to explain."

"I didn't mean to be offensive."

"And neither did I the other day."

"Kenya is so beautiful," Lena said after the movie. "I had no idea. Is this what your home is like?"

"I never saw a lion." Kwamboka's voice grew softer as she spoke so that Lena had to lean in to hear. "I miss home. I don't think I should have come tonight."

"I'm sorry."

"No, it's OK. It's not your fault." She briefly told Lena her story.

"When do you think you'll go back?"

"One day."

Lena was too embarrassed to admit to Kwamboka that it wasn't until after meeting her that she could place Kenya on the map. But since they met, she read several books about Kenya,

When Lena brought up having read of Okech Odhiambo's poems, Kwamboka refused to engage in a conversation about his work, for which Lena was glad. She didn't like his poetry; it reminded her of the leaden socialist poems she was familiar with from her childhood.

There was no beauty in such poetry. Who could live without beauty?

"TELL ME ABOUT him," Lena insisted.

Kwamboka had grown accustomed to Lena's directness over the last several months.

"I admired him. He wasn't like any of the European. So for example, he sponsored Africans who applied to the local sports club. The other Europeans and Asians hated him for that."

"And you liked him because of it?"

"Of course," she said. But it was more than that. He was a decent man and she had come to enjoy his company. Only later did Kwamboka reveal that for a short time they were lovers.

She described to Lena being awakened by birds and watching the sky quickly turn from night-black to lavender each morning.

"You miss it."

"Oh, yes. It used to be hard. But not so much any more. When I first went to London, you know."

"And now?"

"Only when I think about it. When you ask."

Lena looked at Kwamboka, her broad forehead, the back of her hands a deep brown, the thickness of her neck where the color changed from ebony to chocolate. Lena had come to love the smell of her.

"Have you ever worn an Afro?"

"No. But maybe some day I will. African hair is difficult."

"An old boyfriend was bald. I found it sexy." Lena continued. "My hair used to be bright red. Every once in a while I think I'm going to get it dyed, to its original color. But I can't bring myself to do it." She laughed. "Even the thought of this is too bourgeois for me."

"I would *like* gray hair," Kwamboka said. "It's a sign of wisdom, don't you think?"

"It's a sign of getting old, that's all."

Kwamboka shook her head. "You Americans value youth too much."

Lena took Kwamboka's hand as they walked to the subway.

On a crystal clear Saturday they went to the observation deck of the Empire State Building.

"Way over there." Lena said, pointing the telescope for Kwamboka, "is where I grew up."

"You're proud of your home."

"Once."

"The world knows us for its animals, but what do we know? Elephants and lions. I learned about bears and voles, not the creatures nearer my *shamba*. We have cows and goats and donkeys, domestic animals."

A chilly wind gusted on the outdoor observatory. Kwamboka put another coin in the high-powered binoculars, pressed her eyes against it and slowly scanned the cityscape. Lena stood behind her, wrapping her arms around her friend. Kwamboka stiffened for a moment, then relaxed.

"It' strange. From here the city looks beautiful. But over there," Lena pointed, "and there. Those are slums. I love the city from a distance. Up close is hard. But that's the part that really matters, doesn't it? Loving up close."

Lena leaned and kissed Kwamboka on her head, as they stood silent staring at the hazy hills rising on the Hudson's far side.

The next time they meet, to take in a movie at the Waverly, Lena gives Kwamboka a copy of *A Field Guide to Mammals of East Africa*.

〰〰〰〰
〰〰〰〰

THE TWO-BEDROOM RENTAL on the ground floor of a brownstone was ideal for the two women. On their joint salaries, the West 13th St. brownstone, with a common backyard big enough for a café table and chairs, was within their means.

In Vermont Lena had grown tomatoes and looked forward to growing them again; Kwamboka longed for the taste of fresh vegetables. But the few hours of sunshine in the backyard made it unsuitable for growing produce. The following year they substituted shade-loving flowers, lampropanos: "a valued garden plant native to Siberia, northern China, Korea and Japan," the brochure from the garden center read, "a member of the poppy family. The outer petals are bright fuchsia-pink, while the inner ones are white. The flowers strikingly resemble the conventional heart shape, with a droplet beneath—hence the common name, bleeding heart."

The name and the color attracted Lena, as much as its ability to flourish in unlighted areas. Lena found a Japanese legend regarding the flower's origin.

> Once there was a suitor who wanted to win the heart of a beautiful woman. The woman was presented with the gift of two rabbits. —*"These are the first two petals of the bleeding heart."*— But she was indifferent to the entreaty.
>
> Then she was given a pair of slippers.—*"These are the next two petals."*—Still she was unmoved. Then she received a pair of earrings.—*"These are the remaining two petals of the flower."*—But she continued to rebuff the efforts to win her as a lover.
>
> Her suitor's heart was finally broken. In despair, a sword was lifted and thrust into the rejected heart.—*"This is the middle part of the flower."*— The bleeding heart of the rejected lover gives the flower its name.

"What a sad story for a beautiful flower," Kwamboka said. "I think that you are lonelier that me, Lena." She added, "I think that I am disappointing you. You need something else than a roommate."

"Not *someone* else."

"But you're missing something."

"You are, too, aren't you? There is no man in your life."

"That's never been important to me. But for you . . .?"

"At one time it didn't matter who I slept with. But now what's most important is who I'm with."

"Don't live in disappointment. To regret having lived with me."

"Never regret, Kwamboka. You are the person I want to be with."

What Lena wanted to say she couldn't; Kwamboka would misunderstand. She chose not to read this poem to her: "In the beginning,/ there was lust./ Out of lust,/ God emerged in flames./ Lust/ is God's nature./ Everything God creates/ is in God's nature./ Whoever gets more/ of God's nature—/ A teardrop more—/ Becomes an artist, a poet./ One more drop—/ A murderer."

〰〰〰〰〰〰
〰〰〰〰〰〰

THE WINDOW AIR-CONDITIONER wasn't enough to cool the apartment on this blistering Memorial Day weekend. Dishes and silverware filled the drying rack. Too hot to cook, they went for dinner in Little India, a neighborhood crowded with storefront restaurants.

Tawa Delight, filled with Formica tables and fluorescent lights, smelled of spices and souds, vindaloos and pulaos. The open door and ceiling fan did little to provide relief. Having eaten there often, they didn't bother to read the menu. Kwamboka ordered vegetable samosas.

"That's all?"

"I'm not hungry."

"What's wrong?"

"The neighborhood reminds me of Nairobi, all the Indians. I remember where I bought my clothes, the women with their saris, the mosques. I think about home again. I've been away too long. It's almost nine—what?—ten years. You've never been away. This is your home."

"Brooklyn is a different country. And don't forget Vermont," Lena said, trying to make light of Kwamboka's pain. She took Kwamboka's hand in hers.

"I don't know where I belong. I long for home sometimes and I cry."

Kwamboka looked at Lena's hand resting in hers.

"It's so strange, Lena. You know I've really only had two friends in my life. You and Dexter. Two *wazungu*. Not Africans but whites have been my friends. Sometimes I think about him and what happened to him."

"Why don't you go back then, for a visit? We'll figure out a way to pay for it. Isn't there an academic conference in Kenya you can attend?"

"When I was recruited, the part that was most attractive was the idea that I would be able to return home, to continue to talk to the old women and collect their stories.. Maybe I should have taken advantage of that. It certainly is easy to get sidetracked. But now? What for? It's too late, I'm afraid. Most everything is gone. I'm like the donkey between two piles of hay. I don't know which way to go. So I stand in the middle."

"And starve."

"And starve, yes, I guess so."

"Even if I go with you?"

Kwamboka smiled. She separated their interlaced fingers, then looked at Lena's freckled arm.

"How strange color is," she said. "It means so much to some."

"Is that what you see when you're with me?"

"It's no different here. In Kenya it was the colonialists. And here, what should I say? You're a woman, so there is something against you. But I am a black woman, so there are two things against me." She ran her fingers along Lena's arm.

A police car careened down the crowded avenue, its flashing light pulsating on the plate glass Tawa window.

"Sometimes, Kwamboka," Lena began, then started again after the wail of the siren dissipated, "sometimes I look at myself in the mirror and I think something is very wrong, very wrong. And I'm ashamed. For what I've done. For what I haven't done. There are times I just want to give up. Maybe I should never have left Vermont." Lena raised her head to look into Kwamboka's eyes. "The truth is I'm a coward. When I see a bunch of black boys, I'm scared."

"I am more afraid than you, Lena. Let me tell you, I was afraid to come to America. For good reason. This is a frightening place, but you grew up here. You know your way around. In Kenya, we all think the streets in America are full of gangsters. And they are. There's no reason to be shamed because you are afraid. Only mad people aren't afraid."

"It's also that I haven't done anything. Nothing's really changed. I want to be of use, Kwamboka, to do something more than indulge myself."

When they left the restaurant, a caravan of squad cars and paddy wagons passed by. They were used to the police presence in the area. Anarchist squatters had taken over abandoned tenements, cardboard shelters had gone up around a park that had become a haven for drugs and the city wanted them all gone.

The friends held hands as they began their stroll home. Turning a corner they encountered a blockade of saw-horses erected by the police. In the dusk flames lit the park's far side. More sirens filled the air; fire trucks reeled out hoses; mounted police sat astride their disciplined horses.

"Let's go." Kwamboka shivered as she heard a window shatter.

"No, wait."

Lena dropped Kwamboka's hand and approached the stanchion. Three cops glanced at her and continued to talk to one another. When she tried to pass the barricade, they stopped her.

"Come on, Lena. I want to go," Kwamboka said as she grabbed Lena's arm

"I can't leave yet. If you want to go, go ahead. I'll meet you at home."

Kwamboka wouldn't leave her friend.

A shout went up in the park—Parks Are For People! Parks Are For People!

The horses were turned in the direction of the chants.

"Come!" Kwamboka squeezed Lena's arm.

"Let go, Kwamboka." She yanked free from Kwamboka's grip. "Not yet."

A policeman reproached Lena: "Who are you?"

She didn't respond.

"There's nothing to see. If you don't live here, go home. Get out of here."

A water balloon splattered at the cop's feet. Kwamboka released Lena's arm and turned away.

A man jumped on a shopping cart overflowing with plastic bottles, rags and cans. Shoved by a policeman, he stumbled from the cart, scrambled to his feet and quickly pushed his cart away as he shouted biblical verses. He ran into another cop, who cuffed the vagrant's hands behind his back. The man demanded they not touch his cart.

"I ain't garbage! I ain't garbage!"

Lena shouted, "Just leave him alone, you pig!"

"Come on, Lena," Kwamboka called, but as she turned to walk away a cop shoved her from behind. One shoe flew from her foot, blood ran down her leg. With a piece of cloth torn from her blouse, Lena wiped the trickling blood. Kwamboka sat on the curb and when she regained her strength, grabbed Lena's arm.

A policeman came over.

"Do you need help?" he offered. "You look pretty bad." He reached to help Kwamboka.

"Fuck you," Lena said.

The following morning they saw the *Daily News* photo of a policeman in battle uniform. In front stood a man wearing a baseball cap, a hand on his hip, leaning on a pile of plastic bags. Sanitation workers were wearing gauze masks. In the center of the photo was an "unidentified woman sitting on the curb being helped by a stranger."

Lena washed Kwamboka's leg and changed bandages several times throughout the day. She brought her boiled tea.

"Lena, I have made up my mind—to return to Kenya—go home."

Lena said nothing. For more than a minute, she stood silently, then sat beside Kwamboka, their shoulders touching.

"If I don't go back now I'll never go back. Dexter warned me to stay away. But it wasn't supposed to turn out like this."

Lena rubbed her friend's back.

"This isn't my home. It can never be. I don't want to die in a strange land, as a refugee." She turned to Lena. "Look at me. Look. The police left you alone. Not me."

Lena pulled Kwamboka into her.

"There's dignity in dying for a cause. There's none in dying because of what you look like. I have to go, Lena. I can't stay."

"I'm afraid for you."

"It's worse here, isn't it?"

The chairman of her department tried to persuade her to stay; she was a good professor, he said, everyone respected her. He was confident she would be promoted to full-professor.

Lena helped Kwamboka file papers, fill out forms, close accounts.

"Do you think I am running away, Lena?"

"Why do you think that?"

"I'm scared."

"Me too."

Lena tightly embraced her friend; Kwamboka gently stroked Lena's hair.

"It's beautiful," Kwamboka said.

"It used to be."

"You still are."

"I've never been," Lena said. She looked at Kwamboka, removed her friend's glasses and gently kissed her.

"I wish this could have been different, Lena. With all my heart. I really don't want to leave you. Please believe that." She backed away from Lena and put her glasses on.

"We'll see each other again. You'll be back. I know that."

"Someday. But I think you'll be to Kenya before I come back the America. And I promise you I'll learn the names of all the animals."

When Lena returned from the airport after seeing Kwamboka off on a midnight flight, she found an envelope on the bed. She read:

Once there was a girl who enjoyed running in the fields. She counted how many pumpkins she could carry in her arms and liked to throw stones into the river. After a rainstorm she ran to the edge of the hill to find a rainbow that arched into the valley below.

Her favorite bird was the roller because of the way it flew. The roller swooped this way and that, flying up, then down, flying sideways, then straight, a gay bird. When it sang, it said, "Look at me. Watch how I dance." And the girl learned to dance by watching the roller.

One day the bird dived from high in the sky but before it could stop its rolling, it plummeted to the ground. When the girl found the bird in the thick bush, it was nearly dead.

The girl tore a leaf from a banana plant and carried the roller back to her house. For days she gave it bugs to eat. When the bird gained some strength, she fed it a small lizard.

The bird was very frightened of the girl. It knew that caught birds were to be eaten and it thought it was being kept to fatten up and when the time came it would be boiled with spinach and sweet potatoes.

But that's not what happened. Instead, when it was strong and its broken wing healed, the girl released the roller. Eager to escape, the bird flew into the air and disappeared into the forest.

"Good-bye, my little bird," the girl said.

Where the girl lives there are two seasons. When the dry months came, the red dust that settled on the land weighed down her spirits. The girl sat on the ground with her legs straight in front of her.

At first she thought the sound was leaves rustling in the wind. But when she heard it again, she looked over at the nearby tree and saw a roller on the limb.

The bird sang to the girl, "I can make your life a little happier. I want to give you a gift."

With that the roller flew up high. It brushed its feathers with the blue from the sky and the white from clouds; flew down to the ground and touched the grass for its green; it went to the lava beds and gathered black; it flew to a nearby lake and took a touch of pink from the flamingoes. Yellow was borrowed from hibiscus plants. The roller sipped lilac from the lantana shrub.

Roller returned every few days.

The bird said to the girl, "For several months you have too much sun. You can't have rainbows without rain but you need to have beauty in your lives. So here I am, for you to look at until the rains return. I will be nearby and you can gaze on me until your heart's content."

The bird was true to its word. Over there—over there!—is the lilac breasted roller, as beautiful as a rainbow, waiting to be seen by children and you.

Lena couldn't rid herself of the poem: "The moon has left the sky/ And the Seven Sisters have also gone. / Midnight comes / Hours slip by/ And solitary still/ I lie."

Mother Tongue

〜〜〜〜〜〜
〜〜〜〜〜〜

BECAUSE GOVERNMENT BURSARIES were reduced, students demonstrated. All public universities were to be shut for the remainder of the academic year. Kwamboka's hope of finding a teaching position would have to be put on hold for at least several months.

There was no hurry. What savings she had from America would easily stretch into the foreseeable future.

Letters she sent to Conway after arriving in New York had gone unanswered. She never tried calling him; he never contacted her. Now back in Nairobi she tried to find him.

"I don't know who this is," the stranger said at the other end of the line. Thinking that he had changed his phone number, she consulted the telephone directory. No Dexter Conway. As there were few street signs and no house numbers in Nairobi, she directed a taxi to Parklands, but the city had so expanded it took hours to locate what she thought was the house. Barbed wire topped a concrete wall where the cypress hedge once stood. An African held tight the leash of a snarling dog as he talked to Kwamboka from behind the gate. He knew nothing about its former owner.

Berrycloth's publishing company had moved to a building on a long street of warehouses. In the dim waiting lounge of Progressive Press, as she waited for the receptionist to summon Berrycloth, Kwamboka saw her book on a display rack, one in a series of folktales from various Kenyan tribes.

"Kwamboka?"

Berrycloth's left incisor was missing and his thin hair, combed straight back, didn't cover the ink blue mole on his crown. The tattersall shirt was frayed at the collar.

"Mary, bring us some tea. Come on in, Kwamboka," he

said as he led her down a hallway lined high with cartons. The few lights cast harsh shadows on the concrete walls. The foul smell of the toilet assaulted her as she walked by to his office.

Kwamboka explained she had been in New York and now was returning to Kenya.

"We didn't know where to send your royalties," Berrycloth explained. "We've kept an accounting here." He told her that the hope for her book being adopted by the government didn't materialize right away but now it was doing quite well. "It doesn't amount to very much. We sell it for only a few shillings." He called in the accountant and asked him to prepare a statement for her. Berrycloth said would gladly pay her what was owed, but that it would be helpful if she didn't take her money just yet. The company needed the sales from its successful books to subsidize publishing new works. Kwamboka agreed to postpone the payment.

"Perhaps I'll ask for it in the future, Tom" Kwamboka said. What she wanted to know was what had happened to Conway.

Berrycloth told her that he hadn't seen much of him after she left for London, a few of times at the City Market buying flowers and that sort of thing, that's all.

"It seems that his house boy went back to his *shamba* . . ."

"Maranga, you mean?"

"I didn't know his name. In any case, it seemed Dexter didn't employ anyone else, and did his own shopping," Berrycloth said. Conway had turned down every invitation for drinks or dinner and no one had seen him in ages.

"We all thought he must have returned to England."

"So he's gone."

"Well, yes, so to speak. I'm sorry. I'm being gauche here. There was a death notice," Berrycloth continued. "A brief one in the *Nation*."

"About Dexter? He died? What did it say?" A pang of regret swiftly passed over her.

"You know how these things are. Nothing but some simple facts about his life."

"Who placed it?"

Berrycloth shrugged his shoulders. "I don't know. Everyone was as surprised as I was. But I am glad to see you, Kwamboka." She allowed the conversation to take a turn towards the non-consequential.

"You need to ring me up so we can get together sometime. Here's my home number," he said. "You know, Njeri, my wife, died last year. There are a few decent restaurants around town where we can meet for dinner."

Without a compelling reason to stay in the city, Kwamboka decided to visit Kisii. This, after all, was what she missed most about Kenya. Nairobi never attracted her, now less than ever as the streets were clogged with traffic and unkempt sidewalks with pedestrians. She longed for the hills and the smell of the red land after the rains, the bananas and papaya, maize porridge, roasted meat and beans, the brisk morning air, being awakened by the chatter of birds. Most of all she wanted to hear her mother tongue.

〰〰〰〰〰

THE BUS TO KISII laid over in Nakuru for an hour. In the roadside restaurant, Kwamboka ate a couple of samosas and savored her orange Fanta. This town, too, had been transformed, from a farm supply center to an aggressive place teeming with vehicles of every sort.

A woman, no older than twenty, sat on a bundle of cloth. She flirted with a driver whose truck was across the road. Kwamboka caught snatches of Gusii and smiled. When the tout announced the bus's departure, Kwamboka hurried to ensure getting a window seat. The trucker tossed the young woman's cloth bundles to the top of the bus, climbed up and secured them with sisal rope. The young woman followed Kwamboka aboard and, although there were empty seats elsewhere, sat next to her.

Malaika told Kwamboka she was from Kisii and had been in Nakuru to purchase material for her dressmaking business. For the next hour what Kwamboka had expected to be a quiet journey turned into a lively monologue as her seatmate captivated her with observations about men and politics. By the time they reached the edge of the Mau Forest, Malaika, allowing for a few words from Kwamboka, found out that Kwamboka had taught in an American university. To Kwamboka's astonishment, Malaika insisted that the famous American stay with her at her place, a house used both as a domicile and shop.

"I am going to stay at the Kisii Hotel," Kwamboka said, referring to the half-century old lodging, which, when she was last in Kisii, was already more than shabby.

"Who is meeting you?"

"I will find some old friends," she responded without conviction.

"No," Malaika insisted, "you will stay with me."

"I can't."

"I will get a bed for you," Malaika continued, as though not hearing Kwamboka's objection. "I will move my goods into a spare room. If I had known you were going to be my guest, I would have gotten sheets and blankets in Nakuru. No problem. There is a market near my home."

"I can't do that. I don't know you." What a stupid thing to say, she thought.

"You don't know the people at the hotel either. So you will stay with me. This is something great!"

Kwamboka demurred again but Malaika ignored her

protestations. Resistance faded as Kwamboka's curiosity was stronger than her objections. Whatever trepidation Kwamboka may have had disappeared. Certainly there would be less concern about her safety at this woman's house than being alone at a hotel.

Kwamboka offered to pay for her board but the seamstress responded with a well-known proverb: *"Siku moja mgeni, siku tatu mpe jembe."*

Kwamboka laughed. "OK," she said. "The first day I'll be your guest and if I stay after that . . ."

"Of course you will."

". . . I'll do my share."

"You, Doctor Professor Sarah Kwamboka, are my guest. Don't you worry," Malaika said. "When the time comes, you will get a proper hoe. You have been to America. You know what needs to be done to make our country better."

Kwamboka thought that in all likelihood she was being set up to be touched for money for a scholarship perhaps, or for a plane ticket to America, supplies to build a new house. The reality, she knew, was that she was rich beyond Malaika's imagination, and if Malaika profited instead of a hotel, that would be good.

"I will stay for a short while."

"A month, at least!"

"Well, for three days," Kwamboka smiled. *"Siku tatu."*

"Until universities reopen."

"We'll see."

"Yes, yes. In a year then," Malaika said, having outbid Kwamboka. She grasped Kwamboka's hands. "Until then, you are with me."

MALAIKA TOOK KWAMBOKA around the location, introducing her to the women who were her customers. Instead of paying for her room, Kwamboka bought food and incidentals from the market item. At the end of two weeks Malaika presented Kwamboka with a dress she had sewn for her.

Making copies of her resume was difficult; the closest duplicating machine was in Kisii Town, nearly thirty miles away. Mini buses frequently plied the road, but still it would be an all-day ordeal.

"Now I have a big idea for you," Malaika said as she pumped the treadle on the Singer sewing machine. "Women tell me about their children's school. Too many are crowded and there are few teachers. So I said to them that you will be a new teacher. You are a professor, a great teacher."

"You didn't do that, Malaika! You can't tell people what to do. You have to ask . . ."

"You went to America from Kisii and you came back. This is something great. Do you know another Kisii woman who has done this? You are a teacher, aren't you? I am a dressmaker, I sew. You are a teacher, you teach. That's what we are meant to do."

"Yes, and I am going to teach, at a university. Classes will begin soon, I'm sure."

"Children need you in Kabungu. Now."

"It has been a long time since I taught little children," Kwamboka said. "A very long time ago. Your mother's generation."

"You are a teacher. You don't forget how to teach. If you teach big people, you can teach little people. Children are easier, isn't it?"

"I don't think so."

"You teach here until universities open. Then you can leave."

"If you put it that way. But I can't walk in and announce myself, 'Here I am. Hire me.' "

"Tell me why you can't do that?"

"It's not how it's done."

"How should it be done?" she challenged.

"There are rules."

"You have already been announced. The rule is to get the best teacher. Everyone knows you."

"Hardly anyone knows me."

"They know about you."

"That's different."

"I've talked to the sub-chief. I told him there are too many children in the school. And now we are lucky, like other schools that have wealthy patrons. We have a famous teacher from America to be our teacher. I told Ochako you can teach important things, things you have seen with your own eyes. You are a professor, a great thing. Ochako said yes, a big teacher will be good for our children, so he went to Headmaster Ondari and told him you will be a new teacher next week."

"What? What did you do?"

"Ondari first said no. There is no money for another teacher. That's what he said. There's always money for his own pockets, that's what I think, but I didn't say that. I went to him and I said the professor doesn't need your little money. She's an American."

Headmaster Ondari reluctantly agreed to take her.

"Temporary," Ondari told Ochako. "Only temporary."

Kwamboka agreed to volunteer at the school until the end of the semester. If an opening came up for her before then, she would leave, she told Malaika. Whatever little teaching she could provide was better than nothing, she reasoned.

Instead of the traditionally greeting of new teachers with song and dance on the grounds in front of the school building, on the first morning Ondari took her directly to a classroom and introduced her to pupils there. Forty children, doubled- and tripled-up at rough-hewn desks, stood at attention when she and Ondari walked into the room brightened only by outside light coming through a window without glass.

"This is your new teacher, children."

"Good morning, teacher," they shouted in unison.

"Good morning, children," she responded.

"Children," Ondari continued in his stentorian voice, "her name is Miss Kwamboka. Can you say Miss Kwamboka?"

"Miss Kwamboka!"

She had been in such schoolrooms before; it was in one like this that attended primary school; she once taught in one like this before attending university. Kwamboka was glad to be here again, no matter that she had been pushed by a young woman she hardly knew; no matter what Malaika's reasons may have been, her heart was eased by the familiar muffled sounds of children in a cramped room, the memories of long ago.

'My place,' she thought. 'This is my place.'

〰〰〰〰〰〰
〰〰〰〰〰〰

AT THE KABUNGU GIRLS PRIMARY SCHOOL, Kwamboka told the pupils folk tales from Kisii; she told them fairytales from Europe and Asia, and created stories of her own making, such as the origin of rainbows. She enchanted them, the smallest sitting on her lap, resting against her large breasts, others at mud stained shoes. Kwamboka realized, to her amazement, that if life had unfolded differently, she in fact may have been a grandmother herself and several of the children sitting in front of her may have been her own progeny.

At first, she told the stories in English— all lessons at the school were conducted in one of the two national languages, English and Swahili. Occasionally she told one in Gusii and discovered that the children were even more attentive and responsive when she spoke in their mother tongue. In less than a month, Kwamboka began to speak more frequently in Gusii, telling them the tales from her research. She used stories to illustrate lessons, from arithmetic to geography.

When she switched to entirely to Gusii and substituted folktales for standard curriculum, Ondari called her to his office in a building not much larger than a cooking house. Thick earth walls kept the inside damp and cool during the rainy season, but when the sun beat on the corrugated roof the room became insufferable.

The head teacher closed the door behind Kwamboka. It took a moment for her eyes to adjust to the dark.

"Yes, Miss Kwamboka," he said. "How are things going for you? Take a seat."

Kwamboka sat on the wooden folding chair across from Ondari's desk.

"I'm pleased to be here," she answered.

"Is it?" he said. "This is good news. I didn't know if someone as big as you would be happy in our little school." Ondari rubbed his chin. "As you can see, we have very little at Kabungu. We are a poor community. But we do the best we can, isn't it? Because of the *harambee* of parents and teachers alike we have a school with a good reputation. Without that, we would be failing the children. We all do our part to make the school a success."

Ondari, a portly man with deep lines running from his nose to the mouth, wore a sports jacket, dingy white shirt, and a tie emblazoned with the national flag, a symbol of his loyalty to the ruling party. Kwamboka estimated that he was several years younger than she.

"Certainly," Kwamboka said. She knew that it was not a compliment that was to follow.

Ondari stood up and placed his hands on his desk. He leaned forward into Kwamboka.

"So having you as part of our staff is something wonderful for this sub-location," he said. "Few of our teachers are secondary school graduates. The teachers are not as educated as you. Thank you for doing your part to bring progress to our Kenya." He stood upright. "One did attend a private college in Mombasa. Even me myself, I went for one year in Kakamega."

"I understand the difficulty." Kwamboka folded her hands on her lap.

"I know you do," he said. "Having you will make many parents want to send their children to the Kabungu School, without a doubt. We thank you for joining us in our effort to bring education to everyone. It is important that today all children attend school. Not like the old days."

"Certainly not like the old days."

"Today education is for everyone. Universal, isn't that the word?"

"Yes it is," Kwamboka said. "But not compulsory and not free."

"The seeds have been planted," he said. "It takes time to bear fruit."

Kwamboka acknowledged his remarks with suitable noises issuing from deep in her throat.

"It takes much money to send a child to school," Ondari said. "It is no easy matter."

"I know it is a hardship."

"Not hardship, but *harambee*," he chided. "It is *harambee*, but there are books and supplies and uniforms to pay for. It is a sacrifice that good parents willingly make."

Ondari opened the shutter. The room brightened as the sun broke through the clouds.

Kwamboka saw children on the field playing, their feet bare, their ball a tangle of twine.

"It is important that the children learn their lessons well. We must do our best to make certain they pass their KCPE so they can go on. We have to do our best to see to it that our students receive high marks. We can't just make up whatever we want to teach." He grew excited, raising his finger to wave at Kwamboka. "We must teach them so they can pass the examinations."

Kwamboka remembered the rote learning she endured in order to qualify for the next step on the educational ladder. She wanted more for her pupils.

Ondari continued. "I must instruct you, Miss Kwamboka, there is government policy. All schools must comply with it, even ours, even in this village. All our classes, professor, must be conducted in English." He pulled his collar from his throat with his index finger. "You must not be aware of this. I take responsibility for not informing you when you arrived. I believed that as an educated person you knew the regulations. Every teacher knows them. The government makes no secret about them. But you have been away for a long time. It's different in America, isn't it?"

"Quite."

"You are more like a beginning teacher, I must remember," he said. "It will take time getting used to. Don't worry."

Kwamboka had mistakenly thought that she would be measured by the success of her lessons, the eagerness of the children to attend school, what they knew, their desire to learn.

"I understand, Ondari," she said. "I am trying to be a good teacher. I teach the best I know. I look at the children . . ."

"There are too many," he said.

"So I ask myself, what is the best way to teach all these children? I think about this when I go home," she said. "I plan each night and prepare lessons for them."

"All teachers do."

"And I look at the results of what I am doing," she said. Kwamboka rose from her chair and looked at the farms across the road. "What do you think, Ondari? The children are eager and responding well, aren't they?"

"There is more to school than making children happy." He returned to sit behind his desk. He picked up a pencil and twirled it between his fingers. Kwamboka continued to stand. "They aren't here for a good time, are they?"

Kwamboka remained quiet.

"No, of course not," he answered himself. "They are here to to be able to move on to the next level.."

"I think they *are* receiving a good education. They can learn and be happy at the same time. That's not impossible."

"It is not what is possible," he said, "but what is permissible."

"I'm not familiar with the reasons."

"You don't need to be, professor. That is why I am headmaster, not you. When there is a regulation, I know it and I tell the teachers."

"Quite so," she said. "But it would help me if I understood why."

"Why what?"

"What the reason is for such a regulation. It used to be this way during the colonial period. But I thought it was different today, that we would respect the children for who they are."

"We respect the children and want them to learn what it is to be a good Kenyan," Ondari said. "We want all our children to perform well on the examination. There are good reasons for children not speaking their home language in the classroom. You know the requirements that are on the examination, don't you?"

"Why don't you tell me, Ondari?"

"English Language, English Composition, and so on," he said. "But not Gusii. There is no paper in Gusii. If you want to speak to them in Swahili now and then, that's good, professor. There is a paper in Swahili. Every Kenyan needs to speak Swahili. But there is none in Gusii. And why don't you tell me, professor, where their paper is on the stories you tell them? "

"There is none that I am aware of," she said.

"Then we won't waste their time with them, will we? When the children play with one another, that is one thing. But not in the classroom. I think I make myself understood, don't I?"

When Kwamboka returned to the house that afternoon, Malaika was at her sewing machine, pumping the treadle furiously, the whirr filling the room. Several customers sat in the room, one on the plump, cushioned armchair, others on a bench placed against the interior front wall. They waited for their dresses and blouses to be mended. They waited to catch a glimpse of the teacher.

"What's wrong?" Malaika asked Kwamboka when the house emptied. She found Kwamboka in her room seated in the armchair, her eyes closed and glasses removed, an arm across her forehead. "I saw when you came in that you were unhappy."

"It's a problem at school," Kwamboka said. "I saw Ondari today."

"Oh, him," she said. "That man puffs himself up like a rooster but he makes noises like a donkey. S o m e say that they will drag him out of the school by his hair little beard, shave it off, and drive him away with stones."

"I don't know about that," Kwamboka said, taken aback by Malaika's vehemence. "But I do know that children are learning."

Malaika poured tea for the two of them. She opened a package of white bread, cut a piece for Kwamboka, and slathered it with margarine.

Kwamboka sipped the milky brew. "I thought we were beyond the mentality that foreign is better."

"Just forget what he says, " Malaika said. "He's a stupid old man."

"He is the head teacher. He's only carrying out government policy."

"Then do what he wants," Malaika said after some thought, "but tell the stories after school hours."

Malaika was right. If the concern was not straying from the lessons in order for children to pass their national examinations, then there would no objection to her talking to them in Gusii at other times. As long as she met the mandated educational requirements, additional work would not be scorned.

Kwamboka ceased substituting stories for the curriculum material; she no longer used Gusii in the classroom. During school hours she spoke to them in English and Swahili. During breaks, and when she was not with them as a teacher, she used Gusii.

Ondari summoned her to his office again.

"This is a problem, professor," he said to her. "I thought I made myself clear to you last week. But you are telling them stories in Gusii again. I know that you talk to them in their tribal language."

"The stories are between lessons. I'm doing all that I'm supposed to. They aren't learning less but more."

"Let me make myself very clear, Miss Kwamboka, so there is no misunderstanding," Ondari said. "You are not to talk to the children in Gusii. Everything is English. Only English."

He walked to the door and stood beside it, gesturing for Kwamboka to leave.

"I understand why you want to adhere to the curriculum," she said. "The government demands it, so you comply. But what possible reason is there for not allowing me to speak to them in Gusii when it isn't a lesson?"

"Because I said so, Miss Kwamboka. I am in charge."

"A fool. He thinks he is so clever. I hate him." Malaika accused Ondari of skimming money from the *harambee* fund, of being stupid and mean.

"Be careful of what you say," Kwamboka warned. "You don't know who will hear you."

"Oh, everyone thinks the same of him," she said. "I don't care. His wife can take her business elsewhere. I don't want his money."

More women came to the shop to listen to Malaika's indignation. They took her line of thought. Support gathered for Kwamboka.

"I have an idea," Malaika said to Kwamboka.

Later that day as they were pulling weeds from the garden, Kwamboka watered the flowers she had planted. She wished she could find bleeding hearts.

"You can't speak Gusii," Malaika said, "and you can't tell them stories in Gusii. But that's just at school, isn't it?"

Malaika straightened up. She rubbed the small of her back.

"My idea is this: tell the pupils stories after school hours. Tell them as they walk home." She offered her shop as a center for the children after hours. "I'll make room for them. On Saturdays they could come all day. You can tell them stories and talk to them in Gusii. It will make my work go faster too to have children around."

Foolishly Kwamboka mentioned the idea to Ondari. He took his handkerchief and wiped his forehead.

"How dare you, professor. I've warned you."

"This isn't at school."

"Do you think you are a teacher only at school? It is amazing how educated people can be so ignorant," he said. "Teaching requires discipline at all times. If it isn't proper to use Gusii at school, it isn't right for you to use it anytime with children."

Kwamboka tried to interject.

"Let me finish, Miss Kwamboka. The government has its reasons. Tribal language . . ."

"Mother tongue . . . "

"Tribal languages can only divide us," he continued. "So if you don't stop immediately, I will have to dismiss you. Ask you to leave Kabungu."

Kwamboka had meant to write to Lena soon after arriving, but she had been absorbed with her new life that it had been neglected. The next time she went to the market, she bought an aerogramme.

She apologized for not having written sooner. On two small pages, she told her where she was and made a brief reference to Malaika. She ended with the plea:

"Who are you writing to?" Malaika asked. She looked over Kwamboka's shoulder.

"My American friend."

"Oh, good. Tell her to come. I will make room for her, too."

"I've asked for her to do that. I hope she'll visit, but I don't know if she will. It's not easy. It is very far from America."

"You told me yourself that being on an airplane is like sitting on a bus. But better. They give you food. And there is a *choo*."

"She works. She needs to arrange to leave the university for a while."

"Another professor!"

"Not exactly," Kwamboka continued. "It's very expensive to get here."

"She's American. No problem."

She and Malaika walked to town to post the letter.

"That man is no good. You can't stop what you want to do," Malaika urged. "Not for him. No one trusts him. You are a real teacher, not like him. He's just a goat. Do you know what I think?" Kwamboka waited for Malaika to continue. "That you should start your own school. Many parents will be happy for their children to go to you," Malaika said.

"I can't do that."

"I've heard women saying that their children talk about you. They want to be in your class. They want you to be their teacher."

"I am only teaching the children for a short while. The universities will be open soon. That's what I want to do."

"No. That's not what you want to do." Kwamboka broke away from her. She walked briskly to a *matatu* and handed the letter to the driver. The sun beat on her head, her skin glistened with sweat. "Start your own school. I know this is what you really want," Malaika said. "This would be great. A school where you could teach what you wanted. You could speak Gusii all day. You could tell stories whenever you wanted. And the children will learn many things. It will be the most famous school in Kisii. And there would be no Ondari."

"I can't start a school because I want to," she said.

"Yes you can," Malaika insisted. "There are many private schools, more all the time. You can use the house." Malaika put her arm across Kwamboka's shoulder. They began walking to the Malaika's place. "Then we can get parents to build a new school. I'll give you the land."

Lena protested.

"Everyone will want to send a child here. There will be *harambee* like there has never been before. No one will want to go to Kabungu School anymore."

Malaika told her customers to bring their children to her shop on Saturday. Kwamboka was going to teach the children there. That morning, soon after breakfast, children gathered in front of the house. They stood by the front door, ten deep.

"Why are they here?" Kwamboka asked.

Malaika smiled. "How should I know?"

Kwamboka stepped outside. She put her right hand on the head of one of the children.

"What do you want, Queenie?" she asked. "Why are you at my house this morning?"

"I've come for your story," the girl said. She sat on the front step. Queenie picked at a scab on her elbow.

"And you, Anna."

"I've come to hear a story."

All the same: for a story.

Kwamboka walked briskly into the house.

"What did you do, Malaika?"

"The children want you to talk to them," she said. "I, too, want to hear a story."

On Monday, when she returned to school, Kwamboka found Ondari waiting at the gate. He told her that she was no longer allowed on the school compound.

By the week's end, so many people patronized Malaika's shop there wasn't enough room to seat them all. Fathers wanted to know more, mothers wanted to learn when the school was going to open.

Wherever Kwamboka went people quizzed her not only about the proposed school but also about alleged embezzlement at Kabungu School. As best she could, Kwamboka tried to make clear that she had no indication of anything untoward at the school. There were a few, however, who expressed anger towards her. Malaika reassured her that they were Ondari's cronies.

"I don't think you realize how involved this is."

"Well," Malaika countered, "I don't think you realize how important this is."

"I know it is important."

"Then you'll do it. I am going to start clearing the land behind the house. That's where we'll have the school."

Competing versions of Kwamboka's reason for leaving Kabungu Primary spread through the area. A professor educated in America teaching at a *harambee* school—no one of her stature would take such a position; she must be a spy. Her leaving Kabungu after a confrontation with the head teacher—this is what happens when a woman gets too educated; no self-respecting man could work with her.

Those who had bribed to the school committee to secure a teaching position led the way with charges against Kwamboka. Who was this woman to turn her back on a position that was coveted eagerly by so many others? Her arrogance was galling. She had been given the job out of pity and now this ingratitude. She called herself a professor, a doctor. Where was the proof that she had gone to university or had taught anywhere for that matter? There was no reason to believe her. What they knew is only what she told them. She flouted government regulations—who did she think she was?

Rumor was that she had lived with a European in Nairobi. Accusations of witchcraft swept conversations back and forth along the main road, on the lanes and footpaths, as jealousy and indignation mixed in a poisonous brew.

Malaika's business flourished with a new vigor as the Kwamboka became more prominent. The dress shop had more work than it could handle. No longer able to keep up with the demand, customers were informed they would have their garments ready within a week's time. Even this was optimistic. No one complained. The busier she became the more she was sought out. Despite the daily darkening of afternoon clouds bringing thunder and lightning with downpours as Kisii moved into the rainy season, people continued to arrive from every part of the district. Clothes that had been neglected for years suddenly were in need of repair. Trousers, hats, shirts, vests, and even shorts succumbed to her needle and deft fingers.

"More money for the school," Malaika said. "It won't be long before we have the new school building."

"I'm afraid you're working too much. You are looking very tired. And I know you aren't sleeping well. You have to rest."

"You do your work and I'll do mine. We'll have enough for the school, you'll see."

Kwamboka was becoming clearer about her goals. Like her grandmother, she said—"A story I am coming."

Malaika and Kwamboka placed wooden stakes in the grass demarcating the site for the new building and they tried to imagine children on the grounds around the house.

Several families contributed small amounts of money. But funds raised from interested parents could meet only part of the expenses, even with volunteer teachers for the first year. The school would not be completely self-sufficient, not immediately, perhaps not ever, she knew. Whatever money she had saved while in the States she was ready to devote to the project. She was ready to spend every cent she had.

〰〰〰〰〰
〰〰〰〰〰

KWAMBOKA BEGAN TO MAKE plans for her friend's visit. She bought another bed, which she squeezed into her room. Kwamboka looked at herself in the mirror that rested next to the washing bowl. How quickly she had become a woman of the land, Kwamboka thought as she oiled her arms and legs and massaged her cracked heels. Her hands were stained with the rich, ferrous soil and she wore a headscarf most of the time.

Some days Malaika worked diligently, but more and more she woke later and worked only a few hours before retiring to her room for long naps.

With sketches drawn, Kwamboka could visualize the school: a compact structure, whitewashed walls, a balcony of the second floor, a tiled room and, as important, a children's flower garden.

"Will you come back?" Malaika asked when Kwamboka told her she was going to meet Lena in Nairobi. "You once left and didn't return for many years."

"Of course I will be back, Malaika. I promise."

Malaika was unable to go to the roadside with Kwamboka to meet the Sakawa Express, but several school supporters with their children were there to see her off.

"Take care."

The bus was filled with passengers each of whom had an opinion about events that were roiling the country as, for the first time, Kenya faced a contested presidential election.

"Tea pickers from Luoland were chased from the estates. They were evicted from their quarters by Kipsigis."—"In Kericho, women and children were taken from their houses." —"The police stood there as they were slaughtered like cows."—"These are rumors. You were fanning the flames by repeating such nonsense."—"What do you know? I tell you, I heard this myself."—"The government is behind this. They are paying to kill people. *Nyayo.* Footsteps. The footsteps are that of an elephant trampling. Moi is stirring this up for his re-election."

Kwamboka listened with her head down, looking at the folds in her dress.

Why hadn't she warned Lena, told her to come another time? Talk about sharpening *pangas* frightened her.

"What do you think?" Kwamboka was challenged. "Are you Kisii or one of them? Let me see your card."

"She's Kisii. I know about her," another passenger responded. "She came from America and is probably running back there now."

"Leave her alone. She's a good woman."

"Why are you on her side?"

"Stop! We're all Kisii here. Let's not kill one another."

"She's no Kisii."

"Shut up or I'll throw you off the bus myself."

Everyone went quiet. The stale air put most to sleep as the bus continued across the Rift Valley and into the highlands on the east side, reaching Nairobi before sunset.

That night Kwamboka sat on a bench in the waiting room outside customs control. Soldiers in combat fatigues and red berets, the barrels of their rifles pointing to the ground, approached her. They questioned her, then let her remain seated under the Sportsman signboard.

At last the doors of the customs area opened. Passengers from three European flights began leaving with their luggage. And there was Lena, disheveled from the nearly 24-hour-long flight, her hair cut to her shoulders and dyed bright red. Her nails matched her hair.

Kwamboka was shaking as she clutched her friend. They held each other without words. Kwamboka took Lena's luggage and brought to a waiting taxi that took them to town.

Genius

~~~~~~~~
~~~~~~~~

*E*ASY TO CALL IT A MID-LIFE crisis but it was something more. In opening himself to the transience of all things, Junius felt as though after having walked in a fog of disconsolation the light of awareness was too bright to bear.

He wasn't looking to return to what he had known; he knew he couldn't retrieve what he had lost but was seeking something different, a kind of acceptance that the cherry festival had pointed to and what the books he acquired there evoked. His trip to Japan, the appearance on Masuda's show, but mostly his visit to Kyoto had cut him loose and set him adrift.

In a business defined by gangsters and drugs, Junius stayed clean. But now he toyed with the idea of finding something to lift him out of himself and allow him walk in a land of beyond vacuity. Japan wouldn't let him go and he turned his back on the endless offers of crack, weed and smack. Drugs would be just one more escape from the world he had glimpsed, one constantly changing yet timeless, the world of gods who laugh. He wanted to be awake, to know the river in which he stood. Junius also believed that the government was behind the drug epidemic, giving it an excuse to declare a war on African Americans.

For a story regarding allegations that record companies stole royalties from black songwriters, a *Rolling Stone* reporter quoted Junius as saying that African Americans were "fucked-over by white owners who dominated the industry."

"Look. I know what I'm talking about," he told the reporter on the phone. "I've been a promoter, a producer, an agent.

I own pieces of record companies. Shit, I wrote songs that were hits and never collected a nickel."

"Which are those?" the reporter asked.

"Nada. Some connected guy put his name on it."

"What do you know about Mo Levy?" he was asked.

Junius avoided answering.

"Off the record," the reporter assured him.

Junius didn't believe him.

"It obvious, isn't it? How many African Americans do you know besides me who are in the business end?" he challenged the reporter. "Why do you think white kids own mansions while black artists are given prison bunks?"

After the article appeared, other magazines reported on the exploitation of African American musicians.

"Hey, Genius," he heard the caller announce.

Did he say Junius or genius?

"Someone told me you don't like octopus no more," the deep voice continued. "That's not a smart thing for a genius to do. You know, it kind of gets in your blood this octopus thing. I thought you liked it."

Junius kept quiet.

"Once you take a bite, you know, you just gotta stay with it, you know what I mean? Not go for another fish or nothing. Do you know about food poisoning? It can kill ya."

Octopus, Levy's street name.

"So listen. Genius. I'll give you a little lesson in etiquette here you shouldda learnt from your mother. When you eat, you keep your mouth shut. That's what my mother taught me, you know what I mean? She also said you don't shit where you eat. That's what my father used to say. So you outta thank me, genius. You know, keep me in your prayers and shit. I'm just telling ya for you own health. Stick with octopus."

"Yeah, well," Junius finally said, "I never liked octopus or any other fish." He couldn't think of anything else to say. From then on, Junius carried his gun on him.

He took down from his shelf a book, one he acquired in Japan, one he hadn't read since his trip two years before. When he opened the book, it fell open to this story:

A student came to a teacher to learn the way of wisdom. For years he sat with the master but not once did the teacher teach a lesson. Not once did the master perform a miracle.

Finally the student said, "I came to learn the way of wisdom from you but you haven't taught me anything."

"You haven't been paying attention," the teacher said. "Every day I have been teaching."

"What have you taught?"

"When I am hungry I eat; when I am tired I sleep."

'There are no coincidences,' Junius mused when he finished reading the parable. For the next few weeks, he evaluated his life through the prism of the story: what was he hungry for, what does he do when he's tired? Business deals, contracts, bank accounts, meetings, travel, auditors, lawyers, advisors, wise guys and gangstas pushed music so far away that it was beyond his hearing. Junius recognized how he was nearly deaf to the sounds and rhythms to which he had danced and sung and made love.

He opened another book. This time a poem: "An octopus pot—/ swimming there a fleeting dream/ beneath the summer moon."

Reporters assumed he had something to hide when he refused to talk to him. He had made a decision—he would rid himself of all interests in the music business, no matter the loss He sold his cars and Manhattan condo, and bought an apartment in Brooklyn Heights not far from the harbor.

At first as phrases came to him, snatches of melodies, riffs, then entire songs that he heard in his head. Once more he sought out music to listen to and many nights he put on Miles and there was "Bye, Bye, Blackbird," and then the music rushed in; he hummed and finally sang and when he did he dreamed of walking with Candace on a strand of warm beach.

Leaving the life that had always been wrapped around music in one way or another was one thing; starting over was another. Junius didn't know what he would do without his work. What would he do when there was nothing but more time?

〰〰〰〰〰
〰〰〰〰〰

AT THE GOTHAM BOOK MART he bought books on mystical philosophies and at Kinokuniya Bookshop purchased novels and poems. He read them slowly and aloud, repeating the Japanese poems several times, learning to appreciate blank spaces.

Stocks that bought on the advice of his broker were spectacularly successful. But the sense of inadequacy he felt became clearer to him. For a long time he had attributed the feelings of inferiority to racism, as his accountant and lawyer were white. The feeling of deficiency, he now recognized, had surfaced at times with Candace when she talked about plays. He shook his head as if understood her references. He could hear his mother's dismay the day college was traded for the army.

For years Junius had been educating himself but this, he admitted, was like the self-taught musician: while a prodigy might succeed without a teacher, all talent benefits from instruction. His thinking needed to be molded. Correction, direction and encouragement—that's what was missing.

He applied to City College, hoping to pick up what he had missed more than decades before. He could receive life credits, he was told, if he majored in business or music. But Junius didn't want either. He needed new ways of understanding. There is no quick way to enlightenment; he needed the discipline of time.

~~~~~~

JUNIUS SAT AMONGST STUDENTS at least a generation younger than himself; sometimes he was with teachers his junior. For each class he had a notebook that by the end of the semester was filled. He always arrived early took a seat in the front row.

"Hey, old man," a student would tease. Junius didn't mind.

At the end of his sophomore year, needing to declare a major, he chose history because he did well in the introductory course. When he took "The History of New York City from 1624-1900," the excitement he felt when he first read about Weeksville was resurrected. His advisor quickly approved Junius's proposal for his senior thesis, "The lives of free blacks in New York before the Civil War."

Most of Junius's research took him to the Schomberg, in Manhattan, but when he heard about the newly-opened Weeksville Heritage Center, he made several visits to Bedford-Stuyvesant to examine their archives.

"Is this the first time you've been back to that neighborhood since you were a teenager?" his advisor asked. "Have you been avoiding it?"

If Dr. Brooks weren't black, he might have taken offense.

"What's it like?"

"The alley I used to play in had a name, Hunterfly Road. When I was coming up, the houses there boarded up. Now they are being rehabbed."

"How about your old street?"

"I guess pretty much like everything else around there."

"You know, I once went back to my neighborhood in Detroit. I was surprised. Things looked different when you were a kid. You need to see it again, get a new perspective."

Although his childhood house was only a few blocks from the Weeksville Center, Junius said he hadn't gone to his street.

"The subway's the other way."

"Walk around the next time you go," Brooks urged. "By the time you're finished with your paper, you'll know as much about Weeksville as anyone. You ought to see everything for yourself. It's a great chance. History is often turning over old ground with a new shovel. But here is new ground to till."

Junius said that when he completed his paper, he would be through with academia.

"What do you plan to do then?" Brooks asked.

Junius didn't know, but Brooks' question gnawed at him. He accepted the challenge to find out for himself what had kept him away.

After walking several blocks in what he thought was the right direction, Junius took out a street map from his windbreaker to get his bearings. Most street names were unfamiliar and where he thought Dean should be was Bergen. He swore that Saratoga was Howard. Had there been a Kingsborough Walk? The only certain landmark was the railroad above Atlantic Avenue. A few blocks on he found his old street.

The area was as bleak as he had feared. Every house was gone, in its place a graffiti-covered concrete wall on one side and the other nothing but a lot with weeds, a few dandelions and a lone ailanthus tree. He stood for a few minutes trying to place exactly where his house would have been on the block.

According to his map, there was a subway stop on another line just a couple of blocks away that would take him back to Brooklyn Heights.

Something poked his back and Junius turned.

"Give me," was all the teenager said in a flat voice, his eyes glazed in the all-too familiar gaze of a crack addict. As he rocked on his heels to steady himself, he brandished a butcher knife in Junius's face.

"Sure, man," Junius said reaching towards his back pocket. He pulled out his pistol. The teenager lunged at Junius, slashing open the side of Junius's windbreaker. Junius raised his gun and fired. The mugger ran into the doorway of an apartment house.

Blood stuck to Junius's fingers. Wrapping the gun in his handkerchief, he tossed the pistol onto the shredded seat of an abandoned car.

His side began to ache as he continued towards the subway. He stopped, placed his hand through the rip in his jacket and pressed his palm hard against the wound.

A patrol cruiser approached Junius and slowed next to him as he continued his halting walk. The cop scrutinized Junius as the car continued to roll next to him. Junius remained silent, not turning to acknowledge the cops; the cop continued to watch him. Junius now stopped, dazed and teetering. The car stopped beside him but still Junius didn't turn to look.

When Junius began to walk again, the car followed at his side until the end of the block, then turned at the corner.

Junius stopped again. His hand was covered with blood. There were dark red drops on the sidewalk. He couldn't remember if he had wiped his fingerprints from the gun.

A TEENAGER FOUND JUNIUS's discarded pistol in the hulk. He used it in a street fight that ended in the murder of another teenager. The dead youth had no identification and when the police cursorily inquired about him, not a single person claimed to know the victim; no would say who the shooter might be. The police department didn't send detectives to investigate. It was only one of 1,348 registered homicides in the city that year.

The teenager was buried in a pauper's grave in Long Island Sound, on Hart Island, next to David's Island.

Junius didn't know how he got to the hospital, but after a four-hour wait in the emergency room, he received five stitches and released.

Ogres

〰〰〰〰
〰〰〰〰

*G*ROGG*Y* FROM THE TIME CHANGE and the four-hour trip in the Peugeot taxi from Nairobi to Kisii, some months after receiving Kwamboka's letter Lena began her three-month long visit. She pulled herself out from under the woolen blanket that had kept her warm during the cold night and opened the curtains. The cawing of crows and owl-like hoot of mourning doves, the lowing of cows and the motor of a long-haul truck shifting gears on a nearby road drifted into the room. The air was redolent of morning dew and wood smoke.

By a hedge next to the house Kwamboka was standing with a young woman with ashen skin. The woman gestured to the little farm beyond the hedge.

"The night you were gone," she heard the woman say. "There was a storm. Lightning, lots of lightning and thunder and hail that covered the ground. But look," she continued. "The plant is chopped. It's from a *panga*. The maize, too. They've been cut to the ground. This is the work of nightrunners. They are jealous of me. And you. Witches— last year they killed a cow. The cow was healthy one day and dead on its side the next morning."

"You think witches are behind this, Malaika?" Kwamboka asked.

"No question. Last year they caught one after a trap was laid. She was burned by her neighbors. After that the nighrunning stopped. But another has come. These people want for you to go away with your school plan."

"If they are after me," Kwamboka asserted, "I have to put a stop to the school. I can't put you in danger."

"I've dealt with worse men. Besides, stopping the school won't do any good. We are successful. They are jealous. I know who they are these witches. They will be taken care of. Not to worry."

As Kwamboka and Malaika walked away from the house, Lena couldn't make out what they were saying. She only overhears: "You are not leaving the school."

Malaika caught sight of Lena at the window.

"Your American, she is awake. Come. Everyone wants to greet her. Bring her out." Malaika was short of breath. She rubbed her neck.

Kwamboka walked back to the house.

"This is the guest I have brought, my American friend, Lena. Lena, this is Malaika." The gathering has followed her to the house. Kwamboka continues in Gusii, addressing the small crowd. "Our guest from America has come to say hello to us. Let's all greet her. Her name is Lena Morrell."

Malaika said has never seen anyone with her hair color.

"You are nyekundu," Malaika said.

"Red, in Swahili," Kwamboka translated.

"You are tall like a giraffe."

Lena couldn't help noticing Malaika's pallor.

Ululations issued from women's throats and children arranged themselves in a line.

"This is a song for you, Lena. A praise song," Kwamboka explained as she takes her hand. "I told them you were coming. I described my red-headed American friend to them."

"A white bird has flown over the water/ Welcome red-head bird/ Welcome, professor's friend/ Come and dance, tall bird/ Come, white and red/ Our new American friend."

Malaika watched. A chair is taken out for Lena. Malaika sits on her haunches next to her.

"Some day," Malaika began, "I'm going to have a bath tub in the house and a television." With her fingertips she lightly rubs the back of Lena's hand. "Are all Americans like this?"

"What do you mean?"

"This," she explains, as she touches the marks on Lena's skin.

"Some. Not all."

"What are these spots? Are you sick?"

"Freckles. I've always had them."

"So you're not sick?"

Lena assured her she wasn't.

Malaika fingered Lena's hair.

"This is something amazing," she says. "I've never seen hair this color."

"When I was young, it was like this. Now that I'm getting old, I have to buy something and put it on it to get it this color."

"Like fire," Malaika said as she stroked Lena's hair. "You feel like a cat."

〰〰〰〰
〰〰〰〰

"I SAW ONDARI AT THE MARKET," Kwamboka told Malaika.

"Ondari?" Kwamboka hadn't meant for Lena to hear. "Have I met her?" Lena asked.

"He's an ugly man," Malaika inserted.

"He has been giving me a hard time about opening a school," Kwamboka offered.

"He uses witchcraft."

"You don't know that, Malaika," Kwamboka reprimanded.

"The reason I am telling you is that this time it was different. He said that with the elections a new government might institute a new policy. He said maybe I was right after all."

"Don't believe him."

Lena watched the two women, trying to make sense of the conversation.

"I think he is hedging his bets." Kwamboka explained the expression to Malaika. "He doesn't want me to think he was behind our problems."

"Like my being sick. He has put a curse on me. You'll see how I'll get better once he's gone."

Malaika hunched over with a hacking cough.

"Has the doctor given her medication?" Lena asked Kwamboka.

"I don't go to doctors."

"See if you can convince her, Lena. I've tried my best. As you can see, she has a mind of her own. Sometimes like a donkey."

As Lena and Malaika sat together for most of the afternoon, Malaika played with Lena's hair. She asked about her red nails; Lena taught her how to apply polish. Lena talked about New York, the two of them laughed about all the men they had known. Lena regretted her levity when she connected Malaika's illness with how she had saved enough money to open a shop of her own.

Malaika reiterated. "I will get better once the witch is gone." Her fever spiked that night, although it returned to normal by morning, Kwamboka summoned a doctor without Malaika's consent. He listened to her wheezing. The doctor wrote a prescription, took a syringe from his medicine bag and wiped the needle with a cloth and pricked Malaika.

When the doctor left, Malaika's fever subsided. She took Lena by the hand and led her outside to show her a bathtub propped against the house wall.

"Do you have a tub in your house?" she asked. "Soon I will have this inside and I will sit in it like I am at the great lake." She calls Kwamboka over. "Do you know that professor tells stories?" Before Lena could answer, she commands Kwamboka to tell one to them. "I want to hear about ogres again. Tell Nyekundu about ogres."

A long time ago there were only human beings. There were other animals, of course. But animals that walked around on two legs—for that there were only people.

Human beings had good lives and were mostly good people. There were the usual squabbles and disagreements but, all in all, life was agreeable.

There were times when people went hungry and had to scrimp to stay alive. So everyone worked hard to make sure that there was enough food for both good times and bad.

Everyone, that is, except one fellow. He preferred sleeping to sowing, playing to weeding, and running to reaping. The village elders met with him but always with the same result—nothing.

So the elders sent him away. However, while banishment to the forest solved one problem it created another. Now on his own, he became mean and vengeful. This caused bumps to grow on his skin and his eyes to narrow. He became so ugly he was frightening.

One day he abducted a girl who had gone to the riverside for water. At first people said that it was a crocodile that snatched the girl. But finally everyone agreed: it was the dreadful man who was responsible for the deed.

The monster had many children and each with a temper worse than its parent. The children were called ogres and these creatures were no longer thought of as belonging to the human family.

"That's a very good story," Malaika said. Turning to Lena, she added, "But I don't think the elders should have sent him away. They should have burned him, then the girl would be safe and that would be the end of ogres."

Each day children came to see the white stranger with red hair and painted nails, the woman from America who was sleeping in an African's house and walked to the market to buy vegetables and fruit. The noiseless children startled Lena the first time she saw them staring at her, sometimes by the door, sometimes by the window, wide-eyed and intent on watching her every gesture.

"Do you want me to close the curtains?" Kwamboka asked.

"Am I so strange to them?"

"When I was a girl, I used to do the same with the European missionaries. I watched everything they did: the way they walked, the way they ate sitting on chairs around a table, the sounds they made and the way they waved their hands while talking. We girls would boost each other up to look into the window. The priests and the nuns would chase us away, but we always came back and they eventually stopped trying."

"It feels a little like I'm on display, like an animal in the zoo. But I don't mind, really I don't."

"You are a wonder to them."

〰〰〰〰〰
〰〰〰〰〰

A NOTE PINNED TO THE DOOR of one of the school's supporters.

THIS IS KIPSIGIS COUNTRY
LEAVE OR YOU WILL BE FORCED TO LEAVE
ALL KISII MUST GO BY THE 5TH

NO EXCEPTIONS

THIS LAND BELONGS TO KIPSIGIS!!!

Near Kabungu sixteen people were found with charms. The chief of police urged residents not to take matters into their own hands by burning, beating or lynching the suspects.

More pressing to Kwamboka was Malaika's deteriorating health and Lena's impending return to the States.

"My visa is for a few months," Lena said. "I don't want to leave you here. You can't work on the school and take care of Malaika. I'll arrange for a leave of absence."

"You can't do that."

"And I'll change my plane ticket."

"You have to get back," Kwamboka insisted.

Kwamboka feared that she wouldn't be able to protect Lena and care for Malaika at the same time. While her friend was a great support, she was also a burden.

"What you can do," Kwamboka continued, "is find a clinic in the States to treat Malaika. We'll send her there for treatment."

Lena knew there was no cure.

Again Malaika insisted that she didn't need better medical care.

"I'm not leaving here."

"I'll go with you," Kwamboka assured her.

"Take me to Mombasa. There are famous sorcerers there. I want to see the ocean with my own eyes. That water there is bigger than the lake, isn't it? Then when I am all better, then we will visit Nyekundu."

Ondari encountered Kwamboka in the market.

"I am worried," he told Kwamboka as at a table behind a tin shack restaurant. He ordered a beer for himself and a soda for Kwamboka. "Maybe you are sick, like Malaika.

That's what some are saying. I don't believe such a thing. But if you want a diviner, I will take you to one, a woman I consulted myself."

"You are too kind," Kwamboka said, barely able to control her sarcasm. But to walk away would only invite more enmity. "The only sickness I know is children not getting a good education. I will have my school, Ondari, I am telling you."

"Yes, I hope you do, professor. The more schools the better. Yours will be a great one, I know. But I want to talk to you about something else. In Bosongo there is a meeting place, by the Mwalimu Hotel, the headquarters of the new party formed against the president's. There is discussion about supporting Kisii candidates, not toadies who do the president's bidding. And these people, they say they are worried about you."

"Oh, get to it, Ondari. I have work to do."

"Your name was mentioned. I am not a political person myself. I wasn't there. But a good source, a friend who should know told me . . ."

Kwamboka rose to leave.

"Your name was said, that you should stand for parliament."

Kwamboka couldn't control her laughter.

"Don't laugh. They said a woman needs to be in parliament from Kisii."

"Who said that?"

"I don't know names. But it is true."

Kwamboka stared at Ondari, who drained his bottle.

Despite her desire to leave, she added, "No one knows me."

"You are a famous person, professor. You came back from America to start a school. You came from America to Kabungu and in every location in Kisii you are known."

Kwamboka could smell his beery breath.

"There are other women."

"Not educated like you. A doctor. A professor. Who could win against you?"

"You are a funny man, Ondari," Kwamboka said, picking up her bundle of vegetables. "I have to get back to my work. Find a better way to spend your time."

As she walked to the road, Ondari called, "You are a great woman, professor, a great woman. Remember me when you are even greater."

<hr />

GIFTS WERE BROUGHT AS FAREWELL PRESENTS: a *kanga* with the Swahili inscription *Elimu Ni Nuru Isiyo Zima*—"The light of education never goes out," Kwamboka translated—a large packet from Nyansiongo Tea Factory; a wooden, beaded stool; a basket with a cowhide base; and a six-inch high soapstone carving of a mother cradling a child. Kwamboka and Lena discussed Malaika's desire to go with them to Nairobi. She had never been there and wanted to see tall buildings made of glass. Perhaps visiting the capital would lift her spirits, the women thought. They decided, however, that it would too much for her.

"Come back," Malaika told Kwamboka.

"I will return on Friday," Kwamboka tried to re-assure her but Malaika wasn't assuaged. Without saying goodbye, Malaika went to the house before the minivan arrived. She believed that Kwamboka would go to America with Nyekundu.

Dozens of checkpoints along the highway, some established by police and others by civilians demanding a toll to travel the road, slowed their journey. Money passed hands at each stop. Detours took them on narrow, dusty roads, one deviation putting them behind a carrier that rattled with crates of bottles.

After passengers alighted at Chepseon, Kwamboka and Lena continued as the only passengers. Where the road hugged the edge of the Mau Forest, three men stepped in front of their vehicle. One pointed a *panga* at the driver.

"What's he saying?"

"He's telling everyone to get out."

The driver and the two women stood next to the van. The gang looked at them and one engaged the driver in Swahili.

"He wants to know where we've come from. The driver told him we're from Kisii."

The leader walked to Lena, his *panga* dangling on one side, a club on the other.

"What does he want?"

Before Kwamboka had a chance to respond, the man wearing a blue shirt and black shorts asks Lena, in English, "Are you missionary?"

Lena stood several inches above the man. Her breath steadied," she said, "No. I am a visitor." She straightened to appear even taller.

""Let me talk," Kwamboka whispers.

"You keep quiet," he says as he waves the club at Kwamboka. "Who are *you*?"

"I am a teacher in Kisii."

"Are you Kisii?"

"I am Kenyan. I am coming from Kisii."

"She's not Kenyan! Look at us," he says as he scrapes his *panga* on the ground in front of Lena. "We're Kenyans. But you look like Kisii." She stared at Kwamboka. "You're educated, isn't it?"

"I studied in America," Kwamboka offered.

"Me. I wasn't so lucky. Did this woman get you a scholarship?" He gestured towards Lena.

"No. I met her there. In America."

"Now I met her here."

The driver intervenes and asks how much the bandits want.

"Look at her," the man in the shorts calls to the others. "The teacher says we're all Kenyans. So maybe this white woman she is Kenyan, too. She's thin like Maasai. And her hair is the color like theirs. I think she *is* Maasai. Albino Maasai. That right, isn't it?"

They laugh. Lena stares at them. Her face flushes with anger.

Kwamboka takes out two fifty-shilling notes.

"Don't insult me." He holds his *panga* against Lena's throat. Lena stiffens.

"This one is worth a lot."

"Take what you want," Kwamboka says, gesturing to the luggage on the roof rack

The leader lowers the *panga*, rubs Lena's arm, as if trying to see if her freckles will come off.

"Listen," Lena says. "I have something in my suitcase for you. Take it down, please. I'll show you."

One of the young men tosses the suitcase to his confederate. She shows him Walkman and puts in a CD. She attempts to put the headphones over the leader's ears. He shoves her hand away.

"When I get back to the States, I'll mail you whatever you want. Tell me where to send it."

"Your shoes," he says, pointing at her feet with his *panga*. "Give me your shoes."

"You want these? You can have them. I have more in my bag. These are dirty, but if you want them you can have them. And when I get back to New York, I'll get a pair of Air Jordans for you. You know those sneakers? Pump ups. Everybody has a pair. What's your size? Five inches? I bet you're five inches."

He stares at her.

"I see you can use a jacket. I'll get a leather jacket for you."

"Shut up!" He raises the *panga*. "You are what I want."

Kwamboka says, "She's expected at the American embassy tomorrow. She's a famous person . . ."

"Who is she?" the leader interrupts.

"She was on television last week. She's the most famous librarian in America. She is here to set-up libraries in Kenya. Her picture was in all the newspapers."

As Lena begins to speak, the leader says to Kwamboka, "Shut up or I'll cut your tongue out."

Lena glares at one of the subordinates.

"Leave her alone," Kwamboka says. "You want something, take it from me, but leave her alone. You don't know what you're doing. Do you think the Americans will let you get away with this? The vice-president himself will be at the meeting with her tomorrow. If she doesn't show up . . ." Kwamboka lets the sentence hang.

The leader turns to Lena and runs his eyes up her body.

"You're right. We don't harm anyone. It's just a little sugar to make our day sweeter." He points his *panga* at Lena's temple. "I like this."

Lena removes her dangling earrings.

"And the shoes. I'll take these."

She removes her walking shoes.

"And something for the boys," he says, gesturing to the young men leaning against the van.

She gives them her portable player and CDs. They take out the discs from the jewel cases and hold them up to reflect the sun like mirrors.

The leader places his *panga* on the hood the taxi and shakes Lena's hand, then Kwamboka's. He says something in Swahili and continues, "Nice doing business with you. Be careful. There are killings going on."

He helps the driver secure the luggage.

"What did he say to you?" Lena asks as they pull away.

"He said you weren't an albino after all. He called you a *chotara*, a half-caste."

Lena laughed.

"He also said you were an idiot."

The *matatu* continued, crested the Mau Escarpment and descended onto the valley floor. Several more police blockades slowed their trip. The taxi wended its way up the switchbacks on the steep face of the east escarpment. In the Nairobi suburbs they encountered roads made slick by a brief downpour and were further delayed by minor accidents and traffic jams on city streets.

What should have been a four-hour journey had stretched into ten.

The room in the New Stanley was down a narrow, dark corridor with a threadbare carpet. Lena dropped her suitcase on the floor and Kwamboka sat on the bed in the cramped room. They quickly rinsed off the red dirt. Lena went to the bathroom, delighted to find a soaking tub and working hot water.

"I'll draw a bath for you. It'll be ready soon. I'll take mine after you."

"Malaika would have loved this" Kwamboka said. "I'll have to make sure I get her tub connected as soon as I get home."

"It would be a wonderful present for her."

Kwamboka took a Coke from the refrigerator, removed her shoes, took a sip and closed her eyes. Lena had removed her own sweated T-shirt and tossed it under the bathroom sink and waited for the water to slowly fill the long, narrow tub.

She gently woke Kwamboka.

"The bath's ready."

"Here," and before Kwamboka could protest, Lena had unbuttoned her friend's blouse. Kwamboka said nothing as piece-by-piece her clothes were removed. Kwamboka stepped into the tub and sank into the water that rose as high as her neck. Soap bubbles crackled and cascaded over the tub's side.

Lena stood in front of the mirror.

"I'm getting too old for this."

"What?"

"I'm just wondering, Kwamboka. Do you think it could have been different for us?"

She turned to face Kwamboka. Kwamboka sat upright and water glistened as it ran from her shoulders.

"I love you, you know."

She kneels besides the tub and takes Kwamboka's hand to place against her cheek.

"You know I can't. It's not natural."

"For you."

"Yes, for me."

"For me what is natural is doing what is right. I know my love for you is right. Acting on those feelings is natural and right."

Lena untwists the top of the shampoo bottle and pours the cream-colored liquid onto her hands and massages it in to Kwamboka's hair.

"Close your eyes."

She kisses Kwamboka on the cheek.

"Please stop, Lena." Kwamboka steps out of the tub. "I love you, too, Lena. But I can't." She takes a towel and dries herself.

In the room Lena takes a piece of paper from her suitcase, unfolds it and sits in the leather chair next to floor lamp.

"This poem, Kwamboka, is one of my favorites. I was waiting for the right time to read it to you. It's by William Carlos Williams. Do you know his work?" Kwamboka shakes her head. "He was a physician but also a poet. He became partially paralyzed from strokes and was deeply worried about nuclear war. He writes this to his wife to ask for her forgiveness. "There is something/ something urgent/ I have to say to you/ and you alone/ but it must wait/ while I drink in/ the joy of your approach,/ perhaps for the last time." She stops to look at Kwamboka. After a few moments, she continues, "I cannot say/ that I have gone to hell/ for your love/ but often/ found myself there/ in your pursuit."

"What is it that you want from me, Lena?"

"To have me here."

"What? In Kenya?"

Lena nods.

"You are asking something impossible." She shifts on the bed. "I can't have both you and school."

"Lena gets into the bed beside Kwamboka. She shuts off the light. She turns on her side and holds Kwamboka as they fall asleep.

PLANNING ON BUYING household goods not easily available upcountry, Kwamboka switched to the Hotel Embassy, a modest hotel next to the city market She would also make sure she collected the royalties from her book. Berrycloth's promise to send her the money never materialized. She walked to the Progressive Press, politely accepted a cup of tea, and when Berrycloth told her he would send her the money before the end of the month, she threatened him with a lawsuit. She walked out with a check.

As she walked along Muindi Mbingu Street looking for a cooker and utensils, from animated talk on the avenue, with people rushing down Kenyatta Avenue, it was clear that something unusual was happening in Uhuru Park. Clutching her *kiondo* under her arm, she walked towards the swelling noise. Political protesters demanding the resignation of the president had replaced exhortations of evangelists calling sinners to Jesus. Kwamboka stood across the road for several minutes before crossing to get closer.

"The women are over there," said a barefoot man in a clear white shirt pointing to a circus-size tent in front of which was the signboard: Freedom Corner.

Men stood on chairs with bullhorns, men milled around, men cheered.

Kwamboka walked to the tent. A woman at the table recorded Kwamboka's name in a ledger. Inside, only women, most wearing country clothes: *kangas*, headscarves and sandals. A few wore T-shirts demanding the release of political prisoners, the faces of their relatives silk-screened across their chests in murky black-and-white photographs.

"*Karibu*," a young womn welcomed Kwamboka. "Thank you for your support. Do you have a husband or son in detention?"

Kwamboka explained that she was there to support their cause.

"It is important to know that others stand with us."

A military truck rumbled by and the crowd outside scattered amidst shouts and cries. One woman took a chair outside, stood on it and appealed for calm. The Bedford military truck continued down the highway in the direction of the university. In the tent women broke into song. Kwamboka knew a few of the hymns and joined the chorus. When they sang in Gikuyu, she listened.

A police officer, his chest emblazoned with ribbons, appeared at the entrance and demanded the women dismantle the tent.

"Go home. This is an unlicensed and illegal demonstration."

"We go home when our men go home."

"Return to your kitchens."

He is hissed by the younger women.

"I am warning you. We have a right to act as we do."

Later the paramilitary wing of the police moves in. Stones are thrown in their direction. Gunfire, traces of tear gas seep into the tent, the entrance flaps are tied tight.

The officer who had appealed to the women early returned, this time delivering a letter from the president's office.

The strike leader opens the sealed envelope.

"Your actions are a "potential threat to security in Nairobi," she reads aloud.

"You must leave immediately," the office repeats.

"When our men are released. That's when we will leave," the woman says in a soft voice. "Please tell the honorable president that is what we want."

Riots erupted on the streets, cars were torched, buses stoned and shops owned by Indians looted, boys running off with shirts, toilet paper, tea and trousers.

In the dark the police raided the tent and battered the protesters with their batons. Several protesters bared their breasts, daring the police to beat them. They were obliged. The women were corralled outside while the tent was bulldozed. A police carrier arrived. The only sound Kwamboka could hear from inside the van was the keening of sirens.

No one took the women's names at the police station. The detainees were put into cells without electricity, water, cots or toilets. A song broke the silence and just as quickly faded. The strikers were tired, in pain, exhausted.

The following morning, without explanation, the women were released.

Malaika died not long after Kwamboka returned. There was no cure for the slim disease in which the body wasted away.

The Thing Itself

〰〰〰〰〰〰
〰〰〰〰〰〰

*I*N THE LABYRINTHINE STRAND Book Store, a place Lena patronized not only for its stacks of obscure, out-of-print and valued books but also because it was one of the few that employed a unionized workforce, she bought a book by a poet she had not heard of before. She liked the title—*26 Ways Of Looking At A Black Man*—and puts it in her tote bag. At home she reads, "Always I hope to find/ The blackman I know,/ Or one who knows him."

Lena wasn't a collector as much as an accumulator. She culled a few books each time she moved, from Manhattan to Brooklyn to Queens and finally to Washington Heights, but it didn't take long before new purchases replaced their discarded predecessors. She considered her accumulating as benign or, when she was in a generous mood, as a socially beneficial habit.

She put the book down only to discover a copy of a Wallace Steven's poems buried amongst the jumble on the floor. She picks it up and compares it with its new-found offspring. "A man and a woman/ Are one./ A man and a woman and a blackbird / Are one."

Lena called crossing paths with Junius a coincidence, as she always did to explain chance encounters and while Junius didn't exactly believe that everything happened for a reason, he had some notion of karma or destiny.

"Two books about black men and now we meet again and you think this is merely a coicidence?" he said.

In the past, she would have retorted that you can't square determinism with free will, but this line of engagement no longer interested her. People believed all sorts of illogical things and she had come to accept that no idea—however irrational—predicted the character of a person. Stevens guided her—"not ideas about the thing but the thing itself" is what matters.

Lena was no longer working at NYU, having been denied promotion from associate to full curator at the library in 2004. Her tenured position protected her from being fired but it didn't shield her from harassment. The administration didn't want a woman who sided with graduate students petitioning to form their own union. Anti-labor was built into the university's bones, Lena believed, knowing that the first union strike was against NYU when, in order to keep down construction costs for the new college they by-passed skilled stonecutters by using prisoners from Sing Sing.

After retiring she worked for a Manhattan councilwoman developing legislation around workers' rights.

The office staff was invited to an inaugural celebrations, at a id-town hotel. Banners, streamers and cascading balloons filled the chandeliered room and there, by the jumbotron, she was sure that was Junius, bearded now, sitting alone, a wan smile on his face. She waited until she was certain, then sat beside him.

"Junius?"

He turned to look at her.

"Do I know you?"

"Don't you remember?" she asked. She thought she saw a glimmer of recognition in his eyes.

Junius squinted slightly and stared. His expression changed.

"Should I?"

Lena composed herself and began to walk away.

"Sorry," she said. "I thought you were someone I once knew."

She wouldn't allow him the dignity of rebuffing her.

He reached for her arm. Looking at her hair cut chin-length on its way to gray, he asked, "Your red hair. I wasn't sure for a minute."

"Everything changes," she replied coolly, not believing him.

"Don't go away," he said. "Are you with someone?"

She made a slight gesture with her head.

"And you?" she asked.

"Your earrings are lovely," he replied. "Sit with me. Do you want something to drink?"

Lena saw a half-empty glass of wine on the sill beside him.

Their conversation revolved around their disbelief that Obama had been elected president and how they were worried that someone would try to assassinate him. They moved to a quieter table in the lobby and little by little they explained to each other how they had wound up invited to the party. Junius had contributed the maximum amount allowed by an individual to the Obama campaign and the National Democratic Committee; he also had arranged house parties where he had raised considerable funds from several of his wealthy friends.

"So you've been successful. Good for you," Lena said sincerely. Behind the obvious excitement of the occasion and the tiredness that came at the end of a long evening, she detected something else.

"Tell me about your music," Lena said.

"I haven't been involved for years," he answered.

"But you loved it."

"Everything changes."

He told her that he had been married and when his wife died, he needed to do something different.

"Do you remember when I read about my old neighborhood? It got me started. So I moved back to Brooklyn and I began to buy up buildings, rehabilitating them and reselling."

"You gave up music to become a real estate developer?"

It was incredulity, not criticism that she expressed.

"In a way you could say that," he replied. "But that's not quite the way I'd put it."

Lena breathed deeply. She seemed to have offended him.

"I just happened to be at the right place at the right time. I'd buy a wreck, work with a general contractor and resell it to a family for a fair price, to people who needed a decent place to live."

"Gentrification."

"At the very beginning, before the brownstones became a million dollars. In any case," he added, "I stopped that, too. I've made enough money. I don't need any more."

Junius refilled their glasses.

"I'm on the board of a group, the Bedford-Stuyvesant Restoration. I advise them on housing in around my old neighborhood. Rehabbing houses got me involved in preservation."

"So no music at all?"

"Not completely true. I help out kids. In an after-school music program. I wanted to do something in my old neighborhood, help a little. There's a center there now and I volunteer to help out. I've also been involved with something called Soul Summit. It's a musical festival and dance party. The city is giving them a hard time about a permit. I contacted some people I know. I think we've gotten it secured for the summer."

"If you need some help, let me know. I'll talk to the councilwoman. Maybe she can do something."

Lena finished her drink.

"Maybe we can get together sometime," he said.

"Yeah, sure."

When the giant TV screen filled with the new president and his wife on the dance floor, Junius left his seat by the ballroom door and looked for Lena in the crowded room. She was talking to a group of women. He took her hand. He held her loosely, at a distance, as they dance, and Lena's face turned red. She didn't see the tears that welled in the corners of Junius's eyes—for a black president?; for his wife? Lena, too, was overwhelmed by moment.

"I never married," Lena said when the music stopped and they returned to the hallway where the din of celebration was dampened by the carpet and cushioned furniture. "I shared a place with an African woman for a few years. I met her at NYU. She was a professor there and was my best friend."

"What happened?"

"She returned home, to Kenya," Lena said without detail. "I live alone now. Ever since she left." She expected Junius to ask a question but he waited for her to continue. "And you? Did you have children?"

""Children?" he said.

She wished she could take back her indiscretion. Her pale face flushed.

"No." He hesitated. "We wanted to. I wanted to be a father. It didn't work out."

Lena rose to leave.

"Stay," he said, turning to look directly at her and spoke to her in a way that pierced her heart. "Candace died young. We were married for only five years. I've been alone— single—since. A long time."

"I'm so sorry," she offered, stifling a cry, uncertain of its source.

"So am I."

Later she asked, "No other woman?"

"I'm not a monk," he said, "but none I ever wanted to live with. I've been happy alone."

Lena wanted to call him a liar.

They sat side-by-side, Lena with her hands on her lap, Junius tilting his chair on its back two legs. They sipped their drinks and listened to the music drift in from the ballroom. Finally they returned to the large room and danced a little more.

Lena introduced Junius to the women she had been with, her co-workers.

She called later that week.

"Can I see you?" she asked.

"If you like."

"Very much," Lena said.

They met at a midtown restaurant.

Junius asked, "Why did you leave that day?"

"That wasn't my choice."

"Yes, it was. I wanted the baby, you didn't."

"I wanted to stay. You wanted me to leave."

Junius put his arm on the brass railing beside the table and leaned forward.

"That's not how I remember it."

They said nothing for a long time.

"I'm sorry the way it worked out."

"Well, yes. But I don't like living with regrets. I wouldn't have met Candy if you stayed. I loved her. Talented, beautiful . . ."

Lena picked up the napkin that had fallen.

"Can you forgive me for what I did?"

Junius slowly answered.

"I'm not a good enough Christian for that," he said. "Or Buddhist. Some things I can't let go of. When I think about it, Lena, you know, when I really think about it"— "no, I don't forgive you."

"It sticks with me, too." Words from a Gwendolyn Brooks poem came to mind—"Abortions will not let you forget/ You remember the children you got that you did not get"—but kept it to herself.

She changed the subject to Kwamboka.

"I went to Africa once, to visit her at her home there. She's built a school for young children. I've often wanted to go back."

"Why don't you?"

"You know, we each got caught up in our own things. I would like to see her again. I often think about it. She emails every so often. You know, there's still dial-up in Kenya. She has to go to an Internet café about fifteen miles from her home."

"Did the school open?"

"Yes. She's retired now, but the school she started is successful."

The next time Junius told her about a trip to South Carolina.

"To see where my father's family came from and to see what else I could about Junius Stinney. You know, the connection between my name and his."

From his search through the Clarendon County records, it appeared that none of his father's family lived there any longer. But he did find relatives of Stinney who wanted to reopen the case and he visited Stinney's grave at the Paxville Calvary Baptist Church.

"I couldn't get the image of that young boy out of my mind. He was electrocuted, but all I could think of was 'Strange

Fruit'. You know the song? About lynchings of blacks in the South?"

"It was one of the few songs my father let me listen to," she said. "Because it was about how awful America was."

"The image of blacks swinging from trees. Lynchings and burnings. Wherever I walked I wondered if maybe it was from this tree. Whenever I saw an old white person, I couldn't help thinking about where they were, what they'd done. I couldn't get it out of my mind. I had to leave. I know things are different now, but I understood why my father's family left."

"You know the writer of that song . . ."

"Strange Fruit?"

" . . . adopted the Rosenberg kids after their parents were executed."

Junius confessed he didn't know who the Rosenbergs were and Lena talked about the Cold War, her parents and the case of the husband and wife put to death in the electric chair for passing on atomic secrets to the Soviets.

"I always thought Billie Holiday wrote the song," Junius said.

"It was Abel Meeropol, a Jew and a communist."

"Really," Junius responded. Junius remained skeptical, remembering how his songs were appropriated.

The next time they met, Lena told Junius what more she found out about Meerepol.

"He wrote the song to work for passage of an anti-lynching bill in Congress. But I also found he wrote this poem: 'I am a Jew/ How may I tell? The Negro lynched/ Reminds me well/ I am a Jew.' His poetry was really awful."

"But the lyrics, they are brilliant. You know, 'Strange Fruit.'"

And the time after that, Junius said, "The name of the commune you were at in Vermont, Hard Times, right?'

"Good memory."

"Yesterday I downloaded a song, 'Hard Times Come No More.' Tell me you still don't believe in fate."

She smiled.

"Play it for me."

Junius stood across the room as the music played; Lena stared at him. "'Tis the song, the sigh of the weary,/ Hard Times, hard times, come again no more/ Many days you have lingered around my cabin door;/ Oh hard times come again no more."

"Are you ever happy?"

"It may not seem that way to you, but I am happier now than I've been in a long time."

"But why choose such a sad song to play for me?"

"I thought you would like the coincidence." Then he added, "Somehow it lifts me up, like a spiritual, I suppose, a song of travail but also hope."

They sat together, knees touching. She then turned, put her head on the couch armrest and lay down. Junius rubbed her feet.

"Not long after she died I went back to Japan on business. It turned out to be my last time there. I sang a song on a TV show. That was the last time I've sung for anyone except myself." He stopped and glanced at Lena.

"Sing for me?"

"I can't."

She held out her hand mottled with liver spots.

"No," he said and began: "'Tis the song, the sigh of the weary."

Junius told her about how the books on Buddhism and his daily meditations had helped him and about how he attended church every so often to listen to the music. They talked about beauty and sadness.

When they next met, she read to him a poem: "It is not possible to express the most precious insights,/ To see all that craves to be seen,/ To visit even the closest neighbors in the universe,/ To learn all that needs to be learned,/ To live without dying,/ And I am sad about it./ But I lived/ And I am happy about that."

〰〰〰〰〰〰

LENA TURNED ON HER COMPUTER to read her overnight emails. She didn't recognize the sender's name and nearly trashed it.

Dear Lena Morrell

I regret to inform you that I must bring you sad news about our dear friend Dr. Kwamboka. Our beloved friend passed away by shooting. The police arrested three men. We don't understand what they wanted. This is a shock. I remember you from your visit. Kwamboka spoke about you many times. You need to know that there is a funeral service for her on 28 Feb. Words from you can be in the programme.

Prof. Kwamboka's friend and yours,

Lucy Kombo

She gasped, her legs buckled. She read it again, looking for more information, hoping that it was an email prank, but knew that it wasn't, that the worst she had feared had come to pass.

It would be days before anyone would get to the cyber café to read the reply she sent. She had Kwamboka's cell number in her contacts. She let it ring a dozen times, then tried again and again throughout the day, hoping that her friend would answer, anyone would answer, someone.

The phone buzzed in the desk drawer of the Keroka police station.

Lena called the Kenyan embassy in Washington to apply for a visa and was told that it would take several weeks to get.

"But my friend died. I have to go to the funeral."

"Send us your passport with an extra fee. We'll get it as fast as we can, but there's no guarantee. But," the clerk added, "you may be able to get a visa at the airport when you land."

"Maybe?"

"It's possible, yes."

Taking a strongbox down from her closet shelf, Lena pulled out her passport. It had lapsed. She went to the post office to have it renewed. The clerk told her that even if her application were expedited, it would take several weeks.

"I need it immediately."

"Maybe if you have an urgent reason."

"My friend died and I need to get to her funeral."

"Put that in writing. But there's no guarantee that you will get it soon. It will cost you $60, plus delivery charges."

"Fuck it!"

Searching the Internet she found an article about Kwamboka's murder on the front page of the *Standard*.

> Heavily armed gangsters on Tuesday morning gunned down a retired university lecturer in her home in Nyamira County.
>
> Prof Sarah Kwamboka died in her bedroom after three gangsters raided her home at 3 am. Kisii police boss Paul Njenga said the three youths were in police custody.
>
> No motive was given for the crime.

Prof Kwamboka lived in Kabungu since returning to Kisii, where she had been born.

The police boss said security officials had launched investigations into the killing.

Her neighbour, Lucy Kombo, told the press that the gang broke into the house through the kitchen door then moved into the bedroom where they shot her in the chest.

Lena sent another email expressing her regrets that it wasn't possible for her to attend the funeral. She extolled Kwamboka's character and commitment to Kisii, especially its children. Both emails had been received and Lucy read Lena's eulogy in the middle portion of the three-hour funeral service attended by more than a thousand people. A month later she received a DVD of the funeral and watched Lucy, surrounded by children in school uniforms, read her words to the gathering.

〰〰〰〰〰
〰〰〰〰〰

AS THEY WALKED IN THE BROOKLYN Botanic Garden by the *torii* gate when the ground was pink with freshly fallen cherry blossoms, Junius and Lena watched a ibis wade in the reflecting pond. They ate lunch at the Terrace Café.

"That TV show I told you about in Japan," he started to explain, "well, it's weird, but it made me into a celebrity there. The show has been in re-runs forever and the song I sang that day was released as a single. They never asked my permission. What else is new? But at least I get royalties. It is amazing. I've gotten many invitations to come back, but couldn't do go."

"And why are you telling me this?"

"I won't sing that song again. Not even for you. Not anywhere. But that's OK with them. My former associate,

Ito, wants me to do interviews and for me to make some guest appearances."

"This garden reminds you of Japan, doesn't it?"

"Yes." He ran his hand down the side of the glass of juice and looked into the garden. "I think being there saved me. What I saw, what I read."

A chickadee landed on a nearby table. Junius breaks off a piece of bread and holds it in his palm. The bird takes the crumbs and flits to a nearby tree. It returned several times to the table. Junius looked at Lena and said, "I'd like you to go with me."

"You're kidding. To Japan?"

"Yes."

"I don't know what to say."

"Say what you feel."

Lena turned to the garden. "The trees are amazing. So beautiful. How can I never have been here before?"

Junius waited. The chickadee sits momentarily on a branch of a budding maple and doesn't return.

"I feel like I need to think about this. Give me some time, Junius."

"I've called Ito. We're discussing it. We're thinking about December."

Junius imitates the birdcall with a whistle.

"C, D," he said. "Those are the notes."

"What?"

"The bird. C and D." He sings, "With me. With me. Me you. Me you, Ja-pan. Ja-pan."

In mid-summer Junius raised the matter of the trip again.

"I don't think so," Lena said. "I really can't afford it."

"I'm requesting you to go with me. My guest."

For weeks they talked about Junius's desire for Lena to join him.

"I'll pay for my own ticket," she said.

"Do you really want to sit cramped up all those hours? Alone? I mean, without me? I fly first-class. I have the money to make things easier. Why not take advantage of it?"

Lena remembered the endless flight to Africa, with her knees crushed by the seats in front of her, not being able to sleep.

'What do we live for if not to make life less difficult for one another?' One of her favorite aphorisms, she recalled.

She bargained with him. She'd pay the difference between first-class and an economy ticket, still an amount that hurt her bank account, bothered by the unfairness of separate classes of passengers.

In December they were on a JAL flight to Tokyo. Lena handed Junius a small package wrapped in crêpe paper and tied with a red ribbon. For the next several hours he read a book of poems by Rita Dove while Lena listened to Junius's playlist on his iPod. When he read, "I can't wear it/ on my sleeve,/ or tell you from/the bottom of it/ how I feel. Here,/ it's all yours now—/ but you'll have/to take me,/ too." he took Lena's hand and read the poem to her over the hiss of the engines.

"And you me."

The record company publicist drove them to the Park Hyatt Tokyo, where a suite had been booked for them. The next day he was interviewed by a reporter from the *Tokyo Shimbun* and later featured on television news shows, which played his record. He made an appearance Music Station.

When Junius finished his Tokyo obligations, he and Lena rode the bullet train that sped past Mt. Fuji. They visited the temples and gardens. For the first time Lena caught him smiling.

"There's one more thing," Junius said after they returned Tokyo, the night before their return home. "I have to rent a tuxedo. And you need to buy a white blouse and black skirt."

"Where're we going?"

"Ever since I heard about this, it is something I've wanted to experience."

He wouldn't explain further.

Lena couldn't remember the last time she had worn a skirt, no less so prim an outfit.

On Sunday night they took a taxi to Smida Triphony Hall. Every man was wearing a tuxedo and every woman dressed exactly as Lena, everything black and white.

"This is *Daiku*," Junius said. "That's what the Japanese call Beethoven's Ninth Symphony."

"We've come for a concert?"

"Yes, in a way. But it isn't to listen to. I've arranged for us to be part of the chorus." He continued to explain. "Except for a few professionals, every singer is an amateur. Anyone can participate. It's first come, first serve. The company arranged this for us. We're VIPS. It's an invitation from the musical director."

"I still don't understand."

"We're in the chorus. We sing the choral section of the 9th Symphony. All the singers, thousands of them, we all sing."

"You've got to be kidding me, Junius. You're going to sing, in front of a concert hall."

"Not in front of. With."

"Still."

"I hope."

"But I can't sing."

"Yes you can. Remember, 'Yes we can?'"

"No I can't."

"You'll see. Don't worry."

"There are words."

"No one understands them. No one speaks German. We probably the only ones not Japanese. The whole thing is about the feeling, about joy, Lena."

" 'Ode to Joy.' I know. I'm familiar with the music. But I can't sing."

"Just open your mouth and let sounds come out. You don't need words. Just sing the melody."

"I always need words."

Junius pulled out a piece of paper from his jacket pocket.

"I made copies of the chorus. Here," he said.

"It's in German. I don't know German. I won't be able to sing it."

"I've practiced a little. But I don't think I'll be able to sing in German either. So make it up. It doesn't matter as long as you open your mouth. Let it out, even if you're mumbling. You know the melody," he said, as he hummed it for her. "I read once someone said, 'I don't sing because I'm happy; I'm happy because I sing.' Come on, Lena. Lift your voice. I want us to sing."

Junius handed the letter of introduction to a greeter in the concert hall lobby. Lena was led through a door to the women's side of the balcony; Junius went to the men's section.

As the orchestra began the triumphal music, a rush overcame Lena and she felt herself being pulled up and out of herself and when the chorus of ten thousand voices filled the hall, she longed to be next to him. She searched but couldn't find Junius in the black and white sea.

Was he singing?

Epilogue:
Sungusungu

〰〰〰〰
〰〰〰〰

HE WOULD HAVE joined the community patrol in Kisii even without the promise of earning 2,000 shillings a month, an amount far exceeding what Josek earned in the *jua kali* sector. Being recruited was itself a sufficient honor, he believed, one given in recognition of his steadfast service with the *chinkororo*.

Being enlisted into *sungusungu* was a promotion according to Sokoro, although there was no formal structure to the organization that had sprung up in the last few years, replacing the *chinkororo* as the self-declared defenders of Kisii, no officers, no bureaucracy, no uniforms, no anything but working with the police, and that appealed to him. S*ungusungu* had become, in reality, more than an auxiliary force; it was, in fact, doing the work the police were incapable of carrying out because they were understaffed, poorly trained and corrupt. If there was anyone in Kisii who trusted the police, Sokoro didn't know him.

Who to ask for what and where to get it quick and cheap, that was Sokoro's skill. There was no substitute for experience and cleverness. What's more, those in charge knew that he was capable and loyal, two indispensable qualities for success, far more important than being able to pass school examinations or being a *kimbelembele,* pushing himself in front of everyone else.

Sokoro hated those *sonko* who became wealthy by sucking the blood of ordinary people, something he would never do. What was the point of defending against Maasai and Kipsigis if criminals in your own midst stole what wasn't rightly theirs? While he still dreamed of owning a car, a big one that someone else would drive for him, and having a mansion with rooms enough for all his friends and benefactors—he wouldn't forget those who had entrusted him with defending the homeland—and longing to see with his own eyes the mountain with snow on top, for the moment serving his fellow Kisii was enough. Until he was rewarded for his good work in fighting crime (and he had no doubt that his reward would be substantial), Sokoro was content with sharing a two-room flat in a new apartment on Cemetery Road. There was always enough to eat and when he couldn't afford a piece of meat for the week, there was the supermarket where it was easy enough to drop a small package in his pocket and walk out of the thieves' den—that chain of shops owned by Indians—undetected.

But if something more could be had, if he had more cash, Sokoro would be happy to have it. He wasn't averse to wealth. Just a few years back it was rare to see a *bodaboda* in Kisii but now there were *pengs* on every street and dozens of young men sitting on their sputtering and noisome taxis waiting to transport people and their satchels throughout the hills around Bosongo. Sokoro had wanted to have his own but even these inexpensive Chinese *pengs* were beyond his reach. That, however, was no reason why he couldn't learn how to operate one. He was sure he would be able to afford his own bike soon.

He went to one of the locations where motorbikes idled. Although many drivers didn't have licenses, Sokoro wanted to do it right. Besides, there were too many road accidents involving *pengs*. Being killed while on a *bodaboda* wasn't the warrior's death he wanted.

"Teach me to drive," he told one men straddling his motorbike in the staging area near the supermarket. Dozens of young men sat astride their bikes waiting for a customer or, just as happily, watching girls walk by with swaying bottoms and shiny legs.

"Two red," the driver said.

Under other circumstances, Sokoro would reject the initial price. But with his pockets bulging with fifty and one hundred shilling notes, pay for bringing justice to a teacher who had molested a school girl, Sokoro immediately accepted the asking price. He flaunted his cash and handed over two one hundred shilling notes.

"And a liter of petrol," the owner with a heavy, green sweater and sandals added.

"I'll give you these *fegis*," Sokoro countered with a fresh package of cigarettes. "King size. Filter. Never opened."

The owner grabbed the Sportsman and stuffed the pack into his windbreaker pocket.

"Get on."

On the dirt roads by Kanyimbo Primary School and Getwanyansi Coffee Factory, Sokoro learned to drive. Getting his license was easy. He did well on the road test but just to make sure, he slipped the officer of the Driving Test Unit a red, thanking him for being a good inspector.

Knowing how to drive a bike but without having a motorbike was useless. He couldn't even afford a used *peng*. No one would give him a layaway and his account at Postbank was always next to zero.

'Problems were made to be solved,' he had heard more than once. And hadn't his late mother told him that God helps those who help themselves? So when the opportunity presented itself, Sokoro snatched it. A friend told him several motorbikes were at the police impound yard.

"What do they do with them?"

"Most are wrecks. They were in accidents. But there are others like new."

"What does this have to do with me?"

"You want a bike, don't you?"

"Aren't they keeping them for evidence?" As soon as he asked, he realized how ridiculous his question was.

" Answer that yourself."

"I didn't know they sell them," Sokoro said.

"For the right price."

His friend came back the following day with the cost. Still too much.

"There must be another way," Sokoro suggested.

For agreeing to unlock the yard, keeping the dog muzzled and chained, and taking a piss at the right time, after vigorous bargaining the night security guard accepted Sokoro's offer.

Sokoro now had a 150 cc, 4-stroke Reshine that he passed off as new. When asked where he got it, he "connections." The bike did look as though it had just been taken out of its shipping container and as far as Sokoro knew, it may have been confiscated before it made it to a first buyer. The odometer was at zero, but that wouldn't mean much since everyone rolled back the meter.

Charging whatever he could with strangers was standard practice amongst *peng* drivers. But for those whom he knew he charged the same rate regardless of weather; even if roads were thick with red muck after an afternoon rain or the destination was atop a steep hill, Sokoro's fare didn't vary. "Fair Fare" was his slogan.

Hacking wasn't his work, Sokoro thought, but a means to while away his time and to make enough to pay for petrol while he continued to catch and punish malefactors. Utilizing what he learned about engines in his *jua kali* jobs, with a few basic tools and a daily wash at the Nyakomisaro River, Sokoro kept the bike running as smoothly and spotless as the day he acquired it.

First as a defender of the homeland, then as a protector of the weak, Sokoro viewed his *peng* neatly filling out his pride as a Kisii. So when he encountered an old person shuffling along the road or a woman struggling with packages as storm clouds bulked up for the afternoon downpour, he would offer them a lift, no charge. He didn't single out attractive girls but gave free rides to anyone who looked in need. These generous acts, Sokoro believed, were subsidized by the higher fares he charged strangers. This was part of his fairness doctrine.

Some laughed at Sokoro's foolishness; business is for making money, nothing more. The only satisfaction was financial success, then the things you could buy. To others, though, Sokoro wasn't a fool but a threat. His actions would undermine the *bodaboda* taxi industry itself. If he gave away his services, everyone would demand the same from other drivers. This would lower everyone's revenue.

"Fair Fare *mafi*! What you are doing is unfair competition. We'll all go *sota* because of you."

They lectured Sokoro on the law of supply and demand and other matters that held little interest for him. If he wanted to remain in business, he was warned, he must abide by the rules.

"You can't stay in business this way," he was told. "We'll all go poor because of you."

Sokoro saw their point. They knew more about how to run a business than he did. He assured the drivers that he wanted them to succeed and wouldn't do anything to undermine them. But when he saw a woman walking with a jerry can filled with water on her head and a child beside her and the rain was coming down in torrents, he asked where she was going and had them hop on behind him and drove them home without charge. Another day he saw an old woman wandering beside the highway. He took her home. And then there was a lame man leaving the municipal hospital.

On a straightaway on the Kisii-Kisumu road, with a paying fare seated behind him, chewing his favorite flavor of Gogo gum, a Subaru Forester overtook Sokoro and sideswiped him. The bike skidded as he tried to keep it upright, and then it flew out from under him. He hit the pavement and rolled onto the grassy verge.

The Subaru didn't slow; it didn't stop.

Sokoro's jacket was ripped from his body; his left leg seared with pain. For a few moments he couldn't feel his arms. He hadn't hit his head and while he was battered, nothing was broken. Dozens of people came out of shops to look at the two riders and the *peng* that leaked fuel from its ruptured tank.

Before the police arrived the passenger died.

Sokoro sat on the roadside while a policeman questioned him. He took Sokoro's testimony, talked to witnesses, impounded the motorbike. A police truck arrived and took it away. When Sokoro asked where he could retrieve it, he received a laugh in reply.

More papers, more notes and "Come with me."

He asked what more the police wanted from him and was told he was being charged with vehicular homicide. He wanted to tell the highway patrol constable he was *sungusungu* but there was no way to predict what reaction that would produce.

Sokoro touched his shirt. The money purse was still hanging from his neck. He took everything that was in it and placed it in officer's hand.

"My *peng*?" Sokoro inquired.

Perhaps he didn't hear, Sokoro thought as the constable walked away without acknowledging Sokoro's question. The policeman got in his car and drove off.

After waiting hours to be seen by a doctor at the hospital's outpatient clinic, Sokoro was sent away with a prescription for a topical antibiotic and analgesic for the abrasions that extended from shoulder to thigh. The examination lasted no more than five minutes. When Sokoro stepped into the afternoon sun, he looked at the paper in his hand and decided against going to the hospital chemist. Whatever the cost of the medication, it was more than he wanted to pay. In all likelihood, he would wait another hour, only to be told the pharmacy was out of the medication but the chemist could get it for him for a 'little something.' Sokoro decided he could put up with the pain and was certain the wounds would heal by themselves. As long as he kept them clean with soap and water, he would be fine.

〰〰〰〰〰
〰〰〰〰〰

SUNGUSUNGU'S ACTIVITIES CONTINUED to increase. Sokoro relished each assignment: catching adulterers, punishing thieves, returning stolen goods to their rightful owners. But after the last assignment—to a stop a witch— he decided that he wouldn't carry out such a task again. A tire was placed around the sorcerer's neck, doused with petrol and lit. Sokoro raced to the maize field and, hidden in the rustling stalks, puked. In his apartment he used an entire kilo box of Omo to wash his clothes, but it took weeks before the odor of rubber, petrol and flesh began to dissipate. Still he smelled of it, although no one else could sense it. He finally threw the shirt and trousers in the trash, replacing them with clothes taken from the supermarket.

As the latest round national elections approached, *sungusungu* armed itself. Payments of Kshs. 500 per day attracted additional recruits and Sokoro eagerly volunteered even without the cash incentive as a prod. It was his duty to protect Kisii against the Kipsigis harriers. There were drills and speeches and free flowing beer. Organizers made sure everyone had a *panga*. If Sokoro hadn't been sideswiped from behind, he would have recognized the Subaru SUV that ferried bows and arrows to *sungusungu* in town.

Riots broke out following the presidential election and Sokoro joined with others in Chepilat, a trading post divided by B3, one side Kisii, the other Kipsigis country.

The *sungusungu* jostled with Kipsigis youths, glowered at one another, sneered and cursed. The flour mill went up in flames and the battle began, fought along the highway, on farmsteads and in the Sema Academy playing field.

Two shot by the police, the official report stated, four hacked to death in the trading post. In the surrounding vicinity, eight others died by poison arrows or by machete blows. On the Kipsigis side, ten civilians died and the crowd killed a policeman. Burning houses lit the hills on both sides of the road.

At the end of the daylong battle, Sokoro claimed to have killed one Kipsigis with a spear, although another took credit for having first wounded the opponent with a poison arrow. Sokoro was unscathed.

As political matters settled when the vying presidential candidates reached a compromise, the warrior band was dissolved and Sokoro returned to Kisii town to carry on the crime fighting aspects of his work.

In the aftermath of the political calamity the demand for *sungusungu* increased proportionately as the reputation of government functionaries plummeted. *Sungusungu* became guardian, judge, jury and enforcer.

Sokoro gladly assumed new duties finding culprits and meting out justice. His greatest accomplishment came in gaining a confession from a father who defiled his own daughter. Neighbors stoned the man to death as Sokoro watched.

Outlawed homebrew alcohol, a mixture of grains often adulterated with formaldehyde or battery acid, plagued the district. Sokoro wanted to raid the brew sites but was rebuffed.

"There are more important matters," he was told.

"It is killing people. They need to be shut down."

"We'll decide on the actions, not you."

~~~~~~

DOUBTS BEGAN TO NAG AT SOKORO. He didn't expect big rewards for what he did, but something seemed wrong; he was no better off than he had been last year while those in senior roles were gaining rapidly. He wondered why the top benefited from confiscated goods and were always the ones to wind up with title deeds to disputed land, never the displaced refugees. Sokoro wasn't alone. Popular sentiment swung sharply against *sungusungu* as they were viewed as more dangerous than the police.

Promised a big reward for the next job, Sokoro agreed to carry out the assignment against a retired teacher who, he was told, had grabbed land for herself. She had been spoken to several times and offered a fair price, but she refused to sell the property to the neighboring brick company.

"She is standing in the way of progress."

The assignment called for three enforcers. Sokoro expected to be put in charge of the group but that role was given to one of the others.

They hadn't fought at Chepilat, he complained.

"That is true. They were in Nairobi then. Part of the militia. So they have experience. You will do this big work under their direction."

When Sokoro saw how young they were, having been passed over for command troubled him.

On some other assignments, Sokoro had to do a little detective work to find those that needed punishment. He would grab them on the road, in the market or shop or on their *shamba* while tilling the rich soil. This time they needed to break into a house, they were told, rough up the woman and make it clear that if she didn't move out immediately the real deal would follow. Surely she would gladly rid herself of the home and that would be the end of the matter.

This didn't seem more difficult than anything else he had done and he wished he had been given the lead. But questioning orders was never ingratiating. A good soldier was a loyal soldier. If he carried out his undertakings well, in time he would get his promotions.

"There won't be a problem. She lives alone and doesn't even have a dog."

"Why do you want me if I'm not the head?" Sokoro asked.

"You know the area better than they do. We trust you three guys can carry this out together."

The house, off the Kisii-Kericho highway, near Kabungu, was unlike others in the valley, mansions owned by lawyers, religious leaders and successful businessmen. This was the oldest and smallest in the location.

With a pry bar they bent the metal fence to the compound and squeezed through the pried door. They dismantled the window grate to the house and knocked out the glass with the handle of a *panga*. They pushed open the unlocked bedroom door and found the teacher in bed. She was startled when she heard the window break and saw the silhouettes of three men standing in the doorway.

"Who are you?"

She searched for her mobile phone but couldn't see in the dark. One of the gang knocked into the bed stand and phone skidded across the floor.

Sokoro went to the sitting room, shined his flashlight and found in a sideboard filled with crockery and an envelope. It was filled with thousand shilling notes. With the other two in the bedroom, he stuffed the money into the pockets of his fatigue jacket. Two flashes lit the bedroom. Sokoro head the pops. He tightened his grip on the *panga.*

"Let's go!"

The gang bolted from the house and scrambled through the twisted door. Sokoro directed them down footpaths that laced the location. They made their way to Ikonge before dawn. From comments made by his companions, fresh questions arose for Sokoro. They said the mission was to kill the teacher that night and it was meant to resemble the work of *sungusungu.* They couldn't fully explain to Sokoro who had hired them or what the assassination was meant to accomplish.

They couldn't be right, he thought. They must have misunderstood.

At the Ikonge Hotel they ordered roast meat and pints of beer. As they were draining another bottle of Tusker, a squad of policemen arrested them. They were brought to the police station in Kisii Town and placed in a windowless cell with one bed and a slop bucket. The only light came from the dangling bulbs in the corridor.

〰〰〰〰〰
〰〰〰〰〰

KENYA TELEVISION NETWORK, REPORTING FROM KISII, said that three men were arrested for the murder of a well-known, retired schoolteacher. A police spokeswoman said that three hardened criminals had confessed to the crime.

Sokoro had said no such thing. Uncertain whether the police at this station condoned or condemned *sungusungu*, he had kept his mouth shut; all he gave was his name.

Since the arrest none of the three had been mistreated or shackled. Neither had they been searched when brought to the station house and nothing had been taken from them. Sokoro continuously kept on his jacket for warmth. It was clear to him the police were putting on a show to demonstrate they were enforcing the law against *sungusungu*. It bothered him that after two weeks, his superiors hadn't gotten them released. But he was confident that would soon be would be out.

Every few days the three were called in separately for questioning by the investigating detective while Sokoro continued his polite silence. From what he gathered during the interrogations, the teacher was a prominent figure in the area and a large funeral was planned for her, with local and national dignitaries paying their final respects.

Weeks after the murder they were told they were being transferred to another facility out of the district. This was for their own protection, the boys were told, as the police anticipated the jail to be stormed by mobs whipped up at the teacher's funeral. They were hustled into two unmarked cars occupied by men in civilian clothes that night. Sokoro's concerns grew into fear when the vehicles veered off the main road past Sotik and drove onto a dirt road near the Kapsongoi gate on the Finlays tea estate.

The cars stopped and Sokoro was shoved out. A hand grabbed his arm and pulled him from the car. Sokoro yanked free and ran down a muddy lane and then into a footpath used by pickers that crisscrossed the undulating hills of tea bushes. He heard shouts, then the raised voices of his companions pleading before the familiar sound of a pistol fired. He froze him in place. There was more shouting and his pursuers went into the fields to find him but they set off in the wrong directions. Only by luck would they be able to find him amongst the waist-high plants. He crouched nearly breathless for what seemed like hours. At moonset and a blackened sky, car doors slammed and engines churned. Sokoro stayed put, terrified of confronting a naked night runner with a glowing tongue who spits fire and consorts with a leopard, until the first cock crowed and his body turned wet with morning dew. He could hear morning traffic along the road and followed the sound to the crest of the hill, then made his way to the highway as tea workers arrived to begin the day's plucking.

By late morning he was in Kericho Town.

Blending into the street scene, Sokoro stole a *mandazi* from a street vendor. He lifted a moneybag from a merchant in the market, then went to the bus stage and left for Nairobi. Whenever the bus halted for license and registration inspections, his back stiffened as he watched the negotiations between drivers and policemen unfold. Sokoro had heard enough about Nairobi that before dark he had made his way to the Kisii Village, in Fuata Nyayo slum, and imposed on a stranger there to give him shelter for the night. For Kshs 100, he slept on the dirt floor in a single-room house made of mud and wattle.

THE SLUM SHOCKED SOKORO. Why anyone would choose to leave the real Kisii and come here was incomprehensible: no electricity, buildings slapped together out of corrugated sheeting or mud, dirt floors, no running water. Nowhere in Kisii did people live on top of one another like this, where a plastic bag was used as a flying toilet. He, along with everyone else, tossed the polythene bag into the slow moving sludge, that decaying, fetid drainage ditch, the Nairobi River. Only once before had he smelled anything as nauseating but at least that odor was temporary; this smell clung to everything, all the time. What wasn't in the sewer-river piled in the lanes: goat and chicken excreta, vegetal and solid wastes discarded from the outdoor market just beyond the border of Kisii Village.

Repulsed by his new living quarters, Sokoro did find one attraction: the jet liners, which he had never seen before, roaring overhead, flying in and out of Kenyatta airport, just a few miles down the road. Their terrific rumbling and other strange noises, their silver bodies fascinated him. How could anything so big stay in the sky? Where did they come from, where were they going? Did you sit down inside like in a bus and have to stand when it became too crowded? How often did it stop? What happens when you need to piss?

Earning money at the *jua kali* market was easy. But he couldn't return to Kisii, not for a long time. He thought about the planes and how they could take him where no one would find him, to faraway places he had heard about.

He thought it through. He would need a passport; it was easy and cheap enough to buy a forged one. A plane ticket would be more difficult. No one was in the business of printing them; there wasn't enough of a demand. He didn't want to use counterfeit bills. Too risky.

Whenever possible, Sokoro walked to the airport perimeter. After months of planning, he got the metal saw he would use to cut the fence. That was all he needed, that and *kitu kidogo* to be doled out to an airport maintenance worker who lived in Kisii Village.

Weeks passed until one day the worker told him this was the night. He was advised where to snip a hole, the section where the electrification wasn't working. That night there would be only one plane on the tarmac, far from the terminal.

Sokoro squeezed through the opening and took more than hour crawling low to the ground to reach the plane. Before he was lifted into the wheel well of Kenya Airways Flight 102, the worker demanded another payment from him. Fearing that an argument would attract attention, Sokoro emptied one of his pockets and handed over a wad of bills.

In the crotch of his underwear Sokoro had a stuffed a stash of bills sufficient to tide him over when he arrived. It didn't matter where. There was enough to start again, to be independent. He could not imagine such freedom.

Notes

〰〰〰〰
〰〰〰〰

Foreword: A Body Falls From the Sky

1. There isn't agreement about the origin of the word or of the function of the *chinkororo*. Below is one explanation.

Chinkororo is a term used to describe the traditional warriors of the abagusii community much like the morans of the maasai community. They are to be found in Borabu and gucha districts which border the two communities the abagusii have since time immemorial had adversarial relations with, namely the kipsigis and the maasai. Chinkororo are mobilized if and only when there is an ethnic conflict and the government is not quick enough to provide security. They protect the abagusii families living along the two districts' borders, pursue stolen livestock and sometimes– admittedly–engage in acts of cattle rustling in order to compesate [sic] those whose livestock is stolen but never recovered.

More recently, chinkororo - just like the maasai morans - have proved popular as watchmen in the urban areas of the greater kisii district. Because the local community considers their role noble and crucial to the community's security, chinkororo enjoy immense goodwill all over Gusii.

"SUNGU SUNGU, CHINKORORO AND AMACHUMA: GET THE FACTS RIGHT" (http://www.kisii.com/commentaries/45-sungu-sungu-chinkororo-and-amachuma-get-the-facts-right)

2. Border conflicts and cattle raiding between the Kisii (also called Gusii) and Maasai have historical antecedents. See: William Robert Ochieng's *A Pre-colonial History of the Gusii of Western Kenya From C. A.D. 1500 to 1914.*

Every Voice

1. George Junius Stinney, the youngest person ever executed in the United States. He was tried before an all-white jury, which took less than three hours to deliberate. Three months later he was executed. Stinney was so small that he used the bible he carried to the electric chair as a bolster. In late 2014, a South Carolina judge vacated the trial conviction and sentence, calling the trial and the execution "a great and fundamental injustice." The judge found that the prosecution had failed to safeguard Stinney's constitutional rights.

2. The Myers' family move to Levittown, Pennsylvania, revealed the racism inherent in the formation of the suburbs. From the New York Amsterdam News:

In 1957, Bill and Daisy Myers bought a home in Levittown, Pennsylvania, not to be greeted by a neighborly welcome wagon but by a crowd each evening singing the national anthem, jeering and stone-throwing. A cross was burned on their lawn. When the mobs dissipated two weeks later, after police protection arrived, they were replaced by phone calls threatening to shoot Bill on sight. Milk and bread deliveries ceased, and the house next door raised the Confederate flag.

3. Additional information about Levittown, excerpted from "Levittown: The Imperfect Rules of the American Suburbs," from *U.S. History Scene.*

The Levitts' level of control over the appearance of Levittown did not stop at the yards and houses, but extended to the appearance of the inhabitants themselves. Bill Levitt only sold houses to white buyers, excluding African Americans from buying houses in his communities even after housing segregation had been ruled unconstitutional by the courts. By 1953, the 70,000 people who lived in Levittown constituted the largest community in the United States with no black residents.

Originally, the Levitts' racist policy was enshrined in the lease itself, which stipulated that "the tenant agrees not to permit the premises to be sued or occupied by any person other than members of the Caucasian race." That provision was later struck down in court as unconstitutional, but Bill Levitt continued to enforce racial homogeneity in practice by rejecting would-be black buyers.

Activist groups across the U.S. and even individuals within Levittown, who united under the Committee to End Discrimination in Levittown, protested the Levitts' racist policies. In 1955, the National Association for the Advancement of Colored People (NAACP) sued federal mortgage agencies which had helped future homeowners finance the purchase of homes in the community, basing the suit on the denial of six black veterans from purchasing homes. Thurgood Marshall, the lawyer who had successfully argued *Brown v. Board of Education*, represented the plaintiffs, but a Philadelphia court dismissed the suit after ruling that the federal agencies were not responsible for preventing housing discrimination.

The Levitts and [Senator Joe] McCarthy joined forces in promoting Levittown as a more American, capitalist alternative to public housing solutions. McCarthy posed with washing machines to be placed in Levittown homes, and praised Levittown as a model of the American way. Bill Levitt himself once said, "No man who owns his own home and lot can be a Communist, he has too much to do." Later, Levitt vilified those who questioned his segregationist policies as communists.

www.ushistoryscene.com/uncategorized/levittown

4. Excerpts from the *Afro American*, April 28, 1956:

Consolidation of longshoremen's locals in Brooklyn into one "big local" under the direction of "Tough Tony" Anastasia has brought together all but two Brooklyn longshoremen's locals—one of which is Local 968, the all-colored unit struggling for existence on the world's toughest waterfront.

Members of this local work all over the port and are not expected to join any one union sector.

To understand what happens in longshore work, it is known that "locals" of longshoremen, long have been identified with certain piers, which they regard as their "territory." Therefore, if the pier is kept busy loading and unloading vessels, the longshoremen will work.

Every local has a pier except local 968. The members of this local depend on the goodness of Anastasia to secure work. At one time, 968 did have a pier, but in some mysterious way, it caught fire and was destroyed.

That was many years ago and as yet, no pier has replaced the one destroyed by the fire. At one time, local 968 boasted 2,000 members. Today, it has perhaps half that number, all working in Brooklyn.

5. From an interview in the New York Post, September 20, 1961.

You know what it is to be a Negro on these docks? It's to be a nigger again. To the boss, you're a nigger. To the guy next to you, you're a nigger. And to yourself, you're a nigger. That's the worst part of being a Negro on the docks.

6. The Coasters' Searchin', which remained on the top of the Rhythm and Blues Chart for twelve weeks in 1957 was also a hit in the national pop charts. (https://www.youtube.com/watch?v=WR2FvrU-NIM)

Big Red

1. During the siege of Leningrad, women took on many tasks, including serving as air raid wardens.

The Soviet Union also created three exclusively women's air squadrons during WWII. Each pilot of the 588th flew over 1,000 missions in wooden and canvas biplanes. Thirty died in combat and twenty-three received the title Hero of the

Soviet Union. The women flew at night at low altitudes and idled their engines as they released their bombs that glided to their target. The Germans called the pilots Night Witches, a name they evidently adopted for themselves.

Marina Raskova formed a regiment of women night bombers. The 588th Regiment consisted exclusively of women, from mechanics to pilots. The 40 two-women crews flew 23,000 sorties beginning in 1941. Raskova is shown with one of her crews, Valyentina Grizudobova and Polina Osypienko.

2. The lines "grab stones, etc." are from a poem by Bolshevik poet Vladimir Mayakovsky.

3. Brighton Beach, a center for immigrant Jews during the Depression, was a hub of left-wing activities. Along Brighton Beach Avenue were headquarters for the Communist Party, the Socialist Party, the Labor Zionist Party, the Workmen's Circle, the Democrat and Republican Parties. The neighborhood also housed meeting halls for garment and shoemakers unions and there was a branch of the Emma Lazarus Council, a community-based housewives union.

4. As a member of the Communist Party, Meridel Le Sueur was blacklisted by most publishing companies. Through her books about American folk heroes, she presented "the egalitarian, diverse and cooperative elements of American history and folklore . . . Le Sueur paid tribute to America's democratic folk heritage and heroes of the working class . . . in an attempt to discredit capitalism."

See: "Communist in a Coonskin Cap? Meridel Le Sueur's Books for Children and Reformulation of America's Cold War Frontier Epic," Julia L. Mickenberg, *The Lion and the Unicorn*, 21, 1, January 1997.

5. Major publishing houses blacklisted novelist Howard Fast, who wrote for the *Daily Worker* during the 1950s. Richard Wright, the Harlem editor of the *Daily Worker* in the late 1930s, was blacklisted by Hollywood in the 1950s.

6. The explanation for Henry's name change is found in anti-Semitism, which reached new depths in the US in the 1930s. Anti-Semitism became "no more unfashionable than white racism" in this period. Jews were considered a separate race. Father Coughlin's weekly broadcast, which was laced with anti-Semitic remarks, was the nation's most popular radio show. Colleges instituted quotas to keep from being overrun by "pushy Jews who had little training in the amenities and delicacies of civilized society." As a result of this policy, for example, in 1920, 47% of Columbia's College of Physicians and Surgeons were Jews; in 1940, Jews were 8%. Throughout the country Jews in medical school fell from nearly 60% in 1925 to 15% in 1939. It was in this environment that Henry changed his name and went to pharmacy school instead of medical school. See: *Anti-Semitism in Times of Crisis*, Sander L. Gilman and Steven T. Katz (eds.), New York University, 1991.

7. "Not a step back!" was the slogan widely publicized by the Russian press during the summer of 1942, when German forces were inflicting heavy losses on the Soviets in the Great Patriotic War.

8. Antioch College accepted a student from Bayside High School, in Queens, when Edward Jahn refused to sign the loyalty oath, in 1960. Two more high schools made national news that year: Westbury High School, on Long Island, Stephen Bayne refused objected to receiving an award from the American Legion; at Stuyvesant High School, in Manhattan, graduation ceremony was cancelled when many students jeered and hissed the unpopular principal.

The Rooster Gives Way to the Hen

1. These are from the diaries and correspondence of the British regarding the taking of Kisii:

A.

On termination of hostilities in Kisii country and in continuation of my letter of this date, I have the honour to inform you that in my opinion the expedition has achieved the objective for which it was mobilized. The Kitutu section of the Kisii tribe has been utterly demoralized and has been taught a severe lesson. Undoubtedly the prestige of the government has been maintained in a most striking manner.

John Ainsworth, Provincial Commissioner

B.

I have found from years' experience in this country that the native will never fight or be brought to action until his flocks and herds are laid hands on; and after my first days' experience of the Kisii tribe I found he was in no way different from any other of the Protectorate natives and could not be brought to attack us. I therefore decided to make every effort to capture his stock with a view of bringing him to action or at least to attack the camp at night when hampered by large numbers of cattle, but I never could induce him to come to close quarters.

From the date I commenced active operations to the end of the expedition on 6th February 1908, the enemy suffered heavily. They lost over 7,000 cattle captured and 5,000 sheep and goats taken, many living and cattle bomas burnt while over 200 casualties were inflicted on the enemy, who were completely demoralized, fleeing with their families into the Kavirondo country for personal safety.

From the diary of Major Kirkpatrick, Chief Staff Officer for the British expedition against the Kisii.

C.

I do not like the tone of these reports. No doubt the clans should be punished, but 160 have now been killed outright without any further casualties on our side. It looks like butchery. If the Head of Chancery gets hold of it, all our plans in E.A.P. will be under a cloud. Surely it cannot be necessary to go on killing these defenseless people on such an enormous scale.

Telegram from Under-Secretary of State for the Colonies Winston Churchill to the Secretary for the Colonies regarding the massacre in Kisii, 31ˢᵗ, January 1908.

2. A half-century after Kwamboka wrote about the attack on Northcote, a member of the Kisii County Assembly directed a petition to the British government.

PUBLIC PETITION STANDING ORDER NOs.   195, 198 & 200

TO THE COUNTY ASSEMBLY

OLD MUNICIPAL BUILDING

P.O. BOX 4552-40200,

KISII

PETITION: FOR THE RETURN OF MR. OTENYO NYAMATERERE'S HEAD (OUR WARRIOR'S HEAD)

I, Hon. Samson Nyagaka Matoke a resident and representative of the people of Nyamasibi Ward and a member of the Abagusii Council of Elders seek the intervention of the Government of Kisii County, the Government of Kenya and all the relevant authority to Petition the British Government for the return of the head of our warrior Otenyo Nyamaterere who surrendered to the colonial rulers in Getembe now Kisii, but was beheaded and his head shipped to England where it is kept in one of the British Museums.

It is in the public domain that the British Government partially apologized over atrocities committed against ex-Mau Mau freedom fighters of the 1950 and compensated them with over 2 billion shillings the same did not include the Kisii warriors. This was an admission [sic].

Reason whereof I took this decision as the people's representative to bring this Petition to this Honourable house.

The following are the grounds for our prayers:

1. That in 1905–1908 colonialist invaded Gusii land killed more than 500 people seized more than 300 herds of cattle, raped women and destroyed property.

2. That Captain Jenkins led more than 300 Kings Rifles in [a] four month expedition termed to teach treacherous Kisii tribesman a lesson leaving a trail of destruction.

3. That in 1907 a further contingent led by Northcote a colonial administrator, invaded their land killing more than 9,001 people, confiscated 6,000 herds of cattle and destroyed property.

4. That it does not need judicial intervention to bring back the head as it is of no value to the British Government. But has immense Importance to the Kisii people.

THAT I hereby confirm that efforts have been made to have the matter addressed by the relevant authority through the Gusii Culture and Council of elders and it has failed to give satisfactory response.

THAT I hereby confirm that the issues in respect of which the Petition is made are not pending before any Court of Law or constitutional or legal body.

Herefore [sic] your humble petitioner prays that the County Assembly urges the Kisii County Government, the Government of Kenya and all relevant Authorities to seek an apology, compensation and return of our warrior's head from the British Government so as the aforesaid warrior can be accorded a proper burial as per the Gusii Traditions.

Dated this 23rd day of July, 2013.

SAMSON MATOKE NYAGAKA

ID/NO.9148010,

MEMBER OF COUNTY ASSEMBLY

NYAMASIBI WARD

P.O. BOX 69, KEROKA.

"Elders demand British apology," Jackline Moraa, *Daily Nation*, June 12, 2013.

Author's note: in a private correspondence, a lecturer at the School of Oriental and African Studies, University of London, who is familiar with Kisii, investigated this claim of the beheading on my behalf. She informs me that there is no record that Kisii heads were taken.

3. An historical account of the British incursion into Kisii can be found in *Conflict and Accommodation in Western Kenya: The Gusii and the British 1907-1963*, by Robert M. Maxon.

4. *Nyansongo: a Gusii Community*, by Robert LeVine, explores the role of witchcraft in Kisii. A more thorough examination of witchcraft in Kenya is found in James Howard Smith's *Bewitching Development: Witchcraft and the Reinvention of Development in Neoliberal Kenya*, Chicago: University of Chicago Press, 2008.

Farewell Until Eternity

1. President John F. Kennedy delivered to the nation announcing the Cuban blockade.

(http://www.americanrhetoric.com/speeches/jfkcubanmissilecrisis.html

2. "Farewell Until Eternity," is from Comte de Lautréamont's *Les Chants de Maldoror*.

The Kisumu Train

1. Information about school trains in Kenya can be read at: (http://www.mccrow.org.uk/eastafrica/eastafricanrailways/KampalaNairobi.htm)

2. When the East Africa Railway was built from Mombasa to Kisumu at the turn of the 20th century, the cost nearly bankrupted the British Empire. Called the Lunatic Express by Europeans, Africans referred to the railroad as the Iron

Snake. There are many trestle bridges between Nakuru and Kisumu. Derailments weren't uncommon.

3.

> THE LUNATIC EXPRESS: POEM
>
> Aboard the Lunatic Express
>
> What it will cost no words can express;
>
> What is its object no brain can suppose;
>
> Where it will start from no one can guess;
>
> Where it is going nobody knows;
>
> What is the use of it none can conjecture;
>
> What it will carry there's none can define;
>
> And in spite of Georg e Curzon's superior lecture,
>
> It clearly is naught but a lunatic line.
>
> *Truth*, London, 1896

4. *Speaking with Vampires: Rumor and History in Colonial Africa,* by Luise White, provides an historian's view of the widespread fear on the part of Africans that Europeans were vampires who took Africans' blood.

5. Country and western singer Jim Reeves was enormously popular in Kenya, having been introduced by American missionaries. (http://www.youtube.com/watch?v=Smlaq1ezQRM)

Shape-up

1. Connie Hawkins, a graduate of Boys High School where he scored 60 points in one game, was recruited by University of Iowa but never played a game there because while still in high school he had borrowed $200 from Jack Molinas, a major figure convicted in a college basketball point shaving scandal. As a result, Hawkins lost his college scholarship and was barred from playing in the NBA. He played for the ABA, then was admitted to the NBA in 1969 where he played until 1976. Hawkins is now in the Basketball Hall of Fame.

The NBA Encyclopedia writes, "Hawkins was voted into the Hall of Fame in 1992, an acknowledgment that he had been unjustly denied the opportunity to show his talent in his most productive years, and that most basketball fans had likewise been denied the opportunity to see the best that this innovative player had to offer."

2. Malcolm X's speech, his first after leaving the Black Muslims, was delivered a month before the New York riots:

We declare our right on this earth to be a man, to be a human being, to be respected as a human being, to be given the rights of a human being in this society, on this earth, in this day, which we intend to bring into existence by any means necessary.

(http://www.youtube.com/watch?v=WBS416EZsKM)

3. The High School of Music and Art was one of New York City's specialized schools. It required auditions for admission. The roster of notable alumni is extensive. In 1984, it merged with the High School of Performing Arts to become LaGuardia High School of Music & Art and Performing Arts.

4. Sam Cook sings "Little Red Rooster," a crossover hit in 1964. (https://www.youtube.com/watch?v=1vnADZikpnA &spfreload=10)

5. During the 1940s and '50s, New York City constructed low-cost housing projects. Many were put up in Brooklyn, several in and around Weeksville itself. Kingsborough Houses, with 16 buildings housing more than 2,000, was completed in 1941. The two developments known as Albany Houses, completed in 1957, has about 3,000 residents in nine buildings, several of which are 13 and 14 stories. By the early 1960s, the projects had become centers of poverty, drugs and crime.

6. The Harlem/Bedford Stuyvesant riots involved more than 4,000 rioters and most of New York City's police force. Large swaths of the two neighborhoods were left in

smoldering ruins. The riot set the stage for many urban race riots over the next several years.

7. Willie Duckworth sang the first cadence song in the military in 1944 while marching at Ft. Slocum. As an African American, Duckworth would have been familiar with Negro work songs. He composed several more verses and choruses to be used by soldiers during their drills. The Pentagon recognized the value of cadence songs and copies of Duckworth's original cadence call was distributed by the War Department to soldiers around the world.

Welcome Hard Times

1. Founded in 1967 by Craig Rodwell, the Oscar Wilde Bookshop was the first bookstore dedicated to gay and lesbian literature and authors. The first gay pride parade was planned there. The bookshop also published the Hymnal, a monthly newsletter about gay and lesbian activities. It closed in 2009, like many independent bookstores, deeply affected by the economic recession and unable to compete against chain stores and the Internet.

2. The Delmore Schwartz's poem is "A Dream of Whitman Paraphrased, Recognized and Made More Vivid by Renoir."

3. One theory regarding Donovan's hit song "Mellow Yellow" was that the title referred to smoking banana leaves as a hallucinogenic. Years later Donovan explained that the reference was, as Lena thought, to an electric vibrator.

4. The topless radio interview was photographed and published by the Village Voice.

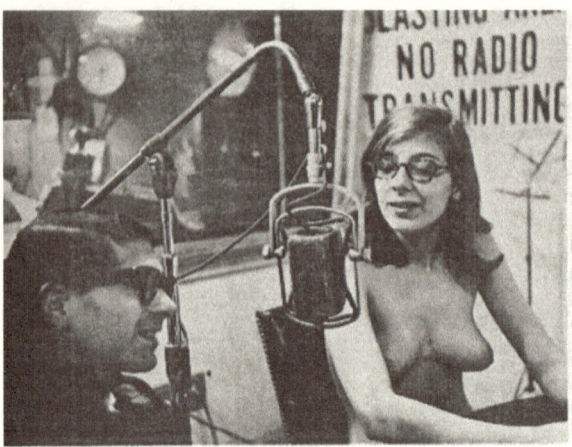

(Joy F. Good, Village Voice Archives)

6. An account of the psychedelic vaudeville can be found at: (http://blogs.villagevoice.com/runninscared/2010/04/hippie-strippie.php)

7. "Rise up and abandon the creeping meatball!" was a slogan of the Yippies, coined by Jean Shepherd in an article in *Mad Magazine*:

> People today have a genuine fear of stepping out and thinking on their own. 'Creeping Meatballism' is this rejection of individuality The American brags about being a great individualist, when actually he's the world's least individual person . . . The guy who has been taken in by the 'Meatball' philosophy is the guy who really believes that contemporary people are slim, and clean-limbed, and they're so much fun to be with . . . because they drink Pepsi-Cola. As long as he believes this, he's in the clutches of 'Creeping Meatballism.'

8. "He who binds to himself . . ." is from William Blake's "Eternity."

9. An estimated 35,000 young people living on Vermont communes in the 1960s and 70s.

10. Norman O. Brown's book *Love's Body,* published in 1966, was one of the most widely read books on college

campuses at the time. The book rejects politics since "the rule of law is the rule of force." He writes, "The prototype of all opposition or contrariety is sex."

11. "There's No Forgetting," from *Residence on Earth*. [*Residencia en la tierra II*], by Pablo Neruda was translated by Clayton Eshleman, a frequent visitor to Greenwich Village bookstores.

Why Is This Night Different?

1. At the time of independence, December 1963, Kenya gave Europeans and Asians two years to become Kenyan citizens. Only 20,000 of the 180,000 Asians chose Kenyan citizenship. The Kenya Immigration Act and the Trade Licensing Act, both passed in 1967, made it increasingly difficult for non-Kenya Asians to find employment. Reacting to the increased immigration of fleeing Kenyan Asians, the British government considered new policies for entry into the country. Enoch Powell galvanized public opinion. Soon after his speech, the UK withdrew the right of entry from Asians in Kenya with British passports.

Addressing a Conservative association meeting in Birmingham, Mr Powell said Britain had to be mad to allow in 50,000 dependents of immigrants each year.

He compared it to watching a nation busily engaged in heaping up its own funeral pyre.

The MP for Wolverhampton South West called for an immediate reduction in immigration and the implementation of a Conservative policy of "urgent" encouragement of those already in the UK to return home.

Mr Powell compared enacting legislation such as the Race Relations Bill to "throwing a match on to gunpowder".

He said that as he looked to the future he was filled with a sense of foreboding.

"Like the Roman, I seem to see the river Tiber foaming with much blood," he said.

He estimated that by the year 2000 up to seven million people - or one in ten of the population - would be of immigrant descent.

Mr Powell, the shadow defence spokesman, was applauded during and after his 45-minute speech.

(http://news.bbc.co.uk/onthisday/hi/dates/stories/april/20/newsid_2489000/2489357.stm)

3. In 1902, after a pogrom in Russia, Britain proposed a Jewish homeland in the Uasin Gishu area in what was then in the Uganda Protectorate and is now in Kenya west of the Rift Valley. Joseph Chamberlain, as Secretary of State for the Colonies, set aside 5,000 square miles for Jewish emigration. (By comparison when Israel was founded, in 1948, it was 7,800 square miles.) The proposal was known as the Uganda Plan. As head of white settlers in Kenya, Lord Delamere sent a letter of protest to the London *Times*, writing, "Feeling here very strong against introduction of alien Jews . . . . flood of people of that class sure to lead to trouble with the natives, jealous of their rights . . . Englishmen here appeal public opinion against the arbitrary proceeding and consequent swamping bright future of country." In a public meeting, white settlers unanimously protested against locating "alien Jews in our midst and are prepared to resist the same by all means in our power."

Zionist leader Theodor Herzl supported the idea. A handful of Jews took the proposal seriously enough that they settled in the Kenya colony, establishing the Nairobi Hebrew Congregation in 1904. The Uganda Plan was rejected at the seventh Zionist Congress, in Basel, in 1905.

Further reading about Jews in the early white settlement in Kenya can be found in *The Kenya Pioneers*, Errol Trzebinski, W. W. Norton & Co., 1985.

4. The British government to mount an exploratory expedition by Jews to the Uganda colony to determine the

feasibility of a Jewish settlement there. The area under consideration was later transferred to the Kenya colony.

5. The Zionist Congress sent a delegation to survey the area proposed by the British government. They concluded that the area was too small to support the number of Jews expected to immigrate to a Jewish homeland. A few years later other Europeans settled there on about 600 farms.

See *The Jews of Nairobi, 1903-1962,* Julius Carelbach, Nairobi: Nairobi Hebrew Congregation.

6. Furniture manufacturer and seller, Issy Somen, one time president of the Board of Kenya Jewry, twice served as Nairobi's mayor between 1957-1959. Somen was also Israel's Honorary Consul in Nairobi. He was instrumental in establishing close ties between Kenya and Israel. He later immigrated to Israel and died there in 1984. At the time of WWII, three other congregations were established in Kenya, in Kitale, Nakuru and Mombasa. They never number more than a few dozen members.

At its height, in the 1950's, there were about 150 members of the Hebrew Congregation in Nairobi.

Blue Spade

1. Thomas R. Jones was an activist in the Bedford-Stuyvesant neighborhood from the 1950s to 1962, when he was elected to the NY State Assembly. As chief counsel to the local branch of the NAACP, he specialized in cases of police brutality. When Jones accepted the position as Civil Judge in 1964, Shirley Chisholm was elected to take his seat. Soon after she won election to the U.S. Congress and in 1972 made a bid to become the Democratic candidate for the presidency.

2. Hubert's Flea Circus, located in a subway arcade at 42nd St. closed in 1969.

3. On April 28th, 1967, when he received his draft notice, Muhammad Ali reported to the Houston induction center as directed, only to refuse to take the oath. He was convicted of draft evasion. In 1971, the Supreme Court overturned the conviction. Here is Ali's statement regarding his refusal to serve:

Why should they ask me to put on a uniform and go ten thousand miles from home and drop bombs and bullets on brown people in Vietnam while so-called Negro people in Louisville are treated like dogs and denied simple human rights? No, I am not going ten thousand miles from home to help murder and burn another poor nation simply to continue the domination of white slave masters of the darker people the world over. This is the day when such evils must come to an end. I have been warned that to take such a stand would put my prestige in jeopardy and could cause me to lose millions of dollars which should accrue to me as the champion. But I have said it once and I will say it again. The real enemy of my people is right here. I will not disgrace my religion, my people or myself by becoming a tool to enslave those who are fighting for their own justice, freedom and equality... If I thought the war was going to bring freedom and equality to twenty-two million of my people they wouldn't have to draft me, I'd join tomorrow. But I either have to obey the laws of the land or the laws of Allah. I have nothing to lose by standing up for my beliefs. So I'll go to jail. We've been in jail for four hundred years.

(http://alphahistory.com/vietnam/muhammad-ali-refuses-to-fight-1967/#sthash.ciirVhJy.dpuf)

4. There were few protests against the war by African Americans. Junius was unaware of them. Many blacks, including Carl, supported Ali's refusal to be drafted because they were impressed with Ali's integrity and disturbed by the unfairness of drafting blacks while at the same time granting exemptions to white celebrities. See *The Brothers' Vietnam War: Black Power, Manhood and the Military Experience,* Herman Graham III, University Press of Florida, 2003. Below is a photo a protest that linked the war to racism.

5. Soldiers of the 26th Army Band published this broadside in 1968 in response to the military's crackdown on their anti-war activities. An explanation of what happened to band members was printed in Xpress, no. 1.

Ft. Hamilton Amends The First Amendment

On July 8 of this year, CW3 Patrick E. Flores, the present commanding officer of the 26th Army Band, appeared before his unit to enunciate a series of radical and immediate changes in the band's duty status. Duty hours were extended, fatigues replaced class A's as the duty uniform, command reveille was instituted, periodic Saturday training was added, instrumental lessons were eliminated from the training schedule, and civilian performing commitments were to be spurned in favor of commitments which were hitherto ajudged [sic] by CW3 Flores as being unnecessary and non-productive.

Mr. Flores went on to relate the justification for these changes: they were based on four antiwar actions by several band members, including an antiwar petition which appeared in the New York Times, and a protest march by several band members at a July Fourth parade in Staten Island in which the band performed.

.   .   .   .

Not all members of the band had participated in these activities, yet mass punishment was implemented with uncompromising thoroughness. The entire unit was harassed for minute infractions, punitive reassignments were threatened, additional work details came about, abusive language came into vogue when officers spoke to enlisted men, and Article 15 convictions rose dramatically.

On July 21, Sp/4 David Cortright, the band's Drum Major, and also a leading figure in the New York antiwar movement, was ordered out of the band on seven days notice. He was to report to the already overstrength 62 AG Band at Fort Bliss, Texas. Upon Cortright's arrival, he was not allowed to sign into the band but instead was shuffled off into an artillery unit. He was later reassigned as a chaplain's assistant. Finally he was transferred into the band.

Sp/4s Paul Dix and Thomas Bankston received Vietnam orders. Simultaneously 4 bandsmen were ordered out; three to Korea, two more to Vietnam, one to Germany, and one to Ft. Lee, Va. On two weeks notice, making the total to this date of ten GIs punitively reassigned [sic].

(http://www.sirnosir.com/archives_and_resources/library/articles/xpress_01.html)

Your Heart Will Be on Fire

1. One of Russia's greatest poets, Anna Akhmatova suffered under the Stalinist regime. When she died in 1966, she was acknowledged by the Soviet government for the great artist she was.

2. Anna Akhmatova's poem "You Will Hear Thunder," is in *You Will Hear Thunder*, D. M. Thomas, translator, Ohio University Press, 1985.

3. The Whitman quote is from the 1856 collection of *Leaves of Grass*.

4. Gangs ruled the New York streets in the 1970s and Kevin Donovan was the leader of the Bronx division of the Black Spades. He adopted the name Afrika Bambaataa and founded the Universal Zulu Nation, which created music and dance cultural events for youths. Bambaataa is one the prime originators of break-beat deejaying and is known as the Godfather of Hip-hop Kulture, along with DJ Kool Herc.

5. Bambaataa denies that he was the leader of the Black Spades. He says,

The leader's name was Monk. I was a warlord in the 1st Division, 1st Chapter of The Black Spades under Kool Dee, famously known as Kool DJ Dee. You can never find any article where I said I was the leader of The Black Spades, that is unresearched media/journalists who write whatever they want to write to sell the papers, articles or blogs. Be care of all you read without proper research in everything. Always look for the Factology versus the BS."

www.solo138.com

6. "Seven different census tracts in The Bronx lost more than 97% of their buildings to fire and abandonment between 1970 and 1980; 44 tracts (out of 289 in the borough) lost more than 50%. 'The smell is one thing I remember,' says retired Bronx firefighter Tom Henderson. 'That smell of burning — it was always there, through the whole borough almost.'"

"Why the Bronx Burned," Joe Flood, New York *Post,* May 16, 2010.

Not Now

1. Most independent investigations into the events surrounding Kariuki's murder conclude the government, under the direction of President Jomo Kenyatta, was responsible. The bombings were a ruse to paint Kariuki as a terrorist; his murder rid the government of a popular critic of policies that favored the wealthy.

(http://www.kenyan-post.com/2013/04/detailed-report-on-how-kenyatta-killed.html)

2. James R. Hooker, the head of Michigan State's African Studies Center, was on the payroll of the CIA. He used his position to document political events in Africa for the American spy agency. A report on the work of the CIA at American universities can be found at "The CIA on Campus," Robert Witanek, Covert Actions Publications and Institute Media Analysis, 1989.

Beatmatching

1. During the 1977 Yankee World Series, sports announcer Howard Cossell said, "The Bronx is burning" as ABC showed the exterior of the stadium and an uncontrolled fire burning blocks away. The fires in the city's slums were finally extinguished when there were few buildings left to burn. Between 1970, 97% of the buildings in the Bronx were either burned or abandoned. In 1976, the city reported an estimated 14,00 arson fires.

(http://burned.journalism.cuny.edu/the-history-of-burned-new-york-boroughs/)

2. Junius Morel was an activist even before moving to Weeksville. His remarks to the American Colonization Society, published in the abolitionist newspaper *National Enquirer*, March 1837, caused a fissure in the "moral movement" composed of blacks and whites, when he opposed relocating blacks to Africa in favor of abolition

Sir, we have not been unmindful of its cruel persecutions, its base destractions, nor its unceasing and certain tendency to inflict on us, and our unhappy and down-trodden brethren, all of those evils which embitter life, and make it burthensome to man. That society, Sir, has addressed us and advised us to go to the death- dealing shores of Africa.—Yes, Sir, they would recommend to us that Golgotha of Colonization Glory!—And for what? Why simply to transform us into men and citizens.

Sir, were we born—here we drew our earliest breath —and here, repose in peace the bones and ashes of our fathers— (revered be their memories) and here by their graves, are we determined to die.

I ask it, particularly, at your hands; because I have repeatedly, and with much pleasure, witnessed the good effects of the wholesome and salutary advice, given time after time by abolitionists, to our people.—I sincerely believe that, under the guidance of the Divine Being, the abolitionists will save our common country from the natural consequences of Slavery—insurrections, bloodshed, and confusion.

http://research.udmercy.edu/find/special_collections/ digital/baa/item.php?record_id=2485&collectionCode=baa

3. Weeksville, the second largest known independent black community in pre-Civil War America, was the only free African American community with an urban rather than rural base. Weeksville residents established schools, orphanages, old-age homes, churches and benevolent associations. It also printed *The Freedman's Torchlight*, the earliest educational periodical produced by and for African Americans.

4. After moving to Weeksville, Morel was "A steadfast supporter of integration, he petitioned for white students to be allowed to attend class. The success of this experiment

greatly aided the effort to desegregate Brooklyn's public schools."

The Elite of Our People: Joseph Wilson's Sketches of Black Upper Class Life in Antebellum Philadelphia, Julie Winch (ed.), The Pennsylvania State University Press, 2000.

5. Susan Smith McKinney Steward, New York's first African American female physician grew up on her father's pig farm in Weeksville. She practiced pediatrics in the neighborhood. Dr. Steward died in Brooklyn in 1918, the year Susan Cassel was born. She was named after the physician.

6. "Peter Quince at the Clavier" is found Wallace Stevens' *Harmonium*. The Dylan Thomas poem "Fern Hill" is published in *Deaths and Entrances*.

7. Penelope Grill worked as a cashier at the Loft and later became an artist. She writes:

When I lived at 99 Prince Street, in SoHo, I worked at the Loft party, which was downstairs on the first floor and basement of the building. I was the cashier and reception/reservationist. I collected the contributions from hundreds of partygoers every Saturday night for years. The doors opened at midnight and the weekly celebration lasted well into the late afternoon the next day. The crowd was a diverse mix of the New York after-hours dance subculture. Watching the dynamics of the dance floor and refreshment areas was fascinating. The dancing was the best and the music and atmosphere electrifying, far beyond what any other party in town offered.

8. Donna Summer sings "Love to Love You Baby." (https://www.youtube.com/watch?v=s250Wplm70M)

On a Barren Branch

1. During the 1970s, several airlines flew 747s that had a piano bar on the upper deck. One of the passengers on

Junius flight snapped the photo in which he appears on the piano's left.

2. Pyrrhus Concer sailed the Pacific on the whaling ship *Manhattan*. In 1848 the crew rescued 33 shipwrecked Japanese sailors and brought them to Tokyo. Japan was closed to foreigners at that time but the government made an exception. Concer became a celebrity in Tokyo and a local artist painted his portrait. Never having seen a black man before, Concer related that his hosts tried to rub off his black skin, stared at his teeth and listened to him speak.

3. In the 1970s, a group of Japanese tourists made a special visit to Long Island's East End in search of Concer. At the time of his death, in 1897, the Hamptons considered Concer one of its most respected citizens.

One More Drop

1. Clara Lemlich moved with her family to the US in 1903. She joined the ILGWU and was elected to the executive committee. By the time she roused the women textile workers to go on strike in 1909, 19-year old Lemlich had been arrested 17 times. She had several ribs broken by the police only weeks before leading the strike of 20,000 women workers.

2. Laborers who worked in the Asch Building (now called the Brown Building as part of the NYU campus) initiated the first large-scale strike by women workers in the country when they called for increased fire safety. No action was taken. The women were locked out. Other workers supported the women at the Triangle Shirtwaist Factory and soon there were walkouts by women throughout the garment industry. The strike earned the title "Uprising of the Twenty Thousand."

The Jewish *Daily Forward* predicted that "With blood this name [Triangle Company] will be written in the history of the American worker movement, and with feeling will this history recall the names of the strikers of this shop-of-the crusaders."

Two years later, in 1911, the fire at the Triangle Shirtwaist Factory became one of the worst industrial disasters in US history. It broke out on the eighth, ninth and tenth floors of the building at 23-29 Washington Place. The factory employed mostly immigrant women to manufacture women's blouses. When the fire broke out, there was no way to alert workers elsewhere. Exits were locked and there was only one fire escape. Fire department ladders reached no higher than the sixth floor. The tragedy led to legislation mandating fire extinguishers, alarm systems, automatic sprinklers, better eating and toilet facilities and limiting working hours for women and children.

3. "In the Café," is by Anna Margolin.

4. Malka Heifetz Tussman's poem can be found in *With Teeth in the Earth: Selected Poems of Malka Heifetz Tussman*, Malka Heifetz Tussman, Marcia Falk (translator), Wayne State University Press, 1992.

5. More than 400 cops were engaged in the Tompkins Park riot. Police Commissioner Benjamin Ward placed the blame on the local precinct.

Mother Tongue

1. Community schools, often referred to as *harambee* schools, are built, managed, financed and run by private individuals or organizations and do not receive funding from the government.

2. Spurred by Kenyans keen desire for education combined with the government's constrained economic resources, the harambee movement began to expand rapidly in the 1970's and has continued through the beginning of the 21st century. A significant percentage of Kenyan students attend community schools. See: "Community schools in Kenya: Case study on community participation in funding

and managing schools," Eldah Nyamoita Onsomu, John Njoroge Mungai, Dramane Oulai, James Sankale, Jeddidah Mujidi, Paris: International Institute for Educational Planning/UNESCO, 2004.

Genius

1. A 1989 Senate Foreign Relations Committee report documented secret funding by the US for the Contras in Nicaragua in their attempt to overthrow the Sandinista government. The report stated that nearly $1 million was paid by the State Department to "four companies owned and operated by drug traffickers." So while the Reagan administration was waging a campaign against drugs resulting in the arrests of tens of thousands of African American, the CIA was at the same time funding the drug trade that was devastating American cities. Eleven Reagan administration officials were convicted in what became known as the Iran-Contra Affair.

2. Morris Levy, dubbed "the Octopus" by *Variety* magazine, once owned Birdland jazz nightclub, several record and music companies and a chain of 60 record and tape stores. He was also noted philanthropist. The FBI claimed Levy was involved with the Mafia, which influenced the sale, distribution and promotion of popular records and tapes. In 1990 Levy was convicted of extortion and died before being sentenced to federal prison.

3. Miles Davis playing Bye, Bye, Blackbird: https://www. youtube.com/watch?v=jlZdvDkQrGA

4. Hart Island, off the Bronx in Long Island Sound, is the site of Potters' Field, the largest tax funded cemetery in the world. It is where New York City buries its poor and unclaimed bodies, now numbering more than one million. Inmates from Rikers Island dig the graves and bury the bodies.

5.

The fatal shooting of a 19-year-old man on Staten Island Saturday night was the 1,842nd killing, according to Police Department figures. It broke the record of 1,841 set in 1981.

The surge of violence is being widely attributed to the drug epidemic, particularly the use of crack, a smokable and highly addictive form of cocaine.

Mayor Koch, asked about the homicide statistics as he served food to the homeless in Manhattan yesterday, singled out drugs as the main culprit and said that adding more police was not the solution.

He said as he has before that he favored giving judges and juries the option of imposing a death penalty on major drug pushers. He also said he supported better interdiction of drugs, more jails and more state and Federally financed drug-treatment programs.

New York *Times*, December 26, 1988.

6. A law journal article sums up police relations with the African American community in this article:

Two years ago, a provocative assertion appeared in the editorial pages of the New York *Times*. It read: "The black American finds that the most prominent reminder of his second-class citizenship are the police." The author of this sentence, Don Jackson, knew what he was talking about because he is a former police officer, who also happened to be a black man. Part of the foundation for Mr. Jackson's charge is a deep-seated distrust between police officers and black citizens. The evidence in support of this distrust has been available for a long time. Scholars and observers of the police, for example, have known for decades about the negative and anxious attitudes police officers hold toward blacks.

"Black and Blue Encounters' Some Preliminary Thoughts About Fourth Amendment Seizures: Should Race Matter?" Tracey Mclin, *Valparaiso Law Review*, 26, 243-279, 1991.

Ogres

1. The following is from a Kisii website:

A nagging 'ghost' in Nyamataro village in Kisii has been throwing pebbles on people's rooftops in the wee hours of the night, excreting on people's doorsteps and wiping itself on the door and uproot [sic] crops. Villagers were so fed up with the night runner. Recently, a smart Mzee Okari who was tired of finding faeces smeared on his door, came up with a solution. He fixed several sharp blades on the door and applied pepper so that when the culprit smeared faeces, the blades and pepper would offer the sweet burning revenge. In the dead of the night, the night runner did the usual rituals from one house to another.

The night runner's journey was eventful [sic] until she reached Mzee Okari's house. She defecated on the doorstep and as usual smeared the stuff on the door. A razor sharp scream that tore into the night awoke Mzee Okari as he jumped out armed himself with a rungu ready to rain blows on the night runner who had caused the village untold humiliation. Shock was written all over his face when he opened his door to find the local pastor's wife lying on the doorstep and writhing in pain.

"Please forgive me," pleaded the pastor's wife. Mzee Okari called his wife and together they screamed to alert neighbours who responded immediately. Villagers came ready to kill a creature that has been terrorising them in the dead of the night.

Everyone was shocked when they finally laid their eyes on the 'ghost'.

"It was my parents who taught me the habit," she pleaded as some insisted she be lynched. Even the pastor woke up to find out what was happening. He was beyond words when he realised it is his wife who was doing the evil things. The locals were so enraged and were baying for her blood, but the pastor who is highly respected pleaded with them. She was spared the lynch but was mercilessly chased from the village to return to her parent's land.

http://kisii.com/the-news/532-villagers-bust-pastors-night-runner-wife:

2. An analysis on nightrunners and witches was broadcast on Kenya TV after 15 people were burnt alive in Kisii after being accused of witchcraft.

(http://kenyastockholm.com/2009/04/21/info-on-15-witches-burnt-alive-in-kenya/)

3. Albinos are widely discriminated against, as they are viewed as abominations of nature. Some sorcerers use their body parts in their potions. In 2012 more than 100 albinos were kidnapped and murdered in East Africa. (http://sabahionline.com/en_GB/articles/hoa/articles/features/2013/07/10/feature-01)

4. FORD-Asili was the name of one of the opposition parties formed before the first-ever contested presidential elections in Kenya, in 1992. Human Rights Watch accused President Daniel arap Moi and Vice-President George Saitoti of engineering the ethnic violence surrounding the election. More than 2,000 people were killed in tribal conflicts that year, which occurred mainly in the western part of the country.

5.

Land, Food, Freedom: Struggles for the Gendered Commons in Kenya, 1870 to 2007, Leigh Brownhill, Africa World Press, 2009.

The Thing Itself

1. "26 Ways of Looking At A Blackman," is from *26 Ways Of Looking At A Black Man and Other Poems,* Raymond R. Patterson, Award Books, 1969; "Thirteen Ways of Looking at a Blackbird," is from *Harmonium,* Wallace Stevens, Alfred A. Knopf, 1923.

2. The *torii* gate in the Brooklyn Botanic Gardens is part of the Japanese Hill-and-Pond Garden. With more than 200 cherry trees, it is one of the major cherry tree viewing sites outside of Japan.

3. One of the first labor strikes in the US took place during the building of NYU, in 1835.

The contractors for the building of the New York University found that they could purchase dressed stone at Sing Sing, the work of the prisoners there, much cheaper than in New York, and so concluded to use it. This, the stonecutters of the city said, was taking the bread out of their mouths, and if allowed to go on would destroy their business. They held excited meetings on the subject, and finally got up a procession and paraded the streets with placards asserting their rights and denouncing the contractors. They even attacked the houses of some citizens, and assumed a threatening attitude, that the Twenty-seventh Regiment, Colonel Stevens, was called out. Their steady, determined march on the rioters dispersed them and restored quiet. Apprehensions were felt, however, that they would reassemble in the night and vent their rage on the University building, and so a part of the regiment encamped in Washington Square in full view of it. They remained here four days and nights, and the work could go on unmolested.

Pen and Pencil Sketches of the Great Riots: An Illustrated History of the Railroad and Other Great American Riots, Including all the Riots in the Early History of the Country, Hon. J. T. Headley, E. B. Treat, 1882.

4. Judge Tom R. Jones helped establish the Bedford Stuyvesant Restoration Corporation, in 1967. (http://www.restorationplaza.org)

5. "The Mother," *A Street in Bronzeville*, Gwendolyn Brooks, Harper & Brothers, 1945.

6. In 2013, Junius Stinney's family petitioned South Carolina for a new trial. A year later his conviction was vacated.

7. Abel Meerepol and the adoption of the convicted atom bomb spies Ethel and Julius Rosenberg can be found in "Abel Meeropol (a.k.a Lewis Allan): Political Commentator and Social Conscience," Nancy Kovaleff Baker, *American Music*, Spring 2002.

8. Mavis Staples sings the 1854 Stephen Foster song, "Hard Times Come No More: (https://www.youtube.com/watch?v=-ixbah9u234)

9. "Sadness and Happiness, is from *Ourmedia*, Dejan Stojanovic. (https://archive.org/details/SadnessAndHappinessByDejanStojanovic)

10. "Heart to Heart," from *American Smooth*, Rita Dove, W. W. Norton and Company, 2004.

11. Each year in late December people gather in many Japanese cities to sing 'Ode to Joy,' the choral section Beethoven's 9th Symphony, known in Japan as *Daiku*. The origin of the tradition is uncertain.

Afterword: Sungusungu

1. At the 2008 exchange rate, Kshs. 1,000 was about $15 US. Shilling notes are often referred to by their color. One hundred notes are called reds.

2. *Sungusungu* may have evolved out of *chinkororo*. Initially conceived as a clan-based militia to protect the homeland, young men were encouraged and recruited by the government to engage in community policing to quell rampant crime in Kisii. Falling out of favor with some sectors of the government, *sungusungu* were subsequently characterized as vigilantes and warned to curtail their zealousness. Finally, many in the community saw them

as a brutal gang used by powerful forces for personal and political gain.

3. A beating and burning of a witch is captured on this video: (https://www.youtube.com/watch?v=nsDtsWJ5ibE)

4. The Truth, Justice and Conciliation Commission of Kenya reported 1,500 killed, 3,000 raped and 300,000 internally displaced over a period of 59 days after the 2008 elections. It is likely that the Kisii who fought at Chepilat were *sungusungu* members.

5. The Commission of Inquiry into Post-Election Violence was composed of a Kenyan judge, a former police commissioner from New Zealand and a lawyer from the Democratic Republic of Congo. It contains the following testimony:

On 5th February, early in the morning my husband woke up and went to till the farm. Shortly after he went out he came running back to the house. He ordered us to close all the doors and windows. He told us that he saw a group of Kalenjin youth coming towards our house. A few minutes later we heard their voices outside. They were calling us by our names and they asked us to come out. We recognized their voices. One of them was our neighbour.

At around 9.00 a.m. they started breaking the doors and the windows of the house. They could not break into the house because of the grill reinforcement. I called the Chief to come and help us. He sent a vehicle and administration policemen. They could not reach us immediately because all the roads leading to Chepilat were barricaded by Kalenjin warriors. They came to us around 6 p.m. and they escorted us out of the house.

(http://reliefweb.int/sites/reliefweb.int/files/resource s/15A00F569813F4D549257607001F459D-Full_Report. pdf):

6. Marcus Bleasdale's photographs of the violence were published in *The Telegraph*. He was in Chepilat when the fighting began. He quoted by Isabel Albiston, "Kenya: Marcus Bleasdale's pictures of the valley of fear," *The Telegraph*, March 8, 2008.

There are gangs of a couple of hundred people walking through the town with machetes, bows and arrows, spears and stones, setting buildings alight. A lot of people look on in disbelief, unable to understand what has happened to their peaceful country.

The ongoing crisis is being spearheaded by gangs of men from different areas who are shipped into towns and paid (probably by a small number of politicians and political activists) to burn down houses and mark the doors of people who are in the wrong tribe. If they are lucky they are told they have 24 hours to leave. In other towns they are just shot.

7. Belief in night runners is strong in Kisii. Night runners are people who are possessed and run naked in the dark scaring people. The are believed to have magical powers and can tame wild animals as companions. Although not intentionally malicious, Kisiis are afraid of them and there are reports of people having been frightened to death.

8. In the mid-2000s nearly 10,000 people in Kisii Village. There were fewer than 10 latrines in the settlement and there were no drainage ducts. Water flowed directly into the nearby river. There was no electricity connection. Most houses were rentals, with charges about Ksh.500 per room.

9. In 2014, twelve senior police officials were dismissed from duty for "lack of discipline, integrity, violation of human rights, financial impropriety and engagement in criminal activities among them bribery, human trafficking, rape and defilement, as well as smuggling of commodities such as sugar, illicit brews and drugs," according to The National Police Service Commission. The report also noted

that the General Manager in charge of safety and security at Kenya airports was subject to further investigation. (http://allafrica.com/stories/201405290154.html)

10. More than 100 sq. miles in Kericho region are planted with tea bushes. Dirt roads and footpaths create countless reticulated sub-plots of tea bushes cropped at about three feet high. This is a tea farm on the road between Sotik and Kericho.

Glossary

〰〰〰
〰〰〰

abasongo (Gusii)	Europeans, white people.
arigatou (Japanese)	Thank you.
Bosongo (Gusii)	The Gusii name for Kisii Town.
bwakiire (Gusii)	Morning greeting.
bwana (Swahili)	a boss or master, used in the colonial era as a form of addressing any European man, now sometimes used as a polite form of addressing any man.
chang'aa (Swahili)	An illegal brew.
chinkororo (Gusii)	Traditionally a name was applied to Kisii youths who defended the homeland, similar to the *moran* of the Maasai.
choo (Swahili)	Toilet.
Haggadah (Hebrew)	The book read at Passover that tells the story of the exodus from Egypt that also contains special blessings and rituals to commemorate the occasion. Since there is no official or sanctioned version, it is often rewritten by individuals or communities.
harambee (Swahili)	a slogan used during Kenyatta era (1963-1978), meaning let's pull together. It also referred to self-help projects that the government endorsed but didn't fund. It was also used, for example, when pushing a stuck vehicle. It was the slogan used by President Jomo Kenyatta.
jua kali (Swahili)	Literally: fierce sun. A phrase used to denote a workplace in the informal sector, typically outdoors.

kanga (Swahili)	A printed cotton cloth, mainly used by women as a skirt, often with a Swahili adage.
kanji (Japanese)	The logographic Chinese characters used in the Japanese writing system.
karanza (Gusii)	Sit down.
karibu (Swahili)	Welcome or come in.
kimbelembele (Swahili)	A show off.
kiondo (Swahili)	Sisal handbag widely used in Kenya.
kitu kidogo (Swahili, slang)	Literally: a little something. A bribe.
konnichiwa (Japanese)	Hello.
mafi or mavi (Swahili)	Shit.
mandazi (Swahili)	Fried dough.
matatu (Swahili)	A minibus used as a shared taxi.
mono no aware (Japanese)	Literally: the pathos of things. The phrase refers to the feeling evoked by knowing that everything is temporary, thereby bringing a greater appreciation for what is loved in the moment.
mzee, sing., *wazee*, pl. (Swahili)	Old man; the affectionate name for President Kenyatta; any honored elderly man.
mumiani (Swahili)	Mummy.
nachire aa (Gusii)	I've come here.
nani huyu (Swahili)	Who is this?
ning'o (Gusii)	Used when responding to a caller at night whose voice the inquirer doesn't know.
nyayo (Swahili)	Footsteps. The word was used as a slogan by President Daniel arap Moi, meaning that he was following the path set down by his predecessor, Jomo Kenyatta.
panga (Swahili)	A machete.

peng (Sheng)	A motorbike. Also called *bodaboda* throughout East Africa.
rungu (Swahili)	A wooden club, typically one-to-two feet in length. It has a long shaft and knob at one end.
ryokan (Japanese)	An inn, often run by a family.
sahib (Urdu and other Indian languages)	A form of address for a man in position of authority. Widely used in the British Raj.
sakura (Japanese)	The Japanese cherry tree.
seder (Hebrew)	The ritual feast to mark the beginning of Passover.
seiza (Japanese)	Kneeling on the floor with legs under the buttocks. Special stools are available for those who find the position uncomfortable.
shamba (Swahili)	A farm.
siku moja mgeni, siku tatu mpe jembe. (Swahili)	A Swahili proverb that means, You are a guest the first day, you get a hoe on the third.
soa (Gusii)	Enter.
sonko (Sheng)	A rich person.
sota (Sheng)	Broke, no money.
sungusungu (Swahili)	A type of large black ant. It is a name applied to community vigilante groups in the Kuria and Kisii communities.
torii (Japanese)	A gateway to a Shinto shrine.
wananchi, pl.; *mwananchi*, sing. (Swahili)	Literally: citizen. The common people.
*Sheng is a Swahili based argot.	